AN EXCITING FUTURE

The second novel in the series

Behind The Smile

The Story of Lek, a Bar Girl in Pattaya

by

Owen Jones

Copyright

any form of binding or cover other than that in which it is published and without a similar condition including this condition being imposed on the subsequent purchaser.

Contact Details

BlueSky: owen-author.bsky.social
Facebook: AngunJones
Instagram: owen_author
LinkedIn: owencerijones
Pinterest: owen_author
TikTok: @owen_author
X: @owen_author
Blog: Megan Publishing Services

Join our newsletter for insider information
on Owen Jones' books and writing
by entering your email address here:
http://meganpublishingservices.com

Owen Jones

Behind The Smile Series

The Story of Lek, a Bar Girl in Pattaya

Dedication

Dedicated to my brother Rhys, without whose encouragement this book would not exist, and to all the Pattaya bar girls that I have ever met - they gave me the material that inspired this series.

Also to my wife, who gave me the time to write.

Thank you one and all.

Owen Jones
Thailand
March 2025

Inspirational Quotes

Believe not in anything simply because you have heard it,

Believe not in anything simply because it was spoken and rumoured by many,

Believe not in anything simply because it was found written in your religious texts,

Believe not in anything merely on the authority of teachers and elders,

Believe not in traditions because they have been handed down for generations,

But after observation and analysis, if anything agrees with reason and is conducive to the good and benefit of one and all, accept it and live up to it.

Gautama Buddha

Great Spirit, whose voice is on the wind, hear me.

Let me grow in strength and knowledge.

Make me ever behold the red and purple sunset.

May my hands respect the things you have given me.

Teach me the secrets hidden under every leaf and stone, as you have taught people for ages past.

Let me use my strength, not to be greater than my brother, but to fight my greatest enemy – myself.

Let me always come before you with clean hands and an open heart, that as my Earthly span fades like the sunset, my Spirit shall return to

you without shame.
  (Based on a traditional **Sioux prayer**)

"I do not seek to walk in the footsteps of the Wise People of old; I seek what they sought".
  Matsuo Basho

"Have I not commanded you? Be strong and courageous. Do not be afraid; do not be discouraged, for the LORD your God will be with you wherever you go".
Joshua 1:9

"Whatever misfortune befalls you [people], it is because of what your own hands have done- God forgives much-"
Quran 42:30

Myself when young did eagerly frequent
Doctor and Saint, and heard great Argument
About it and about; but oft-times
Came out, by the same Door as in I went.
Omar Khayyam
The Rubaiyat XXIX.

Table of Contents

1 STARTING AGAIN

As the wheels of the aircraft touched down on the runway at the new Bangkok International Airport called Suvarnabhumi, Craig knew that he was going to have his hands full with Lek. She suffered badly from travel sickness – it was her one big weakness, but she even got sick on the bus going to the market, so a flight of 11,500 kilometres and fifteen hours was always going to be a problem.

Lek had taken five of the green tablets which were her favourite anti-travel sickness pills. She always seemed to have about twenty of them in her bag. One tablet would make her appear a little drunk, but five made her seem like an escapee from a lunatic asylum. He had seen it on the outward flight. He looked at her sitting next to him; her eyes were glassy and she was humming something quietly to herself.

"Are we there yet?" she asked, "That was quick. Have we stopped off somewhere?"

"We're in Thailand," he replied a little too testily.

Craig was fifty years old and had never asked a woman to marry him so far, but he thought he might like to ask this one. She was a handful, as they say, that was to be sure, but there was also something about her that he found very special.

He didn't like her taking those pills though, but he knew how badly affected by travel-sickness she could get. She'd had to throw up in her new crocodile skin handbag once – her pride and expensive joy – because they had gone on a short bus ride and she had forgotten to transfer all her paraphernalia into the new bag. It was either be sick in her new bag or on the floor of the bus and she would rather die than do that and lose face.

Later, she would have to be assisted like a drunk through the airport, baggage control and immigration and suffer the stern stares from the Thai officials who would assume that she had drunk too much cheap alcohol on the plane.

He was glad that she had chosen to wear long, baggy trousers.

The plan of the day was Lek's usual one whenever anything unusual or exciting happened to her, namely to get down to 'Daddy's Hobby' in Pattaya and tell her friends all about it. In fact, it didn't have to be anything unusual at all, it was just the place where Lek felt most at home in the world. 'Daddy's Hobby' was the name of the bar that Lek's cousin owned and where he had met her. Craig didn't mind going there one little bit. The two dozen bar girls always made a big fuss of him and Lek even encouraged them to do it.

Within a couple of hours, he'd have girls hanging off his shoulders, sitting on his lap and plying him with drinks while Lek recounted the details of her recent adventure in the UK. She should have come round a bit by then too.

Just in time to share a couple of bottles of whiskey with her ex-colleagues.

Still, it would be very pleasant and the apartment that he had booked before they had left was not far from the bar.

He was wondering whether that would be a good time to propose – in front of her friends, when she least expected it and when she would get the maximum amount of attention and admiration. It would certainly give her face a boost, not that it was flagging in Pattaya. All her friends thought she was a star - one in a million.

Craig thought so too.

However, first things first, he thought; people were starting to disembark. Craig thought it best to wait for most people to get off before he tried to coax and manhandle Lek down the aisle, so they just sat there and he tried to get her to get a grip on herself.

Without much success.

The cabin staff were helpful – they understood about the tablets – and Lek and Craig eventually made it to immigration, which was pretty straightforward, although Lek did attract a few of the expected stern looks from the Thai officials and Craig got more than a couple of knowing nods from them too. He just smiled back weakly in reply.

They made it to the carousel, where Lek fell into a chair and Craig picked up the luggage, which he loaded onto a trolley. He considered putting Lek on it too, but that would have been just too embarrassing, so he settled for letting her push it, so that she had something to lean against. No problems at baggage control and then out into the heat.

He had more or less forgotten the overpowering heat and the everyday bustle outside a Thai airport. Taxi drivers and their touts all shouting at once for your custom. This was one of the occasions where having a Thai girlfriend helped a lot. She shooed them all away and they stood in the queue for a proper meter taxi to take them to Pattaya, which was only about an hour away.

They were supposed to go to the British Embassy to have Lek's six-month visa cancelled as it was still valid for three months and allowed multiple entries into the UK, but the Embassy would be closed now and Lek was in no fit state anyway. They would have to do something about it another day.

They arrived in Daddy's Hobby after an uneventful journey. Lek had tried to talk to the driver a few times, but he thought that she was drunk so he ignored her and tried to speak to Craig, but in Thai, which Craig could not speak, so that quickly fizzled out too and Lek, being ignored, soon fell asleep, which was probably the best thing she could have done anyway.

Lek had wanted to speak Thai though. She was excited to be back in her own country, where she could hold a proper conversation in her own language and where she could feel that she belonged again. They had had a few months in Craig's home town of Barry in South Wales and everyone had made her feel very welcome. She liked European food and she could speak English reasonably well, but ...

It wasn't her town, it wasn't her favourite food, it wasn't her language and they were not her people. She had had a fantastic holiday –

her first trip to Europe – but she was glad to be home and she just wanted everyone to know it. She couldn't wait to see her old mates.

They got to Daddy's Hobby at a good time: nearly six o'clock. All the girls had arrived and were ready for action, but there were no customers yet and so the music was low. It would seem like a totally different place in two hours time. Once it got dark, the punters would be out and the volume would rise to deafening.

But between four and eight o'clock, the girls had time to talk and the volume was low enough to be able to hear them. It had been Craig's favourite time to visit the bar before they had gone on holiday. He had come down to the bar for an early drink and a chat almost every day then and he and the girls had got to know each other pretty well.

He often translated messages, texts and letters from and to their 'boyfriends' for them. Not that he could speak Thai, but he translated good English into pigeon and vice versa. It was fun although sometimes the messages were rather intimate and the girls would blush and giggle and run around telling each other in fits of laughter.

It was a good 'job' to have: It earned him a lot of brownie points from the girls, even if it went unpaid in monetary terms. They genuinely liked to see him, although he was quite well aware that he had only gotten his foot in the door because he was Lek's boyfriend. Many of the girls were from Lek's village in the north and she had worked with others for years. She was like a big sister to them and many of them called her just that.

At thirty-two years of age, Lek was also the oldest woman in the bar or at least joint oldest with her two best friends: Goong and Ayr. Her cousin, Beou, was a few years older again, but no-one ever mentioned that – she was the boss anyway. Despite her 'advancing' years (most of the girls were in their early twenties or younger), Lek was acknowledged to be the most beautiful woman in the bar by everyone, although no-one ever mentioned the obvious fact that that would not be true for many more years to come.

However, for now, she was still the beauty queen amongst beauty queens, for they were all very good-lookers in their own right.

When the taxi pulled up outside the bar, it was as if a film star had arrived, all the girls crowded around Lek, took her handbag, led her up to the bar by the arm, fired a dozen questions at her and whooped and whooped and whooped.

Craig paid the taxi driver and carried the luggage to the bar. He had expected a bit more attention for himself than that.

Once he was at the bar, a few of the girls noticed him and flung their arms around him, kissing him repeatedly on the cheek and arms. A few of the girls took the luggage to store behind the bar and Lek and Craig sat down for the start of what they both knew would be a long and lively session.

All the women were talking at once and, although Craig wasn't being totally ignored, he wasn't getting served either. He was dying for an ice-cold beer. He couldn't follow the conversation, maybe nobody could, but he could see how happy they all were, so he went behind the bar and got three beers. The first one didn't touch the sides. He downed it in two mouthfuls, but the other two he took back to the bar and handed one to Lek.

"Oh, so sorry, telak! Nobody take care of you. So sorry."

She said something and a few girls were detailed to 'take care' of Craig. Then she said loudly:

"You only buy two beers, this is not enough!" and she leaned over and rang the bell, signalling a drink for everyone at her expense.

Craig finished his beer quickly and accepted another.

Two of the girls detailed to 'take care' of Craig were unknown to him. They had obviously joined the crew while he and Lek had been away. They were very friendly, but when Ayr thought they were getting a bit too familiar, she sent them behind the bar to serve.

"So, sorry, Craig," she said, "these girls new. They don' know Lek and you together. I tell them later. Nice to see you again. You have good time in Wale'?" and she was gone without waiting for the answer.

Ayr and Goong were Lek's oldest friends, came from the same village and had shared a room in Pattaya before Craig came on the scene. Neither of them held any ill will against Craig for taking their friend away though. They were happy that she was happy, because they were true friends.

"Oh, well," he joked with himself, "Shame about that. Still, never mind. At least, I didn't get into trouble on my first day back. Saved from myself by Lek's friend. Saved from whatever-their- names were too."

It did the trick though. He was not ignored by Lek, her friends or the strangers again. Everyone was keeping an eye on him now. He was served, kissed and complimented without long intervals in between and it suited him fine.

The girls quietened after about twenty minutes and they all sat around Lek, or as near as they could get, to listen to her favourite stories. It wasn't long after that that the first bottle of whiskey was broken out and a few small glasses appeared. The girls preferred whiskey because it was less fattening than a bottle of beer and it was easier to finish quickly if a punter wanted to talk with one of them.

Craig sat nearby too and listened out for landmark words like: Barry, Wales and family names. Sure enough, they were all mentioned often and he was sometimes called upon to corroborate the details, although no-one actually waited for him to finish speaking. He just about had the time to nod and smile, even though he didn't know what was being said. He trusted Lek though.

She was speaking softly so that the girls would have to listen hard:

"We set off on a typically beautiful, balmy Pattaya evening... a bit like this evening, in fact, and at about the same time of day, to catch the overnight flight to Britain. We were going to Wales, where Craig's family lives, but we had to go to London first, of course.

"Naturally we had to be at the check-in desk two to three hours before the flight, but there was nearly a disaster! Really! We nearly couldn't go! All because, unfortunately, Craig had forgotten that he was carrying an old souvenir pen-knife in his pocket that his father had given to him twenty years before.

"I thought they were going to arrest him. I was horrified! I thought I might have to go alone and wait for him over there and I didn't want to have to do that now, did I? Anyway, we were lucky, they only confiscated it. He was very sad about it, especially as the airline gave us metal cutlery to eat with anyway and the knives that they gave us were bigger than the one they had taken off Craig. Weren't they, Craig? Bigger knives?

"Craig said it was stupid to take his one-inch blade from him under such circumstances and I think that I have to agree with him, don't you?

"Anyway, the ten-and-a-half hour flight to Bahrain was very comfortable. The food was not to my liking because I am a Buddhist that does not eat beef or dairy products and the only two other choices were Indian curry or vegetable pie. I didn't mind though. It all looked very nice and I swapped my main course for Craig's ice cream.

"Bahrain was a shock from Suvarnabhumi airport. Oh, my God! It was OK, really, but we didn't have any of their money, Dinar, I think, so we just had to sit there and watch people for the two hours until the connecting flight to Gatwick. That is in the UK. The time passed slowly and I was a little cold because it was 20°c there, much colder then Bangkok. Virtually freezing!

Did I tell you that a man died on the flight? I nearly forgot. Shock or travel-sickness, I think. When they opened the doors to take him off mosquitoes as big as birds flew in! Oh my Buddha! I was sure we'd get malaria...

"Anyway, the second leg flight was also OK; not as good as the first, but at least I could eat the scrambled egg and pork sausage. I had Craig's too, because he took my feta salad. Feta is cheese by the way. Greek cheese, isn't it, Craig? Craig? He's not listening again... Anyway, they eat a lot of cheese in Europe. The coffee was much stronger than I am used to too, but it was lovely. All in all, I liked Etihad Airways and would fly with them again, wouldn't we, telak?

"It took five hours to get to Gatwick and if Bahrain was a shock, Gatwick's 5°c was as good as icy to me. As soon as I got off the plane, I was looking for the Ladies! It was that cold, honest. If you haven't been abroad, darlings, you have no idea what cold is. We are so lucky here in good old Thailand. Anyway, fortunately we only had twenty-five minutes to wait for the bus to Cardiff via Victoria Coach Station – that's in London again, of course.

"The tour coach was good and the driver was friendly, but the weather turned so bad as we crossed the Severn Bridge, into Wales, that is, over the Bristol Channel, isn't it dear? that we were late arriving in Cardiff. We got there just in time for the eleven o'clock traffic jam. Just as bad as Bangkok, but you're in the dark, which makes it a lot worse!

"It was hor-ren-dous!

"So, then our friend Nick, you know Nick, he comes in here sometimes took us in his car through Dinas Powys and Penarth before coming into Barry through Cadoxton.

"Craig suggested getting out at the King William IV – called The Billy – that's a pub, so that we could have a drink. It was typical of him; well, you know my Craig, but it was bitterly cold, and it was close. We had been travelling for thirty-three hours and now we were ten minutes from my Welsh Mum's house.

"Ooh, I'm parched, well, when we got to Mum's, which was a day and a half after we started out from here... No, more about that later.

"I met so many handsome men, Oh my gosh! Our friends Colin, Ray, Billy, Digger, Danny, Sam, Paul and Selby, the father of two famous Welsh boxers, Andrew and Lee (he gave me one of Andrew's jackets – I'll show it to you one day) - they were in O'Brien's and Mike, or Henry as his friends call him, in the Buccaneer and so many others. Those places are in the centre of the town of Barry, of course, Holton Road, near the King's Square. When they come over to visit us, we could introduce you, if you like...."

Lek had them spellbound. It was exactly what it must have been like to watch Hans Christian Andersen telling fairy stories to kids in

Denmark, although Lek's stories were true even if a little dramatised. They just stared at her, sometimes looking at Craig as if to say 'What with him?', but actually saying "Ooh, really?" and "Ahhh, really? None of them had been to Europe before, although it was the dream that every single one of them had.

In fact, they would happily go to live anywhere abroad so long as the job was better and there was more money, which everybody believed that it was 'abroad' – meaning Europe, Australia and the USA. Not many of them had heard of Canada or New Zealand. Second choice was northern Africa, but most of the girls had heard rumours of sex slaves there and none of them fancied that.

Beou arrived on her motorbike and the commotion started all over again. Some girls jumped up to pretend they were working and others got out of the way to allow the boss easier access to her favourite cousin. She put one arm around Lek and, as she leaned in to exchange kisses, took Craig's hand with the other.

"Hello, both! How the devil are you? Did you have a good time? Sorry that I couldn't be here to greet you when you arrived, but someone was late coming to see me. (They'll never do it again though). So, he didn't sell you into slavery then? Or did you do a bit of part-time sex-slaving? Did she tell you, Craig? She was rather worried that you would sell her as a sex-slave to a bunch of old men in a nursing home! She might not have minded if it was to a football team. Or what do you play over there in Wales? Ah, rugby, is it? Yes, rugby."

Lek was blushing deeply and she thought she would die if any of the girls knew what was actually being said about her, but it was a bit too fast for most them.

"No, she didn't say anything. What's this all about, Beou? And how are you anyway?"

"Oh, I'm fine. A few of the old women back home warned Lek to be careful that you didn't sell her into the sex industry. A lot of people are worried about it, but I told her that the old biddies in the village were just jealous."

Lek could still barely speak so she covered her face below her eyes with a hand to hide her blushes.

"Oh, Beou! How could you? I didn't really believe them, but you hear such terrible things, don't you? And I never said anything about an old men's home or a football team! And I didn't even know what rugby was until a few months ago." Then in English: "Don't believe her, Craig..... Well, not all of it anyway."

"I don't know what you are all talking about. Don't believe all of what? What did Beou say?" asked Craig

"Oh, don't worry, I tell you later. It is not important now. Ladies in the village tell me to take care nobody sell me into sex slavery, that's all. Don't worry."

"Oh, is that all," he replied, still not completely understanding. One thing he had learned though was that if Lek said 'later', it usually meant either 'no' or 'never', so he just let it drop. He trusted her and her judgement and, besides that, they were back on her turf now where she knew far more than he ever would.

Beou sat down and a gin and tonic was put in front of her, she lit a cigarette and rang the bell, which was an uncommon thing for her to do. Half-a-dozen of the girls jumped up to see to their boss' order, but they all came back to find out how the story would develop. Beou didn't mind that, she was a pretty good employer and the majority of these girls were not there to clean glasses anyway.

Lek recovered quickly from her embarrassment and she seemed to have thrown off the effects of the tablets too. The adrenaline and excitement of being with her friends again had 'sobered' her up faster than a cold shower, a coffee or even a car crash ever could have. She was flying high and everybody else was up there with her, so Craig just settled back to drink his beer and watch the proceedings.

Customers came and went and girls got up to keep them company and either came back when the man had left or went with him. Some girls had their regulars, whom they were grooming so that they too might have an adventure like Lek's. Everybody wanted what Lek had and they were hoping that she would pass on some secret, insider tips on how to accomplish it.

No-one was surprised that Lek had been the first to manage going abroad in years and no-one begrudged her her good fortune either. She was their big sister, the legendary heroine Lek, and they all wanted to be like her. Even the new girls had heard of her, they had just never met her in the flesh. This put Craig on a pedestal, because they all assumed that a woman like Lek would have had many chances to get out, but just didn't take them for one reason or another. That meant that Craig must be something special.

No Adonis, so must be kind and wealthy, most of them assumed. Or at least well-off.

Sometimes, Lek wasn't sure why either. Some things were coming to a head in her life, it was true: she was no spring chicken any more; but more than that, her daughter, Soomsomai, was twelve, and she didn't want her to know that her mother was associated with the seamier side of life. She also liked Craig a lot, even loved him and he was kind. Not wealthy, but well-off by her standards and still of an age that he could work.

For his part, Craig really loved Lek. He had never met anyone like her before. True, he had worked, studied and travelled nearly all his life and had never been married, but he wasn't totally inexperienced with women either. He had just never met one quite like Lek before. Or maybe he just happened to meet her when the time was right. He didn't know and was not much interested in why anyway. He knew that he wanted to stay with her and that he wanted to stay in Thailand, a place he had come to prefer over his own country.

The only problems from his point of view were that he had always been wary of marrying someone from abroad because of his limited financial resources and the huge travelling costs involved with visiting two sets of parents on two different continents regularly. He would not be able to work in Thailand except perhaps as a teacher and he was sure that he lacked the patience and confidence for that. There was savings money and a few investments for the time being but how long would it last?

That was the big question.

He would have to get out of central Pattaya as soon as possible; that much was clear, but go where? He only knew Pattaya. Bangkok was sure to be even more expensive and he didn't like big cities anyway. They both liked Pattaya, so maybe they could move to the suburbs. He and Lek had not broached the subject yet, but they had pre-booked an apartment for two months, so they had some time to work something out.

Craig spent the next six or seven hours day dreaming and drinking, while Lek spent them drinking and talking. It wasn't boring.

Not at all. It was peaceful. Relaxing.

He had even managed to filter out the awful, loud music that he so detested. He was just so pleased to be back in Pattaya and Thailand. He was tempted to go and look at the sun setting on the sea, but couldn't be bothered.

At sometime near one o'clock, the official closing time in Pattaya, jet lag and the alcohol were winning out over the excitement and adrenaline and Lek reluctantly wanted to call it a day and go to their room. Beou called them a taxi which arrived too soon. They had hoped it would take ten or twenty minutes to get there, but it arrived in two. Lek knocked her whiskey back in one and Craig took his bottle with him. The driver put their bags in the boot and they were off. Glad to be going to their new home for the next few months.

Their apartment was in the Diana Estate which was not far away in Soi Buakhao so they were there in less than ten minutes despite the busy streets. The security guard on the gate was waiting for them with the key to the apartment, because the concierge had already gone to bed. Not that that was a problem. They refused the security guards offer to show them the way as Craig had inspected the apartment three months previously before paying the deposit.

They went up to the room, stripped off and showered together. When they fell onto the bed, Craig was starkers and Lek was in her customary towel; pleased to be wrapped in a towel like she had been for some time every day of her life in Thailand and which she had missed in the UK. She had never thought that such a simple thing like a towel could bring so much pleasure. She hadn't realised that she had missed it in Britain, but now that she had its protection around her again, she knew that she had.

Or maybe it was just Thailand and her friends that she had missed when she was in Europe, despite the fact that it had been her ambition for ten years to make that journey.

It didn't matter for now really; neither of them had much chance to analyse anything because they were both fast asleep in minutes.

That would have to wait until the next day, the real start of their new life, their exciting future, together.

An Exciting Future

14

2 SETTLING IN

They woke up at nine o'clock, which was a bit later than had become normal for them. When Lek had been working, she usually didn't get up until midday or even later, but if she was with someone, it depended on the friend.

She had been with Craig for almost a year now and she had adapted quite easily to his lifestyle. In fact, she usually got up a couple of hours before him in order to get most of the chores done first. She had also gone back to eating rice soup first thing in the morning as she had done when a girl in the village, like most people did in the countryside.

There was no food in the apartment, so Lek went for a shower, in order to go out to the shops nearby. Craig put the TV on to look for Pattaya People's News, a local news channel that broadcasts mostly in English. He lay there catching up with what had been happening in the last seven days. As usual, a Scandinavian had jumped, fallen or been pushed off a balcony and somebody had been robbed at knife-point by a couple of lady boys on the beach at three a.m.

Some things never changed.

His mobile phone rang and it took him by surprise until he remembered that they had both put their Thai SIMM's back in the day before. It was Lek, but then who else would be phoning him, he thought.

"Hello, darling. What's going on? Are you OK?"

"Sure, telak, but there is a good-looking café on the grounds outside the room. I don't want to cook, so will you come down here and we can eat in there or outside in the sunshine? They have Thai and falang food. The coffee looks good too."

"OK, don't cook. I'll have a quick shower and see you there. Where

15

is it?"

"Go onto the balcony, look down to the left and you see me. I stand outside the café."

Craig did as he was told and saw Lek waving up at him enthusiastically.

"All right, go inside. I'll be down in ten or fifteen minutes."

He didn't rush. He fancied a coffee, but he didn't usually eat soon after getting up. Lek, on the other hand, liked to eat within minutes of getting out of bed, unless she had to go outside when it would be minutes after her shower. She was one of those people who start to feel ill, if they don't eat regularly. Lek grazed throughout the day, whereas Craig liked one or two large meals.

When Craig caught up with Lek, she was eating a bowl of rice soup – the Thai equivalent of porridge. She had learned to drink tea and coffee because of the company she had kept, but left to her own devices, she preferred ice-cold water.

Although a lot of the apartments were owned or occupied by foreigners, farang or falang in Thai, the staff in the café could not understand his English, so Lek ordered him an English breakfast and a coffee. It was meant to be a treat, but Craig wasn't really hungry. It was a poor imitation of an English breakfast too, but he pretended to enjoy it so as not to disappoint anyone.

It was a glorious day and the sun glinted off the small pool nearby. There was also a big pool just under their balcony and Craig decided to go swimming every day to loose some weight. He hoped that Lek would join him, but doubted it somehow.

"Telak, what you want to do today? I love this compound and I love our room. What shall we do?"

He could almost hear her think: 'Say, go down to Daddy's Hobby, go on say it.'

"I don't know. We need to discuss where we are going to live and how we are going to make a living, but I suppose we don't have to start doing that right away..."

"We can stay here! And you can swim and work on the computer. Same as before; and I will take care of you and maybe find a small job, although that is not easy. You want me work in a shop or a hotel – make bed – or in a bar?"

"We are booked in here for two months, but after that, I think we need something permanent. And yes, I will try to do something on the Internet, but no, I don't really want you to do any of those jobs. That can wait for now anyway, unless something comes your way that you would like to do."

"OK, good idea. You want to swim after breakfast. I go get towels and costumes and book for you," and she was gone. Craig suspected that she had a plan of some kind. Thai women, and a lot of Thai city men, do their best to stay out of the sun because they want to keep their skin white, so why would she volunteer to sit at the poolside with him?

Lek came down with a duffel bag with his things in and a towel around her waist, which made him think that he must have misjudged her. While he went to get changed in the toilet, Lek rearranged two of the sun loungers to be as much in the small amount of shade as possible. She also put a couple of parasols up.

The pool was deserted and looked very inviting even though it was eleven a.m.

Craig swam for an hour and Lek watched and pretended to try to sleep. When he got out, Lek handed him a towel and began pulling on her jeans.

"I cannot sit here, darling, it is too hot and the sun move and give me black skin. I want to go to Beou's house and eat lunch with her. You stay here, swim and read your book. It is boring for you to sit listen to me and my cousin speak in Thai, I think. No?

"I want to know everything what happen here when I stay in Wales. Too boring for you, eh? I want to speak Thai and eat real Thai food from north Thailand. Beou phone to me and ask me come for lunch. She ask you too, but I say I think you not want. You want to come, telak?"

Craig knew that he had been outmanoeuvred, but he didn't really care. Lek was right, he would find it boring and this way, he could slip out to a bar and see who was about.

"No, that's OK, don't worry about me, Lek. I'll see you later."

"OK, thank you so much, telak. Don't drink too much and I phone you later. Maybe see you in Daddy's Hobby bar at four o'clock. Good idea, neh? OK, good idea. Bye-bye."

She looked around furtively and then gave him a quick peck on the cheek. She was back in Thailand now and kissing in public was frowned upon even in Pattaya. He watched her walk away and could not help thinking how beautiful she was yet again. It was still too early to go out, so he took Lek's advice, rummaged in the bag for his book and started to read.

He decided to wait until twelve-thirty to start his first tour. At midday, a fat, old man made a huge splash in the pool. It took Craig by surprise because he had been engrossed in his book, but he looked up to see if a greeting of some kind was in order. The man was not looking at him, but he caught sight of a small, young woman hiding from him behind a bush not five metres away.

She was looking at him, then at the man in the water and giggling. The old man shouted at her: "Spring ins Wasser" – German for 'jump into the water'. The woman was obviously shy of Craig, so he looked down at his book, until she ran past him, dropped her towel at the last moment and slipped into the water.

Craig watched her for the last few seconds and she knew it and wasn't too happy about it either. They were probably used to having the pool to themselves, he thought. Ten minutes later, an old couple came down, also German, as it turned out. They were both as brown and as wrinkled as walnuts. He was twenty kilos overweight and she was about twenty kilos underweight. They were lappers – swimming up and down the pool, obviously counting out a predetermined number of laps before they could go for lunch.

The first German was quite adept at keeping out of the way of these serious swimmers, but his girlfriend, just hung onto the side as if an undertow would suck her away if she let go. Each group, the man and his girlfriend, the couple, and Craig studiously ignored one another, although Craig had not started it.

'Very friendly, he thought, 'very friendly indeed'.

Meanwhile, Lek had got on a Baht Bus outside the compound, gone right to Pattaya Klang and then had to change bus to turn right again as the one she was on turned left towards the beach. She was in her cousin's house fifteen minutes later. Beou's daughters were in school, so they had the place to themselves.

"How did you get on in Craig's town, Barry, isn't it? Did you like his friends and family?"

"Oh, yes," replied Lek, "I wasn't joking yesterday when I said that I loved everything about it except being away from my daughter and a few others in the family. I want to go and live there, but that will take some work too, because Craig has his heart set on living here. With me, of course. Still, I can work on that one. There is time enough."

They both laughed and hugged. It was great to be in cahoots with each other again. They really got on well, more like sisters than cousins. Lek had worked for Beou in the bar for ten years but even then Lek had had a special position that none of the other girls could ever have achieved.

"Well, look at it this way, telak, Soom is still only young and cannot speak English anyway – well, not fluently, eh? So, maybe it is better to get Craig to teach her before you all go over there anyway. That will take a couple of years and by then he may want to go home again. Don't worry. As you say, you have plenty of time. Let's see what fate has in store for you all."

Lek had told a white lie to Craig, she hadn't been invited to lunch, well, not a prepared lunch anyway. The two friends wanted to cook lunch together as they might have done if they were back in the village, where it is normal for visitors to help prepare the food. There, if you are not asked or allowed to help, you know that you are not being considered a close friend.

So, the first job was to call another old friend from the village, Noi, who also worked at Daddy's Hobby but as night watch woman. She had arranged to get off early to be with her oldest friends. They met up in the market and when Noi and Lek saw each other they ran at each other and hugged.

"Oh, Noi, I have missed our chats together. I tried to wait for you to come on shift at the bar last night, but we were so tired and the taxi came early. Still, here we are together again, all three of us. Like 'The Three Sisters', three peas in a pod, eh?" and they walked off arm-in-arm to shop for their favourite foods.

They spent an hour shopping, an hour washing, chopping, preparing and cooking the food and an hour eating it, although, in proper Thai country style, they prepared three or four dishes and started eating them first, but cooked other courses at the same time, so that there were always half-eaten and totally fresh, different courses on the table at the same time

By the time they had finished they were truly stuffed and there were still kilos of food both cooked and unprepared. After an hour dozing, chatting and watching TV, Beou, put the left-overs into cartons and put the cartons into three carrier bags so that they were shared equally.

Noi would take hers home, because she had to meet her daughter after school, but Lek and Beou weren't finished yet. They would take theirs to Daddy's Hobby and start the party up again, but with a lot more people this time.

Craig thought that he had got away with a free pass as he nodded to the security guard on his way out of the hotel compound, but in fact he had been granted one, so that Lek could do what she wanted. He thought he would stroll quietly down Soi Buakhao, the same way Lek had gone, but turn off before the end and make his way down to one of his favourite places the 'Pig and Whistle' on Soi Seven, which was not far from Beou's bar.

He intended to stop at quite a few of the intervening bars along the way though and get to Daddy's Hobby between four-thirty and five – late, as is normal in Thailand. He knew that Lek wouldn't consider an hour as being late.

As he had hoped, every bar along the way was devoid of customers, because it was still too early for most people, but they were full of bored bar girls and he got come-ons from every bar. They took a standard form, which was usually: 'Hello, sexy man' or /and 'Come have drink with me'. He took more than a few up on their kind offer, but he had no intention of doing any more than drink a few beers.

Most of the girls were beautiful and scantily-clad. Not many of them could speak English well enough to hold a decent conversation, but if the truth be known, they weren't really interested in talking either. If you didn't want sex and you wouldn't buy them a drink, you were soon left to your own devices. This was not a problem, because there were literally hundreds of bars on his chosen route and thousands of girls. He could not possibly have even one small beer in even five percent of them.

There were usually some nice surprises too though. You would meet a girl who was willing to just talk for a beer or even for nothing, because it kept you spending money in her empty bar and because she was bored out of her mind. If there were clients then it was only fair to move on. These were the sort of contacts that Craig was hoping for today. Just a few nice chats with young, beautiful, half-naked, female strangers.

He always made a point of telling the girls the truth, although he would never reveal were he was staying. After all, the last thing you need is some drunken, desperate woman knocking on your hotel room when you and your wife are asleep. And that had been known to have happened, or so he had been told. You never knew what to believe in Pattaya, but it sounded plausible enough to make him cautious.

Today he could tell the girls that this was the first day of his holiday. That always caught there attention, because it could mean that you will stay with them for a month (most people go for a month's holiday), or at least take them out often or it could mean that you didn't know your arse from your elbow with regard to Thai bar girls, so they would get more money out of you. The second question was usually: 'How long you stay here' and the third, though less important question for most girls was: 'You have Thai girlfriend already?'

Most girls didn't mind ousting another Thai if she didn't know them and some didn't care whether they did or not, but those were rarer – much rarer. It was usually the older, desperate pros who fell into that category – and the loners and the free-lancers.

As a bar girl had once told him: 'We bar girls don't cheat on wives, we are just the rope that cheating, husbands hang themselves with.'

In time, he got to the 'Pig' and went inside to see who was there. It was four o'clock, not the busiest of times, which revolved around meals: midday, five to six and seven to ten, but there were a few faces sitting at the bar that he recognized from his previous visits months before.

"Hello, Craig, how are you?, When did you get back?," said a voice from down the bar. It was one of the people who either owned or managed the bar/restaurant-cum-hotel.

"I'm fine thanks, Rob. How are you? We got back yesterday evening."

"How's that little darling of yours, Lek, isn't it? I thought I saw her walk past here a few minutes ago with another woman arm-in-arm, but I thought, no, that can't be Lek, she's in Wales with that Taff."

"It probably was her – with her cousin, maybe. She went for lunch at her house and I'm supposed to be meeting her at about now. But she's all right, can you ask one of the staff for a pint of Guinness, please? Do you want one?"

"Nah, not for me, thanks. I've got an hour off, then I'm on till closing. It'll start getting busy soon. Can't be pissed on parade, can I? Well, not every night anyway."

The pint of Guinness duly arrived. The taste of burnt wood or charcoal that characterized Guinness for Craig was always a lot stronger in Asia than in Europe. Probably because of the water supply there he thought.

"What's the news then, Rob? Anything monumental happen while I was away? A few more Scandinavians fell off their balconies pissed, I suppose?"

"Nothing much has been going on. The season has been quiet and hot. Except for Songkhran, of course. That was busy, but then it always is. Even if there were no falangs the Thais would make up for it. It's always good. A couple of jumpers, yes, if you believe that. I think most of them get pushed. Pissed, robbed and pushed. Not only Scandinavians either. Quite a few Germans too."

Rob left and Craig had another Guinness. Nobody else seemed to recognize him and he couldn't be bothered to start a conversation with any more strangers, so he just sat there and watched the girls walking to work and the falang coming back from the beach, wondering about where all this living in Thailand lark would eventually take him.

In truth, in private, in his head, he had no idea at all, although he was more confident when talking to others. He knew what he wanted to do: live in Thailand with Lek and support them by working on the Internet. And that seemed possible, but so much was beyond his control that anything could go wrong any day with just minute changes in the law or the exchange rate. It seemed unlikely that no law or no currency valuation would not go against him in the twenty-five years that he reckoned he had left to live there.

That was too much to hope for. What then? Would he have to go home broke with his tail between his legs? Would he be able to take Lek, even if she wanted to go with a pauper? The future was exciting, but it was also very uncertain and there was nothing he could do about that at all.

He and Lek were riding a canoe in white water on an unknown river.

So, on that sobering thought, he finished up and ambled down to see Lek, who he assumed would be waiting for him at Beou's.

And there she was, looking as beautiful as ever, standing behind the bar chatting with Beou and a couple who were sitting in front of it.

She saw him coming and waved and whooped as if she been doing it for years. "Hello, sexy man. You want to have drink with me? Where you come from?," she shouted. The three women laughed out loud and the man smiled broadly. When Craig got closer, he stood up and held out his hand.

"Hi, my name is Bob. I've heard a lot about you. How are you doing?"

"I'm fine thanks, Bob. How are you?"

Craig struggled with the man's face as he shook the girl's proffered hand. He knew her all right though – that was Mia, an old friend of Lek's from up-country, but Bob with the Australian accent, Craig was sure he'd never met him before.

Craig had met Mia before though and in such a way that it would take senile dementia for him ever to forget her. She had behaved even more 'friendly' in the past than the new girls last night, although Mia had been shrewd enough to avoid being seen doing it. Mia was dangerous, but he liked her. However, they were all sitting right in the front of the bar with Mia's fairly long-term boyfriend so that should be all right, Craig was reasoning.

He sat down next to Mia, Lek put a beer in front of him and Mia squeezed his knee.

"Oh, Bob! I love this man. He is very good friend for my good friend Lek and he help me too. You un'erstan'? You not jealous, neh? Craig only good frien'."

Bob nodded and smiled at Craig. Craig smiled, but grimaced inside knowing the truth that was being shared between him and Mia, but which had not been told in its entirety to Lek and Bob. He felt as if he were being held to ransom.

"We good frien's long time, neh, Craig? You, me and Lek?," she said as her hand moved up from his knee to his thigh and squeezed it.

"I know Lek very long time and I love her friend, same she love my friend, neh, Lek?"

Lek nodded enthusiastically, saying: "Mia and I know each other from baby school and we met Craig nearly one year ago."

That elicited another squeeze on the thigh, but higher up and a kiss on the cheek. Lek was sitting behind the bar, so she couldn't really see exactly what was going on, although she knew from the direction of Mia's arm where it was roughly.

Bob knew exactly and he wasn't too pleased about it.

He realized that there was more going on than he knew about, but didn't know what. Lek, for her part, could see the growing consternation on Bob's face, but she put it down to jealousy — an emotion that she detested and had given up when she had left her husband more than ten years before.

Craig had asked Lek before whether Mia was an exhibitionist, and Lek had reacted with surprise, but he knew from previous experience with Mia that she was 'up for anything' as long as there was a reasonable chance of not getting caught, although he suspected that she did want to be observed one day really.

Mia was like a 'shy' convent girl who drops her towel while changing and is so flustered that it takes her three minutes to cover up again.

The only one sitting there who knew that except Mia herself was Craig, because he had been on the receiving end. He would happily be there again, if the truth were known, but the stakes were higher now for him and he had had his fun.

Still, she tempted him more and more as the drinks flowed and Bob was becoming more are more cheesed off.

When Bob went to the toilet and everyone behind the bar was working because of the rush, Mia leaned over, put her hand on Craig's bulge, slowly undid his zip and said in his ear:

"Your trousers are open, do you want anything while I'm here?" and she stroked him inside his trousers.

'Where was Lek and her guardians when you needed them', he thought, 'when resistance was low?.' Bob came back and Mia said:

"Craig you zip kaput Look!"

Three or four by-standers looked and laughed.

"The zip is broken, I'll go fix it and go pee-pee," he said in pigeon-English.

Craig slinked off to the toilet with his hand over his crutch, trying to keep up the illusion than the zip was broken. Lek blew him a kiss from behind the bar. Once in the toilet, Craig did his business, zipped up and walked outside, only to be grabbed by Mia.

She pulled him into a shadow, lifted up her skirt and put his willing hand into her knickers.

"I shave my pussy," she said, "but you think I do good job? You shave for much longer than me; can you help me learn to shave pussy good same your face? Have little bit hair here, by pussy, what you think? Feel here. Oh, too wet, not have hair here. Sorry, what you think? Cannot grow hair in there, eh?"

After a fondle and with a great deal of will-power, Craig said: "Mia, you said that you had finished all this stuff because you had your own boyfriend. Bob, I suppose. If you are happy with him and I am happy with your friend Lek, what the hell are you doing?"

"Nothing," she said, "Just having some fun" and she walked back to the bar.

Craig followed a few yards behind, but he was troubled.

This was beyond his ability of deception. Not that he wanted to deceive Lek anyway. The problem was that he couldn't help feeling flattered and attracted to Mia. In fact, this was the first time anything like this had ever happened to him. Mia was unique amongst his friends or even casual acquaintances.

When he retook his seat, Lek smiled at him from where she was standing in font of the customer she was serving and Mia smile at him too.

Bob was looking the other way quite studiously.

Eventually, Lek tired of helping out and went to sit with Craig. Lek was on his left and Mia was on his right, so to talk over the din, they both had to lean across him and shout in one another's ears. Lek put her hand on Craig's thigh to steady herself and Mia put her hand about a foot higher on the other one.

Whenever Mia thought that no-one was paying attention, she stroked Craig's crotch lightly by wiggling her little finger. She pretended to be really drunk too, but maybe that didn't take much pretence. Eventually, the night finished and everybody went their own way.

On the way home, Lek said:

"Mia likes you, I can see. If I didn't know any better, I think I might have reason for concern."

"Ah, don't worry.," said Craig, knowing that he would never shag Mia or swap her for Lek in a month of Sundays.

As much fun as Mia was.

An Exciting Future

3 WHITHER NOW?

One afternoon, while they were drinking iced coffee on the balcony, the conversation turned to the future.

"So, Lek, we have had a bit of a holiday, so now it's time to start making some plans. What do you think? What would you like to do?"

"Well, first of all, I want to go see Soom and my Mum."

"Yes, OK, we'll go in two days, if you like, but I mean longer term than that. Where do you want to live for a start?"

"That is up to you, darling. I give you two choices: here in Pattaya or in my village, Baan Suay."

"OK, that's a start. I must have the Internet, so if we can get the Internet in the village, we still have two choices, but if we cannot, then we live in Pattaya. We could buy or rent a condo or house here and have a small 'hunting lodge' affair in the village for holidays."

"Hunting lodge? What is 'lodge'? No hunting in the village. Only hunt frogs, not tigers. Cannot hunt tigers now. Police take you and not have tigers any more. I don't understand."

"Yes, all right, wait a minute, calm down. I don't believe in hunting for fun anyway. I mean a small house. A hunting lodge is just a small house. Like a cabin. A small wooden house."

"Ah, I see! We have many hunting lodges in the village. Not many for chow though – I mean for rent. Maybe buy land and make small house. Can do?"

"Do you have Internet in the village?"

"I don't know, telak? I think nobody has a computer, but I don't know. We can go look in two or three days."

"Yes, good idea. I want Internet in our room too, so today I want to go buy a USB wireless modem. It's a bit like a mobile phone, but only for the Internet. I saw one yesterday in Pattaya Klang for 3,500 Baht, so not too expensive. Then I don't have to pay 20 Baht every hour in an Internet shop. Now I pay 100-160 Baht every day. Then I can work from the room or the beach or anywhere I like."

So, they drank up, grabbed the laptop and set off. Once in the shop, Craig spoke to the assistant:

"I am interested in that wireless modem."

"Eh?"

"That wireless modem there."

"Eh?"

Then she said to Lek in Thai:

"What is the falang talking about? I cannot understand him. Does he speak English? I can speak a little bit of English."

"He is speaking English, but I don't know what he wants either. I don't understand computers at all. Ask him again, but tell him to speak slowly."

"What you say? Say again, but speak slowly, please, sir."

"OK, I want that wireless modem there. That one, right there."

"Ah! Wi-Fi? Internet Wi-Fi. OK. Here. Look."

Craig inspected the device, took out his laptop and switched it on.

"I can try now?"

"No, cannot. Not have ca's."

"What? Not have 'cars'. What are Internet 'cars'? Lek what is she saying? Can I see the instruction book, please, Lek?"

There was a flurry of Thai and the manual was handed over.

"I don' know how to tell you, but we don't have 'ca's' for modem. I don't know what is ca's."

So he sat down to read the manual.

It was only in Thai. He couldn't read it and Lek couldn't understand it. Then the sales assistant took out her mobile phone, took the back off it and pointed to the SIMM card.

"Not have ca's in modem. Must buy, then can use for Internet."

"Ah, I see. Must have SIMM card." The two women smiled and

nodded. "OK, if I buy Wi-Fi and a SIMM card will it work every-where?"

"No," she said, "only in Thailand. If you go to Cambodia, stop working."

"OK, does it work everywhere in Thailand? Everywhere? Even Sukhothai, Uttaradit, Phitsanulok, in a village up there? Or only in big city?"

"Everywhere, sir. It working everywhere in Thailand. Even in vil-lage."

"OK, I want one Wi-Fi and one SIMM card, please."

He was putting his laptop away, when she said:

"You can buy Wi-Fi, but cannot buy ca's. Not have."

"What?," he was starting to become hot and bothered now. "Why not?"

More Thai, then Lek said:

"You must get SIMM card from a DTAC telephone shop."

That meant nothing to Craig, but he bought the modem and they left. He wasn't sure about the DTAC SIMM card, but Lek led him straight to a shop near the apartment. When he saw the shop, he real-ized that he'd seen hundreds of them before. There were several in every main street in Pattaya. DTAC is one of the biggest mobile phone providers in Thailand and with thousands of girls and several million tourists a year, Pattaya could support hundreds of phone shops selling DTAC SIMM cards.

Craig's cost 750 Baht a month for unlimited usage, which worked out far cheaper than the roughly 4,000 a month he was spending then and it was much more convenient. It also still left them with two choices of where they could live.

Things were looking up.

They went down to Daddy's Hobby, where Craig plugged in his new toy and was chuffed to find that it worked like a dream. They sat there until the battery on the laptop ran out and then Craig wanted to go home. Lek had a simpler solution and she had the laptop plugged into the mains. The adapter was always in the bag because the battery only lasted two hours and Craig regularly spent eight hours working in the cyber cafés in one session.

He was off again and, with a beer, was as happy as a sand boy.

Lek admired the way that Craig could sit self-contained, detached and completely absorbed in whatever he was doing. At times like this, she had noticed, he would be the only person in his world. Nothing would distract him, yet he would react to his name. It fascinated her. Lek found it hard to concentrate on anything for more than fifteen minutes at a time. For that reason, reading novels was not her favourite pastime.

Lek was telling everyone how excited she was to be going home for a few days to see her family. They all made the appropriate noises, wished they could be going too and those from Baan Suay asked if she would take small presents home for their families for them. It was a custom and Lek naturally agreed. Some girls even rushed off there and then to get something from a local store, while it was not busy in the bar.

Gifts would be things that were impossible to get in the village like chocolate for the kids and dried squid for the grown-ups. A pineapple from Chonburi, the Province that Pattaya is in, is also a luxury as they are famous for being the sweetest in Thailand. Children's clothing was also often sent back by mothers missing their children.

Some of the girls who knew how to, wanted a go on the Internet. It would save them time and money not to have to go to an Internet café and Craig found himself reading, translating and writing some quite pornographic message to amorous falang lovers. Little did they know that a bloke was writing them, he thought. The image of their faces if they had known made Craig smile.

"Ha, ha! Man tell man he want to kiss him all over. Funny, neh, Craig? If my boyfriend John know you send message, he want box you and me. Tell him I wan' to kiss him down there. Good joke, neh?"

Craig was not very impressed but wanted to help out and so did so.

It went a log way to getting him back in with the girls and he loved every minute of it. It would become a regular part of his frequent visits to Daddy's Hobby.

They went to the apartment quite early at nine o'clock, but both were tired after a week of parties. They went to bed after a shower and Lek fell asleep almost immediately as she often did. It was a knack that Craig envied.

He had had problems getting to sleep all his life; for as long as he could remember. Even as a very young child, he could remember going downstairs to ask for a drink of water, just because he was bored that he couldn't get to sleep. His parents' advice had always been to just lies there with closed eyes as 'a rest is as good as a sleep'. He didn't believe it any longer, but he still couldn't get to sleep.

Usually, he just got up and read, but this evening he had a new toy, so he switched the computer on and got ready to work. It would set the trend of the way things would be for the rest of his life, but he didn't know that yet.

Craig had made a few web sites before, but he knew that they were amateurish, so he set about looking for instructions on how to do it properly. He didn't want to have to learn HTML thoroughly, so preferred the route of using an editor.

After three hours of research he had selected a British HTML editor from a short list of six. It was not cheap, but by two a.m. it was on his desktop and he was preparing to launch it. This was typical of Craig, he always wanted to be 'doing it'.

By six a.m. he had created a web site that was better than he had ever made before. At least it looked good in preview, so he looked around for a host for the web site. Within the hour, the web site was uploaded to the host and a decent-looking web site was live on the Internet. When he looked up, Lek was standing behind him.

"You get up early, telak? I think you not go to bed. Why you not sleep, my dear?"

"Don't worry, Lek, it's just that I'm excited with this new modem.

It allows me to do what I want at any time of the day or night. I love it. Look, I made my first web site in Thailand. Not bad, eh?"

"Very nice. You can make money with that?"

"Well, no, not yet. As it stands it will not make money, but...."

"So, I don't understand. Why you work all night for web site that not make money? Seem stupid to me. I don't understand Internet and web sites. Tell me later, I go to sleep again for one hour."

He didn't feel too discouraged, but he knew that he could not ever be certain of being able to make enough money on line to keep them together either. It was another facet of their new life together that was not guaranteed. In fact, so far there was nothing guaranteed except that anything could happen.

When Lek woke up again at eight thirty, Craig had applied for a Google Adsense account, a PayPal account, an Amazon account and several others. These would allow him to monetize his web sites, if he were accepted and it would mark the first step to being able to live in Thailand without financial worries whether it be in Lek's village, Baan Suay, or Pattaya.

There was little more he could do now except think of an idea for a good web site, so he undressed and crept into bed beside Lek with sun-light streaming in through the French windows leading to the balcony.

Moments later, he heard:

"Telak, I go get tickets for go to the village tonight. OK? I want to see my daughter and my family. See you later. We go tonight, if I can get tickets. Or tomorrow if I cannot."

Lek was getting up, before he was completely asleep – this too would become a regular occurrence in their future.

4 BAAN SUAY

Craig got up at midday, showered, went for breakfast and a swim and was back at his computer within the hour. He was in his element. There had been no confirmations of being granted accounts, but he hadn't expected that there would be. Every firm that he wanted to work with was either in the USA or the UK and the time difference varied from seven to fourteen hours.

In his head, he was still working on what would be a good theme for a web site, while manually, he was building a site about Wales, just to get to grips with the new site-building programme he'd bought the night before. Or that morning really. Craig didn't need much sleep.

When Lek came back at about two p.m. Craig had decided to create a site on Thai food and was getting stuck into making it.

"Hello, telak. How are you? We have ticket for go tonight at six p.m. You want to eat something?"

He didn't. "No, thanks. I want to work, but I would love a few cans of beer. Can you get me six, please? It's very hot in here and the aircon is not good."

Lek was not impressed, but went out anyway. She returned ten minutes later with six large bottles of Chang beer.

"Craig, you stay here? I must go to Daddy's Hobby get presents from friends to take to their families tonight. Here is one bottle for you and I put five in the fridge."

He agreed with a grunt and she left.

He was on a mission and so was she, but they were starting to go separate ways already, although neither of them could see it yet.

Craig worked for three hours and drank three beers in the time that it took for Lek to get back. When she arrived, she packed the case with a few things and the presents she had just collected. They showered and took a taxi to the VIP bus station which was not too far away except that they had to get there in rush hour. Having to get anywhere in Pattaya between five and six is best avoided. However, Lek had taken that into account and they got to the bus station with fifteen minutes to spare.

Lek was not a particularly good traveller. Not only did she get travel sickness really, really badly, and the tablets that she took for it made her half-dopey but she worried constantly about having left things behind. Now that they were waiting for the bus, Craig was waiting for her anxiety attack to start. Sure enough, after a few minutes of sitting there she was frantically searching in her bag.

"What's the matter, darling?" he asked.

"Oh, the tickets. I give you the tickets, yes? I don't have. I think you leave the tickets by the TV in the condo. Maybe we must buy more tickets. Not have."

"I never saw the tickets. You didn't even show them to me. Just slow down and look carefully." He was tempted to look for himself, but he had never liked looking in a lady's bag. "Just don't worry, we can buy more like you say, if we have to."

"Maybe not have more. Maybe must come back tomorrow or next week. Oh, Craig, I want to see my Soom. I tell her already that we come tonight... Ah, here are the tickets. I put by Soom's photo in my purse. Good job, neh?" Craig knew that, unless he could get her to fall asleep, there would be eight hours more of this. Sometimes, it was worse than listening to a drunk full of remorse at a bar when she was on these tablets. He hated them.

They got on the bus, which was only five minutes late and after phoning her daughter to say that they were on their way, Lek kissed him and fell asleep. Craig put the blanket over her and turned to look out of the window. Lek never sat by the window because the reflection in the glass and the scenery whizzing past aggravated her travel sickness. This was ideal for Craig the insomniac, because he could spend all night gazing out of the window. Mostly into impenetrable darkness, but they did pass through a few cities.

On occasions like this, since he had lived in Thailand, Craig liked to look for UFO's at night. He wasn't quite sure why he was more confident of spotting one in Thailand one night, but he was. Maybe Thailand just seemed naturally more exciting that the UK. In the day time he would look out the window hoping to catch a glimpse of a snake or a crocodile.

He knew that here was about as much chance of that as seeing a UFO, but it didn't stop him looking. In fact, there are no more wild crocodiles in Thailand, they are bred in farms, as westerners breed cattle, for their meat and skin. Sometimes, a few escaped during the monsoon seasons when the crocodile ponds overflowed and the crocodiles could swim out over the walls. That always caused quite a commotion among the locals. Very few living Thais knew how to be safe with four metre long crocodiles swimming in the river these days.

Now he wished he hadn't had those three pints of beer, because he would have to scramble over Lek to get to the toilet and he didn't really want her to wake up. Bugger, he thought. Yet there was nothing for it, so he clambered over her, heard her say something unintelligible and rushed down the aisle to the back of the bus, which was bouncing and swaying down the road at about 80kph. He woke up more than a few people on the way trying to steady himself.

After peeing everywhere in the toilet but down the pan because of the unpredictable swaying of the bus, he ran the gauntlet down the aisle again, annoyed a few more people, woke Lek up properly this time, got cursed for it and took his seat. He swore that that would be the last time he would ever drink beer before a coach trip again, even if there were a toilet on board.

To his amazement, his brain soon got bored scanning the empty skies and, now that his bladder was no longer troubling him, he too fell asleep.

When they arrived in Phitsanulok it was one thirty a.m. but the bus station was still quite busy. Around all four sides of the station there were situated small cafés, a few restaurants and even fewer tiny hotels. The last time they had come up (or the first time, whichever way you want to look at it), they had been met, but this time they had to sort things out for themselves. They both wanted the toilet and Lek knew Craig well enough to know that she wouldn't upset him if she suggested a beer, so she invited him to choose a café-cum-bar.

He made his selection after a few seconds careful deliberation, but the nearest one wasn't 'good enough', so Lek gave him another chance. That one wasn't right either, so she led him half-way around the block to one that she had used before. He wondered why she had bothered asking him in the first place, but didn't say anything.

Craig had a large bottle of Chang, a bucket of ice, with which to water it down to a sensible ABV and a glass. Lek would share the beer with him, but had her own glass and a very large bowl of Pad Thai, which is basically noodles and whatever else the cook puts in it, although most chef's would say they have a set, private recipe. They were followed every inch of the way to the café by several taxi touts offering their patrons' services, but when they sat down the touts went away grumbling.

"Right, telak, we have three options, an' it's up to you. The bus to the village comes at five o'clock, so we can sit here drinking and eating until then or we can take a room upstairs and wait for the bus; or we can take a taxi now. If you want cheap, we stay here drinking, if you want expensive, we take taxi. We have three hours for wait. What you want to do?"

Thinking about his recent experiences on the bus, Craig asked: "How far is it again to Baan Suay – er, how long will it take? About ninety minutes? OK, lets just sit here, watch TV, read a book and eat and drink until the bus comes." It wasn't a financial decision for Craig, he just didn't want to be lying awake for three hours with nothing to do.

Craig was the first one to need the toilet and it changed his mind.

He said to Lek: "Crikey, that bog is stinking!"

"What, telak? A problem?"

"Yes, if the places I chose were not good enough, they must have been very horrible, because the toilet here is not clean at all. Smell very bad and I mean very, very horrible. Please ask how much is room for two hours." Lek called the woman over.

"One hundred Baht? Is that all? Go look at the room, Lek and if the toilet is clean we take it." Lek said something and followed the woman to the first floor room. When she had returned, she said to Craig: "It is not same as hotel in Pattaya, but OK. It has UK toilet, shower, TV and bed."

They took it and two bottles of Chang. Lek was pleased to be able to shower, but there was only one small hand towel and they hadn't brought any towels with them. They didn't own any towels either, so she put on one of Craig's shirts and lay on the bed wet. She was asleep in minutes, leaving Craig to drink his beer alone and look through the five TV channels for something in English in vain.

He couldn't be bothered to test his new wireless modem by switching on the laptop, so he just sat on the edge of the bed, listening to Lek snoring softly, watching TV from time to time, reading from time to time and drinking his beer. This was beginning to feel more like the first day of the rest of his life. Pattaya was just a fantasy, a fun city, the most Fun City in all of South-East Asia by all accounts and he could well believe it, but could anyone really live there for a long time without going slightly mad?

The time passed quickly and he was soon waking the bleary-eyed Lek for the next stage of the journey. That bus was thirty minutes late and Craig had never seen an older-looking vehicle in public service. It looked American, maybe from the Fifties. It was bare aluminium or tin, with some streaks of blue. It was quite ornate actually and had two rows of double seats with rotating fans above them and a bench seat in the back.

They took half the bench seat so they could sit by their luggage and because Craig didn't fit in the narrow space between the other seats, which were obviously laid out for Thais or children. Not for 18 stone men anyway, that was for sure. When the bus started up, he could see why all the windows and doors were wedged open – only the one fan above the driver's head worked, but the bus was cool enough when moving, even if the air was very dusty.

An orange-robed young monk got in at one of the dozens of stops. He gave a cursory glance at Lek and started to sit down next to her on the bench seat. She leaped up and swapped paces with Craig. "Lady cannot sit next to monk. Cannot touch monk," she explained. The monk smiled briefly at Craig and they were off again. When the conductress came for the monk's fare, he thrust a iffy Baht note into Craig's unsuspecting hand. He had no idea what was going on, but the conductress took it from him and replaced it with a twenty Baht note, which the monk took with a smile. "Lady cannot touch monk," whispered Lek in his ear.

When the bus stopped for them, it pulled over onto a bare patch of earth by the side of the road and they climbed down into a swirling cloud of dust, which was made worse as the bus pulled off. It hadn't been worth showering less than three hours ago, he thought, but knew that that was not the Thai way and certainly not Lek's. She seemed to take a shower, whenever she had ten minutes to spare. She was on the phone in an instant and within ten minutes a car pulled up to take them to the village. It was not far, but when they got there it was eight a.m. It had taken 14 hours to travel the 700 kms to get there – more than the time for a non-stop flight from Bangkok to London.

The last time they had come up together it had been for a national holiday and there had been a large welcome party waiting to meet Craig, but this was a normal working day and people had been hard at it in the fields since about six o'clock. The village was practically deserted except for old ladies and pre-school age kids. Lek's Mum was there though and a few of her friends, cooking as usual. He waaied everyone that was older than himself – that is everyone but the children – as he had been instructed and sat down.

Three plates of food and a beer appeared in front of him instant-aneously and he wondered if this visit would be like the last one – a seventy-two hour party with sleeping breaks. He was shattered and just wanted to go to bed, whereas Lek had slept whenever she could and was raring to go. So, after a length of time which made it polite to leave, Lek took him for a shower and put him to bed in the large room that they had used before.

Lek was too excited to sleep though. She had to tell all her stories again to the old ladies who had warned her about the dangers of be-coming a sex slave. Her daughter would not be back from school until five-ish so she had plenty of time for visiting. After a couple of hours with her mother and her mother's friends, she borrowed a scooter and went to the village Wat or temple, which always doubles as a monastery in Thailand. Most, if not every village has at least one Wat, just as west-ern villages have churches, but a Wat has a colony of Buddhist monks too.

Lek had made a pact with God before she had left for the UK: if she returned unharmed, she would donate a pig's head to Buddha and put on a Lickay, which is a little like a pantomime. Although there is only one storyline to Lickay, a good troupe will rewrite the script fre-quently to include references to topical, current events. Lek wanted to hire a good troupe as she had promised, so she had come up to give thanks and arrange a date for her offering.

The Lickay would or could take weeks or even months to arrange as the best touring companies were always in high demand, but the of-fering of the pig's head was set for two days time, which was plenty of time for her and her mother to arrange a party.

Having taken care of business, she couldn't wait to talk to her friends, whether they were working in the fields or not. Some of them would be home looking after grandchildren anyway.

Craig woke up at three, went for a shower, tried to phone Lek, but couldn't get through, so set up his equipment. He couldn't wait to get back on line.

It didn't work anywhere in the room, so he went outside to the huge communal dining table-cum-family bench that all rural families sit at just as Americans like to sit at the kitchen table to talk.

It didn't work there either, but by the time he had found that out, his 'Mum' had spotted him and food and beer were placed before him again. With a sigh of resignation, he knew that he was trapped for a while.

It was extremely disappointing that the wireless modem wasn't working as he had been promised but there were black spots for mobiles, he knew that, and he was still hopeful of finding somewhere he could work. As soon as he was finished eating, he got up and went for a walk. Baan Suay had no bars or hotels he could sit in and the small café didn't sell beer, so he thought he would buy a few bottles and sit in one of the shelters that he assumed were bus stops. The purchase, in Thai, went well enough, but when the shop keeper saw him cross the road to sit in the 'bus shelter' she ran after him.

This conversation did not go so smoothly, because neither party understood a word of what the other was saying. In desperation, the shop keeper took his arm and led him back to the shop. Craig assumed that he had underpaid her or something, but she pointed to a table, then brushed it down and pushed him into it. This shop and this table was to become the nearest thing that Baan Suay ever had to a bar and Craig would use it often.

The only problem was that the modem didn't work very well there either, so he decided to phone the company that provided the equipment and tell them about it.

"Hello, Hutch? Good. I hope you're well too. Look, I am up in northern Thailand and I can't get decent reception on my USB wireless modem, is there a problem?"

"No problem, where are you sir?"

"I'm not sure, in the juncture of Phitsanulok, Sukhothai and Uttaradit. Where those three provinces meet."

"Oh. Wi-Fi not work in Uttaradit sometimes, sir. Please move."

"What? Move where? My wife lives here. I can't just 'move'. I was told that this device works 'everywhere in Thailand'."

"Yes, sir, everywhere in Thailand sir, but not yet in Uttaradit maybe in two month." We put new mas' everywhere soon. Can get signal from Phitsanulok, if condition is good. You have tree between you and signal, sir?"

"Phitsanulok city is seventy-five kilometres from here, I imagine there is a tree between here and there yes."

"Sorry, sir, you say 'yes'? Can you cut it down? Then you get good signal maybe. Or move. Bye, bye. If you have problem please phone again, my boss not here an' I not speak English' good. Bye, sir."

Great, he thought, I've either got to move to a different province or cut down all the trees between here and Phitsanulok.

Lek turned up while this conversation was going on having tracked Craig down on the jungle telegraph with her network of spies. He tried to get her to phone the Wi-Fi company but she would not. "I know nothing for computers," she protested, "You want me look stupid?"

This was the truth, computers had passed her by, but Lek did not like to cause a fuss either and certainly not with people 'in authority', which basically meant anyone with a better job than she had. Being unemployed that meant practically everyone, although she was married to a 'wealthy falang' and not destitute, which counted for something.

The truth was that she had a complex about her lack of education and she bitterly regretted the decision to leave school early that she and her parents had taken together eighteen years before.

She could see now what the lack of schooling had gotten her: a ten-year separation from her daughter and family and ten years in the sex tourist industry. It had made Lek fiercely pro education for her daughter as a means to better her life, even if that would mean leaving the village for ever too one day.

So, hoping that lightning would strike every tree between the village and Phitsanulok the next time it rained, Craig ordered another beer, another glass and a bucket of ice and they waited for the school bus, which coincidentally would stop at the shelter across the road. When the bus turned up at four fifty, little Soom was framed in the window and a big smile flashed across her pretty face as she spotted her mother.

She descended and waited for the bus to pull away before slowly and carefully crossing the road towards the shop, the only emotion showing was a glint in her eye and a small smile.

"Hello, Mum. Hello, Craig" and she waaied him. Craig waaied back then it was like a hurricane of Thai between mother and daughter none of which Craig could understand although he could feel the love flowing between them. There was no touching though. Soom sat down and a Coke was brought. They talked politely for fifteen minutes and then got up.

"We are going to do some cooking now, please come home in one hour. OK?"

It was OK, they would go upstairs in Mum's house where he had never been and they would kiss and hug out of sight of all but the closest family, which Craig was not yet quite a full member of. He knew that and wondered how long it took for membership to be approved.

He ordered another beer and went back to his computer, happy to see that the signal had improved.

Maybe somewhere to the south, someone had just cut down a tree.

5 A TOUCH OF REALITY

Lek didn't know how long she wanted to stay in the village, and, although Craig found this naturally frustrating, he didn't really mind. Lek was resenting the fact that Craig had surprised her with that lovely condo now though and the money they were wasting by not sleeping there. Still, it couldn't be helped. Craig had rushed into that decision without consulting her and it was his own money to burn if that was what he chose to do with it. She would have tried to pay by the week, not by the month in advance, although unbeknown to her, that option was not possible.

Craig didn't worry about the condo, but he did miss the swimming pool and the smooth Internet service, because the signal was still a bit temperamental in the village although the shop was as good a location as it got locally, which was a bonus for him.

Life was really quiet. Craig had never lived in a village before. He had always stayed in medium-size towns. Cities were too big for him, but he had always imagined that villages would be too small for him too. This small village was proving to be fine though. He thought that he could live here, especially if he could find a way of improving his Internet connection.

Lek spent all the daylight hours helping her mother about the house and talking with friends, while Craig built and refined his virtual real estate. He was getting better at using the HTML editor and his web sites were looking all right. They were not flashy, but they were sedate and business-like. Built to install confidence in the buyer rather than impress him with the owner's programming skills. He hoped the tactic would work, because up to now he hadn't been able to test it.

Basically, he had nothing to sell and no visitors to sell it to. It was unlikely that he ever would have any physical products to sell either in Baan Suay. In Pattaya, a trip to the market would render a supply of games, sunglasses, clothes and perfume, but there was nothing but rice where he was staying. Very good rice, there was no question about that, but he couldn't see it selling by the kilo all over the world.

He needed something else; non-physical products and finding them was the next challenge. Eventually, authorization to use Google Adsense and PayPal came through, so now he could accept credit card payments (if he had anything to sell) and he could put a bit of code supplied by Google on his site, so that it would display adverts relevant to the content on his site automatically.

Then he faced the brick wall that every Internet marketer faces: how to get traffic to the site. Craig prevaricated on this one, basically because he had no idea how to do it. He thought like they said in the film: 'If you build it, people will come', so he looked around for some affiliate products to sell instead. He found a shop in Britain willing to give him ten percent commission on any food bought from their web site and a travel company offering commission on flights, hotels and car rental in most countries in the world, so he put them on his sites and waited.

And waited, and nothing happened. He could see on his web sites' access logs and on his Google admin account that he had about twenty visitors a day and that half of those were robots scanning the web. He started to become depressed, but not with the village. The worst thing was that there was no-one to discuss anything with. He had the only computer and the only Internet connection for miles around as far as he knew and no-one knew anyone who could speak English, although it was taught in all the schools. Life in the village for him would be an endurance test against cabin fever. He could see it coming.

∞

One day, while scootering around five to ten miles from the village on Mum's motorbike for a break, a foreigner ran out in front of them shouting something. It was the first falang that Craig had ever seen up country and Lek pulled over. He was obviously very upset but Lek could not understand his Thai. "What's the problem, mate?" asked Craig.

"Oh, sanks," he said, "I have big problem with slang. Can your wife help, please."

Craig guessed he was either Dutch, German or Scandinavian and spoke to him in Dutch. He was right. A big black snake had bitten the maid's young son and he was screaming the place down. The man didn't know what to do as his wife and the maid had taken the car to go shopping. He had phoned her but it would take her an hour to get back and the man was worried that if it had been a cobra the boy might die before then. They could see the boy rolling around on the lawn, so Craig got off the bike and told the man to get on with the baby. Lek took them to the local clinic.

Craig wandered around the gardens, which were quite impressive and up onto the verandah at the back of the house which overlooked the river. It was beautiful and just the kind of house and location that he fancied. There was a fridge on the verandah too, nicely stocked with snacks and beer, so he took one out and sat down to await his 'wife' and his host. He felt a little like an intruder, but not too much. He was taking care of the Dutchman's house which had been left wide open.

It was just over an hour or two beers later that a car pulled into the drive followed by Lek on the motorbike. The Dutchman and his Thai wife were in the car and the maid and the boy were being taken to hospital. Anti-venom had already been administered and the boy was out of danger. Craig and the Dutchman were getting on well and the wives were talking to each other too, but not so warmly, as is often the case with Thai women married to foreigners. They forget where they came from and look down on other Thai women who are trying to better themselves too. When the mosquitoes started coming up off the river, Craig made his excuses and they left, promising to call back again soon, but somehow, Craig doubted that Lek would ever find the time.

The following day, while Craig was sitting in the shop trying to fathom out how to get visitors to his two web sites, the Dutchman's car pulled up. "Hi, Craig! You OK? You tell me you have problem with de Internet. I want to help you like you help me" and then in Dutch: "Let's speak Dutch, you speak it better than I do English. You can call me Dutch too, everyone else does. How do you fancy a ride to an Internet shop not far from here? If you get stuck in the future you can get your wife to drop you there. It's not far. Where is Lek? Can she come with us now or shall we go another time?"

Craig phoned Lek, who dropped whatever she was doing, probably eating, and came right over. She was not very impressed, but a foreigner would not have been able to spot it. They all went by car to a large village-small town about ten kilometres west of Baan Suay where there was a new Internet shop – not quite an Internet café yet as they didn't sell any refreshments, but the owner was introduced to Craig and he seemed cheerful and friendly. Then the Dutch couple drove them home. Craig and Lek sometimes passed the house over the following years, but never saw or spoke to them again.

It was rumoured that the Dutchman was playing the field and had been for years even with successive housemaids. His wife and everyone else in their vicinity knew it too, so it was said. One day, Dutch fell ill and was confined to bed for about six weeks. When his wife didn't come home one day, he feared that she had had an accident because he couldn't raise her on the phone either. She also didn't come back that night, so Dutch got on the scooter to get some money from the bank as that was the last thing she was supposed to have been doing.

The ATM swallowed the card, so, Dutch went inside and spoke to the manager whom he had known well for years.

"Sorry," the bank manager had said, "you have no money in your account."

"Impossible," had screamed Dutch, "my pension goes in there every month and we have savings too!"

They had checked the records together, but it was true; Dutch's wife had cleaned him out the day before. So they phoned his bank in the Netherlands, but they had 'acted on his written instructions' weeks ago to transfer all his funds to Thailand and redirect his pension to his new Thai bank account.

Dutch was beside himself apparently. He borrowed enough money to fly home and was never seen in the area again. They had been together for twenty years and she had probably poisoned him to keep him in bed while she rifled his bank accounts. When Dutch went home, the wife came back and sold the house, because it was in her name – foreigners may not own land in Thailand.

It was a big lesson for the local foreigners, although most of them said that Dutch did not chase other women and certainly not local ones, but few people will probably ever know the whole truth of the matter.

∞

Craig started to make more and more use of the Internet café, because his own ISP was very unreliable – what with the distance the signal had to travel and all the trees that kept growing up between him and its source. Anyway, it made a welcome change to get out of Baan Suay and have a chat with Tum the owner of the place. His English was not too good, because he lacked practice but he did have a degree in computers. His Internet source was pretty fast and reliable too.

Craig liked to get there early, as soon as it opened at eight o'clock and stay there until the school kids arrived at about five o'clock. This suited the people who gave him a lift too as they would drop him off on the way to work and pick him up on the way home. The small town was surrounded by working rice fields like Baan Suay – it was just bigger.

It was impossible for Craig to stay there any later anyway because the school kids transformed the place from a peaceful 'international library' into a seaside arcade parlour in minutes when they arrived and during the weekend it was just a no-go area. Tum tried to cordon off a 'quiet area' for Craig, but it was an impossible task given the volume of the twenty machines playing shoot-em ups and the kids screaming and, to be fair, those kids spent a lot more money there every day than Craig did in a week.

The Internet shop was a good short-term solution, but the only real answer was a faster or at least more reliable connection of his own. Tum had discussed a couple of options, but Craig had not had time to check them out yet. There was the Thai national telephone company, TOT, and a new satellite service called IPstar. Neither company had blemish-free, glowing reports from foreigners on the forums and chat rooms. TOT was cheap but unreliable and useless when the kids were home from school due to overload and IPstar was three or four times the cost and sixteen times slower but very reliable and not subject to overload as not many Thai families used it.

However, he was jumping the gun a little. He had proved to himself that he could work in the village or nearby and he assumed that access to the Internet would only improve in the years to come. Therefore, it was possible to live in the village. The next thought was to be about housing.

He favoured the idea of living by the river and owing a small rowing boat or a canoe. Lek liked fishing and he could row her out into the river for play-days on the water. It sounded idyllic.

And they could sit under a tree in the garden on the river bank and watch the water flow past.

And he could put a picnic table there and work on the Internet as long as his own tree didn't sabotage his signal.

A plan, a dream, even a fairytale was beginning to form in his head. Maybe plant a small vineyard and make his own wine. Lek was an ex-farmer, she could learn how to do that and they could work it together. He would be like Don Corleone in the Godfather but without the gangster connections.

And before he had a heart attack.

Marriage was looming too, he had already felt a few undertows sucking him in that direction. He and Lek had been together almost a year and he had 'taken her off the market', so to speak. He still wasn't exactly sure what Lek had done for a living and he didn't really care either, but he sort of knew, whenever he allowed himself to think about her likely past.

Not that Lek had ever mentioned her history in Pattaya, but whichever way you looked at it, he was reducing her chances of marriage by occupying her time at this stage of her life and he would be giving her false hope.

Marriage had to be on the cards, not that Lek had ever mentioned marriage either. However, her friends had.

Many times.

It is a sort of rule of thumb that people consider you common-law man and wife after three months of living together. It has absolutely no legal foundation, but there is a kind of permanence established after three months.

And now he was sleeping with Lek in her mother's house under the very noses of her daughter and family. Not for the first time either. They had shared the room he thought of as a chapel the first time they had visited almost a year ago. In those days, he was 'just on holiday' though and he had hoped that people were naïve enough to think that they shared a room but not the one mattress on the floor.

How naïve he had been.

The fact was though that he would have been mortified if he had allowed himself to think that everyone knew that they were sleeping to-gether. Especially her mother and daughter. Luckily that was all behind them and they could start looking for a suitable house for sale on a beautiful riverside plot.

Meanwhile, unbeknown to Craig, Lek was following her own lines of enquiry. There was an empty house not 50 metres from her Mum's house, which she fancied, but it fronted onto the 'main' road, which meant that it was a little noisy. There were also two more coming up for sale soon. One was still occupied but the occupant would be moving away in a month after she got married and the other was being sold by the relatives of someone who had just died.

Lek was very superstitious and more than a little afraid of ghosts, so she was wondering whether to tell Craig about that house at all, but the other one was just over the back lane of her mother's house – literally no more than three metres! She thought that that would be ideal as well, although it was a little ramshackle. To be truthful, it needed to be taken down and a new house built. She wanted a nice new concrete house, like the ones in the new estates in Pattaya. She thought that the traditional teak village houses on stilts were so outré.

Lek decided that she would try to sell the ramshackle house to Craig by emphasising the noisiness of the one and the eeriness of the other. She knew that Craig was not so worried about ghosts, but she would make sure that he knew that she was and she would try to come up with a few other things wrong with it too. Price, maybe. And mosquitoes because it bordered on a rice field. Snakes too. Yes, that should rule that one out.

All she had to do now was to bide her time and wait for the right opportunity. She could meet him after he came back from the Internet café and suggest they go for a few beers in the shop. Yes, he was always up for that and it would sound good coming from her – her suggestion. They could then go for a walk and 'spot' the three properties by accident and then go back to the shop to talk about them.

In fact, Lek was so excited about the prospect, that she couldn't wait for a 'good time' to raise the matter, so she went to the shop at five o'clock to wait for her uncle to bring Craig back from the Internet café To make the surprise complete, she phoned her uncle and asked him to warn her when they entered the village. When she got the call ten minutes later, she ordered an ice cold beer Chang and arranged some of Craig's favourite mini spring rolls on a plate and put a napkin over them to keep the flies and dust off them.

Sure enough, minutes later Craig could be seen approaching, riding in the Thailand next to her uncle.

Like a lamb to the slaughter.

"Hello, telak, over here. Here I am," she called. Not that Craig could have missed her beside the narrow 'main road'. "I have a surprise for you."

Craig waved and as the wagon slowed to a crawl, he tapped 'his uncle's' arm by way of thanks and hopped off.

"Hello, Lek. Nice surprise. What are you doing here? I don't normally see you till teatime"

"Yes, telak. I want to surprise you. I saw someone sell pompia today, so I buy for you. Your favourite, neh? Spring rolls. And a beer – very cold. It is good after the dust from the road on the Thailand."

She handed him the bottle and uncovered the spring rolls. It was just what he wanted – a bite to eat and a cold beer, because that dust did get everywhere. Most people wore a bandanna or a balaclava when travelling, but Craig hadn't yet got into that habit. He made the first motion to bend over to kiss her, but he caught the meaning of the look in her eyes and just squeezed her shoulder. No kissing or holding hands in the village.

It was the only rule that he had to observe, but it was strictly enforced with no exceptions at all.

"Craig, did you have a good day, darling? You stay in the Internet shop all day or you go for a walk at lunch time?"

"I didn't stop for lunch, I never do. Tum's wife gave me a home-made sweet of some kind. I don't know what it was – very sweet, wrapped in a bit of banana leaf. It looked like blancmange. It was very nice and I bought a packet of crisps. This is just right."

"Oh, good. We can have one more beer and then go for a walk before the mosquitoes come out, neh? You must have some exercise. Sit down all day, not walk, no good for heart. You must exercise too. We can come back here after walk and drink some more, if you want. What you think? Good idea?"

He considered it a good idea, because he thought he could tell her about his ideas for a vineyard down by the river, while she was in such an obviously good mood. So, he encouraged Lek to have a beer too and they chatted about everything but houses, both of them postponing the subject until after their walk and a few more beers.

The time came for the walk and they arranged to pay the bill when they got back in thirty or forty minutes – nobody worried about things like that in the village. Lek suggested a route which would lead them around the outskirts of the western half of the village and past all three of the properties.

The heat has gone out of the day by six o'clock, but it was still warm and at that time of the year, there was still an hour and a half before dusk and the mosquitoes came out to play in force. It is one of the nicest times of the day along with the early morning.

As they turned the first corner to walk past Mum's house, Lek pointed. "This house is for sale. People go away. Work in Bangkok long time, so take all the family go live in Bangkok. It is very sad. My mother's friend go too, because she cannot live here alone. Mum miss her friend very much already."

They walked on for fifty metres in silence, then Lek said, "The lady live in this house get married next month. She want us to go to her wedding. Do you want to go, Craig? You never see Thai wedding before. It is very beautiful. Then she go to live with her new husband in Sukhothai and Mum lose one more friend. This house is only three or four metres from Mum's house. Mum's closest friend. She go away too, so Mum lose two friends very quickly. It is so sad for an old lady to lose friends like this, neh? Mum will be very lonely, I think. Two friends gone in one or two months."

"Yes, sad," said Craig, not catching the drift of the conversation yet, "but I'm sure she has others and she has family and friends at the Wat too."

"Yes, true, but not all friends are the same. One friend cannot replace another friend. My Mum will miss her friends who go away."

They walked on and finally exhausted the small inhabited road that led to the village perimeter and the rice fields. Craig loved to walk along the village ring road here. Rice fields as far as the eye could see. All year around, green, lush fields broken up only here and there by squares of brown where the stubble in a harvested field had been torched in preparation for replanting.

It was beautiful, but Craig really liked walking there because there was more chance of seeing snakes, birds and big lizards outside the village. Not much wildlife that was restricted to the ground made it up the road as far as Mum's house, even though that gauntlet was less than two hundred metres long. Kids killed most snakes and big lizards and their parents ate them. The kids, the boys anyway, also used catapults to take pot-shots at birds for the table.

Here, beyond the houses, the chances of seeing a snake were quite high, because they thrived on the frogs and rodents in the fields. The rodents came for the rice and the frogs came for the small fish that farmers put in the water to reduce the number of mosquito larvae. Craig had never seen a Thai snake yet in Thailand, but he lived in hope and was ever vigilant. Lek knew his passion for wildlife. She didn't really share it, she didn't even really understand it, but then, she knew that there were many things she didn't understand. It just didn't matter – nobody could understand everything, so why try?

As they rounded the edge of the last field adjoining the village and came back onto the main road and shop-bound stretch, Craig was disappointed: "No snakes this time either. I liked the herons though." The herons ate the large snails that fed on the tender stalks of rice.

"You make too much noise. Snake hear you and hide. He is not stupid, he knows people hate him and kill him and eat him. People only see stupid snakes and stupid snakes die soon. Clever snakes hide when they hear you, Mr Elephant Man coming," she laughed. Craig had to smile too, because he knew that she was right. He crunched gravel, snapped twigs and kicked stones as he walked and wondered why he never saw anything. He had seen plenty of elephants and they were very quiet walkers. In fact, much quieter than he was.

As they were approaching the shop with about one hundred yards to go, Lek pulled him up abruptly. "This man die last month. Very sad. He was same age my Mum too. One more friend from Mum go away. I hope he go away. I'm scared of ghosts. Maybe he stay in the house, not want to leave home. What you think? Ghost for man live in there? Can you see him? You not scared ghosts, neh? Look in the window. Nobody live there now, only ghost of old man. Come quickly, I am scared. Nearly dark. Quickly." and she took his arm and hurried him along.

Sitting herself down at their table, Lek said: "Oh, I am very scared now. Look at my arm. I have little bumps. I don't like ghosts at all. Maybe they will never sell that house, because people think pee, um, how you say, ghost lives in there." She ordered two more beers and touched Craig's foot with hers.

Well, she was right about one thing, he thought, he wasn't afraid of ghosts, but he wondered whether the time had passed to talk about his riverside villa, so he started with: "Lek, I think I could live up here in or near the village. The Internet is a bit shaky, but I'm sure it will improve. I've been thinking about it a bit today. What do you think of a house like Dutch's down by the river or by any river that is near here – I don't know what is available really. Is there an estate agent around here we could look in? I don't mean in the village, I mean in town or some-where."

Lek wondered how much of what she had said over the last half hour had gone in. She was amazed. Dumbstruck even. She took a swig of beer to play for time then said: "No, no estate agent. Only have in Pattaya and Bangkok. You must walk and look and talk and ask. Same we do just now. There is no river in my village. You see river in my vil-lage before? I not see one. Why you want to live by a river? Too many mosquitoes. You hate mosquitoes. Too many snakes. I hate snakes. Nobody is happy by the river and when the monsoon come, water come in the house and poop-poop come out from the toilet and go everywhere. It is very bad to live by the river.

"People who live there are very stupid. Maybe they never live here before, buy land by the river because beautiful now, but when they have house for one year, they are very sorry they buy. Nobody born here want to have a house by the river. Believe me, people with house by the river want to move, because they only have problems. You remember boy in falang house nearly die from snake? You remember we come home quickly at seven o'clock because one million mosquito want to eat all your blood? Please, think. No more talk about river house."

He knew he was beaten There would be no riverside vineyard and no little rowing boat to go fishing.

And no more arguments about it.

"What you think about living here in this village. We could take one of the houses we see tonight. Do you like one?" When Craig took his time to reply, Lek added "Please don't say the house with the ghost. I cannot live with a ghost and it is by a rice field too, so have mosquitoes and snakes too. And men come to work in the field all day and make noise. Play radio very loud all day and you hate pop song radio, eh?"

That was enough to put him off that house, but it wasn't what he had been thinking about. He was just wondering whether he was ever going to get a say in anything that mattered. In public she asked his opinion about every tiny detail of where they should go, how they should get there and what they should do once they arrived, but his opinion counted for nothing on the bigger matters.

The 'problem' was though that she was probably right and he was just too inexperienced to see the difficulties before they were pointed out to him. He had always considered himself to be quite knowledge-able and worldly-wise, but perhaps he was the only one who thought that.

It was a hard thing to realise.

"Yes, OK, my dear. I know you don't like that house with the ghost. I don't want to live there either. Are there any more houses for sale?."

"No, not that I know about," she replied feeling a bit better. "You want to look in the other two houses? I can get key for one and lady is friend in other house. She show you house if you want to look. We can look tomorrow, OK, telak?"

"Yes, OK, why not? It won't hurt to have a look will it?" he smiled. Lek blew him a kiss shielded by her hand and the rapidly fading light.

∞

The following day, Lek bounded into their room beaming from ear to ear. She held out her hand, in it were two keys. "Craig, guess what! Lady who marry move all her things out last week. The house is empty. She stay with her mother in mother's house, so we can go look at house alone and I have the key for other house too. Good, eh? Come on, get up, go shower. You want to eat first or go look at house' first? I will make you omelette, while you shower, then we can look slowly, OK? Quickly, go now."

After breakfast, she took him first to the house she was hoping he would turn down and let them in. The door was very stiff and creaked loudly. Lek looked at Craig with a dramatically grim expression on her face and shook her head disapprovingly.

Craig noticed that Lek hadn't removed her shoes on entering so neither did he. The smell of damp inside was quite overpowering. It was a single-storey concrete construction and even in the dim light from the open door, he could see structural cracks in the walls. The house was probably not safe to be in. The jammed front door was almost certainly just that – the door jam had moved and pinched the door.

"Come on, Lek," he warned, "Let's get out of here before the whole place collapses and kills us." Lek didn't need to be told twice, not because she was afraid of dying, but because she didn't want the house even though it was slightly larger than the other one.

"How much do they want for that?" asked Craig out of curiosity.

"I think it is expensive," she replied "five hundred thousand. Lady say special price for you, because you buy your first house in the village."

Soon to be my 'first pile of rubble', he thought.

The other house had a fairly well-tended garden of shrubs that produced edible beans and leaves. There were chillies, aloe vera, limes and a few other plants he didn't recognise. This house was also a single-storey in height but of teak and unusually, not on stilts. Lek kicked off her sandals, went in first and threw all the shutters open and there were a lot of them – eight large shuttered openings, the triple-width, folding front door and the strangely normal, wooden back door.

There was just one large living-room-cum-bedroom, a kitchen and a bathroom. There was no ceiling, just the bare pitched roof and rafters and the walls were unlined, so that there were gaps between the boards that were wide enough to look through.

The house had been constructed around a framework of fifteen massive teak columns that held everything up and apart. The house's electrics had obviously been an afterthought, because a square of board with two sockets and a fuse hung off the most central column. Into these two sockets were plugged two adapters and three leads came from each adapter at the end of which were extension boards. Two had fans plugged in to them, but Lek didn't turn them on. The on-off switch was a large, catapult-shaped lever like you see in American films involving the electric chair. Craig had never seen one actually being used. Sparks flew off it when it was moved.

There was nothing but a small table in the kitchen and nothing in the bathroom either except a French-style hole-in-the-floor, squat toilet. It was very, very basic, but light and airy and cheerful in that it had lots of potential. It looked as if someone had built himself a home and got bored halfway through the project.

A huge green spider appeared from nowhere and made a suicide run at Craig, but Lek was too quick for it and crushed it under her bare foot. It left a sticky mess. Craig walked around the house keeping to the edges in case the floorboards were rotten, although they looked sound enough. There were six eggs the size of ping-pong balls stuck to a wall in the bathroom. Lek smashed them with an old broom. "Tokay. Not nice lizard," she said in justification.

The woman had moved out a week ago and wildlife was already re-claiming their lost ground, he thought. Things grow so quickly in Thai-land. The grass was reclaiming the garden and the animals were re-claiming the house, but he could see himself living there and being happy. In his mind's eye, he could see a typical Thai exterior to the house, but a beautifully modern interior. When people came to the house, they would think 'what are they living in?', but when they stepped inside it would be wonderful. He could see it as plainly as a cottage on a biscuit tin lid.

Lek, on the other hand was thinking of demolishing the whole she-bang and building her dream concrete bungalow or even house, if the money would stretch that far. Or maybe they could add another floor later. She wasn't too sure of the details because houses were not one of her strong points.

Yet.

"This is a lot better, Lek," he said eventually, allowing Lek to breathe normally again for the first time since they entered the garden. "We could make something of this. We could make something really nice out of this. How much does your friend want for it?"

"Oh, this is a good friend. She wants us to be happy near to Mum. She wants two hundred thousand for the house and land together. Not bad, eh? Yes, I think we could be happy here and make a nice house too."

They were both thinking the same words, but the minds' pictures that they were describing were totally different.

"Tell her we will take it subject to survey and valuation," he said. "We will need to see some paperwork. I need to see who actually owns it before I pay up."

This took the wind out of Lek's sails and left her feeling non-plussed. "I don't understand, telak. Mum's friend live here for all my life. All her life, nearly fifty years. It is her house, her land, she can sell."

"Yes, I don't doubt it, but I still need proof. I can't just give her two hundred thousand, move in and then get kicked out by her brother next year, can I?"

"She don't have a brother or a sister. Only a mother."

"But she must have some papers from the government to say that she owns the land and can sell it, surely?"

Lek was crest-fallen, but she smiled and started locking up. She was good at solving problems. This was just one she hadn't come across before so had not been able to anticipate.

∞

They decided to leave the next day, so they hardly saw each other for the rest of the day. Craig stayed in the house writing pages of content for his web sites and Lek went to Phitsanulok to get some bus tickets to Pattaya. She took a friend with her, the mayor's wife, so that she could learn something about buying property in the village. She already knew the bare bones of property ownership or chanoot, but she knew that she needed to know more to satisfy Craig's enquiring, suspicious Western mind.

When the time came to leave the following day, they had to wait for their lift back to the bus station. Craig was a patient sort of person, but he liked to know how long he had to wait or when something would happen. If he was told he had three hours to wait, then he would find something to do for three hours and be ready on time, but he would definitely not be happy if he was then told he had to wait another hour. Lek considered it to be one of his weaknesses.

Unfortunately, this was what happened. They waited for the taxi for hours and then some more; and then some more and yet more. He tried to keep calm and to console him, Mum fed him with her best mangoes. He had eaten at least eight by the time the taxi arrived. They were lovely.

By the time they got to the bus station an hour and a half later, Craig was very lucky not to have embarrassed himself and couldn't get to the toilet quickly enough. Lek was aware of his predicament, but she said there was nowhere to stop.

He learned his lesson that day - he loved mangoes, but he vowed never to eat more than two at a sitting again and never, ever before travelling.

6 THE FINAL WEEKS IN PATTAYA

The final few weeks in Pattaya were a real scramble. Lek was concerned with visiting all her friends several times and then saying goodbye to them all several times too as if she were emigrating on a one-way ticket to a dense jungle in deepest Central Africa. Craig rarely saw her alone and even then it was only to sleep. On the other hand, he was trying to find out if there were any programmes he needed to buy while he could, because there was nothing where he was going. He also needed another visa and wanted to find out about IPstar as a backup in case the trees kept growing in his way. Lek had already assured him that there were telephone lines in the village.

Craig usually started work immediately after getting up and waited for Lek to get back from shopping or the beauty salon. Then they would have breakfast together and he would go for a swim. Craig often felt that he was more comfortable in the water than on land. He thought he was rather slow and ponderous on land, but he could spend hours, literally hours, in the water just amusing himself – his feet never touching the bottom. He could float, swirl, dive and swim very quickly in short bursts, because he was now getting out of condition.

He was naturally lazy, physically, and ten years behind a desk had given him an excuse to do practically nothing in the way of keeping fit. He had once swum a measured mile in cold, north-European October conditions and had the certificate to prove it (somewhere), but now he could barely manage fifty metres at sprint speed. He felt sad about it and expected it to kill him one day, but not sad enough to do anything about it. He was not a Buddhist, but he didn't fear death either.

After swimming for a couple of hours in chlorinated water, his eyes were not up to reading a computer screen, so he usually swam from about noon until two and then went for a beer in the girly bars alone, working his way down to meet Lek at Daddy's Hobby at between four and five. When they got back from there, at whatever time, he would work until he had to stop from exhaustion.

Lek lived the life of a society wife. She lunched here and there, went for coffee with friends and visited before people had to start work. She felt as if she had elevated herself out of her old way of life, but she was not the sort of person to forget her friends or where she had come from. She treasured her past, although she was not yet prepared to share it with Craig. That was far too risky, although in her heart of hearts, she thought he could handle it, if he didn't know already.

His friend Will knew, although Will would probably not spell it out to Craig, unless asked a direct question. He was a nice man and Lek and he had got on well when they had met up the two or three times in Barry recently. In fact, she liked all of Craig's friends. 'Birds of a feather …', she assumed. Her close friends were all pretty good people too, she knew.

She would miss her best friends Goong and Ayr and her cousin Beou when they moved to the village, but her being there would give them an added incentive to go home for holidays and she and Craig could go to Pattaya on various pretexts as well such as to renew their health insurance, have check-ups and register his address every ninety days for his visa.

In fact, Craig needed to do a visa run as the ex-pats called it immediately. A visa run was a trip out of the country, usually to Cambodia or Laos in order to get a visa upon re-entry into Thailand. Some people did it every thirty days, some did it for longer periods – it depended where you went. Re-entry from Cambodia delivered a thirty-day visa; Laos a sixty or ninety-day visa and Malaysia a one hundred and eighty-day visa.

Craig wanted to go to Cambodia now and Laos later, so he booked a seat in a minibus, like he had when he had taken Lek the previous year. He invited Lek to go with him, but she wasn't interested this time, so he went alone. It was a nice day out – a change. The bus set off at six a.m. after a hearty breakfast and arrived at the border just before noon. After getting the visas and having lunch, the bus then turned around to be back in Pattaya by five or six in the evening.

Lek used this time to check up on one of her priorities, which was to find out more about property ownership. Beou was very helpful in this regard. Beou had grown from similar origins to Lek into quite the business woman. She was older and had been in the game for a lot longer that Lek, but she had learned how to leave her working girl past behind her and become a businesswoman.

Lek hoped to do the same but in a different way, although she had no idea which path her business future would take in the village. She had a few tentative ideas, but it depended on how much Craig or she herself were willing to invest.

However, the first thing to sort out was the house, while Craig was still warm to the idea. One day a piece of paper arrived in a registered envelope and she showed it to Craig: "Look, darling, lady from the house send me this. She is the owner of the house."

It was in Thai and looked very official except there were no stamps, names, address or signatures on it. Lek wasn't sure what it was and couldn't translate the legalese into English, so she was wary when Craig insisted on showing it to an estate agent. The agent translated the document as: "This document proves that the bearer owns the property," but because there was no address on it or room for an address, it was worthless.

Both Lek and Craig left the office feeling rather foolish.

It turned out that that piece of paper was not a scam, but an initial document meaning that whoever held it could claim chanoot or ownership of the land where they lived after five years and it had two years left to run. There was no identification on it, because it was a local document issued by the mayor's office and there was no address because it referred to a piece of squatted land that did not have an address yet.

Every villager had a similar document from when the king had granted ownership to whoever was living on certain parcels of land. It would later be converted into a title deed by the mayor, who would also create an address at the same time.

There was no real 'final night party', or if there was it lasted a fortnight, but on the day before they were to leave, Lek collected all the gifts that were to go back to the village quite early so that they wouldn't be in the way of the last night. Lek started her trip back to Daddy's Hobby from her cousin's house as had become the norm while Craig left on his own from the apartment block.

In one of the bars on his way down, he got talking to a girl he 'clicked with'. Craig never went with any of the girls but he was comfortable with 'playful banter'. The conversation started pretty normally with the girl asking: "What your name? Where you come from? How long you stay here? What your job?"

On the last question a thought came into his mind and he said, "I have come to Thailand to start a new business."

"Oh," she said, "what sort of business?" she was all ears, because he could be a good catch.

"I am a hairdresser and I heard about all the ladies in Pattaya. I hear that they like to shave under their arms and around their pussies, so I have come to set up a shop for shaving pussies. What do you think? Good idea or not good idea?"

She looked at him as if he had just dropped to Earth from another planet and said, "But all ladies shave own pussy. I shave pussy me."

"Yes, but I am an expert. I shave hair for thirty years, you shave only three-four years. True?"

She admitted that that was true.

"And, and, I shave all ladies free for one month! After one month, must pay. What you think? Good idea?"

A twinkle of understanding grew in her eyes.

He ploughed on, "You say you can shave good, but I know I can shave better. I take my time and make sure lady is very happy. Show me I want see if you do good job."

She looked at him again, then lifted up the front of her skirt and pulled her knickers down a little.

"It is very dark here. Can I feel? My eyes are not good."

She got it, laughed and nodded and he put a hand in her panties. "Mmm, not bad, but I can do better. You still have a little bit hair here... Feel it? Anyway, next week, I make business cards and you can give to your friends. You help me and you get for free all time."

She had the measure of him now and she pulled away and beamed at him. He offered her a drink for being such a good sport. She was the sort of bar girl he liked to meet.

He walked on, happy to have met that girl, happy that his joke went down well and happy for the feel, but...

There was still a nagging doubt about going up-country. He had only met one foreigner up there. He couldn't speak Thai, but was prepared to try hard and no-one spoke English well enough to hold a conversation... and he loved a good ol' chin-wag. On the other hand, they might just do away with him after he had paid for the house. Feed him to the pigs or bury him in a rice field.

No-one would ever know. None of his friends or family anyway. Weeks after he went missing someone might say that they hadn't heard from Craig 'for a long time'.

He emailed Will about it, but typically Will said: "It's up to you, go with your heart."

That much he knew already. It struck him after a few beers that that must have been how Lek had been feeling before she grabbed the bull by the horns and decided to go with him to the UK. He wandered in the rough direction of Daddy's Hobby, but his heart wasn't in it. He tried his new 'job routine' a couple of times to cheer himself up but it didn't work every time, so he gave up on it for the day.

It was a huge, enormous leap to go from Pattaya to a village that no-one had ever heard of and set up home. More than once, he thought of backing out. It wasn't too late. He loved Lek, he loved Pattaya, he liked what he had seen of the village, so why not stick with Plan A and live in a condo in Pattaya, but have a small home in Baan Suay?

By the time that he got to Beou's bar the die had been cast in his mind – he would keep his word and go through with it.

Lek greeted him with open arms when he arrived at six – at least an hour late even for Thais. She guessed what he had been thinking and realised that he had no-one to talk it through with. She too had realised the similarity between her trip to the UK and his to Baan Suay and she felt for him. She also knew that promising Buddha an offering if she got back safely had given her courage, while that option was not open to Craig.

Craig was a bit more drunk than he should have been, a bit more friendly than he should have been and even a bit more familiar than he should have been, but he excused himself by thinking that it might be his last night of pleasure for a very long time or even in this life. Any woman that came into contact with him on purpose got at least an equal measure of contact back. That was to be his yardstick tonight, he thought: 'You hang your arm off my shoulder and I'll hang my arm off your bum.'

Everyone could see that he was past caring – in his own little world – so those who wanted to avoid him did. Some of Lek's close friends only talked to him when there was a bar counter between them, but that was not fair because he wasn't familiar with just anyone – only those who touched him first. Lek could see what was going on as well and chose to turn a blind eye too.

It was out of character, after all, and the next day would be a momentous change to his life.

For the first time since they had been back, he was hoping that Mia would turn up. She had to, didn't she? Her best friend leaving Pattaya and going back to the village with the trophy 'rich' foreign husband. He just hoped that the Ozzie had already gone back, because he wasn't prepared to put up with disapproving glares from him all night.

He behaved himself as best as he could within his principal for the evening and there were no upsets. He watched Lek most of the time, or tried to, and nodded when she looked at him, but he didn't see when she sometimes looked at him in the mirror behind the bar. He was beyond that, but so was she. Lek was just glad to be going home, where she could see her daughter every day and stand proud in her daughter's eyes. The rest didn't matter.

Or at least, not for now.

Craig felt a tap on the shoulder; more of a squeeze that a tap, but very light. Something like Lek would do when he was talking to friends or busy on the computer. He turned with the words 'Hello, Lek' escaping from his mouth even as he saw who it was. It was the very person he most wanted to see at that moment, Mia, and he foresaw fun.

The bar wasn't particularly busy so Mia had no trouble squeezing a stool in beside him. "Craig! My heart is broken! What can I do?"

"I don't know, how did it happen," he said trying not to smile too much.

"Bob must go home to Australia and you and my number one friend Lek go home too. What can I do without you all?"

"I don't know," grimaced Craig," but let me get you a drink while we think it over. What do you want? A big Chang?."

Chang being the name of a strong Thai beer, the Thai word for elephant and Thai slang for a penis.

"Yes, OK, a like big Chang."

Craig shouted: "Lek, Lek, come here a moment, please, my dear. Look who's just arrived. I want a beer Chang for her, for you and for me, please. Make them big ones too." Lek greeted her friend and moved off to get the bottles. When she returned Mia leaned on Craig's erection to reach her bottle before it could be passed to her. Lek didn't see, because it was under the bar. The two friends chatted for five minutes or so while Mia kneaded Craig's cock like a happy cat flexing its claws in a lap.

"Can I leave you to talk together, please? I want to work one last night before we go away from Pattaya." They both nodded and the game was afoot.

"Your perfume is very nice, Mia, what is the name?"

"It is not special perfume, Craig, but thank you. It is this… wait, oh, dear…" and she spun on her chair and bent over to pick up something that had fallen from her bag. She put her half open fist to his nose. He took her hand and a deep sniff, but moved it back, away from him into his field of vision.

"What is that? Your handkerchief?"

"No, silly boy! It is my knickers! I take them off for you now because you like my smell. You don't like?"

He did, that was the problem.

"Here, you can keep and smell again later, when you miss me" and she half-stuffed them into his shirt top pocket. They looked like a pink silk hanky poking out of his shirt. He hurriedly tucked them in out of sight.

Craig was loving it. He looked at Lek; she was talking to some punter and seemed happy enough, not that anyone in the bar would let anything happen to one of the sorority.

Pushing the point, Craig asked, " Are these from yesterday? I don't want you to have a problem. Maybe mosquito bite you on the bum."

She smiled. "Not bite me. You want to see?" and she lifted her skirt for everyone who was paying attention to see her blemish-free fanny. "It is OK, or not?"

A few men nearby were getting an eyeful too and Craig realised that he was being used as Mia's stooge.

He'd had worse jobs though.

For the rest of the evening, Mia sat facing him crossing and uncrossing her legs to give her audience a free peep from time to time. They talked about Mia's 'worries' about being left alone and his fears of being isolated in the village, but it always came back to her pussy. Like-wise, whenever someone talked to her or Craig from behind the bar, she would lean on his cock.

Even when Lek came to join them for a five minute break, Mia gave up her seat to Lek and sat on Craig's lap. Lek saw no wrong, but Craig knew she was bare bottomed on his lap and it was driving him crazy. When Lek 'eventually' left, Mia stayed put and moved to the music, smiling at any man sitting at the bar opposite that looked at her.

She reacted typically: "Ooh," she shouted above the music as she bobbed up and down, "Lek, can you check if my bag is OK over there?" She only got off his lap when Lek nodded then she went back to her own stool smiling broadly.

Craig didn't feel low or a cheat for touching these women. They wanted it and they knew that they would never be with him. He was with Lek, but a standing prick has no conscience and he thought that he was doing no real harm as long as Lek or her best friends didn't know. It would all be history within twenty-four hours anyway, he 'reasoned'.

At midnight, Lek came over to join them. Again, Mia gave up her seat for Craig's lap. She took care not to sit on her skirt and wriggled a little until she was 'comfortable'.

After a few moments, Lek said: "Here, Mia, have your stool back, I will sit on Craig's lap" and they swapped places. Craig never knew whether he had been caught out, but he suspected that Lek knew what was going on and had had enough. She had probably seen more than enough in the mirrors.

That old trick of people who work or drink in bars regularly.

However, Craig's memory stopped there and Lek never said any-thing about the evening again. They woke up in bed the next day as if the previous evening had been a dream. The fact was that both of them wanted to put Pattaya behind them and see what the next phase of their lives would bring.

Craig didn't know it, but Lek was far less uncertain about the next phase than he was.

7 A LEAP OF FAITH

Thirty-two beautiful, scantily-clad women went to see them off at the bus station and there was not a dry eye among them. Every one of them kissed and hugged Lek and then Craig as if they were astronauts being sent on a perilous journey from which they would probably never return.

Even Craig was starting to believe that he might be better off staying behind, although he would not miss Pattaya hangovers.

This was Craig's third trip up country and he was starting to feel like an old hand at it. The bus left at six thirty, so it was dark within the hour and like everyone else on board, he tried to get some sleep. Lek went out like a light as usual, but he lay back in his partially-reclined seat drifting in and out of slumber for hours before finally nodding off only to be awoken at the half way stage to dine in a motorway restaurant. Neither he not Lek got off for that, but they went back to sleep until they arrived in Phitsanulok at two a.m.

This time they decided to try a different option and headed over to one of the two better guest-houses outside the bus station. The room was small, but adequate and very reasonable at two hundred and fifty Baht, but Lek insisted on setting her mobile phone's alarm so that they could catch the five fifteen bus to the village. It hardly seemed worth going to sleep, but they slept like logs in their clothes on top of the bed with the aircon keeping the temperature down to twenty-one degrees centigrade.

Then it was up, shower and down to board the next bus. Ninety minutes later the bus stopped as near to the village as it was ever going to get and two friends met them on motorcycles to take them the two kilometres to Mum's house which would be their home for the foreseeable future.

Mum had been up for a long time by the time they arrived and Lek's daughter, Soom, had already left for school, but there were half-a-dozen there to welcome them home.

'Home', thought Craig, 'My new home. Five and a half thousand miles from where I was born and my blood family. What am I doing here?'

Lek was not having any doubts about moving home at all. All right, she had been hoping to move abroad for the last ten years, but at least this option gave her her daughter back… and her mother and a few others… and there was still a chance that she would get to live abroad one day. That avenue was not completely closed to her, it was just undergoing temporary road repairs. The first task was to buy the house and make it habitable.

Lek had been giving a lot of thought to Soom recently and where she was going to live in particular. Should she move in with them or stay put with her grandmother? It seemed logical that she should move in with them, but on the other hand, it was traditional for grandparents to bring up the kids while the parents worked.

Besides, her mother had got used to caring for Soom, how would she feel if Soom were moved out? And Craig – he hadn't lived with children since he had left home thirty-odd years before and he had never lived with a young girl in the house.

It was a small problem which she still had time to work out.

Craig thought that it was definitely a much better idea to sleep on the bus. He could feel the benefits. He was completely refreshed and raring to go. He wanted to get on with 'the rest of his life' – his 'new, exciting future', but he hadn't had a new life since the day that he was born and he had never had to do much other than keep breathing.

If he but knew it, that was all he had to do now as well. There was nothing that he could actually do, physically do, to progress their new life together. He got his laptop out, but there was no signal. He knew from previous visits that the TV was a waste of time for him because there were no English-language broadcasts and he couldn't talk to any-one. All he could do in Mum's house was sit there and maybe read a book. So he took out one of the six precious paperbacks that he had bought in Pattaya and read that to the excited background chatter of his new family.

He lasted two hours, but only out of propriety, his heart wasn't really in the book. He wanted to get on line and prove that he could support himself and his new family from the village, although he was still some way from having an Internet presence that was capable of providing enough income. The problem was that he still only had very woolly ideas on how to go about what he wanted to achieve. He was pretty sure that he had the basics, but he suspected that there was a lot more to it than he knew so far.

"I'm going to go to the shop to see if I can get on line, Lek, OK?"

"You want to go for a beer already, Craig? It is early, neh?"

"I'll say it again: I'm going to the shop to see if I can get on line, OK? But now that you have mentioned it, yes, I will have a beer or two while I'm there. It would be rude not to, wouldn't it? After all, I can't just sit there and start plonking away at the computer without buying anything and they don't sell tea or coffee. I'll see you later."

He walked off, having waaied goodbye to Mum and the others. It was strange of Lek to have said something like that, he thought, maybe she had other plans for them. She had made her living from bars for the last ten years and she was not adverse to a good drink herself, so it was definitely out of character for her.

He sat down at his usual table, the only table, and the shop-keeper came over immediately. She was a friendly sort, so Craig decided to try to swap names:

"Hello, my name Craig. You what?"

She looked at him and smiled, but obviously had no immediate idea what he was talking about.

"Beer Chang?" she asked hopefully.

He nodded and smiled, but when she brought the bottle he tried again:

"Pom Craig. Khun alai? I Craig. You what?"

"Ah, my name is Nong," she said in Thai with a broad smile. 'Nong' was the only word he hadn't heard before, so he assumed that that was her name. He smiled, lifted up his bottle of beer and said, "Hello. Chok dee," still not sure enough to speak her name aloud.

He could check with Lek later.

Nong smiled and walked off. Craig was happy though. It was a milestone – his first 'conversation' with a Thai who couldn't speak English. He set his computer up and checked for a signal. He was also half-expecting Lek to turn up and explain her remarks about starting early.

Sure enough, an hour later, Lek appeared at Nong's. Craig didn't see her approaching because he was head-down searching the web.

"Hello, telak, you have keun, uh, signal, here? I not want you to come here early because I think you can come with me to see lady who sell house, but no problem. I can go alone or we can go tomorrow. What you want?"

"I don't need to meet her yet, do I, love? You go alone and tell me about it later."

Lek seemed happy with that solution and walked off with a wave. All sorts of thoughts were running around her mind and she wasn't proud of many of them. The one she disliked the most was that she might have the chance to get a reduction in the price, because the house was not really habitable, but Craig had already agreed to two hundred thousand and she wouldn't have to tell him about the saving.

She hated herself for even having thought about double-crossing Craig, but she supposed it was normal. Definitely not nice, but normal and undetectable. Probably, after all, he didn't speak Thai.

Lek talked to her former neighbour and congratulated her on her forth-coming marriage. The lady, Su, was effervescent. She had never had so much money in one lump sum in all her days and, coupled with getting married later-on in life too, she could not believe her luck. She even kissed Lek's hands and thanked her time and time again for 'getting the foreigner' to buy her land at full market value.

Lek felt bad. Her instinct was to try for a discount for all sorts of reasons, but especially because they were old friends and because she was leaving the village, so had less bargaining power. However, she could not bring herself to ask for a price cut. She wanted her 'old friend' to be happy and Craig could afford it.

Lek knew that she could get ten percent off, because it was built into the price anyway. Su might even accept a fifteen percent discount, but Lek was plagued by her thoughts of keeping the money from Craig. She didn't like the way this woman was assuming that she would cheat her foreign boyfriend for her Thai friend, but she had been near to cheating him, hadn't she, for her own ends? She felt really bad about the whole affair, but decided to let sleeping dogs lie.

"No problem," said Lek. "We will be happy in our new house and I hope that you will be happy in your new house too."

When Lek got up to leave, she was still being troubled by the thought that she was being implicated in cheating her boyfriend. As she mounted her motorcycle, she leaned over to her friend and said ",I wanted to ask you for ten percent discount and I know you would have given it, but my boyfriend, Craig, told me to let you keep it for a wedding present."

"Tell Craig thank you very much from me and my future husband. He is a very kind man and you are a lucky woman to find such a man who is generous to strangers. I will invite you both to our wedding and I hope you can come as guests of honour."

Lek smiled and drove off, happy that she had bought Craig deep gratitude even though it was with his own money, that he didn't know he had.

Lek went straight to Nong's. Craig was still there.

"Darling! The house is ours for sure and my friend say thank you for not arguing about the price too much. She wants us to come to her wedding as number one guests. She is so happy. We can keep the key.

When can you pay her? I want to pay very soon. Is that OK?"

"Yes, sure, dear. I have transferred the money already. It will be here in three days, so we can get it from the ATM on Friday and you can give it to her. How will you make sure the house is ours though?"

"Don' worry about that. The mayor will witness everything. He will know the house is mine."

"Ours, Lek. Ours," he corrected her not for the last time.

"Yes, sorry, telak, 'ours', not only mine. Ours." But she knew that it would never be 'theirs'. It was about to become hers, because foreigners may not own land in Thailand.

Craig was curious about his new home and Baan Suay in general so he decided to ask Lek for some background. She was not normally in favour of talking about the past, but she was in a good mood, so he chanced his arm.

"Lek? I'm going to be living here for the foreseeable future, so do you think you could tell me something about the village? How old it is, some history, that sort of thing?"

"I can try, telak, but no-one talks for old times. It is boring and no-one knows for sure. It is not the same as UK. No-one write history before. People just remember and some people tell lies and some people do not remember good, but I will tell you what I think is true."

"The name of the village is Baan Suay. It means 'Beautiful Village'. Nobody speaks English in Baan Suay except me and you, although most of the people under fifty years of age have had lessons in English at school."

"But Baan Suay is not near the tourist area so very few people in the village have ever met a foreigner or had the chance to speak English since school. You will see that many children will stare at you and cry, because they are frightened of you. You are big and very white. Maybe they will think you are a ghost… or a monster from space." Lek giggled at the thought.

"It is a quiet farming village where almost everyone is involved in growing rice and fruit.

"The village is probably several hundred years old, but no-one really knows. The oldest man lives between here and our house. You have seen him already I think. He is very fit, but ninety-seven. He often walks with a short sword, because he remembers when the Japanese come here in the war. My grandmother is ninety-two and can remember when the village stood in a clearing in the jungle.

"The oldest building now is the Buddhist Temple or Wat. We have seven or eight monks living there now, I think, but I am not one hundred percent sure.

"My grand Mum – my Mum's Mum - told me about a time when it was best for children to be locked up as it got dark because tigers hunted at night and so did bad men from over the border with Laos. There were also giant snakes that could carry off children, dogs and even young cattle. Mum and grand Mum told us we must be good and come in early or maybe animal or foreigner get us, but it was before my time really. Baan Suay was not in the jungle when I was a girl."

"This was why houses were traditionally built on legs, er, stilts - so that the family could go upstairs at night and pull up the door. They stay inside at night because they scared and must work early. No pubs, clubs, bars, restaurants or hotels in Baan Suay. Nothing for have fun. Only work. Slowly, in the Fifties and Sixties people cut down the jungle to make fields for rice. I remember my grandfather cutting down trees and making big fires. Then he put the ashes on the fields to make the rice grow quickly.

"The ground was good anyway because trees and leaves fall for thousands of years. It is very good land but it could only make one crop a year because we not have much water. This was a problem until well into the 1980's when I was a teenager working with my dad and grand dad. But people in the north, Chiang Mai, Uttaradit, Chiang Rai cut too many trees and the water cannot stay there any more. The water go in the rivers and come down to us.

"Now Baan Suay and land here have very much water and we can make three crops of rice every year. The extra water and better types of rice allowed clever farmers to produce three crops a year and the region get rich. If scientists ever make a faster-growing kind of rice, the farmers will be able to grow four crops a year because we have the water and good land.

"If you stand outside Baan Suay there are fields of very green rice for as far as the eye can see. Land in Thailand is sold by the 'rai' or forty by forty metres, sixteen hundred square metres, so when you look at the land, you see small plots marked out by narrow, raised strips of earth that keep the water in the fields and allow the farmers to look at the rice without getting wet feet."

"Oh, our new house is twenty by thirty metres, so six hundred square metres" interjected Craig.

"Yes, a little more than one third of a rai. Anyway, before we had too many tigers, big snakes and crocodiles but people put them in a zoo in the Sixties. Sometimes you see very big snakes, but not every year. The biggest wild animal these days is a heron. Big snakes like reticulated pythons can grow up to eleven metres, but it is very rare to see one over five metres any more, telak.

"We used to use elephants and buffaloes a lot on farms to pull the ploughs and carry the crops but no longer. Now farmers have tractors, combine harvesters and trucks called 'Thailands', although when the price of rice gets very high, some farmers go back to the old way of planting and harvesting by hand to get the most rice from land.

"Many falang think na, er, rice fields are flooded with water all the time, but rice not grow like reeds, or at least the rice around Baan Suay does not. When a crop has been harvested, the farmer sets a light to the old rice. Some, maybe ten percent, burns. When it is burnt out, he pumps water into the field to a depth of maybe four or six inches and lets it stand for a day or two.

"Then we get really horrible big snails in the water and maleng, er, insects, especially mosquitoes, but other flies too. The farmer sprays a chemical in the water to kill the snails and then ploughs all the dead snails and rotting rice stalks back into the ground. This makes a kind of mud several inches deep. Then maybe a farmer tops up the water to six inches or more again, but every farmer has his own favourite way and it can change with the season, if monsoons come.

"Rice seed may be scattered into this mud, but more and more often, farmers are using six or eight inch plants grown elsewhere and sowing them by hand or by machine in order to get an early start. If a patch of land has no rice for some reason, the farmer can use these young plants to keep the field one hundred percent full.

"Then the snails and mosquitoes come back and the farmer sprays every week or two weeks to kill insects and snails that eat his rice. Many farmers try to reduce the need for expensive chemicals by putting small fish into the field to eat the baby mosquitoes. Frogs come for the fish and snakes come for the frogs. Herons come for the frogs and snails.

"If the water rises too much because of monsoon rain, farmer pump some off and take fish out of the water. Shrimps grow in it too. These small fish and shrimps make a tasty omelette. I will make one for you next time a farmer sells some fish or shrimps from his field. The people in the village also eat the frogs and snakes and the rats that steal the rice. A rat or a frog cost more than a chicken! Maybe two-three times more. You eat frog before, Craig? I like very much.

"Rats are very, very nice to eat too – very sweet. There is no - how you say? - toilet water in the country, so rats not live in shit. Rats only eat clean, fresh rice and fruit, so people not think rats dirty animals. Nobody eat a town rat. Thais who believe Buddha only eat poisonous snakes, because it was python that keep Buddha out of the water when he prayed. It coiled up like a cushion and Buddha sat on it. But some Thais eat all snakes, not my family, but some do. Not nice. I don't like snakes – I am scared, but not kill 'snake not bite die'. Only eat, uh, poisonous snakes.

"Baan Suay is in a region where it is easy to grow mangoes, longon, bananas, lemons, jack fruit, custard apples, chillies, peanuts and pumpkins so we always have many things to eat with rice. We also have fish, shrimps, crabs, pigs, chickens, rats, snakes, small birds and frogs This land is some of the richest farming land in Thailand, so you are very lucky you meet me. I not take you somewhere very poor. My family don't have big money, but people here not poor same in other regions in Thailand.

"When you live here, you can have good life, if you work hard. Only cannot have fun. Everybody must make their own fun. People like to give party for birthday and for big Buddha Days, like Khao Phansa, Songkhran, New Year... Oh, we have many big days for Buddha."

It was quite a lecture, but Craig was happy to know a little more about his surroundings.

"That reminds me. My visa will expire in a few days, where can I get a new one up here? Phichai? Phitsanulok? Uttaradit? Surely any big police station can do it?"

"I don't know. I never do before, but I think you cannot do here. Maybe we must go to Chiang Mai, Bangkok or Pattaya. No idea. Can you look on the Internet?"

So, Craig went on line and looked up the web site of the Thai Immigration Police in Jomtien near Pattaya. The nearest places that he recognised were four hundred kilometres away – Bangkok and Chiang Mai. It was not a big problem, they could fly there, but it was a big shock because he only had three days to expiry.

"We have three days to get my visa and we have to go to Bangkok, Pattaya or Chiang Mai. What do you think? Fly to Bangkok tomorrow?"

"We can fly from Sukhothai to Bangkok tomorrow. It is easy, but why you not think of this before? Rush, rush now. I don't like to hurry. Now I must change all my ideas for tomorrow."

"Hey, Lek, how was I supposed to know that I couldn't get a visa up here. It's bloody ridiculous that we have to go four hundred kilometres to get a visa stamp. What do you want? To be able to go about your business in your own sweet, slow way and have me deported or help me stay here?"

"Not ridiculous. Not everyone can put a stamp. Not everyone in the country can speak English and you cannot speak Thai. Maybe if all falang can speak Thai, all police can put stamp.

"I will help you, of course, but you are not a baby. You must learn to take care of your own business. This is my country, I don't need a visa. I know nothing of visas. You must learn for yourself."

The next morning, Lek's brother Ngat drove them to Sukhothai airport, where they boarded an internal flight to Bangkok with Thai Airways at ten o' clock. Thirty-five minutes later they were in Bangkok and an hour later in a taxi heading for the immigration police. Craig got a one-year retirement visa before the close of business that day and they decided to take a sleeper train back that evening at six thirty.

They arrived in Phichai at five o' clock and went to a noodle shop by the station for a coffee. The owner, Ben, always got in early to cook breakfast for the early commuters, shop-keepers and market traders, many of whom wanted to eat before six a.m. It had been a whirlwind of a twenty-four hours, but it showed that it was possible, so was comforting too.

It had also been lucky that he had brought over one million Baht to cover buying and converting their new property, because he had not known until recently that that was a requirement for the visa. Later the law would require that the money had stayed in a Thai bank for three months before a visa extension could be granted and later still this would be reduced to two months. One of the biggest bug-bears was that visa regulations seemed to change with each government, but they were still far laxer than Britain would have been to Lek.

Ben made a fuss of Craig and Lek because she and Lek hadn't seen each other for a very long while, Ben was glad of the company and she was a friendly sort of person anyway. She could hardly believe that they had been to Bangkok and back in twenty-four hours and wanted to see the visa - not as proof, but because she had never seen one before.

So long as the two women were happy chatting, Craig thought he might as well have a Chang, so he reached over and took one out of the fridge. Lek tutted when she heard the bottle pop open and Ben turned around from cooking to see what was going on, but they both smiled and Lek asked for a can too. There were plenty of pick-up taxis to take them home whenever they wanted to go but neither of them had a lot to do that day anyway.

8 THE NEW HOUSE

Lek usually got up at the same time as her mother and daughter, at about six o' clock, Craig got up about an hour later, so the routine wasn't really disturbed when Friday came around, but there was definitely a new sense of urgency about the house. Lek prepared him an English breakfast as best as provisions allowed and it was on the table at eight o'clock. By eight fifteen, he was being ushered into the shower and by eight thirty, Lek was standing by her Mum's motorcycle.

"Shall we go into town now, darling, and get the money for our new house? Don't forget, it is Friday. If we go too late have too many people and must wait long time. It is good to give the lady the money for the house for her wedding soon too. You want to go now? I am ready and can take you."

Might as well, he thought, get it over with. He wasn't too sure of the directions yet, but he knew that it was about thirty minutes away.

They pulled up outside the bank just after nine and Craig drew two hundred and twenty thousand Baht out. It caused quite a stir, because it was an unusually large sum of money for those parts, not that it was every day that Craig drew such large sums or bought a house and land for cash either. Lek was definitely impressed and very proud that her 'husband' could call on such a fortune too.

The security guard escorted them to their motorcycle and saluted as they rode off. Lek wanted to go straight home and buy the house, but Craig wanted to do some exploring first.

"Do you know this place, Lek?" he shouted in her ear. "Stop. Stop here. I want to go shopping." He didn't. He wanted to look for a bar, but he knew the word 'shopping' had more stopping power than the word 'bar' – the word 'shopping' was the verbal equivalent of a forty-four Magnum.

Lek turned around and headed back the way they had come.

She parked up near the police station which was near the railway station in the centre of the small town of Phichai, only just across the road from Ben's coffee shop. She waived and called to Lek.

"There is a market in there and some shops, but Phichai is not like Pattaya. Not big. Not have too much." They walked around for a while, but Lek couldn't understand what he wanted to buy. "You want to buy some food?" she asked trying to be helpful. "Or you want to buy something for the house? Or you want to buy some gold for me?" she joked.

"It is not that I want to buy anything. I just want to see what sort of place this is and what kinds of things it has to offer."

"There are no bars here and no girl bars either. Nothing like Daddy's Hobby here. Daddy's Hobby is only for tourists, Phichai is only for farmers."

She had read his mind, fair enough, but it wasn't important to him that there weren't any girlie bars. He hadn't really expected to find any up there anyway and it wasn't his main source of interest even in Pattaya. He did enjoy talking to the free spirits that inhabited girlie bars, but he had his mate and Lek was enough for him.

He would have liked to find some sort of a bar though.

They walked around for about thirty minutes, which was thirty minutes more shopping than Craig could normally tolerate, but at least it was all completely new to him. Just as he was about to call it a day and surrender, Lek said: "You want to eat something?"

He didn't, but he had come this far and 'suffered so much' that he thought he might as well put up with a little more. Lek led him back to the motorcycle and Ben's Coffee Shop.

"This is not a real bar, but you can have a beer here and some food, like we did before. It is the only place I know here."

Ben, a very pretty woman in her mid-thirties, was friendly and greeted them in Thai and English. Her English was pretty good too. Next to Ben's was a newsagent's and they had one copy of the Bangkok

Post, which Craig bought. It was a real treat to read the news in English again. He took the fashion section out and gave it to Lek. She was talking to the couple on the next table, so Ben took it and started reading it. She was the first Thai person that Craig could remember seeing reading English. Phichai was starting to look a lot more promising.

Lek ordered some food and asked Craig what he wanted. He couldn't read the menu, but there were trays of food on display, so he chose what looked and smelled like chicken curry. He wasn't too keen on eating spicy food before lunch, but his life had changed and in more ways than this. Then he remembered the beer Chang in the fridge.

He was happy now.

A bar that sold beer and curry of several types and had a pretty, friendly boss who could speak English well and that had a newsagent's next door that sold English-language newspapers! What more could a man want? The only bad thing was that it was thirty minutes from home.

Craig didn't want to push his luck, so when Lek had finished her food and he had finished his bottle of beer Chang, he gave in the first time Lek suggested that they go home 'before they lost the money'. Craig took a tin of Chang to drink on the bike on the way home though. This became a ritual.

When they got back to Baan Suay, Craig went home, fetched his laptop and went straight to Nong's. Lek was not impressed, but she could go and complete the purchase alone. She didn't need him to be there. He couldn't understand anything that was said and wasn't impressed by the nonchalant way of purchasing the house either. There would be no solicitors, no estate agents and no documentation as far as he could see. It was just word of mouth and trust and he had to pay two hundred thousand Baht.

However, he had tried to sort it out in his own mind, but every time he had asked Lek questions she got angry and said it was the way things were done in the village. She couldn't explain it, it was just their way in this area. Not the same as in the UK or America and not the same way as in Bangkok. It was their way.

And that was that. At which point one of them usually stormed off in a huff.

Craig tried to do some work, but his heart wasn't really in it. It wasn't every day that you bought a house and land for cash, he told himself and had another beer. In a few hours, he would be a landlord in Thailand, he thought. How grand! He bought a pen and settled back to do the crossword puzzle in the paper. This was a rare treat indeed – a crossword, Sudoku, a word game and Scrabble. This was several hours of luxury entertainment and should by rights be rationed over a number of days, but he was ravenous for something new to do after weeks of working and reading.

Lek didn't get back until it was dark and Craig was a little drunker than he had expected to be, but then Lek was a lot drunker than he had expected her to be too. In fact, he had thought she would hand over the money and come straight back to tell him all about it, but that had been pretty naïve.

Lek, the vendor, the mayor and a few friends that had acted as witnesses to the sale-purchase had bought a case of Leo beer and a few bottles of whiskey to cement the deal and hadn't given up until it was all gone. They had also killed a chicken and made some food to help the alcohol go down as is the Thai custom.

It didn't bother Craig much that Lek hadn't tried to tell him that the deal might or even had turned into a party. Sometimes, he felt that there was too much stress in being the only foreigner 'in town'.

He was permanently 'performing'. Some people wanted to stroke him, mostly the older people, unfortunately for him, some wanted to try talking to him in Thai or English, which made no difference because their English was too fragmented and his Thai was too poor, some just wanted to sit near him and help him by pouring his beer or passing him food, and yet others just sat there and smiled. Nobody actually wanted anything from him except his attention.

This was so far different from what many expats had told him to expect that sometimes it was hard to believe that they were talking about the same nation. Craig had had no bad experiences at all – not even one that might have been considered not nice on a bad day. He found rural Thais charming, helpful and inquisitive, although not well-informed about anything outside Thailand.

Craig remembered how one evening, while he was looking at the moon, a woman asked him if there was a moon in Wales. He hadn't been sure whether she had been joking or not, but he had smiled and said, 'Yes, the same one as that'. 'Really?' she had replied, 'Well, I never. You can see our moon in Wales too."

He hadn't thought it was worth trying to explain.

Lek stopped for one beer and a chat and explained between hiccups how the transaction had proceeded. It seemed to have been quite an affair, which, if he had bothered to think about it, he would have known it would be.

If the bank thought that withdrawing two hundred thousand Baht had been a big deal, then handing it over in a small village was a once-in-a-lifetime event. People had turned up to see Lek lay the money down and it had been counted, all two hundred one thousand Baht notes by Lek, the vendor, the mayor and all four witnesses.

Lek had wallowed in the glory of having so much cash, but no-one could understand why Lek's husband had not wanted to be present. Lek had been typically quick-witted:

"Oh, it not big money for him," she had explained, "He has a house in Wales and his family has houses in Spain too. He trusts me to do this job, while he is working on the Internet. He is in Nong's shop because the signal is stronger there and he can work faster."

Everyone, including the mayor, had been suitably impressed and Lek had gained a lot of face and so had Craig.

Craig wanted to sleep in their new house right away. He thought they might Christen it. Maybe Lek could cook something in their garden and they could take it indoors to eat as there was no lighting outside. But Lek was having none of it. She had no intention of 'roughing it in that house' until it was just the way that she foresaw that it should be.

In his inebriated, slightly deranged state, Craig thought that this was the time to be masterful and show Lek who was the boss around the house, so he demanded 'his' two hundred thousand Baht key, bought three beers and a few cakes to take away and went back to the new house alone. Lek went to bed in her mother's house.

Three minutes after letting himself in, he knew that he had been stupid.

He didn't have a bottle opener.

That was the first problem, but it was fairly easily solved. He had seen Thais faced with this problem use one bottle to open another, but he didn't know how to open the last bottle. Still, he would face that problem when he came to it. The fans were still there and the electric was still on, so he would be all right with his beer, cakes and computer. He laid everything out before him and thought he would check his email.

There was no signal whatsoever. Not even a glimmer. Why, O why had he not checked that out before buying the house? he wondered.

He had checked the country, the province, the county and the village, but he had bought the only house in it that could not receive the Internet!

Or so it seemed.

All right, he would write some new content for one his web sites on 'travelling by bus' or 'buying a house in rural Thailand' and discuss the 'problems of using the Internet abroad'. So he had something he could do, something to eat and something to drink in his new house and he felt pretty good. Until he looked up for inspiration and noticed two large Tokay lizards looking at him.

He was happy enough with geckos, or jin-jok in Thai, but Tokay were a lot bigger – a foot long and fat too, maybe six to eight inches in circumference. They certainly weren't dangerous and not at all interested in human flesh, but he was not happy sleeping with them all the same.

'Oh well, this is Thailand and this is my new life', he thought.

It took about twenty minutes for all the insects in Thailand to notice that the light was on in his property that had been empty for a while and that there was a new flavour of blood to be had in it – foreign food in a white wrapper.

They found the temptation irresistible and flocked to the table in swarms.

And there was nothing he could do about it. The cracks between the floorboards and the walling were showing light and the insects were coming in. He turned off the light, but there were already millions of the flying torturers in there already. With the light out, he couldn't see the spiders and whatever else that might come out. He put the light back on and searched the empty house for a solution.

He found an old rice sack in the kitchen and so got into that, but he had to put his arms in too, so he couldn't type or hold his beer bottle and they were still biting his face.

Desperate situations call for desperate measures, so he took off his underpants, got back into the sack, aimed the fan at a corner of the room, put his underpants over his head and curled up in the corner.

He was as miserable as he had ever been in his whole life.

He didn't sleep a wink all night despite being tired and drunk, because he could hear scurrying and buzzing and whining going on all around him.

He was so grateful when at last daylight came and he could get up. As he was doing so, Lek's mother appeared in the doorway. She was grinning from ear to ear when he took his underpants off his head and saw her. Craig was so embarrassed and felt really foolish.

"Bai baan. Lek tam ahan – Come home, Lek is cooking." He didn't need to be told twice and rushed out after switching off the fans.

"Did you sleep well, telak?" asked Lek straight-faced as she put his breakfast in front of him. "I come to see you at midnight, before I go to sleep, but you were snoring so I leave you there. Nice house, neh?

You have many friends with you last night, neh? First time you sleep in a Thai house. Did you like it?"

"How can you live like that? Those sodding insects ate me alive last night."

"We don't live like that. You were stupid. We sleep under mosquito nets and wear pyjamas. You wear an old sack and underpants over your head. We are not stupid like you. Why do you think I don't want to sleep there last night? The house is empty a long time. Not clean and too many insects live in there. Must clean and kill all insects first, then sleep there. Not sleep there first, feed insects and then kill them.

"You have a lot to learn about life in Thailand, darling, and I am happy to teach you, but you must listen. You understand Europe or UK or Wales, yes. I do not, OK, but I understand Asia or Thailand and you do not. In fact, you not have any idea at all. If you don't have me, you die soon. You understand me?"

Lek walked off smiling to herself having made her point and sure that it had been taken on board.

9 CONSTRUCTION

With the house in her pocket, so to speak, a milestone had been achieved and Lek appeared to go off the boil, but this was only to the casual observer like Craig. In fact, she was already working on phase two of the master plan – how to get the existing building knocked down and her dream concrete bungalow built. Craig suspected nothing of this of course. Craig still wanted to live in a house that looked traditionally rural Thai from the outside but modern from the inside.

He had learned the hard way though that he needed to plug all the gaps to stop insects getting in again.

A few days later, Lek offered to take Craig to the builders' merchant in Phichai to buy some proper windows and modern doors. Craig saw it as a good opportunity to get a paper, have a beer in Ben's and get out of the village for a few hours, so that is what they did.

In the builders' merchant's Craig bought a couple of hammers, because Lek was keen to help, a saw and several boxes of nails of different sizes. He also bought fifty, two hundred by one hundred centimetre three-millimetre plywood sheets to be delivered. 'That should keep the buggers out,' he reasoned. They were to be nailed around the walls and over the floorboards, which was a shame, because they were massive teak, but too many creepy-crawlies were coming up through them.

They had lunch in Ben's bought a paper, had a few beers and went back home, but as they were riding away, Craig was sure, or at least half-sure, that he saw a white face in the crowd that was shopping nearby. He didn't want to go and say hello, nothing like that, but he had the first inkling, except for Dutch, that he was not alone. It made him think of SETI – 'We Are Not Alone'.

The next day, Craig set about blocking access to the house to all bugs. He had tried to explain his intentions to Lek, but she had not understood, or appeared not to anyway. In fact, she had understood, but thought it was a stupid idea. Her tactic to deal with it though was to let Craig waste his money on foolish notions and then show him better ones. Ones that would actually work.

Concrete ideas in the form of concrete blocks.

They laboured all day from seven in the morning until six in the evening cutting up and nailing down the plywood boards. The floor and the walls were looking quite chic to Craig and he was looking forward to staining and varnishing them. Lek's mother looked on bemused but could be seen shaking her head from time to time.

Lek just played along; measuring, sawing and nailing as Craig directed.

"What you want to do about the ceiling, Craig? We don't have one and insects come in through the roof. Birds too."

"Mmm, we'll get some plasterboards and make a suspended ceiling. That'll keep them out or at least up there and I don't care what lives up there as long as it doesn't come down here."

"You can do that? Alone?"

"No, no, not alone, but first we must find plasterboards. I've never seen any in Thailand."

"What are plasterboards?" Lek pretended not to know what he was talking about. "Why not get Chang to help us?"

"Chang? How is beer Chang going to help us? I drink the stuff every day for relaxation and inspiration, but it won't help put up a ceiling, will it?" Craig knew he was missing the point, but he thought he was being funny too.

"Chang! Boss! Man or lady who can do something very good. Chang fai, chang mai." Lek was becoming infuriated with him. "Uh, electrician, carpenter. You can also have chang boss for electrician and carpenter."

He knew about tradesmen, contractors, builders and building contractors – he knew what she was trying to say, but was choosing to be stupid too. The worst thing was that she knew he was trying to be difficult and it made her even more angry.

"OK, you want to be stupid, you can work alone." She threw down the hammer, kicked the tin of nails over and was gone. 'Tcha, women,' he thought. It had been fun working with Lek, but it was no fun at all without her.

Yet he was supposed to be on an adventure with the love of his life, not slaving away in a house five and a half thousand miles from home. He knew that something had to change and he was beginning to realise that it would probably have to be him.

He downed tools as well and went looking for Lek. She was not hard to find, she had gone to her Mum's house.

"Lek, I'm sorry, dear. Can we talk? We need to talk about the house and what we want. Let's go to Nong's and have a chat."

They left Mum to her cooking and strolled to the shop. Craig bought an exercise book and a pen and labelled the book 'Baan Rao - Our House'.

"OK, my dear, what do you want for our house?"

"I don't know," she lied, "but I think we must have a kitchen, a bathroom and a bedroom. We must keep out insects for you so we must have a ceiling. This is the start."

"OK, sounds good. How do we do that? We have started with the floor and the walls...."

At that point, thunderous rain came down like a waterfall and they had to move under the eaves of the building.

"You will see, darling, that what you have done is no good. The rain like this will come in through the house wall boards, soak your plywood and make everything smell bad. This does not happen in old-style Thai house because water come in and falls through the floor. Your style let the water come in slowly, but not let it get out again. Cannot work here. Maybe good for Wales, but not good for monsoons in Thailand."

He could see that she was right. How could he not have seen that?

He felt very foolish and was ashamed of himself.

"I see that now, so what do we do about it?"

"I want to get chang here and talk to us. I can do it now if you have the time. He live over there. I see him go home not long ago, maybe because raining too much to work."

Craig made one last feeble attempt at humour: "OK, I have time for chang. Please order one more for me."

She sighed, went inside, ordered another beer, borrowed an umbrella and ran off in the direction of chang's house outwardly frowning, but inwardly triumphant.

Chang suggested taking all the walls and teak corner-posts down and replacing them with concrete alternatives as Lek had primed him to do if he wanted the job. Craig nodded accepted defeat and sanctioned the work, which was to be started the next day. If it was still raining, they would measure up and order the materials, if it had stopped they would start stripping the walls.

The first job was to strip a section of wall, prop up that section of roof, dig out the teak posts supporting it, pour new concrete posts and then fill in between them with concrete blocks. In this way, they could reconstruct the house in modular fashion. After this, the floor could come up. The resulting cavity would be filled with builders rubble and sand and then concreted over. Finally, they would hang a suspended ceiling.

That was the working plan. There were no estimates of cost or time span and no details. The details were to be made up as the job progressed. Craig had never heard anything so preposterous or haphazard in his whole life and he found it almost impossible not to say so.

But he didn't, because he was being proved wrong every time he took a decision. The way he had been taught to do things by his father just did not work in Baan Suay. The people of Baan Suay, maybe all Thais, took far, far more on trust than any Westerner would feel comfortable doing – including Craig.

Lek, of course, couldn't see any problems with the way things were progressing. In fact, she thought that things were progressing very nicely indeed.

∞

The next day it wasn't raining and Craig awoke alone to the accompaniment of lots of banging and cheerful shouting. He had no idea what it could be, but suspected that it must be another big Buddha Day, that he hadn't been told about. He phoned Lek.

"Hello, darling. Where are you?"

"I am in our new house with chang. They start work already. You must come and see."

Craig got dressed, didn't bother with a shower and went over the back-lane to their property. The spectacle that befell him was quite amazing. The house, his house, uh, their house was standing there with no walls at all and thirty-odd men and women moving planks into piles of varying lengths. Some were singing, some were joking, but everyone was working and making a noise. Lek and chang stood in the middle of this circus. Lek was whispering to chang and chang was shouting directions to his workforce.

There was a roof supported on fifteen massive teak pillars and nothing else except stacks of teak boards of different lengths. Craig estimated that there was about ten cubic metres of seasoned teak lying in his garden. He didn't know, but he guessed that if he could get that timber to the UK it would cover the cost of buying the property and rebuilding it. He wondered if there might be a business in there somewhere.

Offering to replace old teak buildings for concrete ones if he could keep the timber.

The other thought that ran through his mind was: what had happened to the plans they had made the night before? Not twelve hours ago, they had agreed with this chang to take down and rebuild the walls section by section and now they were all down and exposed to the elements, not that that really mattered. They were starting to re-move the teak floorboards as well.

He wouldn't be sleeping in there again until it was finished, that much was pretty obvious at least.

Or so he thought.

A week later, Lek had found a buyer for the timber and she proudly handed over the forty thousand Baht that she had been paid for it. Craig was happy too, although he guessed that it was only a small frac-tion of what it would have fetched in Europe. He had to keep remind-ing himself that the path to happiness abroad lies not in comparing, but accepting.

If you compare and find fault with your host, you might as well have stayed at home and not have had the experience. It is a hard les-son to learn because criticism comes easy to expats of all countries who miss their homeland deep down. Bob Dylan's line: "... and don't criticise what you can't understand," came to mind.

It was advice that he would have to remind himself of many times while he lived in Asia.

∞

When Christmas Day came, Craig thought he would have a day on the town, but Lek was not interested in taking him to Phichai, so he settled for a day on the village instead. Craig left the house at ten a.m. He had asked Lek if she wanted to go with him, but she said that there was a day's work to be done before she could go drinking. Craig didn't mind that, he was quite happy to go alone. He was also pleased that she had not asked for a Christmas present, but then she knew that he hadn't bought one because she hadn't taken him anywhere where it would have been possible to get one.

She often went out on her almost-monthly religious days alone, so why shouldn't he? He started by walking the long way around the village to Nong's. He was determined to wish 'Happy Christmas' to everyone he met and buy everyone who was nice to him a drink. One Thailand farm vehicle passed him on his fifteen minute walk and he shouted his seasonal greeting. The driver waved back and moved his lips in an imitated reply, but it was obvious that he didn't know what he was saying: "Ha'Kiss" was all Craig heard, but he waved him away merrily just the same.

When he sat down in Nong's, she was surprised that he was so early and without his computer. He did however have a few sheets of paper and a pen in case he had a brainwave.

"Beer Chang, kap, Nong." She brought it. "Wan nee Happy Christmas — today is Happy Christmas" - the closest he thought he could get to Christmas Day.

"Happy Kissmas?" she asked and walked off, only to hurry back a few seconds later. "Happy Kissmas? Yes! Kist!"

At least she understood what day it was in the Christian calendar. Craig was not religious in the conventional Western sense, but he could use any excuse for a drink and he did like tradition and traditionally, he had always gone for a drink on Christmas morning, so he was doing it in Thailand too.

There was no further social interaction, so he motioned that he would be back and moved on. There were now three more shops that he could visit and the first was half the village away. When he got there a young woman fetched his beer but ignored his greeting, she looked and actually was, terrified that he would try to get her to speak English. Craig would have too, given a small chance, so he took his time over his beer and moved on again.

The third shop was very friendly. The eldest daughter had always given Craig a big smile when they passed each other, but he knew that that was not sexual, just friendliness tinged with shyness. She sat down opposite him.

"Hi, what your name? My name is Craig."

"She giggled behind her hand: "I know al'eady, Mr Craig. Evely-body know you name. My name Bum.""

"Oh, very nice bum" was Craig's joke to himself.

Bum giggled again: "No, I have big bum."

He didn't think she would have understood that, but it was a word that many young Thais did know. If he had known that he would never have said it. He felt like a total buffoon.

"I'm sorry, Bum, I make a stupid joke in English. Sorry. Nice to speak to you. Can I buy drink for you? Cola, milk. Not beer! I am not saying beer, OK?"

Her slight frown changed to a smile. He did know that it would have been very wrong to offer her a beer.

"No, thank you vely much, I am not thirsty."

"Happy Christmas, Bum. You know Christmas?"

"Yes, I remember... Jesu Kist. Number twenty-five. Oh, is number twenty-five today. Happy Kistmas, Mr. Craig."

He allowed her to keep calling him mister, because it made her feel comfortable, although it had the opposite effect on him. When he had finished his beer, he waaied Bum, thanked her for keeping him company and walked the short distance to the fourth shop.

As he sat down there, he felt a little unsteady. He had been drinking on an empty stomach.

"Beer Chang yin yin neung kuwat yai, kap," came out of Craig's mouth and no-one could have been more surprised than he.

He had said: "A large, cold bottle of beer Chang, please." OK, he knew that he knew the words, but they had never flowed so naturally before. The boss came back with his beer and sat down.

Thinking that Craig could speak passable Thai, he launched into a monologue which Craig had no hope of understanding. All that he could hope for was that he nodded and shook his head in the right places. He didn't bother using his greeting and when the next customer came in he thanked God, took his writing paper and pen out and star-ted writing. The owner was too polite to interrupt him and Craig left as soon as he could.

He had one more beer in Nong's and then went home to an empty house. Such was his first Christmas in the village.

∞

Despite the initial burst of action, the house progressed at a snail's pace. Sometimes, there were weeks when nothing was done at all. A few times, this was because of bad weather, but not often. Chang was first and foremost a farmer and so his farm and his rice came first. If it was time to do something in one of his fields, it was done and the house was abandoned. When he had a few free days or even a few hours, he and his crew would appear at their house, which was now just a shell. In short, it took an hour or two to take the walls down but four months to rebuild them in concrete blocks.

It really irked Craig, because he had seen his family build four and five-bedroomed houses from scratch to finish in twelve weeks and chang hadn't been able to manage four single-storey walls in sixteen. It was not a question of money, because they had arranged to pay per square metre of blockwork, it was the time and frustration. It was the broken promises and what seemed sometimes to be downright lies of the 'I'll be there tomorrow' kind, when chang knew that he could not be there tomorrow.

It was the Thai face-saving lies that happened every day in one form or another.

Lek and Craig argued every day, sometimes several times a day, about the house. Not about costs but about style. Lek was willing to put up with far lower standards than Craig. On the few occasions that Lek would convey his criticisms to chang, Craig had to pay to have them put right, whereas he contended that he shouldn't have to pay for something he hadn't asked for or which had been done badly.

It annoyed the hell out of Craig that his wife took the part of strangers over him, but it was what he had come to expect – Thais supported Thais over foreigners, no matter who they were. It was something that he and Lek had been fighting over since he had come back the second time and he knew that other foreigners in Pattaya had had similar experiences, but he was determined to get her onside no matter what.

By the time the walls were up, a lot of the cavity under the floor had been filled too because the builders were using the void to dispose of their debris, but they still needed fifty tons of sand and twelve cubic metres of concrete to finish it off. It was actually starting to look like a house again, albeit a very rough one. Everyday neighbours would take it upon themselves to inspect progress and discuss it with Lek and the builders who stayed behind after work to drink a couple of bottles of whisky before going home.

Lek provided the whiskey every day and cooked or bought food for them to accompany it.

This was something Lek had been brought up to do. Not everyone treated their workers so well, but Lek enjoyed it and Craig didn't mind. The extra three hundred Baht a day that it cost between ten to twenty workers was little enough for the goodwill that it brought them and they were not there everyday anyway.

Craig usually used this time to make notes about the house which he would pass on to Lek when the workers had gone. Then they would fight about what to do about it and Lek would talk to chang the next morning. Craig never really found out what Lek was telling chang, because only a few of his suggestions, demands and corrections were ever heeded.

It was a very hard time for him and Lek, because they fought every day over some detail or other and Craig lost ninety percent of the time and had to pay twice or more for the small victories that he did win. When the floor had dried a few days later, he and Lek stood inside the house. It felt huge compared with what they had become used to. It was one room of eighteen by seven metres and resembled a large shoe-box. There was something too 'regular' about it and Lek came up with a solution:

"Why not knock through here and build an office for you?" she suggested.

At first Craig groaned very loudly inwardly at the thought of knocking holes in what had taken so long to put up and he could feel himself getting angry for neither of them having thought about it before, but it was a very good idea and would give him a room overlooking the front, back and one side garden. If the windows were large, it would not take too much blockwork and would be like working in a conservatory so they went for it and the next day chang set to work with gusto.

He led a small squad of demolition workers and his wife led a larger group of female plasterers who set about rendering the outside of the other walls. They actually finished that before chang had build the office and were able to drop straight onto it for plastering without losing any time. This gave Lek and Craig plenty of time to argue about the other rooms. Lek had no intention of cooking indoors, she liked to cook in the garden, where the smoke and smells could drift away.

Most country Thais preferred to cook that way, so she did not need a large kitchen. Craig did not have a problem with that, but he did want a small 'kitchen' of sorts inside where he could make tea, coffee, sandwiches and the like, especially after dark and stand the fridge in, so they allocated three metres at the back of the house for the kitchen and bathroom – half the width of the house for each, which gave a larger bathroom but smaller kitchen than Craig was used to, not that he was going to argue about it.

Without too much debate, they settled on two bedrooms: one for them and a spare room so that they could have guests over, Soom could stay when she wanted to and Lek could have a dressing room when it was unoccupied. Chang, his wife and four other ladies set about constructing the dividing walls. Craig started thinking about the wiring. Thai houses have surface-mounted wiring 'in case anything goes wrong' according to Lek, but because it is 'cheaper' and you can't bury wiring in single-skin wooden walls, according to Craig.

This caused an argument. Chang was there, but he gave up and walked away in disgust, because Thais hate any sort of disagreement in public – it is not only not cool, it is very, very uncool. They decided to talk it over with chang fai, the electrician. He liked Craig's plan to sink it in, because the walls hadn't been plastered yet and he had only ever seen it done once before when he was an apprentice. He was keen to have a bash at it.

It was also more expensive, so more money for him.

Lek was not pleased at all about having 'electricity running around inside the walls' inside plastic conduits that might catch fire 'if something went wrong', but she acquiesced and chang fai started. He was very quick, but could not put the ceiling lights up because there was no ceiling. He got most of his first-fix done in a day though.

This kind of wiring caused great concern amongst their uninvited advisers. Not one of them liked the idea and they all made sure that Lek knew it. One pointed out to her that they would be living within an electric field and that that was not natural. Another said that they had ruined the house by putting the bedrooms in – they had had a lovely big house, the envy of the neighbourhood, why couldn't they just sleep on the floor like 'normal people?' he had asked.

However, Lek wanted bedrooms too, so she didn't add to their problems. Chang Number One, as Craig took to calling him, called in a few colleague changs to help out: a plumber, a tiler and a suspended ceiling specialist. Craig was not too happy about the ceiling going up yet, because he could see six or eight tiny holes in the old tin roof. Chang Number One assured him that it didn't need a new roof and that the ceiling fixers would plug those holes while they was 'up there'.

Craig let them carry on with grave reservations, but he didn't want to argue with Lek so early in the day as he had grown accustomed to a slanging match after chang and his crew had left in the evening.

Two weeks later and the ceiling was up, the electrics and the plumbing were in, the sanitary-ware and the kitchen, such as it was, were in place and the tiling was complete – walls, floors and worktops. In short, it was looking like a real house, except that it had no doors or windows and was undecorated. To complete the outside, chang and his wife laid a one-metre wide path around the house – partly to hide all the render that they had dropped and not cleared up and partly for ease of access. It did look very nice though.

That night, they had a few extra bottles of whisky and a case of beer and chang announced that he could do no more. He was finally finished after ten months. The house wasn't finished, but he was. He was fed up with the arguments, the chopping and changing and the almost permanent disruption to his normal farming routine. They couldn't blame him, said Lek, but Craig did wonder why he bothered with building if he didn't like doing it.

That night, the 3rd July, they decided to sleep in their own house. Lek got a blanket and a mosquito net and they snuggled up on their living room floor. Lek fell asleep very quickly, but Craig spent hours looking at the stars through the holes where the windows were supposed to be.

An Exciting Future

10 INDEPENDENCE DAY

Craig woke up covered in sweat with the sun beating down on him. He was wondering whether to move, so that the sun could no longer get at him, or whether to just get up and survey his new domain, when he heard Lek scream.

It was not a summon for help, just a scream, but he decided to investigate anyway. Lek was in the smaller bedroom and in the far corner lay a Lion Snake, head up looking at them. The locals feared Lion Snakes, because they are very fast, some are thought to be deadly and there are millions of them around Baan Suay. This one was about a metre long and starting to shed its skin.

It is an uncomfortable time for a snake and makes them short-tempered, which is bad news for the already short-tempered Ngu Singh.

It was the first time Craig had seen one, although he had seen tracks in the wet concrete which chang had said were made by the dreaded Ngu Singh. Maybe it had been made by this one. Maybe they were occupying his home. He could have moved in months ago, but gone into hiding every day when people were about. Lek was busy on the phone while he was thinking all this – his attention riveted to the silver-grey-black snake which seemed just as engrossed in them. Lek's Mum came into the room very stealthily with a yard broom held above her head.

Bang, bang, bang and the snake was dead. It was a sad moment for Craig, but the two women were triumphant. One less evil monster in the world – the first casualty in their new house.

"Did you have to kill it?," he asked Lek when her mother had left.

"Do you want to live with a snake or with me?" she replied coldly

"With you naturally, but couldn't we have caught it or shooed it outside?"

"You never think, do you? You think I like to kill things? Do you think my mother likes to kill things? We are Buddhists. My Mum goes to the Wat every day. We don't believe in killing things, but if you have your way, you send the Lion Snake away and then he goes next door and bites a baby and the baby dies.

"How would you feel then? When the mother cries for her dead baby and you know that you let the snake go free. Wake up, Craig, this is not Wales, where you have more chance of being attacked by wild sheep than dying from a snake bite."

And she left, leaving the snake motionless in a pool of blood, it's head caved in.

A few minutes later, he followed her into the garden, where he could hear something being fried. He sat on a plastic chair in the shade of some bush or other within a few metres of Lek:

"Sorry, you are right. I do have a lot to learn and I want you to teach me, but don't forget, I am European and don't know Thai ways. Maybe I will learn slowly like a stupid boy, but you will have to try to be patient with me and I will try to learn quickly."

Lek didn't bear grudges for long. She had been getting angry very quickly recently – far more quickly than she had used to in Pattaya or the village before she had left it, but she also cooled down quickly too.

"I know, darling, but you question every little thing that I do. It makes me angry that you don't, uh, waai-jai me – trust me. Every time, why this? Why not that? Why not like this? Why not like that? Why? Why? Why? Why? Why? It is because I think it best. That is why. If you think I am too stupid, why do you stay with me? You ever think why you do that? No, only think why did Lek do that? Don't worry about me all the time, think about why you do some things and let me get on with other things."

He didn't have a suitable answer that he thought would help, so he just said: "Did you know that it's Independence Day today?"

"Yes, I know. We moved into our new home and this is our first day and we fight already over a poisonous snake. Great."

"No, I mean it is American Independence Day. The day that America became free from the UK. Before, more than two hundred years ago, America was from the UK and there was fighting for some years and the UK lose and America became independent, free. It was on the 4th July, same today. Everywhere has a big party in America today."

"Oh, good. I see. I can tell my brother he can have his room back too now we go to our new house."

"What do you mean? He sleeps in your temple normally?"

"Temple? What temple? We don't have a temple in the house. Temple is the Wat. We sleep in my brother's room and he sleep in the kitchen."

"What? For nine months? Your brother has been sleeping on the kitchen floor for nine months so that we can have his room? That is incredible. I don't know anyone who would do that – well, except for your brother."

"We are family. We help family. Only family counts. You are family too now, but I am family. My brother helped me, and you too."

"But, nine months? Why didn't you tell me? I feel awful now."

"That is why no-one told you. What good if you know? You just feel awful for nine months. What can you do? We don't have hotel. Family don't want you to sleep in the kitchen. What can people do? We sit, we think and we do the best together. Not your business. Why make you sad?"

"Well, thank him, won't you?"

"What is the matter with you? You think I haven't thanked my own brother for giving us his room twenty or fifty times already? You think you are the only one with good manners? I know how to behave too!"

"Should I say something?"

"Say what? 'Thank You'? Why? You just make him embarrass'. Make you feel good, but make him feel embarrass' by you say 'thank you'. Say nothing, you talk too much already. Learn to say nothing."

He could feel that he was just making things worse by talking. Either something was going wrong for her and she was taking it out on him or he was truly annoying her. Maybe a bit of both, so he decided to eat his omelette, drink his tea in silence and then get out of her way.

As it happened, she left him alone first, while she went in to deal with the snake. She had left it long enough to come around if it was not dead, but it was definitely deceased, so she put it in a bag and mopped up the blood. It would make a good meal for her Mum, or maybe she would cook it herself for Independence Day, she thought.

She was sorry for the way she had picked on every word that Craig had uttered so far on the first day in their new house, but she had not been able to hold back. She wasn't sure why. There were no solid reasons, but she had spoken the truth. She hadn't made anything up but he could be a bit 'holier than thou' sometimes.

It wouldn't hurt to let him know sometimes that he could be annoying. There were a few rough edges to be knocked off both of them before they could fit in the same box together – she knew that, but she also knew that Craig would point out her weaknesses soon enough too. He couldn't help himself – he spoke his thoughts without analysing them first. He was like a child – whatever came into his head came out of his mouth without being processed.

He didn't mean to hurt people's feelings, he just thought that he was being honest, speaking the truth, but the truth was that he was being thoughtless. He just didn't realise it. She could hear him in the shower singing some old Welsh song, at least she assumed they were Welsh because she couldn't understand them.

Maybe she would get him to take her shopping as a consolation. That would make his day! Cruel, but it had to be done and sooner was better than later. If they went shopping for doors and windows there would be no more snakes coming in and far fewer mosquitoes. Luckily the scorpions hadn't found the house yet, but she knew that they would soon. Yes, shopping would be a good idea and she would let him have a beer in Ben's too for being a good boy.

"Telak," she shouted into the bathroom, which didn't have a door either. "We must go shopping today to get some doors and windows to stop your precious snakes from coming in and being killed."

He didn't even put up a token struggle,

"Yes, OK, my dear. Good idea."

'I'll soon have him trained,' she thought and went over to her mother's house to take a shower in some privacy.

While she was gone, Craig measured the openings for the doors and windows. He had been monitoring them during construction, but he wanted to get the sizes right, especially for the doors. The glaziers would want to come and measure up for themselves, but they could give a rough quote off his sizes.

There was only one glazier in Phichai and a few more builders' merchants that sold doors but they all sold the doors made in the wood yard up the road, although there was no difference in price. Craig had been thinking of objecting when Lek placed the order for the doors, because he wanted to compare several prices, but they would have to go at least forty kilometres one way or seventy-five kilometres the other to find more outlets and the delivery charges would have off-set any possible gains, so he didn't bother.

Lek could see that something had nearly escaped his lips and she was glad that he was learning to hold his tongue.

But for how long, she wondered.

They chose aluminium framed windows with smoked, toughened, sliding glass panes. There were also fly-screens built into each window. They looked very stylish and the glazier promised to go and measure up while they were shopping. The doors would also be delivered before they got home, so Lek paid for them in advance.

Craig didn't like paying before delivery, but he didn't say anything and nothing untoward happened. The doors were put in the small bedroom and the glazier phoned his quote through, while they were sitting in Ben's.

It was certainly an easier life not saying anything.

Craig was just contemplating the fact that the windows and doors had just cost him half as much as the property and Lek was chatting to Ben, when he felt a hand on his shoulder.

"Hi there! My name is Murray. How are you?"

"Er, Craig. I'm fine, how are you?" said Craig getting up and taking the out-stretched hand.

"Fine too. Where are you from? Are you on holiday? I'm from Canada."

"I'm from Wales, but I'm not on holiday. I live with Lek here in a small village called Baan Suay about fifteen K from here."

Lek got up and shook Murray's proffered hand too.

"You live here a long time, Craig. You married with this beautiful lady?"

"No and no. I've been here just short of a year and we are not married. How about you?"

"I've been here for years and I am married." He sat down and ordered a beer,

"Can I get one for you and your, er, Lek? Ben you want a beer and sit with us?"

She already was sitting with Lek, but Murray hadn't noticed.

Ben returned with four bottles of beer Chang.

"My wife is out shopping, but she doesn't drink much, she prefers to stay at home. Ben told me there was another falang about. There aren't many of us up here you know. A couple of Germans, a few Norwegians, me, you and one or two others. I think only a few live here all year round. I go home every year for six months. I should be there now by all rights, because it's too hot for me to be here in the summer."

Murray clinked glasses with everyone, took a slurp of beer and turned the label down on his bottle.

"I do that so I know which ones are mine," he grinned, "Ya gotta use your intelligenics. Ben where's my condom, darling?"

She passed him a foam rubber bottle holder to keep his beer cool. It was red and bore the maple leaf. Craig assumed that he had brought it back from Canada with him. There was also a small Canadian flag in a holder on the wall accompanied by a Norwegian and a Thai flag. Craig had noticed them before, but it was starting to make more sense now.

"We've just been out buying doors and windows for our new house. We moved in yesterday, but it's not quite finished yet. We woke up this morning with a snake in the spare bedroom. Lek surprised it while it was getting changed. She quite embarrassed the poor thing."

"What? Say that again?"

Craig ran though the little story again.

"Sorry. You'll have to speak up. Let me move closer, I'm a bit deaf on that side. What did you say?"

Craig repeated the story again.

"Lek was embarrassed when a snake caught her getting changed? I don't understand. What sort of snake? A trouser snake?"

Craig shook his head, leaned in closer and repeated his story again."

"Oh, I see. Very good. You make a funny. What was the snake changing into? I don't get that bit."

"It was shedding it's skin. It wasn't changing into anything. What did you think I meant? A cocktail dress or something?"

Lek kicked him under the table.

"All this talk about trouser snakes and cock … I don't know, Craig, you've got a one track mind. I'm sorry about my hearing, I need to get some hearing aids next time I go back. What does your wife do for a living."

"There she is, ask her yourself. Her English is very good." With that he took his beer off the table and leaned back out of the way so that Murray could get closer to her.

He let them get on with it without listening although he was aware that they were both struggling with each other's accents and Murray couldn't hear Lek's quiet-spoken voice. They both decided to give up on the conversation as a bad job when Lek excused herself to go to the Ladies'.

"You got a nice girl there, Craig. Very beautiful. Lovely smile too. Lek, eh? I've never seen her in town before, I would have remembered her all right. Are you going to be coming in here every day now? I don't live far myself – a few kilometres the other side of the railway tracks."

"I doubt if we can get here every day. It's a pain to get here on the motorcycle to be honest. It's thirty or forty minutes each way. Maybe once a week or so to come to the bank or do a bit of shopping."

"Then it has to be Tuesday. Tuesday is market day. Ask Lek, she will know. Come in here on Tuesday at about ten or eleven a.m. The market closes at noon. The girls can go shopping together – they'll like that – and we can have a few beers and a chin-wag, What do you think? Good idea? We falang have got to stick together and make good business for Ben. I know Ben for ten years. She's a lovely lady too."

After buying the next two rounds, Craig and Lek thought they had better get back while Lek could still drive.

They took their leave of Murray and went home slowly, checked the doors and realised that they had forgotten to buy stain or varnish to protect them. Still they could be painted after they had been hung, so Craig took his laptop to Nong's shop and Lek went to her mother's.

"See you in two or three hours, telak," she shouted as he walked off, "I must do something for myself. OK?"

He wasn't listening, but it was OK. It had been a nice afternoon. Meeting Murray, getting the windows and doors sorted out and having a few beers in Ben's.

It was almost dark before Lek found the time to meet up with Craig, but she had not been slacking and had a few things to tell him.

She had been given a firm price for the windows which was pretty close to the estimate. If they gave the go ahead that day, they could have five percent discount which matched the price of the fly-screens. Craig agreed so, Lek confirmed there and then. It would take three days to make the frames, a day to fit them and then another day in install the glass. So in five days they would be 'safe' from mosquitoes.

The external doors would be fitted the next day, so they only had one more day to worry about snakes and scorpions or they could sleep in Mum's house again if they wanted. Craig preferred to put up with the snakes for one more night rather than put her brother out any more. Lek phoned Ron the carpenter – chang mai – and confirmed him too.

Then she ordered two more beers and sprang the last surprise. The monks had time to bless the house on his birthday, August 14th. Lek thought that was the best bit and she was disappointed that it didn't have the same impact on Craig, but then he wasn't a Buddhist, but didn't matter because she had already booked the monks in anyway.

They went back home for an early night, but neither of them slept much, they were too worried about uninvited visitors.

11 THE LITTLE THINGS IN LIFE

The next morning, chang mai, the carpenter, arrived early and hung the front and back doors as he had promised, but neither of them was happy about the front door. It was a very nice door in itself, but they had become accustomed to the extra light that it blocked out when shut and it had to stay shut in order to do its job, so Lek phoned the glaziers to measure up and price for sliding patio doors. Eventually, they settled on French windows and the glazing firm promised to take the wooden door out, double the size of the opening, fit the new unit and make it all good in two days.

They gave the wooden door to Mum as a gift.

The glaziers fitted the frames one day and installed the French doors, but they had never promised that they would be able to glaze them as well and Craig had to agree that there just were not enough hours in a day to have done all that work, even though they had four men working on the house. However, they did finish the glazing by lunch time the next day. There were gaps in places, but nothing to worry about in a country where keeping warm was never a problem.

Their house was now secure. Nothing could get in or out unless they allowed it, but they didn't have a stick of furniture and nothing to eat drink or cook with that they had not borrowed. At least they could buy stuff and put it in the house, safe in the knowledge that they now had as much chance as anyone else of being burgled and that wasn't very high.

Lek didn't know of anyone that had been burgled ever. A few machines had been stolen from the fields but that was probably by professional thieves from far away. Nobody's house had ever been broken into in Baan Suay that she was aware of.

Craig had done a bit of decorating before and he was looking forward to transforming those lovely carved teak doors into beautiful, stained and varnished doors. He reckoned on a coat of stain, not too dark, and several coats of varnish until they shone like mirrors.

He liked doing little jobs like that, but Craig hadn't put much thought into this house-buying thing at all. He realised that now. The house and land had cost him two hundred thousand, the work so far had cost him one hundred thousand and the doors and windows just over a hundred thousand and there was a long way to go to make it comfortable. Craig had had enough of the house already if he were honest. He didn't regret it, but it was a much bigger task than he had ever imagined.

The fact was that they were, or Lek was, trying to get everything done too quickly.

Although she had given the builders all the time they had asked for, now it was rush, rush, rush. The builders had gone to work at their own pace and it had not been quickly. Now, he just wanted it to end, so he suggested that they go into Phitsanulok and buy whatever they needed in one go.

Lek nearly fell through the floor with shock. Craig was suggesting going shopping! There was obviously a first time for everything, but she got him into a taxi and down to HomePro before he could change his mind.

Just in case.

Craig's method of shopping left a lot to be desired and Lek didn't really like it. HomePro sold everything connected with a house and Craig walked from one department to the next buying one of everything he thought they needed without really checking if it was the best for them or whether he had to buy it right away.

He choose that bed, that fridge, that TV, that cooker, that set of pots and pans, a dozen assorted light fittings, a couple of ceiling fans, an assortment of paint brushes, some turpentine, a couple of dozen other items, two cases of beer Chang and sat in the cafeteria drinking a beer while staff were running around putting it all on trolleys. Lek was trying to direct manoeuvres and make sure they got everything that Craig had ordered.

The floor manager brought Craig the credit card chit to sign and then Craig and Lek spent half an hour checking the paper list. Finally, Lek spent another half an hour checking the goods. A hundred and fifty thousand Baht spent in an hour and the manager was so pleased that he gave them three free juicers.

'Why three juicers?' thought Craig, 'why not three assorted kitchen items?' But he couldn't be bothered to think about it for long. They could give one to Lek's mother and keep one to give as a present to someone else at a later date.

They had everything they needed, it was true and he had spent a lot of money – three times what Lek had thought they'd spend, but she hadn't had any fun. Shopping was fun to her. She liked comparing items and prices; she liked chatting about the pros and cons and generally taking her time over shopping, which was after all her favourite hobby. Craig had not had any fun doing that. She could have made that much money provide her with bags of entertainment for a month or more.

They put a few things in the boot of the taxi and went home expecting the rest to be delivered the following day.

Lek was both impressed and not impressed by Craig's style of shopping at the same time, but she knew that it would make a great story to tell the neighbours and she couldn't wait to tell it.

On arrival back home, Craig got out at Nong's. He had a newspaper and was looking forward to doing the crossword puzzle. It was a very hot day and it hadn't gone very well for him so far.

∞

When the goods arrived in three medium-sized vans the next day, all the neighbours were in the street outside the house watching the items being unloaded. Lek was loving it, but Craig was just pleased that the deliverymen were also prepared to install them. They put the bed together in the bedroom, and they unpacked the fridge and stood it in the correct position in the kitchen. They unpacked the TV and put it on the small table bought for the purpose. It was only when they wanted to turn it on to see if it was working that Craig realised that they didn't have an aerial.

The installer was ready for such a situation and gave Craig a card. It just so happened that his brother fitted aerials. Craig wondered whether he knew anything about how to get an Internet signal, so the helpful delivery man phoned his brother to ask.

He could fit a range of aerials and satellite dishes and, although he did not do Internet packages himself, he knew a man who did. Craig took the card resolving to get Lek to arrange a visit as soon as possible.

Within an hour, the house was starting to look like a home.

At one point, Craig spotted Lek leading a group of men back into the house:

"Craig, did you tell them they can keep this paper?"

"The packing? Yes, I told them to take it away. Why?"

"Why? Because I can sell it. All this packing paper is very heavy. I can sell it for maybe one hundred to one hundred and fifty Baht. Never throw paper, plastic, tins or bottles away. I collect them. I sell and make small business."

The men stacked all the packing cases and boxes in the snake's bedroom.

When Lek had seen everyone off the premises, she inspected everything herself:

"Craig, come here, please. Why you let the men put our bed here?"

"It has to go there, darling, that's why I put those electric points by there. One for your side and one for my side. Then you can put a light or a fan or phone charger by you and I can put one by me. The same as in a hotel."

"No, I will not sleep there. We put dead people in that position. It is very bad luck. We must move the bed over here. Like so."

She demonstrated with her arms.

Craig was beginning to get a bit sick of all this criticism. He couldn't say anything or do anything without Lek jumping on him. He was sure that it couldn't be any worse if he were caught in bed with her sister. What was going on?

He decided to try to find out later over evening drinks, but it would not be easy because Thais, and especially Lek, rarely talked about their inner feelings with anyone other than very close family and it was obvious that Lek didn't consider him that yet, although he had taken her to Britain, supported her off work for a year, bought a house and land and was now paying thousands of pounds making it comfortable.

'All right,' he thought, 'money can't buy you love and you have to earn respect,' but Craig did think that he was entitled to be treated better than that after all the faith, effort and money he had put into their relationship. Just what had he done that was so terrible that Lek felt justified in treating him worse than a, a, … words failed him. Craig couldn't think of a suitable comparison. Not 'dog'. Thais didn't treat dogs well by British standards, but they didn't treat them badly. 'Cat?' That didn't seem to fit the bill either and he didn't know any cat-owners. 'Snake?', well, they got short shrift, but Lek hadn't killed him yet.

"OK, Lek! OK, I get the message. I've paid the bills, you don't need me any more, I'm just in the way. Get some of your friends to help you rearrange the house. It'll be easier on your throat – I've never heard you nag or shout at any of your friends or family. Ever, but you seem to think that you can give me a bollocking whenever you like.

"If you have any more complaints, please put them in writing and send them to my office. I'll read them later. I've got some work to do. See you. Bye-bye." He picked up his laptop and left, feeling a little like a schoolboy in a huff.

When Craig had left, Lek flopped on the bed and wept. She could see that she was behaving like a spoilt cow, but she couldn't help herself. It wasn't a question of not loving Craig, she did, or was pretty sure she did, more than she ever had ever loved anyone else anyway.

No, it wasn't that. He was a nice man, the best she had ever met and got to know well. He was easy to kick though, because he didn't fight back much. Not that that was a good enough reason for her behaviour. Unless she thought of herself as a bully. But surely she wasn't that. She never had been a bully before anyway.

Or maybe nobody had ever been so dependent on her before. Most people would have just walked away if she had bullied them. Not even Soom was as dependent on her as Craig was and never had been – not even as a baby. She hadn't been the best mother a baby could have, even if it hadn't been her fault, but her mother had taken her place so that Soom had not lost out. Yet now that she was back, it had changed her life completely, but it hadn't really affected her daughter's.

It seemed to Lek that it wouldn't have mattered whether she had come back or not. It was a depressing thought and she hoped it wasn't true. To cap it all, she was driving away the only person that did need her. If he left, she might as well die. No-one would be any the worse off. She was beginning to wallow in self-pity, but she was strong enough to realise it, so she washed her face in the bathroom and went looking for her mother.

"Mum," she said when her mother sat down to join her on the big square table in the garden, "do you think I'm going through the menopause?"

"What? Menopause? At your age? How old are you now? Thirty-three next month? If you are then you are fifteen to twenty years early! It is possible, but I don't think you are. Everything is all right every month, isn't it? Well, it probably isn't that then. Why do you ask?"

"I don't know, Mum. I just get so angry and depressed and I'm shouting at Craig all the time. I don't want to and I always regret it, but I just can't stop doing it. He just seems to annoy me. No, it's not even that really. I just take everything out on him. Is it a nervous breakdown then? Have you ever had one of those?"

"I've never had time to, darling. What with you lot; no husband, no money and, well, in my day, we didn't worry about things like that, we just got on with it. Just got on with life. I probably didn't even know what one was back then. Maybe I thought that only rich people got them, but then, you are rich now, so maybe you have time for one."

She smiled and touched her daughter's hand in a rare display of affection that made Lek want to cry again.

"Your life is so new now, isn't it, dear? Look back on what you have accomplished in the last twelve months. You have done more in a year than most people, or at least most of us in the village, do in twenty or thirty years. Think of the changes you have brought into your life.

"You were working in a city every day, now you are retired, well, as retired as a woman ever gets. You lived in a flat, the responsibility for which you shared with two friends and your landlord, but now it is down to you to take care of your own house. You were single, footloose and fancy free, so to speak, but now you are virtually married. You lived in a big city where you could do whatsoever you liked and there was no-one to criticise you, but now you live in a village and there are plenty who are jealously watching your every move. You have a lovely house – one of the best in the village – and a lovely husband, who has enough money to take care of you and Soom.

"But, it is all new to you. Your life has been torn apart and rebuilt. I think that it has been put back together in a better way than it was. Your daughter and I are so pleased to have you around. I appreciate why you went away and we are all eternally grateful, but we missed you. Soom has never spent more than a few days at a time with you, but she has loved living near you for the last nine months or so.

"We are all so pleased that you have come home and we are grateful to Buddha for sending you Craig, because it was Craig's money that allowed you to come back to us. Never forget that. Buddha sent Craig to you. He sent you a good man with enough money. He sent you a man you could love and who would love you back, if you give him the chance.

"I have seen the way he looks at you. I saw it last year when you first brought him here on holiday. I knew then that you would be all right and now here you are.

"We have all waited for this for ten long years. Just take it easy. Slow down a little. Slow down a lot for a while. There is no need to push yourself or to push Craig so hard. You have all the time in the world, so why not sit back and enjoy some of it? Why not enjoy all of it? A cycle of life is soon over, don't wait for the next one to correct your mistakes.

"I have a good idea. It is your birthday next month, why not have a party? You have the monks coming to bless the house on the 14th and that is Craig's birthday too. Isn't that what you said? Well, there you go then. The 12th is your birthday, the queen's birthday and Mothers' Day and the 14th is Craig's birthday and the house's blessing. Five reasons for celebration. You have three weeks to organise something. Plenty of time. Have a small do on the 12th for family and a bigger one on the 14th for friends, family and neighbours."

"Oh, thanks, Mum! I knew you'd come up with something. I think you are right in everything you have said… I have to go now. I'm going to make a surprise for Craig, join him in Nong's and wait for Soom's bus. Then the three of us can plan the parties."

She hopped off the table and went home to prepare her surprise.

Lek cooked a few things. She boiled some vegetables and fried an egg, a few prawns and a handful of Soom's favourite frozen chips in a wok. Then she chopped some fruit, a banana, some papaya and a mango. She also buttered ten slices of whole wheat bread and tipped a few dozen cashew nuts into a small bowl.

Just before five o'clock, she wrapped her peace offering in cling film, placed it on a tray, covered the whole thing with a clean tea towel and headed off to Nong's.

Craig didn't see her coming, so he was surprised when she pulled up a chair.

"What do you want? What have I done now?" he asked trying to hurt her, because he still hadn't forgiven her completely. "I came here

for a bit of peace and quiet. If you're still in a bad mood, you can just...
sod off."

"Yes, sorry, telak, I don't want to disturb you, but I have brought
you something to eat. A surprise. We can wait for Soom and eat together here. Do you want some more beer? I will have one with you if
you have time. Thank you for everything you do today. The house
looks good. Later we must talk about what you want to do in the
garden. You know, for stop dogs and babies come in and for cooking
and eating... but not now. Another day."

As the bus pulled up, Lek ordered two beer Changs and a bottle of
water for Soom. Soom waaied at Craig and then sat down when her
mother asked her to. Craig put his computer into hibernation and
pushed it aside, resigned to having to stop what he was doing for a
while.

"OK, darling, I have made you some lovely fresh sandwiches to go
with your beer. I know you love beer and sandwiches together."

Soom's eyes lit up at the prospect and Lek was obviously pleased
with herself, but Craig had had Lek's sandwiches before so his smile
was not quite so genuine, although he could see that she was trying to
make peace.

Thais don't eat sandwiches as a rule, so they don't have an instinct-
ive knowledge of what makes a good sandwich.

Lek removed the tea towel with a flourish and took off the cling
film. There were five neat-looking double sandwiches cut diagonally
into quarters.

"Very posh!," Craig said to Soom with a big smile as he took one
off the plate that Lek offered him first. "I wonder what's in it."

He took a bite. It was unusual, but not unpleasant. Craig smiled and
opened it up as the other two were chewing a bite of their sandwiches.

"Mmm, lettuce, ketchup, banana and egg. Lovely. One of my favourites. What are the others?" Craig took a look: mango, cabbage and
prawn; ketchup, cashews and scrambled egg; peanut butter and prawn
and finally, papaya, pork, onions and scrambled egg.

"Very nice, Lek, thank you. That is a very nice surprise. I love your sandwiches."

'Making sandwiches is definitely not 'inbred' with Thais,' he joked with himself.

12 MOTHERS' DAY

Craig and Lek had discussed the house over the sandwiches and Soom had sat there wide-eyed as she listened to the fortunes they were planning to spend before the parties in August. Craig still had money and investments, but even he was beginning to worry about the huge imbalance between expense and income. He had already lived in Thailand for a year and had earned precisely no money, whereas he had spent a million Baht and there was no end in sight.

Perhaps a little light, the faintest glimmer, at the end of the tunnel, but no clear end. That evening, Lek had arranged for the aerial fitter and the Internet installer to come around and she had asked her uncle for a quote to build a 'sala' – a covered area where they could sit and cook. They also arranged for someone to give them a quote for railings, gates and garden walls to keep the kids and dogs out of the garden.

Lek had assured Craig many times that it was quite normal and acceptable to Thais for people to take a short cut through someone's garden, but he didn't like it. He found it annoying to be surprised by someone walking through his garden or looking through his windows if he was working. Not that he liked it any time really. He was amazed that it didn't bother Lek. Several times he had been sitting in the office and been startled to see total strangers trying to get a good look through the smoked glass windows. They didn't realise that they couldn't see in, but that people inside could see out.

So Craig needed these last few conveniences. Lek could not be expected to cook on the lawn, such that it was, in the sun and rain, so she did need a sala and he liked the look of them too. A sala looks like the kind of building made of grass and bamboo that you see on tropical beaches. Like a beach bar, but the space under the grass roof is a table,

a huge table with a grass roof on it. It is where the members of a typical rural Thai family spends most of their free time talking and eating.

Furthermore, Craig needed to start making some money without
having to buy beer for the privilege. He needed a working connection
at home. They also wanted to install an aerial for the TV for some entertainment. Craig liked to watch the TV in the UK and in Pattaya, but
wasn't sure what they would be able to receive in the village. Not a lot,
he supposed, and Lek didn't watch much TV anyway, she never had
done. Perhaps they could use the laptop to play DVD's through, Craig
thought. Buying a big TV was beginning to look like a daft thing to
have done.

Lek's uncle started work almost immediately. He used some plank-
ing that they had over from the house to make a three metre by two
and a half metre table and then built the sala around it using teak sap-
lings from his woods for posts, bamboo for rafters and grass for the
roof. It took him and a labourer three days and it cost Craig three thousand Baht. Craig thought that it was the best deal that he had had so far
in Thailand. He liked to look at it and sit in it as one does one's first
car. Lek was not so impressed. To her, it was just a boring old sala like
she had seen thousands of times before in other gardens, but it did
keep the sun and rain off her.

The television engineers had several suggestions. Craig was only
sure about one thing, if there was a reliable way of getting an Internet
signal, he wanted it. The engineer went up on the roof and pointed
some kind of meter at the sky. Apparently, the signal was strong from
up there, so they could erect a fixed dish to receive the signal and relay
it to a computer in the office below. The engineer said the signal was
excellent and very fast and only two and a half thousand Baht per
month for unlimited usage. Craig bought it and it was installed within
three hours. Then he was charged eight thousand Baht for installation.

"What, Lek? Eight thousand Baht for what? You told me that he
said two and a half thousand per month!"

"Yes, telak," she said, looking at him as if he were a slow-witted child, "but you don't think this man work for nothing, eh? You pay IP-star two and a half thousand every month for the Internet signal, but you pay this man for satellite dish and wire and his time for fix everything for you. You un'erstan now? Not difficult. Don't make trouble, darling."

Craig paid up, but it took all he had on him and the other guy was fixing another satellite dish alongside it for the TV. He pointed this fact out to Lek, who graciously offered to lend him the money until he could get to the bank.

"What can I get on this TV satellite dish?" he asked Lek.

"Five hundred more TV stations and three hundred more radio," she replied.

"Any English language?"

"Oh, yes, I ask him already. Many English and BBC."

The Internet wasn't working when the engineer came down off the roof for the last time. "Mai tam nang – it's not working," Craig told him.

"Uh?" He walked off in the direction of Lek. He was not very favourably impressed with Craig's apparent stinginess.

"What's the falang saying? I can't understand foreigners."

"What you say to man, telak?"

"I said 'Internet mai tam nang' – the Internet is not working."

"Oh, he said that the Internet is not working. Is there a problem?"

"No, no problem. I have to tell head office that you have paid and then they will set the signal so that your equipment can receive it. It can take hours or it can take a few days. Sometimes they like to see the money before they will turn the signal on. I'll ring them now and tell them you have paid in cash." He took out his mobile and Lek explained to Craig.

Meanwhile, the TV engineers were tuning the TV receiver into the satellite decoder and they were talking excitedly to each other.

"Lek, will you come in here, please," he called, "I want you to watch this procedure, so if we have a problem, you can fix it." Lek did her best, but she was not at all technically minded.

"What did the Internet bosses say, Lek?"

"I don' know, he got in his car and he drive away. You must wait. Try again later or tomorrow. He say he try hard for you for today."

The engineers were tuning into hundreds of channels on auto-search and it was quite hard to follow. Lek soon got bored and went outside. Craig tried to talk to them, but it was useless really. After a while, one of them smiled at Craig and handed him the remote control with a proud smile on his face.

"Five hun'red forty-seven TV an' three hun'red an' four radio. Try."

Craig flicked through a few channels. He could hear the dish moving from satellite to satellite automatically as he pressed the buttons to change channels. This was more like it, but there was no English-language handbook. He had been looking forward to hours of fun checking the channels and sorting them into 'Favourites Folders'.

The guys went out, Lek paid them and off they went.

"Everything all right now, telak?"

"Yes, it's great! We have five hundred and forty-seven channels in many languages. I have seen fashion and Thai channels for you and I am putting them in folder number one for you. I'll show you later."

At five o'clock, Craig and Lek went to Nong's for a few drinks, but Craig wanted to get back and play with his new toys.

"How much was the TV, Lek? Any extras?"

"No, darling. They say five thousand five hundred for everything before they start work and say five thousand five hundred after they finish work. Are you happy with everything now?"

"Yes, sort of. I am very happy with the TV and will be happy when the Internet is working, but I didn't like the surprise about the extra money."

"Only surprise for you, Craig. Not surprise for me. I forget to tell you. Sorry. But you must have, and you want, so no problem, eh?"

"No, I guess not."

When they left Nong's, Lek went to her mother's for a chat with her daughter as she usually did before Soom went to bed and Craig went home to test the Internet. It was still dead, but wasn't too bothered because he knew that he still had hours of fun to go learning to use the TV. He was particularly looking forward to watching 'East Enders' or 'Coronation Street'. He hadn't watched soaps when he lived in the UK, but he was suffering English-language starvation in the village and was itching to listen to something from back home.

He had never gone so long without watching some British TV in his whole life and he was soon to be fifty-two. It was almost a year since they left the apartment block in Pattaya, which reminded him that his twelve month visa would expire in late August. They had promised themselves that they would go to Pattaya to register Craig's address every ninety days as stipulated by the terms of the retirement extension to his visa, but the building of the house had gotten in the way and they had done it by post instead.

He had never really understood what was meant by 'cabin fever' before, but he was starting too now. Murray was the only person in eleven months that he had met who was from a country where people learned English from birth. Dutch didn't count, but he was the only other foreigner. Murray had talked about a few others 'being up here', but they remained in hiding as far as Craig was concerned.

He was eagerly switching through the channels hoping to be surprised by the next one, because he hadn't found anything in English yet. Still, there were more than four hundred left to check so he was not despondent. It was taking an hour to check about fifty channels, because some were in foreign languages that he partly understood, although most of them seemed to be Chinese or Indian/Pakistani though. There were also a few Arabic channels. Then he found Al-Jazeera.

That was new territory, but not British and no films or soaps – rather repetitive too. Good, but repetitive, he had seen it before in Pattaya. That was one he could put in his own folder though. Lek came back at eleven, showered and went straight to bed. She asked about the

TV and he tried to find something nice to say about it, but he still hadn't found any British TV and no film channels either. There were only fifty or so to check so it was starting to look grim.

Craig hadn't found any British channels when he went to bed, but he was hoping that they shared a channel with something else and that he had simply missed them. He decided to check again in the morning and ask Lek to get the boys back if he were unsuccessful.

There was nothing the next day either, so Lek phoned the TV people. They were astounded that Craig hadn't found the channels and promised to call back in the afternoon to show him.

There was no Internet either, but he said that Craig would just have wait until he had the time to take the cash payment to head office before they would 'switch him on'.

Great, thought Craig, the house looks like an airport control tower but none of it does what it says it would do and I paid fifteen and a half thousand Baht for it. Now he was becoming despondent.

He said goodbye to Lek and took himself off to Nong's with his laptop, mobile phone and a notebook. He was going to write home before he forgot how to use a pen.

At three o'clock, the TV guys beeped him as they passed on their way to his house. He left Nong to guard his stuff and ran back to the house, just as Lek was letting them in

"Oh, thank you for coming. Where is English TV? I cannot find."

They looked at each other and smiled. They had come prepared with a list of the English channels. Craig passed over the remote and sat next to Lek on the sofa, the lads sat nearer the TV. Click.

"There is one."

Lek translated.

"No, that is a South African God channel. Not English."

Lek translated.

"English, no?"

"It is in English, but it is not English."

Lek translated.

"Is English, not African. African is not same as English. I learn English in school little bit. This English."

Click.

"More English."

"Australia. God channel. TV for Buddha. Not come from UK."

Click.

"No, Al-Jazeera. Arab. In English, not from England."

Click.

"American God channel. Not BBC. You say have BBC."

He checked his list and clicked.

"BBC."

"Yes, OK, BBC International. It's crap."

"Thanks for coming guys. Thanks a lot. I am busy now, must go."

He walked out leaving everyone crest-fallen. He had lost face there, and so had Lek, for embarrassing the boys, but Craig didn't care at that precise moment, he was going back to Nong's to cry into a few beers.

The TV boys passed a few minutes later and waved half-heartedly at him through the window and then Lek arrived.

She was quiet and sympathetic, but firm: "You must not behave like that. Everybody lose face because of you. They hear English language, they think England. They don't know. Never go outside Thailand. I go outside, but if you don' tell me, I think UK too. Maybe their boss tell them it is English from the UK because he don't know too. You must be strong and say: 'Goodbye, thank you very much' and give them one hundred. Then everybody is happy..."

"Well, Lek, everybody but me that is. I was promised UK TV and I didn't get it. Why is it my fault that they don't know what they're talking about? I understand what you are saying about hurting their feelings and face, but when do I get something? When do I get what I pay for?"

"You have me, telak. Every day, you got me" and she got up, blew him a kiss surreptitiously and walked off swinging her hips at him like a catwalk model.

Craig had to laugh even though he didn't feel like it.

Saving face was such a big part of Thai life. He had thought about it many times but still wasn't sure whether he had got it right. He had asked Lek too. Sometimes, she would answer other times she got frustrated and walked off. He had not encountered face in other Asian countries, so didn't know whether Thais took face more seriously than other Asians.

One thing was for sure though, if he were going to live in Thailand, he had better learn how to deal with face pretty quickly. In Thailand, they take face so seriously that not only do they try to save their own face, they try to save others embarrassment too. The objective is not to allow anyone to lose face, because it might reflect badly on you. This is what Lek had been alluding to, he knew that.

It showed itself in many ways, but a simple example she had given once was if someone trips over a stone and drops a bag of eggs. In the West, people would say: "Oh, what a shame!," which implies a tragedy and the person who tripped up will feel clumsy. However, in Thailand, people would smile or even laugh and say: "At least eggs are cheap."

Making a joke out of a potentially embarrassing situation is one of the reasons why Thailand is called 'The Land of Smiles.'

In order to cause the least amount of embarrassment, and so save the most face, one should never criticise anyone. Never, ever. Another example she used was: in the West, if the newspaper is late in the morning, people shout: "Bloody paper-boy is always late!," but in Thailand they would not assume automatically that it was the paper-boy's fault.

Instead, they would not cast blame, until they knew for sure and even then they would probably say nothing until one day they had had enough and they would move their order to another shop. But no-one would ever know why that had been done and no-one would ever ask, because it might elicit an embarrassing answer.

Craig already knew that Thais didn't ask: "How are you?" as a greeting for the same reason. They greet each other with: "Where are you going?," because the answer is less likely to be awkward.

He had noticed that Thais are funny with the truth - most Thais are religious about telling the truth. A thief and murderer, when confronted by the police, will say: "Yes, I raped and murdered her and then I ransacked the house," but if you ask a Thai for directions and he doesn't know, he will just send you somewhere. He had seen examples of murderers and thieves on Pattaya TV and had first-hand experience with Thais giving false directions.

They did it because that way, they don't have to admit that they don't know and so can save face. All Thais know this about themselves, so they never ask for directions from a Thai stranger - ever. Craig had heard many foreigners living in Thailand complaining about it - it so frustrating, but they know why really.

The downside of saving face though, he thought, was that no-one ever complains, so people think that they're doing their job well, even if they're completely incompetent. Craig thought that it was a growing problem for Thailand in an age of increased international travel and higher expectations of value for money.

∞

As the day of the first party approached tension rose slowly but surely too. Lek hadn't given a party for more than ten years and she could not expect any help from Craig, or not much more than fetching and carrying anyway. She was glad her mother had suggested two parties, because she could use the smaller, first one as a trial run.

It was not that Lek was not a good cook, she was, she was just out of practice with giving parties. She had been brought up by her own parents, but she had stayed with her grandparents, and especially her grandmother, while her own parents were working in the fields. This is much different to nowadays, when village parents often work away in a city and leave their kids with their grandparents full-time, as Lek had had to do.

Lek had had the benefit of being with her grandparents all day and then her own parents and her aunties and uncles in the evening. Some of these aunties and uncles had worked away or married people from other parts of Thailand, so they had brought variety to her culinary skills. She had had a good childhood because there were always people around her. It also meant that she learned to cook from her parents, her grandparents and all her aunties and uncles. She spent most of the first twenty years of her life cooking with various people.

When Lek was a girl, it was still normal for boys and girls to learn how to cook, but not only to cook, also to slaughter, preserve food and care for livestock. Boys were taught to cook, but they seemed to concentrate on slaughtering and tending rather than cooking. In Lek's family, everyone learned to cook and enjoy cooking.

However the story was not the same for subsequent generations with the result that many modern, city, Thai girls have never learned to cook without a microwave. They were not taught by their parents, who were not interested in living in a village. Furthermore, most traditional Thai cooking is done outside. This is why most town people tend to eat in restaurants or order a take-away. In fact, Thai townspeople eat out far more often than their European counterparts, because eating out is cheap and apartments often don't have proper kitchens.

Lek's village was in northern Thailand where most people ate food with a lot more chillies than a Westerner would like, but their style of cooking was not hot by Thai standards. The hottest food in Thailand is cooked in Isaan and the far south near Malaysia. Lek learned to cook northern Thai style at home, but she learned other styles, like Isaan, in Pattaya, because most of the girls in Pattaya come from Isaan. Besides that, Pattaya is a melting pot for Thailand as a whole anyway because of all the money that tourism brings.

This also accounts for why so many insects are consumed in Pattaya.

Lek liked fried insects, although as a rule they were not sold where she came from. In Isaan, they also ate rice-field snails, but not anywhere else. Lek's favourite 'bush tucker' at home was rat, frog and snake and it went without saying that she could cook them well. However, her normal everyday food usually consisted of pork and fish, for which she knew hundreds of recipes.

Most of them could be adapted for chicken too, but she had virtually given up eating chicken when the bird flu scare spread, not that she knew anyone who had contracted the disease. Lek's diet was traditional Thai, despite the fact that she had mixed with foreigners in Pattaya for ten years. She didn't often drink tea, coffee, lemonade or milk. She didn't eat Western sweets or chocolate, nor bread or dairy. She got her calcium not from milk or cheese, but from eggs and the small bones of fish, birds and frogs, which she liked to crunch up like a Westerner might crunch pork crackling. She also had a passion for pork scratchings, and crisps, but only as an occasional treat.

Having a birthday on Mothers' Day for Lek, was like a Westerner having a birthday on or close to Christmas: it tended to be overshadowed. When she was a child, her family had tried to make her feel special on her birthday, but as she got older it happened less and less so. It was every mother's special day: hers twice, her mother's and her grandmother's. Four parties in one. She didn't mind her birthday taking a back seat, because Mothers' Day is a very big event in Thailand – far bigger than in the West. If there is one day a year that everyone will try their utmost to get home, it is Mothers' Day, if she is still alive.

As head girl in Daddy's hobby, Lek had usually had to stay behind, while some of the other girls and Beou went back to see their mothers. No alcohol may be sold on Mothers' Day, but men still came looking for the girls especially after midnight, when alcohol went back on sale.

Being home for this day was practically a new experience for Lek and she was looking forward to it. The no alcohol ban was not rigidly enforced in the villages, it was more meant for the cities. Perhaps the authorities hoped that more people would go home to their families if the night life was affected. It worked anyway. Travelling around Mothers' Day was a nightmare. The best buses were booked up and other buses and trains were full to bursting. Those who had cars often sat in traffic jams for hours.

A village like Baan Suay could expect to grow by ten to twenty percent with all the people coming back to see their mothers. Fathers' Day, which was on the king's birthday, didn't have the same affect. Most people celebrated the day for the king rather than their fathers. The Thai king is held in very high esteem.

Lek's sister, Chalita, was sure to come back if she could get the time off work, but she still wasn't sure. It was easy to tell when a family had returning children, music would be played louder than normal; there would be more smoke from the cooking fires and more laughter. As with all big Thai parties, the fun started the night before when the ladies gathered to wash and chop vast quantities of vegetables.

Lek's mother's house was no exception and she, her mother, daughter and a few neighbours started preparation of the food on the 11th. Craig took no part in it. Since his Internet connection had been enabled – five days after the technician had left. He had become a recluse. He sat in the office all waking hours, except perhaps a hour in Nong's in the late afternoon. The fact was that he was getting worried about making some money and was anxious to see some results.

The 12th was also an anniversary of sorts for them. It was the day that Craig had gone back home two years before when he had first met Lek on his first trip to Thailand. He hadn't seen a lot of the day. He remembered that the streets had been quiet and that there were more girls in the bars than men, because there was no alcohol on sale. It had not been his favourite day in Thailand for several reasons, but that was two years ago and now he was sitting in 'his' new house in Thailand with a Thai 'wife', a Thai stepdaughter and a Thai mother-in-law.

It was quite overwhelming the difference twenty-four months had made. He hoped that Lek and her family were happy about the changes to their lives too. That first year he hadn't known that it was Lek's birthday that he had left on. He wondered whether his departure had spoiled her day. In fact, Lek didn't celebrate her birthday in Pattaya, because it hadn't felt like it was her down there, just someone pretending to be her, like a character in a play or a dream.

Every day of all ten years of it.

Craig was already asleep when Lek got back just after midnight. It was unusual for him to go to bed that early, but it happened. He woke up just long enough to mumble happy birthday as Lek got into bed and went back to sleep. Lek kissed him on the cheek. She wanted to be up at five o'clock, but that would not be a problem for her. She was asleep as soon as her head hit the pillow.

∞

Promptly at five, there was the usual call to action, loud music from all around. Loud Thai music, which Craig happened to like, but he was glad that he didn't have to live by any sort of schedule. It didn't bother the villagers, because as farmers, they got up at five every day anyway. Something was being announced over the village loudspeaker too, but mercifully, the nearest speaker was about a hundred metres away and it could only be heard faintly even on a quiet day. Craig could just about hear it between tracks, but couldn't understand what the mayor was saying, Happy Mothers' Day, probably. Lek was already in the shower, singing as she often did.

He didn't know whether to get up and try to show some interest, go to work or watch TV – going back to sleep was not an option in that racket. He decided to wait for Lek, so he switched the TV on and idly flipped through a hundred Chinese and Indian channels. There wasn't one word of English. There probably was somewhere, but there was no TV guide to look through – it was all hit or miss – and scanning more than five hundred channels took hours – you could easily miss a whole film while looking for one.

Lek came back in in her towel.

"Happy Birthday, telak," he said. "What are you doing today?"

"First, go eat with Mum and Soom and family. Then cooking and eating and drinking all together."

"A bit like a normal day then, but more."

"Yes," she grinned, "Good, neh? You want to come with me or you want to come later?"

"What do you want me to do?"

"I want you to give me a birthday present."

"But, I don't have anything. You know I can only go to the shops in town if you take me and I haven't been in for ages."

"I know, darling. Only joking. I take you tomorrow. See you later in Mum's house. I stay there all day. Come back for shower again in six or seven hours or maybe shower over there. If you are hungry come see me."

She kissed him lightly and breezed out singing again. The music from the neighbours was still there, but it was funny how the brain could filter it out. Craig was not easily distracted when he was latched on to something. The TV was a waste of time and money, but you have to have one, don't you? Otherwise visitors just ask where it is or, worse still, might assume you can't afford one and Lek could never allow that to happen. He switched it off and got up.

Mum's or the office? It was getting light and warm, so he started the daily routine normally carried out by Lek. He walked around the house opening all the windows to allow cross drafts in and opened the back door, because it too had a fly screen on it. He brought his computer back to life, put the coffee on and went to brush his teeth and wash his face. Then he took a mug of coffee to his desk and checked his email.

Nothing of interest. Nothing from any friends and no sales reports from PayPal, just tons of 'incredible, never-to-be-repeated, special offers' for things he didn't need or even want. He was getting about four hundred spam messages every day, so he set about filtering some out. He didn't like Outlook's inbuilt spam filters because he thought they might trap useful stuff too, so made his own list and decided to add to it every day until most of the junk just never saw the light of day.

The first step was to ban all email originating in Nigeria – he didn't know anyone there anyway; next was to trap any email with 'Viagra', 'Cialis' or 'penis' in it. That dealt with a quarter of them, but it left him wondering what to do next. Maybe wipe Russia off his version of the Internet too? They would have to be careful or they would be next in line for a blanket ban.

Work. Yes, work, but what at? He received fifty or sixty offers to make him a millionaire in weeks 'while working from home in pyjamas' every day too, but instinct told him they were junk. They were tempting though and if he were honest with himself, he didn't have the faintest idea what he was doing. Or going to do. It was quite scary.

Lek seemed hell-bent on spending all his money as soon as she could, but he wasn't earning a bean, yet he was sitting in his new house on the other side of the world from everyone he knew. It was crazy. He knew that some people in Pattaya had the same problem, but they had access to physical goods that they could sell on eBay. There was just nothing where he was, only rice and you couldn't even eat that, because the husk had to be milled off first. Even the biggest and best farmers in the village had to buy and eat some other farmer's rice from the shops. Some farmers were producing three hundred tons of rice a year, but couldn't eat a spoonful of their own produce themselves.

That was a bit crazy too and the thought cheered him up a little.

He was sitting at his desk at five-thirty in the morning, half listening to the music, looking out of the window before him at the birds foraging, and waiting for inspiration. He had done this many times before. Sometimes just as early, but usually equally clueless. It was very worrying.

And that was worrying, because worry builds walls. The more you worry, the less time you have to think about a solution. However, nothing would come so he thought about joining Lek and starting drinking early. It was her birthday and a national celebration after all. You couldn't want a better excuse, and her brothers, Long and Ngat, and sister, Chalita and her husband, Deo, and his own 'wife' would all be getting stuck in already anyway, so why not?

But he couldn't. Not yet. He liked to make some 'progress' every day, even it was ineffectual. He needed to know that he was at least trying everything that he could.

He made a list. He had heard a woman on the radio say that men like lists and he did. So he decided to make a list of what he had and what he could do and then try to match them up into some kind of a job. The first list was web sites. He already had sites on Wales, Thai Food, Travel and Gardening and he thought he could write sites on... well, anything really. He wasn't an expert in anything, but he liked researching and writing, so he reckoned he could create a site on virtually anything that wasn't life-threatening. Then skills and assets; he had the Internet; a moderate ability to write, dedication, an ability to concentrate and a desire not to be sent back to Wales penniless.

However, stare at them as long as he liked, he could not see what to do with this hotchpotch. The web site on Wales would be a dead loss, because he didn't live there and was already out of touch. The same went for the site on gardening. He knew nothing about gardening in Thailand. Travel? He wouldn't be doing much of that any more. Lek was not only not a keen traveller, but she loved being in the village with her daughter.

That left Thailand and surely there were hundreds of loss-making sites by hopeful falang on the Internet covering that subject already. An Internet search confirmed it – Google helpfully reduced the number of sites it returned to a round eight hundred and twenty-two million. Fat chance there then. How about a web site on 'My Quest to Make Money Online'. He could write about his attempts at making money on the Internet. That way, failures would become stories and successes would be doubly successful. He made a note of it on his Outlook 'To Do List' and set a reminder for the next day.

Thailand? Snakes, reptiles, plants, orchids, culture, traditions – there had to be enough material there to write about. He was interested in snakes and had to learn about them anyway for the sake of safety, and reptiles and Lek was always talking about her garden and orchids and cooking. Culture and Buddhism were a part of daily life too and surely, visitors to Thailand and those thinking of retiring there would be interested in life in a village in Thailand.

He added that to Outlook too. They seemed like things he could write about regularly as he had to learn them anyway. He was beginning to feel a bit better, when he became aware of something behind him. It was Lek, she was always doing that – creeping up on him. It didn't bother him and he suspected that she didn't do it on purpose – he just got so carried away.

"Hello, telak. I bring you some food. It was a bowl of Yellow Curry and another bowl of boiled white rice."

"Mmm, thank you."

He rarely ate Thai food before lunch and he had mentioned it dozens of times, but Lek could never seem to remember. Curry before noon, was just not right somehow, but today he fancied it for some reason. He heard Lek switch off the light.

"We must save money. Why you want light? He looked at the clock on the wall. He was surprised. Shocked even. Five and a half hours had gone already!

"And here is a cold beer from me for my birthday. See you later."

And she was gone again. He watched her skipping down the garden path singing out loud. She was like 'Will o' the Wisp', he thought, here one moment and gone the next.

The curry was mild and sweet. It was very nice and he drank his beer with it. It was a chicken curry on the bone and a bit too salty for him, so he knew that Lek hadn't cooked it. Lek was very wary with salt, because of his blood pressure, didn't eat chicken and would have de-boned it for him anyway. Maybe her sister had made it or perhaps Soom was practising again. Lek's mother rarely cooked chicken either.

He had the bit between the teeth now and couldn't wait for the next day to put his new plan into action, so he made another list. A list of the articles he could write to populate his existing web site on Thailand and his new blog on making money on line. The first blog post would be the story of the last five hours and the first article on Thailand would be his recent experience with 'face'. He put them on the list. Then he added: 'A Thai Birthday', 'Mothers' Day in Thailand', 'Common Local Snakes in Northern Thailand' and 'Overcoming Writers' Block'.

He promised himself that he would join the party when he had written and posted the first article. It was a common tactic he used to get that little bit more out of himself.

He wrote five hundred and seventy-six words on 'What Face Means to Thais' and reread it. He looked it up and down, reread it again, posted it to his web site on Thailand and then pinged Google to let them know it was there. Instead of going to the party, he decided to have a shower, get another beer and then set up his new blog so that he would have a flying start the next day.

When he sat back down at his desk with a fresh, cold beer, it was already one o' clock. The music was still playing and cooking smells and the sounds of laughter were wafting in from all around. He was getting hungry again, but he wanted to set up the blog first. He had never done that before but he had read that Wordpress was easy to install. His Internet host provided the service free of charge, so he logged into his cPanel and clicked on Simpatico.

Wordpress was easy to find and he clicked on 'New Installation'. The installer kicked in and all he had to provide were a few names and passwords. It was done. He had a blog attached to his web site on Thailand – http://packageholidaystothailand.org which he had set up previously. It soon became apparent though that a basic installation was not going to be enough, so he looked up articles on 'plug ins' and 'widgets'. When he was happy with that. He reluctantly put his computer to sleep, locked up the house and went to Nong's. He sneaked past Mum's, because he knew that the party was already in full swing. They had all been at it for hours and he would not fit in yet.

He needed to have a few more drinks and come out of his shell, before he could mix with party folk. He knew that from many embarrassing previous experiences. There were few social experiences worse than being the only sober one at a party. It always made him feel 'out of sync' and he couldn't dance or sing unless he'd had a few, but that was probably his Welsh upbringing. His Thai was better after a few beers too, so having convinced himself that he was doing the right thing, he took a seat and ordered a beer Chang.

"Why aren't you at the party?" asked Nong.

"Oh, drong ror nid noy – I have to wait a little." He pulled a frown in explanation, but Nong wasn't sure what it meant. Not surprising really, no-one else in the village would either although he had tried to explain it to Lek several times. When he was working in his head, he seemed to go in so deep, that it took a while to find his way back to the outside world where he could talk to people again. It was like potholing, he imagined, or exploring a deep cave, you go in very deep and the people outside the cave don't seem to register any more. You have to come out to be able to talk to them and getting out takes time.

Sometimes he didn't even want to come out and this was one such time. He would rather have stayed in the office with a beer at his elbow and his head stuck in the Internet, perfecting the appearance of his blog, that didn't really exist. It was just an apparition, an electric ghost, but he felt at home in that world and it seemed to accept him too.

Craig took another swig and looked up. A large black snake was crossing the road about five metres away and heading straight for him. He could hear Lek's voice starting to sing her favourite party piece on the karaoke machine – something about a foreigner breaking her heart.

"Nong! Nong! Kor tort, ther ma leeuw, leeuw! Ngu ma – Nong, sorry, but come quickly, there's a snake coming."

Out she came in a flash. Craig was already, standing ready to run. He liked snakes, but didn't like getting bitten and some cobras were black.

"Gat die? - bite die?"

"No, she laughed. No problem. This one not bite die. It eats frogs. It's a water snake. Can be very big – three-four metres. Very scary, but no problem."

'Very scary' was dead right he thought. Lek was still singing, unaware of his brush with 'death' as he retook his seat and the snake followed the gutter down the road.

"One more for the road, please, Nong," he smiled.

"One more?," it was the only English Nong had learned since she had met him, so the joke went over her head.

Craig liked to joke and he missed an audience. All his attempts at humour fell flat in the village. Even the few who spoke a few words of English missed the puns and when he saw puns in Thai, nobody else did, because Thai words that sound the same to foreigner do not to Thais. What foreigners hear as synonyms are usually spelled differently and or pronounced with a different tone.

It made his life a little greyer.

The party had been going strong for five or six hours by the time Craig got there. As soon as he appeared, Lek and the girl she had been dancing with grabbed him and pulled him to dance with them. It was the last thing he needed really. He just wanted to sit in a corner and slowly slip into the party atmosphere like a wary swimmer into a deep, cold pool.

"Sorry, Lek, cannot. Must sit down first."

She had guessed he would say that, but she had had to do the dutiful wife thing to show everyone that she loved him. She passed him three plates of different types of food, opened one of the bottles he'd brought and rejoined her friend.

"What's the matter with him?" asked Lek's dancing partner.

"Nothing's the matter. He's all right. He get's like this sometimes. He get's too serious and can't mix in. He likes to be alone a lot and think. He does it often really. Nearly every day. I sit with him and watch sometimes, but he hardly seems to notice me. I'm not sure that all that reading and computer stuff is good for him. Maybe his brain will explode one day."

Her friend laughed at the idea.

Craig stayed a few hours until he felt that he could slip away. He waaid Lek's Mum and said 'Sawasdee Wan Mae', which he hoped meant 'Happy Mothers' Day', greeted Lek's brothers and sister and chatted to Soom in English for a while. He even danced with Lek, but he told her he had to go back home. She didn't mind. He could look so grumpy sometimes that it put everyone off having a good time. She waved him goodbye and took the mike to sing another song.

13 BLESS THIS HOUSE

The next day, Lek was 'sick'. She didn't know why. She said that it couldn't be a hangover, because she couldn't remember drinking that much.

Everyone else could though.

So, her sister drove her into Phichai to do some essential household shopping. They didn't ask Craig if he wanted to go, but he didn't want to anyway. Lek would not have gone either if she didn't really, really have to. She had to get some special bits and pieces for the monks the next day.

Chalita was a strong, independent woman, like Lek, although for different yet similar reasons. Chalita had married a local boy too but they had decided to move away as soon as they could after getting married. Neither of them had wanted to work in the fields, so they had moved to Bangkok and found jobs in factories. They had stuck at it and worked hard and now they had a house of their own in the suburbs. No children, but they hadn't ruled them out yet.

Earning her own money and having her own house in Bangkok, had transformed Chalita from being a shy country girl into a confident cosmopolitan woman. She worked, kept house and played tennis. She was fit and pretty. She was also more serious, more middle-class and better off than Lek, but she knew how to have fun too. She liked to dance and cook, but she never drank alcohol. She preferred to sit quietly whereas Lek liked to be out there in the thick of the party.

Lek didn't know it, but her younger sister looked up to her enormously. She knew the sacrifice that Lek had made to save the family from ruin and she knew how much Pattaya had changed her. She was not at all convinced that the change had been for the better either, because

Lek was a farmer's daughter at heart. Lek would not have gone away if she had not had to, whereas Chalita had never had any intention of living on a farm and working ankle-deep in mud all day. She had always wanted shops, nice clothes, a car, a sports club, cinemas and all the other things that a city has to offer.

She was glad that her sister had found Craig and that they had come back to where Lek belonged. She hoped that Lek could find peace at last and calm down again. There was no sign of it yet though, judging by the previous day.

"Little Sister, stop at the bank first, I need the ATM." She flashed Craig's card. I do all the money, because he can't be bothered."

Chalita knew her sister's little ways. "You don't use your own card then?"

"No, Craig pays for all the house expenses. One sec..."

She fell out of the car rather awkwardly and stumbled to the machine while Chalita watched her and parked nearby. She shook her head with mild disapproval but considerable awe. Chalita would not have the nerve to behave like Lek did sometimes.

"OK. We have the money, so let's get shopping!" Lek took her sister's arm and they went off, both thinking how long it had been since they had done that.

Lek needed some presents for the monks that would bless the house the next day and beer and spirits for the guests. The rest they could get in the village. There were no real shops in the village, but there was plenty of food – acres of it.

As they were loading the car with half a dozen bags, Chalita pointed and whispered: "Look, a falang." It was still unusual for her to see foreigners, because she lived and worked in the suburbs of Bangkok, where few foreigners ever ventured. Lek looked up.

"Oh, I know him. Hey, Murray! Murray! Over here!" Chalita didn't know where to put herself as Murray came over with a broad smile.

"Hello Lek, how are you?," they shook hands and Lek introduced her sister. Murray took her hand. Chalita spoke English quite well, but hadn't had any practice for a long time Not a single word of English could she utter, but Murray was used to that and he filled the gap, assuming that she couldn't speak English at all.

"What are you doing, ladies? Come have a coffee in Ben's with me. I pay. Come on. Where is Craig?"

Lek nodded assent and took Chalita's arm. She didn't mind going, but would rather have gone straight back home. She beeped the car locked and stuck close to her sister.

"Craig is at home working, I'm out with my little sister, Chalita."

When offered, Chalita accepted a coffee, but Lek and Murray asked for beer Chang. They chatted for twenty minutes and Chalita's English was starting to return, but the both sisters wanted to get home. As they were leaving, Lek invited Murray to the party the next day:

"We bless the house with monks in the morning at ten o'clock and Craig has his birthday. We have a party all afternoon and maybe all night. Please come and bring your wife. You remember? We live in Baan Suay, just ask for falang house. Everybody knows it."

"OK, nice to see you both. Tell Craig that I will be there."

∞

On the big day, Lek, her mother, sister, daughter and some girl-friends got up at five a.m. and started up the music system that had been set up the night before. They began by preparing food to go with what they had done the previous evening and putting out rows of chairs for those who couldn't get into the house.

Craig took a bottle of cold water into the office and started work again. He had four or five hours before the guests and the nine monks would arrive. He didn't want to waste them, but on the other hand, he didn't want to retreat so much into himself that he couldn't get out again in time to enjoy the day either. It was a gamble that he would have to take, because he had to work.

So did most of the other men in the village, about a dozen women worked together to make the place ready. The garden and the house were already acceptable as Lek always kept things looking nice – just a little short of house-proud, Craig liked to think. Clean but not obsessive. Just how he liked it

Once the crew was assembled and working, Lek turned the music down, so that the ladies could laugh, sing and lark about – have sanuk – enjoyment at work – as the Thais call it. Sanuk is a very important concept to Thais.

Some older men started to arrive at about eight thirty and some of the early helpers drifted off to get changed. People have to look respectable before monks. The dress code for men is long trousers, collar shirt and sandals. The women may wear traditional Thai village dress or modern clothes.

Those men who knew how to, began to prepare the living room for the monks' ceremony. This meant that the walls and windows had to be covered with orange sheets so that the room resembles an orange cell (a monk's cell, not a prison cell!), cushions were scattered about for those who needed them and a row of bamboo matting was put down for the nine monks to sit on. A PA system was rigged up so that those who could not fit into the house could hear the proceedings in the garden.

The nine monks arrived at about ten fifteen a.m. from the local Wat and took their places on the matting. Lek took her position before them and Craig was ushered to a spot next to her. The house was full and very hot. The monks and a 'master of ceremonies' chanted the rites of blessing.

Typically, nobody had told Craig what to expect or what was going on, but he could feel the atmosphere and it was good. Solemn, but good. When the monks had done their bit, Craig and Lek had to present a goody bag of gifts to each of the monks. These gifts consisted of simple items like soap, talcum powder, uncooked rice, a nail brush, a flannel, cooking oil, but no-one had explained what to do.

The master of ceremonies gave Craig the first bag to give to the head monk, who was sitting opposite him. He knew better than to stand up, so he shuffled forward on his knees until he was within reach of the monk and handed him the bag. The monk looked him in the eyes and smiled, but made no attempt to take the net bag.

He tried again, but still nothing. Craig could hear tittering from behind him and the monk was smiling, but he still didn't know what to do, so he crept a bit closer and tried again. The master of ceremonies took pity on him then and pushed the proffered bag downwards onto the handkerchief laying before the monk. When the bag touched the cloth, the monk grinned and nodded. Craig found out later that the monk was not allowed to accept the gift by hand, but he could pick it up off his handkerchief. Craig backed off and Lek presented the next gift. Craig presented the third, fifth, seventh and ninth gifts like an old hand.

He was, if nothing else, a quick learner, but he couldn't understand why he hadn't been told what to do before he had to do it, unless they wanted to have a laugh at his expense, because he knew that his new family and friends were quite capable of doing that.

After giving the personal gifts, the food was brought in for the monks on nine huge trays with many dishes on each. Everyone sat and watched the monks eat. When they had finished, the 'left-overs', at least ninety percent of what they had been given, were taken away to be shared amongst the guests later - a symbolic gesture as there was a hundred times what was left on the trays waiting outside anyway. People saw it as an honour to be given something off the trays that the monks had blessed.

When the trays had been taken away, two of the monks walked around the house, painting symbols and words and sticking gold leaf on some of the wall above doorways. They wrote on the wall outside the master bedroom and inside the office in Pali. One monk held the paint-pot and glue and steadied the chair, while the head monk carried out the artwork.

Monks have to eat their last meal of the day before midday, so they left at about eleven thirty to go back to the Wat for dinner, this food just being a welcome bonus.

As soon as they had left, Lek's mother called on everyone to go outside and join the other guests for an afternoon party in the garden. It was lovely to be outside the house again, although August was not one of the hottest months of the year in Baan Suay. People laughed and joked as they ate and drank to the accompaniment of records and the roadies setting up the stage for the evening's entertainment.

By five p.m. most people had gone home for a shower and a siesta so that they would be fit to come back for the evening do. The dancing girls and the DJ took advantage of the lull to set up their gear and practise a few routines. The men that were left set up the dining tables for the hundred and twenty invited guests, who would arrive between seven and nine.

∞

As the first guests started to arrive, Craig and Lek stood at the entrance to welcome them. They had to have security guards because it was the done thing, not because there was a risk of trouble. Thais give an envelope containing money when they come to parties like this and it was Craig's job to accept them and say thanks. He wanted Lek to do it, but she kept wandering off to supervise elsewhere. Craig understood very little of what the guests said as they entered, so he was relieved when Chalita came to help.

"Thank you, Chalita, I cannot understand, what people are saying. They are giving me money, but I cannot say anything. I don't like it."

"No worry, I un'erstan. I see your face. Look funny, so I think I come to help you. You very funny with the monk too – everybody smile," she put her hand to her mouth to cover her smile. It was a very pretty gesture, but most Thai women did it.

Craig had often wondered whether it started centuries ago because they had had bad teeth then.

When the flow of arrivals had slowed to a trickle, Craig and Chalita went around to the back garden to join in. The usherette, a friend of Lek's was totally drunk and was allowing people to sit wherever they liked. The head table, which was meant for the family, was being occupied by strangers, but Chalita soon sorted them out.

It was quite a surprise to Craig when Murray arrived, since Lek had forgotten to tell him. Chalita made room for him to sit next to Craig because Lek was floating around the tables greeting people and making sure that everything was running smoothly. He had hardly seen her since the monks had left, but she came over as hostess to greet Murray.

"Hello Murray, Thank you for coming to our party. I forget to tell Craig that I see you yesterday and ask you to come today. Where is your wife?"

"She's not really into parties. She likes to watch TV. That's OK by me, I come alone."

"Shame, but very good that you come. Thank you. Craig will talk to you and take care of you. I must take care of everybody else. See you later. OK, Craig?"

"Sure, darling. We'll be all right. Murray, is your wife any good with sandwiches? Lek made me some beauties the other day. Do you think that the ability to make a good sandwich is inbred?"

Craig had been waiting for an opportunity to use his new joke. He waited and watched Murray's face.

"Sure, she makes sandwiches in bread. What else can you use? Do you make sandwiches out of something else in Wales? I suppose you could make 'em out of pancakes, but that's not really a sandwich then, is it? Can you get good bread? I can't find any good bread – it's all too sweet."

It was too loud to talk comfortably, so they both just sat there, drank beer, watched the dancing girls and clinked bottles from time to time.

It was a good party though.

Everyone seemed to have a great time. The eight girls danced their hearts out and so did most of the guests, including Murray, although it was a very hot evening.

When the guests had all gone home at around midnight, the roadies took the stage down and loaded up all their gear in double quick time. Lek asked them if they wanted to stay behind for a drink, but they weren't interested. They did this every day and they just wanted to get home or back to their hotel. They had put on a good show though and Lek took one of their cards so she could invite them back for the next party.

She may not have given many parties in the last ten years, but it looked like she intended making up for it. She loved parties and now she liked giving them too.

The men and some of the kids cleared up the empties that were lying around everywhere and the women gathered up all the paper plates and cutlery. The plates were dumped and the washing up could wait, but when the last person left, nobody would have guessed that a party had ever taken place there. Craig had never seen anything like it.

He was very impressed indeed.

When he awoke the next morning, Lek was sitting on the bed, putting the envelopes of money into some sort of order, because many of them were crumpled where he had stuffed them into his pocket.

"Good morning, telak. Wow, look at all those envelopes! I can buy a nice birthday present with that. I'll tell you what, fifty-fifty because you didn't get any money for your birthday, did you?"

She just looked at him and smiled: "We will see what you say later."

She slit the first envelope open with a knife: two hundred Baht. Lek wrote something in an exercise book. She opened another: five hundred Baht, she made another entry into the book. This went on for half an hour.

"What are you doing? How much did we get?"

"There is fifteen thousand, three hundred and forty Baht. Very good, neh? Now that we live in the village we must do the same everybody else in the village. This money is not present for you. I know you think it is your money, but it is my money really, because I give the party."

"You may have given it, but it was my birthday and I paid for it, but I'll give you half. That's fair, isn't it?"

"Maybe, but you don't understand. Listen: many times, the lady saves money all year for a party. The man not always give or not always have money for give and a party is expensive. So, maybe lady borrow some money for the party. When people come to the party, they give the lady – me – some money to help pay for the party. If they want to give you a present, they give you something – a painting, a photo, a clock, something, but if they come, they must give me some money, but if they are very poor, no problem, they can give twenty Baht.

Then I write in a book who gives me what and when I go to their next party, I give them the same, but maybe a little bit more. Then that lady writes that in a book: Lek, or better, my full name, Leynou Suk-sawat: three hundred Baht. Then next time, I write her name and how much.

"Un'erstan now, darling? Not your money. My money, but you can have if you want to do this job and go to every party. But it is no good, because people ask me to their party. Some people say you can come too, but not everyone. Sometimes have party for ladies only or for babies and you don't care or want to go. See now why this my money?"

"It's like a loan."

"Yes, it is like a loan. People borrow – loan – me money, so I can pay for a party. Good system, no?"

"Yes, it is a good idea. In the West, people just bring a bottle."

Lek folded the notes, tucked them, into her bra and tapped her left breast:

"Very nice, neh? I go give to my Mum to put in the bank for me." She slipped off the bed, kissed her forefinger and tapped his forehead.

"Yes," he said, "they both are," but she had already gone.

An Exciting Future

14 THE CURE FOR CABIN FEVER

They had both been 'up country' since the previous August and the only foreigner they had met properly was Murray and they didn't see him often. Craig was starting to miss foreign company. Lek too was feeling constrained by living in the village. She had thought that they would go to Pattaya every ninety days to sign the TM47 for Craig's visa, but the house and laziness had gotten in the way. The time was fast approaching when they would have to renew the visa extension itself and that had to be done in person.

Lek took Craig's passport out of the wardrobe: "You know you have to get a new visa before the 22nd August, darling, don't you? We don' want the same trouble as last year."

"Yes, I remember. When do you want to leave. I'll go tonight. I can't wait to speak English properly, have pie and mashed potato with gravy, read a British newspaper and best of all, get some cheese. I haven't had any cheese for about a year. Or is it longer? It certainly feels longer."

"Yes, I want a holiday too now the house is nearly finished and we can lock it, but cannot go tonight. Maybe tomorrow or after tomorrow. I must go to Phitsanulok and buy tickets. Maybe my friend can buy for us. I can ask her."

"Look, Lek. Don't worry about all that, let's just go to Phitsanulok tomorrow. If we can't get a seat, we'll get a bed and try again the next day."

"Get a bed? Stay in a hotel? Yes, OK. I am so bored with cooking and cleaning and washing clothes. OK, tomorrow. If we go tomorrow, I must go now say goodbye to everybody. You can put these clothes in the washing machine for me and hang them outside later. Only one basket, maybe we want to take them with us to Pattaya. Thank you darling, I go now see you later."

"What about lunch. Thinking about pie and cheese has made me hungry."

She turned around halfway down the garden path, "We have some fruit. Look. Not want to buy more food now if we go away soon. Not good idea, only go bad. You take care yourself and do washing. I will see you later. Bye-bye, telak."

Craig tipped the basket of clothes into the machine and started it up without checking the colours or the pockets. He didn't care. He seemed to spend his whole day alone working – not at housework very often, it was true – but, alone at his desk while Lek was out 'doing something'. He didn't know what she got up to, but he did trust her not to be playing around.

He looked in the fridge: a couple of raw eggs, a bag of some sort of sauce, some vegetables that looked like cabbage, a tomato and a few bottles of water. Lek didn't really believe in fridges, she said that Thai food was not designed with fridges in mind, but she had to have one, because everyone else had one. There were six or seven mangoes, an orange and a few bananas in the fruit bowl, so he carried that through to the office with a bottle of cold water and started work .

Lek wasn't back by five o' clock, so he showered and took his laptop to Nong's. He drank a few beers, nodded to a few people, did some surfing and took three bottles of Chang home with him. Still no Lek. He would have to get his own phone in Pattaya, it was the only way to get back into the loop, because he felt left out on the edge of things since his old one had given up the ghost a few months back.

Lek got back at nine o'clock carrying a roast chicken.

"Hi, telak, sorry I am late. I bring you this. You OK? Not put washing out? You forget?"

"Yes."

She wanted to say something sarcastic, but thought better of it because she had been out with friends for twelve hours and had eaten well and was also a little drunk, while Craig had been stuck in the house working without much food. She hung the clothes out, put the chicken on a plate for him and took it into the office.

"Look. I put this for you. I vely solly, I go out with friends leave you alone, but we go away together tomorrow. I put clothes out. Not rain tonight. I go shower and go to shleep. Big day tomorrow. Good night." She kissed him on the temple, but he didn't reply.

There was nothing to say.

The next morning, was nothing new. Lek got up early, ate rice soup, showered and left. Craig got up, brushed his teeth, put the percolator on and started work. They wouldn't have to leave for Phitsanulok until six or seven in the evening so there were about twelve hours to go. Twelve hours of sitting alone in the office probably, but then he would be out.

Free again.

And he had a new line he was going to try on the first bar girl who invited him in for a drink. He couldn't wait. He felt like a pit pony must have been when it realised that it was being led up into the light for a few days gambolling in a field in the sun.

He was totally worn out emotionally. Lek had people to talk to, to discuss the news with, to drink and dine with.

Craig only had Lek, and that was not often.

He buried his head in the computer, the Internet and work – biding his time until Lek would come and get him to go for the lift that would take them to the bus.

She came back at five thirty and dived into the shower. Craig was already ready. He only needed to put his laptop in its bag and walk out the door. Lek came out of the shower, dressed and was folding clothes into the suitcase when her brother beeped at six. They were off.

Lek surprised him by passing over a few tins of Chang that she had asked Gnat to pick up for her.

"Sorry you sit alone all day, but now you can see friends in Pattaya, neh?"

Craig didn't care, he just wanted to get there.

∞

When the bus arrived in Pattaya at two o'clock in the morning, they weren't sure where to go, so they got a taxi to Daddy's Hobby. It was still open, Lek had checked by mobile and they were waiting for them. There were plenty of hotels and bars with rooms nearby too.

Beou greeted them warmly as usual and so did Ayr. Goong was 'out' and all the other girls had gone home, but the two friends had waited up. Craig was passed an ice-cold beer Chang as the three women caught up on what had been happening. He was sitting there on the edge of the loop again, but he had something to look forward to now and he knew that the next day would be different.

The next day he would be gambolling in the sunshine in the fields with the mares.

They stayed in Daddy's Hobby until daybreak and then walked the short distance to the Queen's Hotel. It looked very grand and they had both always wanted to stay there. It was surprisingly cheap, but the room they were shown to was a little frayed at the edges. Very nice though and the pool was fantastic. Lek stayed in bed late, uncharacteristically, and Craig went for a swim.

When he returned at ten, Lek was coming out of the shower: "Where you go? Why you not tell me where you go? I wake up alone."

"I only went for a swim in the hotel pool downstairs. You've got a nerve moaning about being left alone, haven't you? You leave me alone every day and never tell me where you've been. You say: 'Oh, Craig, I go talk to Mum'. Three hours later I go to Nong's and look for you in your mother's house on the way and she is sitting alone. I never know where you are."

"You check on me? You spider same 007?"

"Not spider, spy. No I do not check up on you. Sometimes, I want to talk with you in Nong's. You know talk, T-A-L-K? Like we used to before we moved to the village."

In truth, the talking had started to wane a long time before that, but blaming the village suited his argument more. They weren't angry with each other. Not really. It was just a battle of wills. Craig thought it might be because they were both the eldest children in their families and were used to getting their own way. Now it could not happen that each would get his or her own way, but neither was ready to give up yet, so there was a constant frisson of friction between them.

Sometimes it felt like the sound of polystyrene on glass.

"Do you fancy breakfast downstairs or in the Pig?" he asked.

"Oh, you know I like the Pig very much. If you want to spoil me for giving you a good party, you can take me to the Pig and Whistle."

Craig often didn't know when she was joking or being serious. She had to be joking now, he thought, but it had been a good party nevertheless, so maybe she wasn't. He decided to go with the flow and accept what she had said at face value.

"Yes, I want to spoil you, my darling wife, because you are so good to me. You do not make me work hard in the house or garden and give me plenty of time alone to think and 'play' with my computer."

Craig thought that the sarcasm would be lost on her, but Lek just played him at his own game and she knew that she could play it better than Craig.

"Thank you, my dear. It is nice to feel appreciated. We can have a nice breakfast, go for a walk along the beach, have coffee with Noi and then you can do what you like. Maybe you want to go walking alone, looking for inspiration for your web sites. You can talk with people in English and meet new falang and others. Maybe they will give you good ideas, because I think that I cannot and I am very sorry that I cannot help you in your new business with web sites."

The last part was straight from Lek's heart. She did feel inadequate about not being able to help with the web sites and sometimes it hurt when she went into the office to say hello and he didn't even notice that she was there or even shoed her out saying that he was too busy to talk.

Lek was sure that Craig wasn't doing it on purpose; maybe he didn't even realise that he was doing it at all, but it still hurt and it still made her feel 'lacking'. Made her feel more of a house-keeper and less of a partner.

She had tried to talk to him about it several times, but mostly the words would not come out. She knew that they were spending many times more than they were earning and she was all too well aware that her contribution in cash terms was zero.

She also knew that no-one had ever made her feel that pain before.

Craig knew that Lek spent most of her time talking with her mother and friends because that is what she told him she was doing and he believed her and he was right to believe her, because she would never cheat on him, but he didn't know what they discussed, because he never asked and she never volunteered the information.

She didn't like that Craig apparently didn't care what she talked with people about, because that also added to her insecurity, but in another way she was glad, because she discussed work with them and she didn't want Craig to know that she thought that he couldn't provide adequately for her and her daughter's future.

And that was the truth of the matter

Craig was a trier, but she couldn't see how he would be able to earn enough money to be able to stay in Thailand the way that things were going. This left her with two choices. She could either wait for Craig to burn all his money and be deported or she would have to help him support them.

Lek was convinced that she loved Craig, so she wanted to help him stay, but on the other hand, there was no work for her in the village, so soon she might have to invent some work and pay herself with her savings, which Craig knew nothing about.

That would be a hard thing to do. To spend the money that it had taken her ten long years of degradation, heartache and deceit to earn at a job that had taken her away from her family and daughter and dumped her in the laps of lusting men and not only foreigners, to be sure.

Or she could keep what Craig had built up and allow him to be sent home, in which case, her money would go further and she could either live frugally in their house in the village or she could go back to work as a cashier in a bar and take Soom with her, for she felt that she could never be parted from her for long again.

It was a very tough call and she had thought of little else for months. Many of her friends advised letting Craig be sent home, not because they didn't like him, most did, but because it made Lek's money go further. However, Lek's mother was one of the few voices that advised supporting her 'husband' and trusting in Buddha. Her mother was convinced that Lek's and Craig's karmas would be good enough to get them through any crisis.

Not that there was one yet.

No real storm, just dark clouds on the horizon, causing plenty of stress and arguments over whether their boat would sink or float.

They had both added to the problem by fighting, often over petty details. Lek knew that and was sorry for it. She knew what the real cause of the fighting was but she wasn't sure whether Craig did. He just seemed to bumble along as if he hadn't a care in the world, but then he could go home and be taken care of by his family or the government while she would be left behind to fend for herself and her Soom.

She still didn't know which way to jump and too often ended up drinking too much while caught in the debate. She often wondered whether Craig drank too much because he was scared to be so far from home and all the certainty in his life that he had once had. She could ask him, but she knew that he would only deny it, whether it was true or not, so what was the point of embarrassing him or causing him to lie?

When they arrived at Daddy's Hobby at one o'clock, neither of them had spoken for a long time, but they broke out of their world of silence to save face for themselves and their friend. They acted as if they hadn't a care in the world and Noi greeted them warmly.

"Hello, Craig, handsome man! How are you, my darling?"

"Very well, thank you and very happy to see you again. You are looking as lovely as ever."

"Ooh, thank you, bak wan – you flatterer, you. Do you want beer or coffee today?"

Lek replied, "I'll have a coffee but I'm not sure about Craig. Maybe he'll want a cup of tea."

They all laughed, but Noi was already opening a bottle of Chang. She had never seen him drink anything else. Ever, from the first day he had arrived in Thailand and met her best friend.

They sat down together and talked about nothing for an hour then Craig made his excuses and left the two ladies to get on with whatever they did when they were alone, because he honestly had no idea what Lek and her friends found to talk about for so many hours a day.

As Lek and Noi got down to the serious business of Lek's future, Craig wandered off down towards the beach. He looked back as he turned the corner and felt a twinge of jealousy that they appeared to be laughing about something, as friends do.

He walked on to the beach and sat on a wall looking out to see.

He refused several offers of company from several beautiful girls and boys and some that he wasn't sure of, but he was not in any mood for making conversation with strangers. He was feeling very sorry for himself and not only a little lonely. He had absolutely no idea what to do and seemingly no-one to discuss it with. Lek appeared to be bliss-fully unaware of his financial situation, although he had dropped a few hints.

At least Lek had people to talk to though. He didn't and he really needed to talk to someone. In the village there was no-one who spoke his language, here in Pattaya there were many thousand who did, but they didn't care about him, so he was just as alone.

He remembered Lek's words about going out to look for inspira-tion and thought he could give it a try, so he got up, crossed the road and started walking towards Walking Street, which was still several kilo-metres off. He didn't really want to go there – it was just a direction to take. After a while, he found what he was looking for and went inside. Craig didn't know exactly what he wanted but was looking for some ideas.

They had a nice-looking folder into which could be inserted any B5 notebook, so he bought one of each together with a modern ballpoint pen, an HB pencil and an eraser, then he went back out onto the street and continued in his previous southerly direction.

He had had all of those items before when he was in school and university, but he had not bought them all together like that for more than twenty-five years. His intention was to make notes on things that he saw and thought or heard or thought he saw or heard and if nothing noteworthy happened, he would make lists. The pencil was for crossing out ideas once he had used them so that they would not be obliterated.

He took off down the street looking for an opportunity to use his new tools for recording inspirations, feeling somewhat better now that at least he had a plan.

Craig declined a couple of offers to keep ladies company in bars, but they wore him down so he entered the third, ordered a beer and sat in a quiet corner facing the sea. He was the only customer, which was why he had accepted the offer.

He took out and inspected his new equipment while waiting for his drink and the Muses to arrive.

A pretty little barmaid duly arrived with his beer and leaned over him tauntingly to place it on the table. "You want something else, sir?" she asked smiling.

"I want some ideas if you have any."

"You want me sit here talk to you?"

"Yes, OK, if you are not too busy. What is your name? My name is Craig."

"My name is Ann. Nice to meet you, Craig."

"Nice to meet you too, Ann," he said with a smile.

"You are an artist?" asked Ann, pointing at his pad and pencil. "You want to draw the sea? It is very beautiful, neh?"

"You are very beautiful too. I wish that I could draw the beach and the sea, but I cannot. I want to draw people. Real people with reality in their expression. You understand?"

It was not quite true, he had wanted to do that years ago but had had no talent for it and so had given up decades ago, but he thought it sounded like something a pretentious artist would say. He also thought that it might make her laugh.

However, she didn't laugh. Instead, she said, "We are quiet now, do you want to draw me? I want very much for you to draw me. No-one ever draw me before. Please, if you have time."

Craig had plenty of time, but was short on ability.

"OK, but you must sit very still for fifteen minutes. All right? OK, swap seats with me because the light is better and people on the street cannot see you. That's it now look out to sea. Very good. You look just like the figurehead on an old sea galleon. Will you take your breasts out, so I can draw you like a woman on an old ship?"

"I am shy, but OK, no-one can see me here. If someone come in, I close my shirt quickly." Ann smiled at him, undid her blouse and let her breasts fall free.

"Wow, that's great, now just keep looking out to sea and think about something nice." He reached over and raised her hemline so that he could see if she had any panties on. She did; red ones and he left the crotch just visible. She didn't budge, so he took one of her breasts and pretended to move it into a better position. Ann's eyes swivelled towards him, but she didn't say anything. He tweaked her nipples one at a time and then moved her hemline again, a little up and then back down, but as he did so he lightly brushed his thumb across her crotch.

"I want you to feel sexy on the inside and then it will show on the outside," he whispered.

Ann nodded ever so slightly, so he did it again and felt her nipples again, before picking up the pad and pencil and starting to draw. Craig found several reasons to have to touch her again. When he had done his best at drawing. He laid the pad face down and opened her knees:

"To make you feel sexy."

She allowed it, but when Craig started to pay her panties more attention than the note pad, Ann, pulled away.

"Show me, what you draw so far."

Craig willingly showed her his efforts.

"That is horrible! You make me look like an old witch, not a sexy lady. You tell me you can draw."

"No, Ann, I said I would like to draw. I didn't say I was any good. This is the first time I try, but I like to draw now and want to try again."

Ann pouted and clipped him on the shoulder before smiling and saying, "You buy me a drink now. You cheat me."

Craig was happy to buy her a drink and she sat with him until he left. When he got up to go, she kissed him on the cheek and said,

"Can I have that drawing, please? Put your name on it and I will put it on my wall in the room. I will remember you and I will remember that I am stupid sometimes. When you are famous, I will sell it and buy a car."

He kissed her on the cheek back. He knew that there were no hard feelings and he thought he may call in to see Ann again. He gave her the signed drawing and left feeling much better than when he had gone in.

Ann could see that he had cheered up too and was pleased for him.

15 ANOTHER VISA AND HOME AGAIN

Craig had to renew his visa on the August 22^{nd,} It would be his second twelve-month visa, but the rules changed often and seemed to vary from province to province. Craig didn't know whether this was true or not as they or he had only done it once before in Bangkok, this time he would go to Jomtien which was only a short bus ride away. However, visa renewal was one of most-talked about problems of living in Thailand long term.

It seemed quite simple to Craig. In order to get a retirement visa extension for twelve months, you needed photocopies of salient pages of your passport and proof issued by a Thai bank that you had had eight hundred thousand Baht on deposit there for at least two months. You also needed photos and the fee of three thousand nine hundred Baht.

Craig and Lek put the relevant information together and hired a taxi to take them to Soi 5 in Jomtien, directly to the office of the Immigration Police. They filled in the form, a TM7 and waited for their turn.

They were seen within thirty minutes and there was no problem with the visa although Craig had to leave his passport there and collect it the following day because the office was temporarily short staffed. They had not had to wait in Bangkok, otherwise the procedure had been the same as before. Craig readily agreed and they left much relieved.

Lek hated anything official. Craig could not get out of her why that was – he had asked her many times. Lek insisted that she had never done anything illegal and had never been in trouble with the police, which Craig believed, because that question had been on the British visa application form and she had gotten a visa the year before.

Still, there was a problem and he hoped that one day she would confide in him what it was. Or maybe she already had and it was just 'one of those things'. The fact was that he was glad to have got it over with too.

While they were there, Lek wanted to look around the shops and get something to eat, so they went for a meal first and Lek left Craig to enjoy the sea views, while she did some comfort shopping.

Lek really had never been in trouble with the police, but she was still nervous of them because they had so much power. They could persecute someone if they took a mind to. She had seen it happen and they always picked on the vulnerable.

Lek had never been in trouble with the police, but prostitution is against the law in Thailand, so technically she had broken the law, which was why they had such an elaborate system to hide what was really going on. They called clients boyfriends, who paid bar fines or bar finds to compensate the bar owner for the loss of the girl that had already been paid to work that night.

The fact that that girl was paid a hundred Baht, but the bar fine was four hundred betrayed the lie, but it was enough of a smokescreen for some. Not for the police though who knew exactly what was going on. Many of the bars were owned by policemen who then sublet them.

Lower ranks would then be sent around to collect 'tea money' and some of them in turn hoped that the girls would 'be nice to them'. Some complied, but Lek never had, possibly because her cousin had protected her. She had never asked, but she assumed that that was the case.

However, there was more to it than that, for Lek remembered when the police had accompanied the bank's bailiffs with an eviction order for failure to pay a loan on the property that her poor dead father had arranged without telling them.

It was the reason why she had had to go to Pattaya and miss her daughter growing up and her family growing old. On the bright side, she would not otherwise have met Craig and she was grateful for that. He had delivered her back to her family, because although she had paid off the bank loan before meeting him, she might not have had the courage to go back to the village without him.

No matter what people said, there was a stigma to going away to do what Lek had done – there is always a price to pay for what people do - but taking a 'rich' foreigner back and building a nice house was one way of saying 'Up Yours, I don't care what you think. Look at me now and look at you.'

Lek had not been above doing that and Craig was the unwitting instrument. She always felt grateful to Buddha for sending her Craig, but sometimes she pitied him for his stupidity and naivety for not having seen what he had let himself in for. She knew that Craig was a decent man and she knew that she had manipulated him, she only hoped that he would not get hurt and that she could make him happy.

She also realised that nagging him every day would not do that, but the stress of uncertainty and indecision was destroying her.

She looked around for something nice to surprise him with. It wouldn't be clothing with Craig, she had tried that before and just got a grunt of gratitude. Cheese cheered him up and so did gadgets, but being totally atechnical, she steered clear of those sorts of things. However, taking him a block of Cheddar did not seem to fit the occasion well enough either. Still, being an expert shopaholic, she knew that she would spot something sooner or later.

She soon saw something that she thought he would like, in fact she thought that she wouldn't mind having one herself either. It was a simple pocket notebook, one of the small, old-fashioned ones with a pencil that fitted down the spine of a leather cover. It would fit neatly into a pocket or handbag and she had noticed that he had bought a large notepad the other day. This one was far more convenient. Later on, she bought him a bar of chocolate to go with it. His favourite sweets.

Her shopaholism was strangely sated just by buying something for someone else — it didn't even have to be for herself, but as she was making her way back to the bar where she had left Craig, she saw a beautiful pair of heart-shaped earrings. They were really quite unusual and she wished that Craig was the type of person who bought spur of the moment gifts. They were only cheap, but they were just her style, so she bought them and put them on there and then.

She wondered whether he would even notice.

Lek found Craig where she had left him, but he must have gone out for a newspaper, because he was doing the crossword and didn't notice her approach him. It was only when she sat down that he looked up.

"Hello, darling, how are you?" she said.

"I'm fine, thank you. Nothing can upset me today now that I am legal for another year. Do you want a coffee or something?"

Lek didn't drink much coffee or tea, but she liked the occasional cup of something out of the ordinary. To her that meant a latte or a cappuccino and so that's what she ordered.

"Darling, I have something for you. I saw this in the market and I wanted to buy it for you." She handed over the small bag with the two presents in and said,

"I love you, telak. I am very sorry that we have been fighting so much. I don't know why we do it, but I don't like it."

"I love you too, Lek, and I don't know why we're always fighting either. The house, I suppose and the change moving back to the village. Thanks for my presents. I love the notebook, it is just what I need to write my inspirations in, if I ever get any and I'll have a coffee to go with this chocolate." He signalled the waiter for a coffee and leaned over to kiss Lek, but then thought better of it. He didn't want to embarrass her now that things were looking better, so he squeezed her hand instead.

Lek smiled at him.

"I was thinking something else too, telak. I want you to have a good life. You have helped me more than you know, so I am going to tell Soom to take care of you when I die."

That was out of the blue and Craig didn't know what to say, so he tried humour, his usual recourse.

"Well, you're not that old yet, you're only thirty-three or something, so you have a few years left in you yet and by the time you die, I'll probably be long gone and Soom will be married and if I'm not dead, don't you think Soom's husband might object?"

"I said take care of you not have sex with you," she glared.

Craig hadn't meant sex either, he had meant 'move in with', but he judged that it was safer to say nothing.

Although Lek had over-reacted, she knew what Craig had meant, she trusted him with her daughter as much as she trusted any man, although that was still not a huge amount yet. The only man that she had ever trusted was her father and, although she had never openly blamed him, he was responsible for her having to work in Pattaya in the first place. If he hadn't had grand ideas and borrowed so much money, none of this would have happened.

She didn't think like that often because he was her father and he had died and maybe from the worry that repaying the loan had caused him. Medically, it had been diabetes and a lack of insulin that had been the cause of his death, but worry might have been the original reason.

As a peace-offering, she accepted the square of chocolate that Craig was offering her, despite the fact that she didn't like chocolate because she found it too sweet.

"Chocolate and coffee are my favourite combination of tastes," he murmured, "What do you think?" It was anything but her favourite combination, but she felt justified by muttering 'yes', because she felt that she was agreeing that it was his favourite, so she was not technically lying.

"Do you want some more?," he offered.

"Maybe later," she said and Craig knew that that was Lek's polite way of saying 'no'.

He could see that something was bothering her. Her beautiful eyes looked so sad.

"What's the matter, darling? Why do you look so sad? I have seen you happy and I've seen you angry – many times, but I can't remember seeing you sad often at all; so what is it?" he asked quietly

"It is nothing. Don't you worry. It is just something for me. You cannot help, so why tell you? It only makes two people sad."

"I understand but seeing you like this makes me sad anyway, so you might as well tell me, eh? It can't make me any sadder can it?"

"Maybe it can. There is nothing you can do... except... will you take care of Soom if I die before she is married?"

"Hey, of course I will, but what is all this talk of dying? I have never heard you talk like this before? What has happened?"

"Many things have happened, telak, but nothing new. Nothing has changed. It's just that I have never let you see this before. I have done bad things in the past. Things which I had to do, things which I didn't think were so wrong then, but now I think that my karma is bad and that I am not meant to be happy. I think that I will not enjoy being with you for long or seeing Soom grow up. I need to know that someone will take care of her if I die early and I want you to do it. Mum is too old now and Soom calls you 'Paw'."

"I've never heard her call me Paw or Dad, she always calls me Craig, but of course I'll do anything I can – everything I can. I gave up a lot to come and live with you, my dear. I didn't do it lightly and I'm not only here for a couple of years. You name it and we'll see if it can be done."

Tears were streaming down her cheeks and dripping onto the table, but she barely made a noise except to speak.

"I am sorry to embarrass you in public by acting so foolishly, Craig, but I love you and wish things could have been different for us..." she broke off.

Craig wanted to hug her, but he leaned forward with a tissue instead. Lek leaned back to indicate refusal.

"I am not a baby. I got myself into this and no-one can help me. It is my fate and all the hugs, kisses and tissues cannot help. I do not fear death, but I do fear leaving you and Soom without me to look after you. That is why, darling, telak, you and Soom must take care of each other."

Craig was getting really scared. He didn't know what to think. He didn't think that Lek had been to the doctor, but didn't know and didn't think she was the suicidal type especially after what she had just been saying, but he was petrified that something was going to happen and that Lek knew what it was.

"Promise me, Craig, that you will give my half of the house to Soom, if I die first. I do have half of the house, don't I? If I die, you won't sell everything, move on and abandon her? Promise?"

Lek had Craig locked in a melancholy stare, the streams still flowing from her eyes. She was making infrequent, half-hearted dabs at the puddles with a useless, soggy tissue. Craig stared back.

"I will never abandon you or your daughter, I promise and yes, you have half the house and that half is your daughters. But, if I move on I'm taking my half with me." It was a gamble, but Lek sniffed once and tried to hide a smile as she dried her eyes with the back of her hand.

"And if I can't carry it, she can have my half too."

Lek was smiling almost normally now, although she looked very strange with pink eyes. They smiled at each other and Lek reached out for his hand, but instead of the brief squeeze he was accustomed to in public, she held it fast and tight.

"Thank you, my dear, it means everything to me that you will take care of Soom. Now, shall we have a large Chang before we go, I've got a lot of water to put back into my body."

Craig would have agreed to anything after that powerful outburst of emotion from someone who had rarely shown any distress to him before.

When the beers arrived, Lek held her bottle out to clink it with Craig's, just like she had done when he first met her: "Chok dee, telak," they chimed together also just like they had done in the past.

Over the past year, they had grown apart somewhat. Lek drank spirits with her friends and Craig drank beer with his computer. Lek had often declined to join him in Nong's because she said she was worried about getting fat, but Craig suspected that there was more to it than that. They had argued over the house every single day and they were both thoroughly sick of it. Now that the house was all but finished he hoped that they could get back to normal and he was pleased to think that it looked like Lek felt the same way, although she had obviously been worrying about her daughter too.

When they left the bar it was hand-in-hand as they had used to walk and instead of taking the first taxi back to Daddy's Hobby they walked for miles straight back to the hotel.

∞

The following morning they showered and breakfasted together and Craig offered to go and get his passport alone since there was no possibility of any problems, while Lek went to the bus station to book the tickets to go home. They arranged to meet in Daddy's Hobby around noon. They could have stayed a few more days if either of them had wanted to and they probably would have done at any time in the previous twelve months, but the air had cleared between them and they both just wanted to get back to their quiet home in their quiet village.

They stood on opposite sides of Soi Buakhao to each other waiting for Baht taxis. They smiled at each other frequently until of one them won the ten Baht bet on who would get away first.

Craig lost, but he didn't mind.

Both of their tasks were a doddle. There were good seats available on the six o'clock VIP bus for that evening and Craig's passport was stamped and ready for collection. All Lek had to do was return to the hotel, check out, leave the case at reception and walk down to Daddy's Hobby, where Noi would still be on duty either guarding or selling the stock. When Lek arrived at about eleven-thirty, the bar was deserted and Noi was still 'resting'.

Lek banged the flat of her hand on the bar out of sight: "Come on, let's be 'aving you! Service! The fleet has arrived and we want servicing!"

"Go away," came back a voice, "I'm waiting for a friend."

"That's no way to speak to loyal customers is it, O Custodian of the Happy Waters?"

Noi's head popped up with a broad smile on it. She had been lying on the counter out of sight dozing again.

"You're chipper this morning, aren't you? Had a good night, have we? Nudge, nudge, wink, wink."

"No, we went to bed early because we were tired and shagged out after a long walk, if you must know. Well, no you're right if you must know, but we did walk back from Jomtien as well. Hand-in-hand! What do you think of that?"

"Well, a year ago I would have thought nothing of it for a pair of love birds like you two, but today I think it's marvellous. So, you're getting on better then are you? How did it happen, did he propose?"

"Don't be daft. Of course he didn't, but we did sort of cross a bridge together yesterday. As you know, things have been rough for quite a while now, but when I look back on it, we mostly only fought over the house. Craig wanted this, chang wanted that and I ...."

"You wanted the other. I know some things never change, but at least you got it again last night."

"Do you mind! Craig and I are all right in that department, so just watch it, but, yeah... it has been hard – no flippant comments, please. It has been difficult, to put it less ambiguously. He's coming here soon... Craig will be arriving here soon."

"Well, I'm happy for you both. You really were made for each other, but sometimes it seemed that you were the only two who couldn't see it. It was sad to watch sometimes."

"How are Ayr and Goong? I haven't seen them to talk to much this trip and I don't like to keep phoning if they're busy. Are they settled?"

"Yes, they're both well, but still single. I think they still miss you. They still won't have anyone else move in with them and you left quite a while ago now, didn't you? About two years?"

"Yes, unofficially moved out two years, one month and twelve days ago. I met Craig on the 11th July. You know he's got a memory like his computer. He keeps saying things like happy 11th July, the day we first met or remember 12th August when I left or 19th September when I came back and there are six or seven more of them. I'm trying to re-member a few myself so I can get him back, but me and dates or even time... Well, you know as well as anyone and I'm getting worse.

"Oh, just to change the subject and before Craig gets here, I'm thinking of going back to school to get my diploma. What do you think? Does it sound stupid at my age?"

"No, not at all. It's a good idea. Good for you girl, but why can't you mention in front of Craig? You don't mean you have to ask him for permission, do you? That doesn't sound like you."

"No, silly, nothing like that, but I do want to find out more about it before I tell him. So, you don't think I'm being silly then, wanting a bit of paper to prove that I can add up and talk proper, then?"

"No, not at all. Really. Keep it up and one day there'll be mother and daughter going to university together. That'll cramp her style with all those rich college boys - having to drag her old Mum around with her everywhere she goes, won't it?"

"All right, all right, I get the picture, you..."

"No, you don't love. I'm only pulling your leg. I'm sure Soom would be proud to hang out with you at school. Or uni. People will pull your leg, some will probably be jealous, but so what? You've put up with far worse than that, so... Just go for it. I'm sure you'll walk it. You're not daft. You ran this place before, didn't you, Number One Trainee Mama San, or whatever Beou used to call you. To think that that was two... more than two years ago already. And you've got a nice home and a warm husband – I mean the other way around – while I am still sleeping on the counter under the bar. How times change for some. There was no holding you back once your foot was on the rungs of promotion, was there? Talk about high-flyers. Rocket-propelled, you, Lek. Rocket-propelled. And no-one could wish it on a more deserving person. You worked hard for your family and your little Soom and now it's your turn for a bit of pleasure."

Lek didn't know what to say, Noi was such a comfort and a tonic and always had been.

"Thanks, Noi, I needed that. You're such a good friend. You'll have me crying again in a minute and just as my old man has got off the bus. He'll think I'm cracking up." Lek leaned over and gave her friend a peck on the cheek.

"Don't let me stop you two girls from smooching, if that's what you're into when my back is turned," said Craig. "Hiya, both. I got my visa. No problem. Got the tickets, Lek? Great!"

Noi was handing him a beer: "Oh, go on then. I was thinking of having a glass of water, but one won't hurt, will it?"

"You've got to keep your strength up, haven't you? You know, after last night. Lek was telling me. That's right, isn't it, Lek?... You walked all the way back from Jomtien without a rest. It's a long way. You should do it again soon. Take it up as a hobby. Daddy's little hobby."

Lek didn't know where to look and Craig was just looking confused as Noi turned to put the kettle on.

An Exciting Future

16 BPOM AND BPOUY

After Lek and Craig had arrived home from the visa run to Pattaya, they threw themselves into finishing the house. Having identified building the house as the probable cause of all the problems in their relationship, they decided to get it over with as soon as possible. Not that there was a great deal to do and absolutely nothing that they personally could help with — it was all heavy work for professional contractors.

Lek wanted the garden bed raised by at least a foot and they both wanted a perimeter wall and sliding gates. Lek also wanted curtains but as no-one could overlook them, she was prepared to wait until she found something just right.

As it happens, there was always plenty of rich, fertile soil in the area. In fact there was a glut of it, because soil came down in the rivers from the north where it was washed from the hillsides because of over-logging decades ago. The farmers used the river water to irrigate their fields and so, every few years the excess soil had to be scraped off and used as backfill.

Lek ordered a hundred and twenty tons of this and supervised a local farmer with an excavator laying and grading it on what would be her precious garden. The driver and his two labourers were excellent at their jobs, but Lek stood in the thick of the action directing them like a traffic cop at an intersection. Craig found it a pleasure to watch. And that was all he was required to do... nobody wanted his opinion and he was determined not to give anything but praise. The whole job took a day, but they all agreed that there might be uneven settlement, so they promised to come back in seven days and re-level it if necessary.

In the meantime, Lek had a builder from a nearby village give them an estimate for constructing a perimeter wall and providing and fitting wrought-iron, sliding gates. Again, Craig was asked to keep out of it and, since it had worked so well with the soil, he readily agreed. He only had one small suggestion to make and that was to turn one corner of the garden into a shed, so that Lek could pot her flowers on and store things. Lek thought that that was an excellent idea, so she incorporated it into her master plan.

The wall railings and gates took over a month to complete and were expensive by local standards, but they looked the bees-knees. It was a beautiful piece of work and everyone was justifiably proud of it. Lek was planning a big reopening of their 'estate' with a lavish garden party when the work was done and she had planted and grown a few plants and bushes.

Craig naturally agreed to this because they had been almost three months argument-free now and the change that it had made to their quality of life was immeasurable. If he had known that it could have been like that, he thought, he would just have let her get on with it while he read a book. Or maybe she had learned a trick or two from building the house. She was certainly a lot more confident now talking to the male contractors. She no longer just agreed with everything they said. Now she at least wanted to be convinced why she was wrong otherwise she wanted it done her way.

It was as if she had grown up a few inches and it was both great for her and great for Craig to see. He was more proud of her now than he had ever been and if he had really known Lek, the old Lek, he would have been even prouder still.

During the time that the contractors were building the wall and installing the wrought ironwork, a dog started making daily visits to the garden. At first it was just to relieve itself, but after a while it, or she, became bolder and would say hello to people especially Craig. Lek hated dogs, having been bitten a few times as a child, and in Pattaya, but because Craig was behaving himself and he and the dog got on so well, she tolerated her, thinking that the friendship could not last once the gates had been fitted.

It turned out that the dog's name was Da, which was easy for Craig to remember because it means 'good' in Welsh. It soon became apparent that Da was going to have puppies as her teats hung almost to the ground. As the puppies grew inside her, she began to look shabbier and shabbier, so Craig began feeding her scraps. Within a few days of that, Da would go looking for Craig at Nong's shop if he was not at home and Craig would buy her a some duck eggs to build her up.

After a few weeks of doing this, even Lek was beginning to warm to Da, although she stank and was a little mangy. Lek started to save scraps for her and between them they were getting her through her pregnancy. At least, that was what they were thinking, until one day, like Peter Paper, Da came no more. They expected that she had died and Craig was quite upset about it. Lek, the farmer's daughter, told him to adopt another stray and get over it.

One evening, when they were sitting in Nong's shop talking over a beer, Da bounced around the corner looking very happy with herself in the way that dog's can. She was still scruffy, mangy and smelly, but happy too. They made a fuss of her without getting too hands-on and bought her half-a-dozen eggs, which she gobbled up. Then she bounded off.

Five minutes later she reappeared with a little blind puppy in her mouth and dropped it on one of Craig's feet; three or four minutes later she was back again with another one and that was placed on one of Lek's feet. Neither of them, nor Nong had ever seen anything like it before. Nor even heard of anything like it. It even melted Lek's heart towards dogs. Da sat before them and her puppies and nudged them from time to time as they made little squeaking noises. When they picked up a dog each, Da ran off. They presumed to get some more, but she didn't return that night, so they took the blind puppies home with them.

Craig had had dogs all his life, but for Lek, animals either worked, were eaten or were a nuisance. Her natural classification for these dogs was 'nuisance', since they couldn't do anything.

"Can we keep them, Lek, they'll make good guard dogs in nine months to a year."

"Guard us from what? We don't have any crime in the village. They only eat, cost money, poot-poot everywhere, make a noise and give you fleas. I don't want them."

"You won't have to do anything, I promise. I'll wash them, groom them, play with them and clean up after them and they will eat all your scraps to keep the flies down."

"I won't help you."

"Lek, darling, you are a mother, didn't it touch your heart when you saw Da so obviously give her blind babies up for adoption?"

Lek was not keen on this form of emotional blackmail.

"In fifty-odd years, I have never, ever seen anything like what Da did tonight. Nobody around here has. She gave us two of her puppies either because we took care of her or because she knows we can take care of them. Or both. Come on, Lek, they are blind, look at them. First night away from Mum." They were shivering and squeaking with fear.

"We must take care of them tonight, but I am not sure. We will see in the morning. But they stay outside, I am not having smelly dogs in our new house."

"OK, thanks, love, I'll sort them out now"

Craig put the dogs in Lek's laundry basket for a pen and went back to Nong's to get an empty crisp box. Back home he cut one short side down to two inches from the bottom and pushed it in to lay it flat and then put a few old dusters in there for comfort. He warmed some milk from the fridge and tried to tempt them with it, but they were either too frightened to drink or too young to know what it was. Craig dipped his finger in the milk and rubbed a puppy's lolling tongue. It licked the milk and so he fed both puppies for twenty minutes while Lek looked on in silence.

In fact, Lek was trying to look disgusted because dogs were her sworn enemy. She had been bitten as a child for being too rough with some strays, but she had also been attacked by strays in Pattaya when walking home late at night. In many cities the dogs are more dangerous than the drunks at night and there is rabies. She had always thought of dogs as filthy animals, the lowest of the low, way below tasty rats, though she couldn't help but have a soft spot for these harmless, innocent creatures, whose mother had befriended them and then given them her children.

Craig barely slept all night because the puppies were way too young to be away from their mother. When he awoke at seven o'clock, he was horrified to see Lek already outside standing over the puppies who were also awake and bleating.

"Craig! Craig! Your dogs have poot-poot everywhere and are now rolling in it. What are you going to do bout it? Craig! I want something done now!"

He went out with a bottle of water, a toilet roll and some more milk in a saucer. First he cleaned the floor tiles, then he cleaned the dogs and then he fed them again.

Lek just watched.

The puppies were a lot bolder now even after only a few hours and they sort of played together for a few minutes before falling asleep again. Craig put them back in their box, stood the flap up and tied a string around it to lock them in.

This all took place on the patio, but when they looked, Da was sitting outside the front gate watching them, tail wagging.

"Now, what do you think of that then, Lek? Motherly love or what?"

"Maybe Da is hungry again, come for more food. I don't know" and she began her daily routine of watering the garden before it became too hot.

While she was working, she kept looking in on the little dogs and looking out for Da. She didn't want to admit it yet, but she was absolutely flabbergasted by what she had seen of these three dogs. If Da came back she resolved to let her in to see what she would do, but it had to look like an accident, because she didn't want to lose face by appearing to have softened to dogs in such a short time.

She went out to the front gate and opened it, pretending to be polishing it and sure enough, Da came through the gate, went up to her puppies, sniffed them and walked away again. Lek was hooked for now, but she was still trying hard not to be.

"What are you going to call your two fat friends, Craig?"

"Oh, Lek, they are not really fat. Well, I suppose you're right. In English we say they have puppy fat."

"Like I said, what are you going to call you two fat little puppies?"

"I don't know, do you have any ideas?

"How about Fatty and Chubby?"

"Well, if you like, but it's not very nice, is it? They do have feelings, you know? How do you say fatty and chubby in Thai?"

"Ooen and Bpombpouy."

"Well, the first one sounds like the Welsh name Owen and the second one is a bit of a mouthful, so let's call them Bpom and Bpouy, eh?"

"Call them what you like, I don't care. Which is which?"

"The smaller one is Bpom and the other one is Bpouy. OK?"

"Whatever."

∞

By the time of Lek's garden party the dogs were about eight weeks old as far as Craig could judge and they were healthy, mischievous and hungry. When asked, Lek said that the breed was called 'Chinese Fighting Dog' in Thai and although they were more or less mongrels, this type of dog was always born the same shape and size – something like a knee-high, forty-five pound Jack Russell.

Lek was feeding the dogs every day now and even talking to them if no-one, especially Craig, was around to listen. However, they had one feature that prevented them from gaining her true affection. The dogs would only tolerate plants in their garden that pre-dated themselves. They mercilessly ripped out and shredded every new plant that Lek bought, and she did spend a lot of money on her garden, which she was trying to make look nice for the party.

Bpom and Bpouy seemed hell-bent on thwarting her.

Some mornings, Craig would wake up to murderous cries and ghastly yelps from the garden and when he looked outside, Lek would be chasing the dogs around the garden in her nightie with a broom handle or even an axe once.

Every night they would destroy the previous day's plantings, but although Lek was shaking with rage, she never actually hit or caught one of them. All the shouting and screaming was done in Thai and Canine, so Craig didn't know what was being said, but it sounded pretty bad. She threatened to sell them to the dog-catcher many times, but never did. Craig tried to persuade her that they would grow out of it, which they eventually did, after about four months.

The neighbours probably thought it was hilarious, but the occupants of the house did not. Although maybe Bpom and Bpouy did, either that or they had the attention span of a goldfish.

The big day arrived and Lek wanted the dogs tethered to a post, but they made such a racket that even Lek wanted them released. Not many people were invited, mostly people Lek had known all her life such as family and friends, which included the mayor and Lek's best friend from school days who was one of the richest ladies in the village and Murray, who was still the only foreigner that they knew, although rumours of others were beginning to filter back.

Thai parties are pretty informal usually, so when a start time is given it is only an approximation. Lek had suggested that people would be welcome any time after midday. Murray arrived at midday, he was always punctual probably because of his police career and always bore a freezer box full of Beer Chang. The Thai guests, who lived fifteen miles closer arrived between one and two o'clock, which was not a problem, because Lek, being Thai had allowed for that.

The party went well straight from the outset. Those who wanted to help cooked, the mayor brought a chicken in a sack, killed it and prepared his famous chicken curry. Everybody did something, except, the two foreigners, but then they were not expected to. Murray and Craig just sat, talked and drank beer and when the dancing started, they got up and did a bit of that too.

"Are these two little critters yours, Craig?" asked Murray, "They sure are cute." They were chasing each other around everyone's' ankles at the time.

"Yeah, they're ours all right. Or if you ask Lek they are mine. Don't say anything bad about them, please, at least not to Lek, 'cause the little mites get it in the neck every day as it is. They keep pulling up her flowers and then destroying them."

"Yes, siree, I can see they're still in the destructive phase. Is that someone's jacket they're playing with or is it a decoy?"

"Where? Oh, shit!" Craig leaped up to rescue someone's cardigan before it was damaged. "Come on, boys, give me that, before one or all of us gets killed." He managed to get it from them in one piece, but he noticed the mayor's wife coming over with her hand out-stretched.

She was very nice about it, or at least the tone of her voice was nice because he didn't understand what she said and she didn't speak any English.

At that moment, there was no music playing so everyone plainly heard Craig say to her:

"Kapun kap ma."

She looked at him and then at the thirty to forty faces that were facing their way, scowled and then said something in Thai, which he didn't understand again. He looked to Murray for help, but there was none.

Lek breezed over. "What did you say, darling?"

Craig repeated it: "Kapun kap ma."

The mayor's wife smiled and everyone smiled in relief. Some even laughed out load, but neither Craig nor Murray knew what the problem was.

Lek was the only one who could explain it to them. "Sure, 'kapun kap' means 'thank you' and 'ma' can mean to come, a horse or a dog, depending on the tone. The way you said it, was wrong. You did not said 'Thank you for coming', but 'Thank you, you dog'.

When she had seen the mayor and his wife off the premises, Lek came back to Craig and Murray. They watched her coming and saw that she was dramatically mopping her brow to signal a close call, but when she arrived she drew up a seat between them.

"I don't know what advice your wife gives you, Murray, but I am begging you now, Craig. Please, do not speak Thai to strangers, especially men I personally have not introduced you to and absolutely on no account with Thai men who are drunk. Do you understand? If that had been an aggressive man, you might be in hospital or dead now. So, please, promise me."

He wanted to say 'But how am I supposed to learn Thai, if I'm not allowed to speak it until I am fluent?' but now did not seem the right time, so he just looked at her for a second, nodded assent and looked down to the ground.

Lek nodded back and walked off.

Luckily. No offence had been taken, but it was a lesson for Craig.

Unfortunately, for Lek, one that he would often forget, because he was determined to learn Thai.

How else could he talk to anyone in the village?

The party went on until midnight and everyone seemed to have a good time, including the admonished Craig, who didn't bother speaking to another Thai all night except Lek.

In bed, after everyone had gone, Lek said: "I am sorry I shout at you in front of Murray, but you make me very scared sometimes. I love you, telak, and I don' want to lose you for stupid mistake. But listen, I have idea for 'kapun kap ma', next time say 'kapun kap ti ma'. 'Ti' means 'here', if you say that, everyone knows that you say 'come here', even if your accent is awful. OK, my dear? Good night, choop, choop, kiss, kiss."

"Yes, choop, choop, good night, darling, you gave a great party to-night. I'm sorry that I caused a stir, but they were all friends of yours and..."

But Lek was already asleep, he could hear her snoring softly.

17 A SURPRISE VISITOR

A week or so after the party, Craig was sitting in the garden in the mid-afternoon, taking a break from the computer screen and Lek was implementing a new anti-canine security system for her flowers. Craig was doing a week-old Sudoku puzzle that he had saved up and the dogs were biting each other and his toes. When Lek's phone rang, he took no notice because Lek's phone rang several times an hour everyday.

"Wooo! Wooo!," she screamed, and then a flurry of Thai that probably most Thai men would not have had the chance to catch, followed by "OK, darling, we will have madame's room prepared just as she likes it."

Craig was listening bemused, but he didn't have long to wait to find out what the cause of the excitement was. Lek either hung up or was hung up on, because after shaking the phone for a second or two, she jumped into his lap, causing not only a little discomfort.

"Excuse me a minute, I have to straighten myself out, just … hang on and…"

"Oh, there's no time for all that now! Stop playing with yourself. You don't have to impress me any more, I already know what you've got. Listen, this is important. Goong is going to come here in fifteen minutes and stay with us the night! Isn't that great!"

"Sure, it is. I like Goong. So, what do you want to do? Or what do you want me to do?"

"Nothing, darling. Goong and I used to sleep together. She knows everything about me."

This sounded intriguing. He knew Lek better than to expect a three in a bed sex romp, but she had never mentioned this detail of her history before.

"Uh, where was that then, Lek?"

"Oh, long time ago, before I meet you..."

"You mean two-and-a-half years ago or more?"

"Yes, don't worry. I am not lesbian."

"No, I wasn't thinking about that, darling."

Lek was up and off on some secret mission without a word.

Craig wasn't worried about Lek's past – well, to be honest he did have anxieties sometimes, but very rarely – however, he made it a rule never to ask, and she never said anything. This was one of the first times. He would not ask Goong anything, he made himself promise and he would try not to eavesdrop with even his limited Thai vocabulary, which might lead him to make five from two and two – as it had before, but he was a little curious and she was beautiful, which would make it a double pleasure to share his – their – roof with her.

He didn't know what to do: just sit there? Put a clean shirt on? Go to Nong's and give them a bit of space? So, he just sat there, pretending to study his puzzle.

Lek was racing to the bus stop at the end of the village on her Mum's spare motorcycle, hoping to get there before the bus arrived. Goong was also from Baan Suay, but her family had never really forgiven her for going to Pattaya with Lek twelve or thirteen years ago. Her mother was dead and her elderly father and two brothers just didn't seen to care about her, which was why she wanted to stay with Lek instead of her own family. This was one of her very rare visits.

Lek, Goong and Ayr had shared a room and a bed together, where no man had ever been allowed, when they had gone down to Pattaya together all those years ago. For a few moments, she was starting to think of them as 'the good old days', but she snapped out of it and was happy again with what she now had.

The bus was only about ten minutes late, but it seemed a lot longer. When it arrived Goong got off and they both thought that they were going to wet themselves. They certainly did have tears in their eyes. So much water under the bridge, so many shared experiences from school room to hotel room. Things that she would never want anyone else to know except those who had been there and she hoped that the men had forgotten.

It haunted her sometimes, what she, Ayr and Goong had done. The Three Musketeers; The Mountees who always got their men to come, but not always quietly, as they used to joke, but only amongst the sorority of their room and a few select others from the staff at Daddy's Hobby.

"Oh, Little Sister," sobbed Lek, "It is so wonderful to see you again and especially up here."

Goong could not speak yet, she only sniffed and they hid their faces in each other's hair from the passengers on the bus until it had left.

"Oh, Lek, Oh, Lek. Oh, Lek! How are you, Big Sister? Look at us! We're behaving like, like, I don't know what! A pair of wimps. Come on, take me back to your new house and let me have a shower. I stink and now my make-up is all over my face. How on Earth can I embrace Craig looking like this?"

They both laughed and sniffed and wiped their eyes and hugged again, oblivious, almost, to the passing traffic.

"Come on, get on the bike and give me your bag."

As they rode through the village, more than a few people turned to look at the school friends that they had only seen together a few times in more than ten years.

Craig heard them coming up the lane and the dogs went to the back gate too, although they still didn't bark at strangers yet. Craig got up out of his seat and went to open the gate for Lek.

"Hello, ladies! How are you doing? How are you, Goong?" He judged it appropriate not to make a joke about their smeared faces. "Let me take the bike, come in, sit down or go for a shower, whatever you like. Both of you." He couldn't resist it, but neither of them reacted to his joke.

In Lek's absence, and as Mine Host, he had put a couple more chairs around his table and put a few more beers in the ice bucket.

"Come on, ladies, sit down and have an ice-cold beer. Or would you prefer lao? I'll go to Nong's and get some if you like. What do you want?"

They had both composed themselves emotionally, but still looked a mess.

"Just sit down, please, pass us a cold beer and let us catch our breath," said Lek. Goong was more gracious, she took his hand, kissed him on the cheek and asked to just sit down for a few minutes. That suited Craig, so he just sat there in the shade under an evening sun and watched 'the girls' get on with their reunion.

It wasn't a difficult time for Craig, because he had decided years ago that he wanted to be with Lek whatever. At the same time, he had decided never to ask her anything about her past, but to listen if she spoke, even though he might not want to hear what she was saying. He knew what Goong did for a living and he knew that Ayr did the same. Now he knew that the three girls shared a room, although the bed was neither here nor there. He also knew that Lek slept with him on the first night, but that wasn't conclusive either – he'd been lucky a few times in his life, but when all this circumstantial evidence was put to-gether, it was hard not to draw a conclusion.

He had and he hadn't seen it from day one. Hadn't his friend Will advised him to give her a thousand Baht 'in the morning'? It all made sense now, but did it make any difference?

That was the huge question looming in his mind

When he had taken his Mum out for a meal to tell her he wanted to go back to Thailand she had asked: what does she do? He had replied that he didn't know, but worked in a bar – who knows? Mum's reply had been: 'There but for the Grace of God go many women'. So, Mum had suspected what Lek did; his friend Will had told him to pay her after she slept with him on the first night, so... What sort of a dummy was he?

He seemed to have blanked the obvious out of his mind on purpose, but he had been with her for over two years now and he loved her and believed that she loved him. There was no difficult problem for him to resolve in his mind about Lek. Only about himself.

He knew that he would stay with her for as long as she would have him, but he would have to do something about his state of awareness.

Or would he? He knew and had known from day one, but chose to ignore it because there was something about her. He had known from day one that he could stay with this woman forever, visas and money permitting. He stared blankly between the two gorgeous women on his lawn and knew that he would do the same all over again.

If she would have him, knowing what she now knew about him.

Lek woke him out of his reverie: "Are you staring at my friend's boobs, Craig Williams?"

"Er, er, no, I was just thinking..."

"What? You were just thinking about them?"

"No, not that either, I've seen them before..."

"What? You have been peeping in my friend's room? I am shocked, Craig. Shame on you."

"No, I wouldn't do that, I ..."

"Why wouldn't you want to see my boobs, Craig? Don't you like them? Lek has seen them and she thinks that they are nice. Don't you Lek?" Lek nodded enthusiastically.

He knew they were only joking with him and he loved it. There was certainly no other man in the village whose wife would consider discussing another beautiful woman's boobs like she was doing with Goong right in front of her.

That'll do for me, he thought.

∞

They all took it in turns to go for a shower and when they reassembled on the back lawn an hour later, they looked a million dollars worth each, except Craig, because nobody had told him to dress formally.

"Well, ladies, you both look great, do you want me to go and get changed too? Are we going anywhere?"

"You can get changed if you want, Craig. Yes, that would be nice. Put the dark suit on and I'll set up another fan, but we aren't going anywhere tonight – just sitting here and talking. Mostly in Thai, but you can say what you like in English or in Thai and we'll try to understand you."

'Ah, I see, like that is it?', he thought, but went to get changed anyway.

It only took him a few minutes, but the laughter had become raucous. Like all men, he wondered if it was about him, although he didn't mind either way. He loved Lek no matter what – he knew that now – and he had a lot of respect for Goong and Ayr too.

When he went back outside, they had a bottle of French champagne on ice and they were saying something about Wales.

Goong is telling me about Welshmen and sheep. I didn't know that. So, the paintings I have of sheep on the Brecon Beacons, do they disturb you? Make you think of previous lovers, perhaps? If they do, I'll take them down. I can get jealous, you know, sometimes."

They both roared at his expense.

Goong poured everyone a glass of the champagne that she had brought, and said: "So, whose idea was it to have oil paintings of sheep on your walls, Craig?"

"Look, girls, I can't help it if I get homesick, can I? But actually it was Lek's idea. Her surprise to me. Go on, tell her Lek."

"OK, … I visited Wales about two years ago, shortly after I first met Craig, you know that already. We arrived in London's Heathrow Airport on the evening of the 28th February and got to Cardiff very early on March 1st. So, my first day in Wales was Saint David's Day.

"For you, Goong," she said turning to her friend, "Saint David is the patron saint of Wales. What's his name in Welsh, Craig? Dewi Sant?

OK. It is a day of national celebration in Wales. School children usually hold an Eisteddfod, a kind of sing song in the morning and get the afternoon off; some schools hold special rugby tournaments and many people wear a leek or a daffodil on their lapel.

"In fact, these events often take place in Welsh communities all over the world, but I digress. It was a cold frosty night when we arrived and a dark, cold frosty morning when we woke up, but it was nice rather than miserable. There were only a few flowers in peoples' otherwise grass-green and earth-brown gardens and the trees were strangely nude, not that I realised that that was seasonal at the time. I thought all British or Welsh plants were without leaves.

"We went to the nearest pub for lunch and to meet some of Craig's friends. The short walk to the pub was cold but invigorating, which made getting into the warm building something special that I had never experienced before.

"About an hour after we had had our meal, one of Craig's friends called me outside to see that it was snowing. I had always wanted to see snow and here is was on my first day in Wales - my first day in Europe! People later said that I looked like a puppy dancing around catching snowflakes.

"Having seen puppies doing that myself now, I guess that I did. I felt so privileged to see snow on my first trip and on my first day too. I wanted it to go on and on, but everyone else was happy with the two or three inches that did fall. On the way home, Craig showed me how to make snowballs and we had a snowball fight - it was such fun!

"Craig's friends and family really pulled the stops out to make my stay in Wales enjoyable and special. Some of the ladies took me shopping in Cardiff, we were staying in Barry, nearby, and to special ladies-only parties like hen nights and make-up parties. We also went out for meals and to social functions at local restaurants and clubs. We even went to a local Masonic Ladies' Night, something that I had never dreamed that a poor Thai farmer's girl like me would ever attend - it was so posh, yet everyone was so friendly and kind.

"Anyway, one of my favourite experiences of them all though was being driven around the Welsh snow-topped mountains by one of Craig's brothers and his brother's wife. I had never seen sheep before and thought they looked so beautiful standing on the hillsides like balls of white fluff in the patches of snow and bright green grass. I took hundreds of photos of the sheep on the Brecon Beacons, but they wouldn't let me get close enough to pose with them.

"I would love to have a flock of sheep in Thailand, but it would probably be far too hot for them. I have already done the next best thing though and had my favourite two sheep photos transformed into large oil paintings which hang in our living room, as you know already.

"Do you like sheep, Goong?"

"Yes, I'll have a lamb chop if you've got any," she replied and they both started laughing again. Craig could see that silliness was on the cards for the evening and that was not his strong point. He didn't like to ask Goong why she had turned up – it wasn't even any of his business, he was just glad that she had, but he was still curious about why.

"So, Goong, to what do we have the pleasure? What is the occasion of this state visit? Not that you need one."

"I'll keep that till later if you don't mind, but for now, let's just say that I have not seen enough of my best friend and her husband for a long time, so here is to you both and thanks for having me" with that she raised her glass and toasted them.

Craig wondered whether to say now that they were not married, although Goong already knew that, and propose right now, but, as he had done for the last year or so, he thought he should wait for a better time.

"Back to you, Goong. You're as beautiful as ever and you are always welcome in our house. Cheers!" said Craig and he thought he noticed a little extra moisture in Goong's eyes.

"Right! What are we going to eat?" asked Lek. "We can either cook what's in the fridge, see what my Mum's got over there or rope one of my family into driving us to a restaurant. What do you fancy, Goong?"

"If you don't mind, it's been a long day and I would rather just stay here this evening, if that's all right with you two. This is a lovely garden and it is nice to be back in Baan Suay again, even though..."

"Yes, well, we'll see what happens tomorrow," cut in Lek quickly. "Do you want to help me look in the fridge, Goong?"

They both took off like greyhounds from a trap, but now Craig was certain that he had seen tears in Goong's eyes. He politely stayed where he was and took up his paper again.

"What is it, Goong?," asked Lek as they got in the kitchen.

"I don't know where to start, Big Sister. There is good news, bad news and worse news. Which do you want to hear first?"

"Well, the one that affects you the most, of course."

"An American has asked me to marry him and go live over there, in New York..."

"That's great news! You'll be out of it too! Er, mm, but which bit of news is that...?"

"That's the bit you asked for first. The other bits are: first that my family don't want to know and will not wish me well and the other bit is that I have six to nine weeks left to live. Ovarian cancer. You know me, I don't care about dying, but I don't want to spend my last six weeks away from my friends and country. Anyway, it wouldn't it be fair on Bob, the man who has asked me to marry him?"

Lek threw her arms around Goong and started to gush. Goong hugged her back, but had no tears left.

"Don't cry, Big Sister. No woman no cry, remember? I'll see you in the next world and don't be late..."

Lek remembered and knew exactly what she was saying, but it was still painful. She pulled away, but hung on: "Is there anything I or we can do, Little Sister?"

"No, the cancer, the little shit, has escaped my ovaries, we, the doctors and I that is, didn't notice it until late... We kept talking about regular check-ups, didn't we? So there's nothing that can be done about that. I would like to make peace with Dad and my brothers, but not by saying I'm dying and Bob, well, he doesn't even know yet. In fact, only you, me and my gynaecologist know. I'm sorry to hit you with this without warning, but I need to be in the village for a few days and I wanted to see you, Lek, my Big Sister of all my life, my Sister in Arms."

They hugged again, but without tears.

"Don't worry about a thing, 'cause every little thing's gonna to be all right...," sang Lek quietly into her friend's ear. They both loved Bob Marley.

"I know it will... I know that, my friend... Given time."

Craig could see them hugging and kissing through the kitchen window, but he had no idea what was going on. Should he propose tonight, he wondered?

Lek opened the fridge and pulled out a large bag of prawns, which was apt as Goong is Thai for prawn, bacon, bread for toasting, a bottle of white wine and a fish called 'tab tim'. The rice, vegetables and fruit were already outside in the sala. Goong reappeared behind her back.

"Here are another two bottles of 'Moet et Chandon', that's it then. Let's do the lot, eh and see what happens tomorrow? Shall we tell Craig?"

"Oh, that's your decision, Goong. Craig's not a Buddhist like us, but he does believe in life after death and re-incarnation. He's almost a Buddhist, ... as near as damn it anyway. But maybe it'll be better if you or we tell him tomorrow. Is that OK?"

"Sure, good idea. Let's get out there, pop a cork and heat some pans, I'm hungry!"

Craig sat at the kitchen table as the two women cooked, laughed and drank. They were like one in everything they did, Siamese Twins, and they both took care of Craig as if he were their grand old uncle – he was outside the loop, but they were both treating him as if he were part of them equally. Lek was like that with her friends, she was happy for them to be loving to Craig – she did not get jealous of her friends interacting with him. In short, she trusted them – her friends were part of the sorority and they would never let each other down no matter how much a man misinterpreted their actions.

Craig looked on in awe, a very happy man.

When the meal, two bottles of champagne and half of the wine were finished, they moved back onto the lawn to wait for a second wind. Lek brought coffee and brandy.

"Well, ladies, you have excelled yourselves! I must say, that that was the best meal with the best company that we have ever had in this new abode of ours" and he stood up to make the toast. "My toast is to the Ladies," he held his glass up to them and finished it.

They gave a short, light round of applause and thus encouraged and fortified by wine and spirit, Craig got up again, went down on one knee in front of Lek and said:

"My darling, I have been wanting to ask you this favour for more than a year, but I was frightened that you would refuse me. I still am, but I feel that the time is right. Lek, my dearest, would you please do me the honour of becoming my wife?"

He looked up at Lek and she looked at Goong, then the girls clasped hands and burst out laughing.

18 MORAL SUPPORT

Lek and Goong had had to put Craig to bed the night before. She felt sorry for him really as he lay next to her in bed snoring, because she knew how difficult it had been for him to propose like that and her reaction had been pretty dreadful to say the least. He had taken it well though. He hadn't got up off his knee until she had nodded assent, even if she was laughing so much that she couldn't actually voice the word.

It wasn't so much that she hadn't realised that some Western men actually proposed like that outside Hollywood film studios or that Thai men rarely did it, it was the timing. They were about to tell him that Goong was going to get married soon, or at least had been proposed to, when he dropped to one knee and did it himself.

Sad really, but oh so funny.

It had been just what she and Goong needed. It had rounded the evening off nicely and he didn't even get upset. Once she had nodded and laughed yes, he had gone back to his seat, finished his glass and fallen asleep.

She and Goong had let him sit there asleep for an hour to see if he would wake up before dragging him into the house. Bpom and Bpouy had looked rather concerned – they had never seen him in quite that state before.

She could just about hear Goong snoring in the spare room a few yards away when Craig breathed in sharply. He suffered from sleep apnoea and she was lying there listening to them like an anxious mother worried about cot death, as she often did, frightened that his breathing would not kick start again one night and that she wouldn't notice.

'Goong, Goong, Goong.' she thought, 'Always the devil-may-care Buddhist. Not a bit scared of what life could throw at her. The bravest of the three of the Musketeers. She, Lek, considered herself the weakest of them, because she was frightened of what her daughter might think of her and frightened for her daughter's future and now she was struggling to worm her way back into village society and frightened of what people might say or even think! What had become of her?

Her friend, a few yards away, was dying and she, Lek was worried about fitting in again with the very villagers who had reviled her for a decade and more? People who knew hardship, yes, but only where it concerned crops, babies and family. It was a very sheltered life, but they dared to criticize her and she was silly enough to be frightened of what they said or even thought? She had turned from a warrior into a mouse and it would have to stop.

She would marry Craig though and not bleed him dry as some expected of her and if times got tough, she would stick with him too and that might even surprise him, because she knew that she had not been easy to live with for the last year. Maybe that was why he hadn't asked her to marry him before, because she had been expecting him to since they had come back from Britain.

Never mind, she thought, it will all come out in the wash and she allowed herself to fall asleep again, not wanting to get up too much before the others for fear of waking them up accidentally.

Not long afterwards, Lek felt Craig move and jumped out of bed, seconds before he opened his eyes.

"Good morning, telak! How are you this morning? Hangover, mai?"

"Morning, I'm just going to the loo"

"OK, anything you say, future husband."

Craig hadn't forgotten and it brought a huge grin to his face that Lek hadn't forgotten either.

Lek threw all the windows open and opened the doors as was her early morning routine, then went out into the garden to water the flowers, also as she did every morning. As she passed the spare room, Goong opened the window looking a bit groggy.

"Good morning, how are you, Little Sister?"

"OK, but mornings are the worst. Sometimes, I feel as if I could sleep all day. I get tired easily and the tablets don't help. I mean they ease the pain but they make me tired, you know."

"Go back to bed then! Or take a cushion out into the garden and sleep in the sala. Or watch TV in the living room. The house is yours to do whatsoever you want with for as long as you like. Craig's all right with you staying, don't worry. Just make sure you cover up on the way to the shower and lock the door. I don't need any competition."

They held hands for a moment.

"Thanks, Lek."

Lek continued watering the plants and checking on the nocturnal damage the dogs had caused which was becoming less, as Craig had predicted. They were playing around her feet as they did these days and although she might pretend to get angry with them she couldn't really and they seemed to know it, because they took no notice of her threats. She had never taken the time or had the opportunity to get to know dogs before and she was becoming quite surprised how lovable and in-dividual they were.

Previously, she had only seen 'dogs en masse' – dogs, the enemy, all the same, all horrible, disgusting, dirty and dangerous – and yet here were her two dogs – lovable, cute, playful and friendly. She wondered how she could have missed that for all those years.

It was like any form of blind hatred – silly and irrational.

And she had never considered herself any of those things. It was totally beyond her at this moment how she could have let herself feel like that for twenty odd years – more than two-thirds of her life. Tend-ing the garden often had such a philosophically therapeutic effect on Lek these days. She had missed being connected to the land when she had lived in Pattaya, but had forgotten to remember that she had missed it after a few years. She remembered missing it at first, but then her mind must have pushed the memory into the background to ease the pain.

She wondered whether it might be like that for Goong wanting to make amends with her family in this life rather that waiting for the next one. She was sure that Goong was a doer – she would want to solve problems before they became huge problems and if that were not possible then it would not be for want of trying on Goong's part.

She remembered how Goong's father had contacted her through an aunt at her mother's funeral to tell her that she had to give up her life in Pattaya to come home and take care of him and her two teenage brothers now that her mother had passed away. They hadn't cared too much before, but only wanted a skivvy to replace their mother. Goong had gone up to her father and told him straight. Her mother had married him; that was her decision and she would not criticize it, but it was not Goong's. If she was going to look after any man, the man would be of her own choosing.

And that was the parting of the ways, although Goong had been back a few times over the years, but to no warm reception. Her brothers were both married now and her father was old, but their attitude towards her had not changed. She hoped that it would before it was too late for Goong to be there in the flesh.

When she had finished in the garden, Lek started phase two of her morning routine: cooking breakfast. She was still in her nightdress, as usual for this time of day, with one of Craig's shirts over the top for modesty. She took the rice left over from the day before out of the steamer, put it in some water and set it to boil. Then she quickly stir-fried a small handful of chopped meat and vegetables in a little oil with garlic and a chilli and added that to the rice to reduce to a pulp like porridge. Finally, she added more rice and water to the steamer so that it would cook fresh rice by lunch time. The whole process took fifteen minutes and was typical of the way Lek cooked: simple, to the point, but aromatic and delicious.

The smell was enough to draw both Goong and Craig out into the garden to eat.

"Goong has had an offer of marriage too. From an American. She may be going to live in New York. What do you think about that, Craig? Good news, eh?"

"What? He phoned her up last night and proposed?"

"No, silly. He, Bob, asked her a week or two ago before he went back to America. Exciting, eh? A new life – in America! We are both going to get married, but I will stay here and never see my friend again. Oh, Goong, I will miss you so, even though we don't see much of each other any more."

"I may not be as far away as you think. I'll keep an eye on you."

Craig didn't quite catch what Gong had said, but he had learned better than to ask too many questions, so he let it go over his head.

"What are you two ladies going to do today?"

"It's up to Goong. What do you want to do today? Go for a drive on the motorbike? Visit some old friends? Go see your Dad? Go shopping in Phichai? Sit here and talk? Anything you like."

"What about Craig? We can't just leave him out."

"Don't worry about me. I want to get some work done..."

"No, don't worry about him. The day is ours. We'll see him later either at dinner or in Nong's for a drink later. Craig never comes with me in the daytime, he likes to play on his computer with the Internet."

"Work, not play," he corrected her.

"Whatever. OK, 'work' then. It's all boring anyway."

Craig got up to start his own routine of coffee, shower and work. He could hear them laughing as he sloped off and wondered whether it was at his expense. Lek could be quite insensitive sometimes. It was because he 'played with the boring computer on the Internet' that there was food on the table and a nice garden to eat it in, but he was not unkind enough to say it.

Actually, Lek was not trying to hurt Craig's feelings either. She was just trying to be light-hearted and frivolous to cheer her friend up, but Craig didn't know that. She would make it up to him later.

The two friends spent the next couple of hours clearing up the things from breakfast and the night before, then took it in turns to shower, before putting on their make-up together in Goong's room. It was like old times in the cramped room they had shared with Ayr in Pattaya.

"Ayr will miss you terribly, won't she?"

"Yes, I think so. I feel awful for her. She's down there on her own now. I wouldn't be surprised if she packs it in and comes back. I would if I were her. But then what could she do here? Plant rice for some farmer? Work in a shop? Doesn't Craig know anyone for her?"

"Oh, I daren't ask him. I tried once or twice before for other girls and he went mental. 'I'm not a pimp', he said, so I never ask him any more. I don't understand his problem, but then, I don't always understand him full-stop, so that's nothing new. He's all right really... We are just different: different age-group, different language, different culture, different religion, different nationality and different sex, naturally. We are very different. Sometimes, I think that makes it better, but other times I'm not so sure. We can learn a lot from each other and it is fun finding out, but sometimes we clash. All in all though, it is fun.

"Anyway, I bought the ticket and now I'm taking the ride and it's too late to get off, even if I wanted to. Same for Craig, so we just have to get on with it, don't we? He's happy enough and so am I. Soom's glad I'm back and so am I, most of the time. The truth is though that I don't remember village life being this hard. I don't do much physical work, I don't mean that, but fitting in, conforming, being normal is bloody hard work."

"You'll manage. Don't worry so much. Don't worry about what others think too much. You're a nice person. The people who give you a chance will see that and those who don't give you a chance are not worth knowing anyway, so they don't count. Some people will be jealous of you and you can't do anything about that either. Avoid people like that too.

"Just avoid negative people. Stick with the positive and let the others walk their own path. Some will come around sooner or later and you can welcome them into your life then, but don't hold your breath waiting and don't keep inviting them in. Concentrate on those who love you and you'll have enough to keep you busy.

"Craig is a good man, make him feel special, 'cause he has given up a lot to be here with you, and you are a good woman and you deserve him too. Come on, let's get some fresh air."

They popped into Craig's office, put an arm around him from each side and simultaneously kissed him on each cheek.

"Bye-bye, darling. Goong and I are going for a ride. Maybe go to the beauty salon and then visit friends of Goong. OK? You want something or can you take care of yourself? You want more coffee? Do you want more rice? We will cook for you later or bring you something back. See you later."

"No, Lek, I'm OK. I'll get more coffee in a few minutes. You go off and enjoy yourselves."

They kissed him again and left.

The first stop was the Wat. Most of the girls who came back home called in the temple soon after arrival. Lek had always done it too. They didn't often find time to pray in a temple when they were away, but when they were in the village they were usually on holiday and so had time to go. There was something special about praying in the Wat you had grown up around too – it was like a second home or an extension to their home.

A village Wat is always open. There are no walls and so no doors on the main area of public prayer. People can pray or just meditate whenever they like Some people used it a lot and others not at all. For some people it was the only place they could find peace and quiet. Monks were always there during daylight hours and asleep there at night. A village Wat usually has large grounds and so did Lek's. Part of the land was beautifully planted, the rest was cut back, but wild and the public was free to wander and lose themselves in thought.

Lek and Goong climbed the steps to say their prayers and light some joss sticks, before returning to ground level and wandering across the grass.

"I love coming here," said Lek, "I wish I could remember to come here more often. Mum comes every day, after she has got Soom off to school. I should come with her really."

"Yes, it is lovely here. So tranquil."

They passed monks hanging their freshly-washed robes over the balcony of their sleeping quarters to dry. Lek sensed that her friend was looking for something, so she fell quiet. They walked in silence for about half an hour. Lek thought about her friend's predicament and guessed correctly that Goong was too.

Every Thai village has a Buddhist temple, called a Wat, in the same way that every European village has a church. Similar to their European counterparts, many traditional villages have more than one Wat, although there is only one real denomination of Buddhism in Thailand. In Europe, there might be a Catholic Church, a Protestant Church and a Methodist Church, but in Thailand there are only two active forms of the Buddhist religion.

Of these two forms more than 95% of Thais are Theravada Buddhists, who believe in the original teachings of Buddha - that no-one can help another along the path to enlightenment. That is that everyone has to get there by purifying their own life through rightful actions and meditation.

The other form of Buddhism, Mahayana, teaches that a master can remain on Earth to help his fellow man attain enlightenment long after he or she has earned the right not to have to be reborn again and that chanting mantras can also help advancement as well.

The Theravada Buddhist temples, whether in the villages or the cities are maintained on a regular basis by the monks themselves and maybe a few volunteer temple workers. Local women may help out with the cleaning.

Any money needed is donated by the locals living in nearby houses, although the monks do also carry out religious functions for which donations are expected. Specialist, private, contractors are called in if structural or difficult repairs need to be carried out on the Wat. Local businesses, farmers and wealthy individuals will donate money and services to the temple in order to earn 'merit', which they believe counteracts bad karma. The names of donors and benefactors are usually read out over the village loudspeaker system, if a special project has been initiated.

The first contact most people have with the orange-robed Thai monks is in the morning when they go around local houses to collect food. Every Theravada monk takes part in collecting food but some have a lay helper to push the handcart. They got to Lek's house at about seven-thirty a.m. But each monk took a different route so as to cover the whole area fairly quickly.

They would announce their presence by striking two bits of wood or metal together as they walked. Some households provide their own clapper outside their gate for the monk to use. The monks blessed everyone who donated food. Money was not required as a donation at these times.

The food was taken back to the temple and shared by all the monks, but part of the collection was reserved for the last meal of the day, which has to be eaten before noon. This is probably why all functions that require the presence of monks like weddings and house-blessings take place in the morning, because the ceremony involves a feast, in which the monks partake. The recipient of the monks' services donates upwards of a hundred Baht per monk for this and the ceremony requires nine monks. If the service has gone particularly well, the host may donate a further thousand Baht for the abbot or head monk or teacher, ajan, of the temple.

"Well, that's that then! Let's go!" said Goong and they headed back to the motorcycle.

"Where are we going first? How about Ron's noodle shop and see if he'll make us a cup of tea?"

"OK, I haven't been there since we've been back! I've seen Ron obviously, but I haven't been inside to eat. I always cook at home. Craig's not keen on Thai noodles, he says they're too sweet. You know, I never thought about it before he said that. I ate them nearly every day for thirty years, but now he's said that, I don't like them too sweet either. Funny, isn't it?"

"You are learning from each other. I think it's great. You are Borg assimilating one another – becoming one" and they laughed. It was good to have a real friend again for both of them.

As they sat at a table in Ron's both women were hoping that someone from Goong's family would walk in, but neither knew that the other was thinking the same. It would save face for everyone if Goong could meet her family on neutral ground. Goong didn't really want to go to her family, but did want to speak to them. She longed for a re-conciliation, but had been rejected a few times and didn't want to go through it again.

Many people came for their lunch and went again. Every time that someone came in, they looked up hoping. They knew every single per-son who entered and most of them spoke, because they hadn't seen Goong for a long time, but not one of them was related to Goong. After two cups of tea each and a visit to the ladies', they decided to move on. They drove around for a while and then called in to see a friend who lived a few doors up from Goong's father. There would be a good chance that they would see him passing by, if they sat outside, which would be normal practice anyway.

They sat in the sala at Nu's and talked about old times. Nu had been in school with Lek and Goong, but she had taken the traditional path of marriage, work in the fields and babies. She was pregnant again now, which was the only reason she wasn't working at the time.

"I'll be glad when this is all over," she said pointing at her seven-month bulge, "It's too hot to be pregnant. Put me in the rice field any day. I told my old man: 'This is the last one. Four is enough.' We both love kids, but, well, let's just say that four is enough. Didn't you ever want children, Goong?"

"I'm not sure. I think that sometimes I did, but I don't remember ever hankering after them. I didn't want to be a single mother and I saw what happened to Lek. Sorry, Lek, but you were left stranded by your husband, weren't you? I think that if I found the right man, maybe I would want kids. Probably would.

"Yes, I probably would, but don't miss not having had them either. Families can be such a pain in the neck anyway, can't they? Talking of which, do you see much of my Dad?"

"I see him every day now I'm home, but not to speak to. I see him walking to the shop most days. Have you been round to see him yet?"

"No, not yet. I arrived last night and stayed with Lek. We went to the Wat this morning and we were just going there now, when we saw you and stopped for a chat first. Dad's not going anywhere, he can wait and he's not expecting me anyway. You could say that it will be a surprise visit."

There were a couple of face-saving white lies in there, but it made life easier.

"What do you think, Lek, do you want to come with me when I go to see my Dad? What sort of time do you normally see him going to the shop, Nu?"

"Oh, four or five o'clock, late afternoon, you know, when it's a bit cooler."

"Maybe I'll surprise him. Waylay him on his way back from the shop. Can we sit here until then or are you busy?

No, there's only an hour or two to go. I only have to chop some vegetables in preparation for Don's tea later on when he gets home at six. You can help if you like. It's lovely to see you anyway. You don't get back often, do you?"

Goong talked as normally as she could but her eyes were fixed on the first spot where her father was likely to appear. She didn't want him to see her on the outward journey, she wanted to surprise him going home, because it would give him less time to think.

When she saw him walking down his front garden, she made an excuse and went to the toilet. When she returned, Nu said:

"You just missed your father. He's just passed by on his way to the shop, I suppose. You could run after him. It's not far."

"No, it's all right. I'll see him on the way back. Are you coming with me, Lek?"

"Yes, sure."

When the old man passed the gate, Goong sprang out.

"Hello, Dad. Surprise, surprise! How are you keeping? Let me take your shopping for you."

He looked like he'd seen a ghost. He had no idea what to say, especially on the open street with so many people looking on. He allowed Goong to take his small bag, but said nothing and kept walking. Goong made a face at Lek behind his back. It said 'here goes, all or nothing'.

They sat in the sala in the front garden, which was looking very run down.

"Let me cook something for you, Dad."

He nodded, but still hadn't said anything. Lek thought she could see water in his eyes, but it could have been age-related. He was a tough old man of the tough old school. Goong kept asking him questions as she collected a knife, chopping block, a pan and some vegetables. Her father watched her every movement.

"When did you get back?"

"Last night, Dad. I stayed with Lek so as not to disturb you. We went to the Wat this morning. You remember Lek, don't you?"

He nodded. "I'm not mental. She lives with that foreigner. They say he's all right, but can't speak our language. They say he makes real howlers, but they say he's all right. I've never met him. Do you have a foreign friend too?"

"No, Dad. Still single. Footloose and fancy-free. No time for boyfriends or husbands..."

"No babies then? Your brothers have both given me grandchildren..."

"No, Dad, no children. No time for them either, but you have others. Aren't they enough for you? Maybe they'll have more in time."

When the meal was ready, Goong served the majority to her father and a little to Lek and herself. When they had finished, Goong washed up, poured her father a whiskey, squeezed his hand and got up to leave with Lek.

"You take care, Dad. I'll stay with Lek again tonight so as not to get in your way. Bye-bye, Dad. Nice to see you again. I have to go now."

She squeezed his hand again and they left quickly, tears welling up in both the women's eyes.

"Let's go for a drink, Lek. Quickly."

Craig was sitting in Nong's shop as predicted, so they joined him there.

"Nong, a bottle of lao deng, a bottle of soda and a bottle of mineral water, please. Two glasses."

Craig nodded hello, but he was reading and they were speaking Thai in a way that implied that they didn't care whether he could understand or not, so he just left them to it again.

"Pass me that lao, Lek, I need a stiff drink after that. My Dad seems more dead than I am. It was awful. I couldn't tell him about my illness. There was no point. He can't do anything and I don't need him to worry about me. Then there's the chance he wouldn't understand anyway. He didn't seem to be completely on the ball, did he? Has he been ill, do you know? I'll try to send him some money, when I get back to Pattaya. I'll send it you, and perhaps you can get it to him for me."

"Sure, no problem. I haven't heard that he has been ill. I think he's just old and, er, living on his own for so long, he has sort of forgotten the art of conversation. I'll call in from time to time, if you like."

"He wants more grandchildren," she shook her head slowly, "I wouldn't want my kids growing up here or I'd want them to get out to go to university. What is there here for the youth? Eh? We were lucky to get out, no matter what we had to do to achieve it. I'm glad I went and I'm sure Ayr is too. You had to go, I know, but you have done all right out of it too, haven't you?

"I feel sorry for all these kids here though," she continued, "There's not much in the village to hold the youth... Education is better now than it ever has been but that, coupled with the TV and the cinema has persuaded young people to want more than is available locally.

"It's probably happening all over the world, but in Thailand the youth grows up in a village of farmers, knowing that there will be nothing there for them when they grow up. Not only that, but mechanisation has meant that that there are fewer and fewer jobs available every year. I see that, in the West, a disaffected youth has led to gangs of young hooligans terrorising inner city centres and parents losing control.

"Luckily, despite the similarity of circumstances, the results in Thailand are not the same. There is nowhere near the same level of youth violence and crime in Thailand as there is in the West and crime in the villages."

"Well... it just doesn't exist, does it?" replied Lek, "Although it does depend what you mean by crime, I suppose. There is some drug-taking here and people don't leave their doors open any more like they used to, but no-one has a burglar alarm unless you count a dog. My pet hate - and only hate really - is that parents allow young, really young boys to drive motorbikes around at break-neck speeds, knowing that they are uninsured.

"Many boys of eight years or so drive motorbikes or scooters and many of them have modified the exhaust pipe to create as much noise as possible. When these kids come home from school, the quiet village is transformed into a noisy speedway, until they are sent to bed at about seven or eight o'clock.

"Girls never do this. Sure, girls ride motorbikes too, but slowly and they usually need the bike to carry the shopping home with. Thai village girls are always polite and would not want to draw attention to themselves like the boys try to do.

"I suppose that changes when girls get to about eighteen when they become more aloof. But boys, or many of them are rude until they get to about twenty-five or twenty-six years of age, when they revert to polite human beings again. Grandparents are largely responsible for this state of affairs. They treat girls like they were treated: to be helpful and polite; but they treat boys like princes.

"This has a lovely affect on Thai girls but a terrible affect on Thai boys. In fact, the affect on Thai boys is so marked that many people say that girls are grown up by the age of seventeen, but boys not until they are twenty-five, when it finally sinks in that the rest of the world won't put up with their selfish antics like their grandparents did."

"However, stubborn, arrogant and lazy Thai boys often are, at least they're not violent to or a threat to other members of the village community, which is a lot to be grateful for, when you look at Western inner cities... but how long will that last, Lek? Thailand is being Westernised so quickly."

"Yes, Goong, I can see what you're saying. The village is so much different from when we lived here, but it is better in some ways too. The work is less hard and monotonous and the wages are far higher. I don't know what Soom will do. I don't want her to marry a poor farmer and be struggling all her life. She doesn't want that either and she's only thirteen Let's hope she's got the brains and tenacity to get a degree.

"What about you though? Are you going to go into hospital? You said that the tumour is quite advanced."

"No, I don't think so. They did say that it was quite advanced, but also that it had spread all over and I don't want to be cut open. I've had enough anyway to be honest. I'd rather cash in my chips now, go home and come back another day. I don't want to drive around in a broken-down old cronk of a body. I'm used to a Ferrari. It would be too much of a come-down too quickly. I know it's not what you're expected to do these days, but people did live like that for thousands of years and I guess I haven't learned any better.

"It's all only illusion anyway, that's what we were taught, eh? Maya.

Birth, death, and most of what goes on in between is only Maya. I hope it is anyway, because that thought has helped me get through all my adult life. Come on now, let's get pissed and tomorrow I'll go back to Pattaya."

"Why don't you stay a little longer? We can take care of you when you get sick..."

"No, Big Sister. I don't want to keep bumping into my family. Maybe I'll check into a hospital for the last week or so, if I feel really bad, but I'm OK most of the time... at the moment."

"So, you won't be marrying Bob? He can get you the operations and medication you need."

"No, it's not fair on him, is it really? Anyway, I don't want to be an invalid. It's better this way. Really it is. When you have thought about it, you'll know I'm right. Oh, it wouldn't be as easy for you to take the same path. You have a family that loves you, a man that gave up everything for you and a daughter to take care of, but what have I got to keep me here?"

Craig finished his beer and closed his book. He had noticed that their bottle was almost empty and thought that it was a sign that they were ready to go home.

"So, what are you two doing now?"

"We're going to have another bottle. Goong's going back tomorrow. The village is too quiet for this city-slicker. We've become peasants. Go on have one more, then we'll transfer to our garden."

19 MAYA - ILLUSION

The next morning, Goong was the first up. Craig had gone to bed several hours before them and they had finished the second bottle. She still felt a little drunk, but that was better than being in pain. She started clearing up the things from the night before. Craig arose a few minutes later, went to the toilet, put his coffee on and started work. Lek was still fast asleep.

When his coffee was ready, Goong brought it in for him, which he hadn't expected her to do.

"Here you are, Craig. Coffee for the worker."

"Thanks, Goong, but you didn't have to do that."

"Nonsense. You didn't have to put me up and let me monopolize Lek for the last couple of days either or offer me a room for as long as I wanted. You're all right, Craig, and I really hope that you and Lek have a great life together. She deserves it, you know, she's had a really hard life. And you deserve someone nice like her too. All of us think you're smashing." She gave him a peck on the cheek and went back to her work. He could hear her singing quietly in the garden kitchen.

She's happy, he thought.

Lek was not that far behind and after putting her head around the office door to wish Craig a good morning, she joined her friend in the garden.

"A bottle each is too much for me these days. I'm either out of practice, getting old or both. How are you?"

"A bit tipsy, but fine. What are your plans for today?"

"I'm all yours after my rice soup. What do you want to do? Start again and stay here another day?"

"Nice try, but no, I don't think so. I think there's a train from

Phichai to Phitsanulok at two p.m. and then I'll get the first bus to Pattaya – probably some sort of milk train stopping at every village on the way, but I don't mind. I have all the time in the world – my whole life in front of me and I've done all I wanted to do up here or I will have by two p.m. anyway."

So, they performed the rice soup ritual, took Craig a bowl and sat down to eat theirs.

"What else do you want to do then?" asked Lek.

"Not much, a bit of shopping in the village and answers to one or two questions. I want to ask you a few favours too."

"Sure anything. Just name them."

"OK, thanks, but not here. I don't want to be overheard."

"That sounds very cloak-and-dagger, very exciting Goong. Where then? Inside?"

"No, let's leave it until we get to Phichai, assuming you have the time to see me off, that is."

"Of course, I would be offended if you didn't ask me. OK, let's put this stuff away, see if Craig's all right, have a shower and put our faces on, and then I'm all yours to command."

Craig saw them high-five and set about clearing up. He wasn't spying, one of his office windows overlooked the rear garden and the kitchen. It made him think though. Lek and Goong were old friends who enjoyed each other's company a lot and he would probably never experience that feeling of close friendship with anyone other than Lek ever again.

There were no other foreigners close by to get to know. Murray was a friend, but he lived twenty-five kilometres away. No, his life in the village was set to be a solitary existence. He sat alone from morning to dusk and seven p.m. till midnight. It had to be done – he knew that better than anyone, but sometimes he felt like one of the aphids on the roses outside another of his windows. The ants tended and defended the aphids until they were no longer useful and then they ate them. He felt like one of them sometimes.

There was no other way though. Lek couldn't earn money with her qualifications except as a farm labourer and he hadn't brought her back to make her life a misery. On the other hand, if they lived in a city where she could get a job, they would have to pay rent, which would eat her salary up and he would still be on his own all day.

He had painted himself into this corner, but at least it had three windows with beautiful views. He shuddered to think what life on the dole in the UK would be like in comparison. This had to be better and healthier. There was plenty of sunshine and all the fruit he could eat. It was far better to be poor in Thailand than to be poor in the UK, that was for sure.

One of them was showering now, so they would be going out soon, he thought. Not that it mattered. When he was working, he couldn't talk anyway. He had tried that and he just became irritated with Lek for interrupting him.

They were getting dressed and putting on their make up together now, he could hear them laughing and joking. He had never had that sort of a relationship, with men anyway, not even as a boy in school. Maybe rugby or football players had it in the locker room, but Craig had hated sport, so he didn't know. Maybe Americans have it more than Brits, he speculated. They certainly seemed to in the films.

"OK, darling, we are going out for a short while. Goong wants to do some shopping in the village. Do you want anything?"

"No, my giddy ant," he said when she looked around the door.

"Aunt? I'm not your aunty! What are you talking about, Craig? Are you still drunk? We go now OK?"

"Yeah, sure; see you later, anty"

Lek gave him a strange smile and walked out with Goong, saying something that he couldn't hear.

"Craig is strange sometimes. I know that my English is not one hundred percent, but I understand a lot. Now he's calling me his aunt or aunty. I think he's mad sometimes. OK, where first?"

"First stop is the Wat. I want to spend a few minutes there, but if you don't mind, I'd like to go alone. Could you just drop me in the car park and wait for me there?"

Lek did as she was bid. Goong jumped of the scooter and ran up the steps to the praying area. Lek had no idea why she had been asked to wait, but she tried not to be curious. Instead she thought of Maya. She had never known anybody except Goong who not only professed to believe in Buddhist principles but who could actually live by them as well.

Goong cared about other people but seemed to care nothing for her own existence. She honestly had no fear of death because she honestly believed that she would be reborn. She had heard hundreds of people repeat the principles of Buddhism, while secretly or even not so secretly doing just the opposite. They trusted in karma, but wanted the insurance of money in the bank just in case they were mistaken. Goong believed in the storing up of good or bad luck created by actions not only in this life and past lives but by deeds committed while without a body in between incarnations.

She would have made a great teacher or even a nun.

Goong tapped her on the shoulder.

"OK, all done here. Now I'd like to drive past Dad's house, but please, don't you look for him, don't slow down and definitely don't stop even if he sees us, although I doubt if he will. Then we can go to Nong's."

"OK." Lek took off. She set a very moderate pace so that it would not look as if she had slowed down outside Goong's family home. Goong didn't complain. The old man was sitting on the table in the sala just staring into space as he probably did most days of his life now. He looked oblivious to the world, which was good in Goong's opinion. It meant that he was neither too happy nor too sad, which meant that nothing could spoil his state of mind. He was in equilibrium and she didn't want to spoil it. They drove on past and although both women looked at him out of the corner of their eyes, he showed no sign of recognizing, or even having seen, them.

At Nong's shop they both dismounted and sat at the table at Goong's request.

"I don't want tablets today, so I'm going to have a few shots of lao. Don't feel that you have to keep me company. We can just chat for a few minutes and then go back to your place. Where is she? Just wait here a minute."

Goong went inside. She returned alone but with a 'ben' - a half bottle of lao deng and a small thimble glass. Nong was nowhere to be seen.

"It's only eleven o'clock, but there will be a dozen men and boys in the village drinking by now… I'll be the only woman and I don't care! Sod them! Why is it all right for them but not for us? It should be one rule for all and she held a full glass high, before downing it in one. I hope that one of my brothers sees me now. I really do. The hypocrite would be so ashamed."

She offered the glass to Lek, but it only contained a miniscule amount. Lek drank it to show solidarity. Goong refilled it to the brim and drank half.

"You know, Lek, I admire you. The way you went to Pattaya to do a job and then came back when the job was over. I went down with you, sure, but I did it because village life was not for me and your having to go away like that gave me an excuse to go as well… and not have to go alone. I don't know whether I would have had the courage to go alone, but you would have if we hadn't gone with you. You would still have gone, wouldn't you? Because you were on a mission, whereas I was running away. There was no way that I wanted to be ankle-deep in mud or pregnant for the best part of my life. I had always wanted out."

She put the top on the bottle, drained the glass and said: "Come on. Let's go and see your lovely old man."

Lek assumed that Goong had forgotten to pay, but she determined to pay the bill herself later. When they arrived home Craig was sitting in the garden with a pile of boxes in front of him.

"What's all this Craig?

"I don't know first one man came and then another. I couldn't understand them and vice versa."

"It's my going away present. That's all. Some food for lunch and a few beers. Don't make a fuss."

There was a box with two roast chickens and various sauces in it, two cases of Chang Beer and a box with six Heineken and a large bottle of lao deng.

"The Chang is yours, Craig. The Heineken is all of ours and the lao is anyone's."

When Lek and I first went to Pattaya, we thought it was the height of chic to drink Heineken. It was so expensive and no-one in the village even knew what it was. Do you remember, Big Sister? I thought we might have one or two in memory of those early, ancient days of, what? Only ten, no, twelve or thirteen years ago."

She opened three and passed them around while Lek arranged the food on plates.

"Cheers my dears," said Craig and they all clinked bottles before taking a swig.

"We have about an hour, well, just less, before we have to leave, so let's eat and drink and say what we want, because we don't know when the next time will be, if there is another time to come."

"But you will come to our wedding, won't you, Goong?"

"Oh, yes, Craig. That is one thing that you can count on. Nothing in Heaven or on Earth will stop me from being there. I will be there dead or alive. I wouldn't miss it for the world."

The time soon came for them to leave. Goong gave Craig a peck on the cheek, a hug and squeezed his hand. Then she topped up her 'ben' and left with Lek on the motor-bike without any more ado.

Goong needed some photocopies, so that was the first port of call. She also bought writing paper, a few envelopes and three picture post cards.

"That's me done. Let's go buy my train ticket and have a chat."

When they were seated, Lek said: "Where did all that stuff come from? In the house?"

"I ordered the food while you were waiting in the Wat car park and I got Nong to drop the rest off while we had a little tipple in the front. Anyway, forget about that now. Back to business, I still need a few favours from you, please. Thanks. I bought a fake ID in Pattaya. Here is a copy of it. In my dying days, no-one will know my real name, I will be this person. OK?

"Please give me your bank account details or go over the road and get them. You have them? Great. I will transfer money into your account regularly and I want you to give my Dad two hundred Baht every week. Please give it to him in his hand and never to my brothers. You can tell him that I sent it. I will make sure that you have enough to give him two hundred every week until the day he dies and I want you to keep whatever is left over. If he lives longer than the money lasts, well, that's his hard luck, eh? But, I can't see it.

"If or when I go into a hospital, it will be to die. My name will be that one, Nattaporn, and I will pay a nurse to send a card to you and put a bit in the personal column in the local Pattaya paper. It will say: 'Nattaporn had to go home early'.

"I'll ask Ayr to look out for it and let you know, in case the nurse doesn't send the cards. I could do with another drink. Write your address on this while I go find a couple of tins."

Lek wrote her address in the notebook provided.

Goong came back with two tins of Leo beer.

"OK, thanks. Here. A bit like James Bond, isn't it? But the important thing is, I don't want anyone to know what happened to me until after my father's death. Then, well, I don't care what happens then. I have money put aside for my funeral and the hospital will find Nattaporn's bank book with the funeral money in it in my belonging when I die.

"The address on the paperwork in my bag will be false, but I will give all my clothes and jewellery to Ayr before I go in to hospital. Not that I have anything worth having, but if you want something to re-member me by, I'm sure that Ayr will let you pick something out.

"There's no need to come to my funeral. In fact, I won't even let you know when it is or where I am. Don't feel bad about that, Big Sis-ter, please. The only people I'll tell when I die, by postcard, are you, Ayr and Beou. She has been good to me and I truly like her. Any questions?

"Do you know Neil Young? 'If I am just a dreamer, then you are just a dream and you could have been anyone to me'. If anybody ever upsets you, just remember those words. It's all Maya. It's all illusion. No-one can hurt you unless you let them."

"Er, um, you have thought this all out, haven't you?"

"I had to, didn't I?. There is no-one else to do it. One last thing though, you must let me know when you get married, because I wasn't joking, I will be there. You can count on it."

There wasn't much left to say. When Goong's train came in, they hugged like schoolgirls and Goong left, waving out of the window as the train pulled away.

'Wow' was the only word that came into Lek's mind as she walked back to her motorcycle. However, a plan formed in her mind on the journey home and she couldn't wait to put it into action. She found Craig at his desk, working on his web sites.

"Craig, I want to talk to you, but I cannot sit inside, it is too hot. Let's go to Nong's, no-one will overhear us there."

Always ready for a cold beer, Craig grabbed his shirt, laptop and sandals and was ready to go.

"Why can't we talk in the garden? Not that I'm complaining."

"Well, neighbours can overhear us in the garden, but in Nong's we can see anyone hovering nearby. It is more private there. What I have to say will not worry you, so don't be anxious."

Craig nodded. He liked Nong's because it was on the main road through the village and he could see things happening: people coming and going, shoppers, walkers, kids playing, that sort of thing. Their house was in a side-street, a soi; it was very quiet and there was nothing to see. It was ideal for working and resting, but not for living – there was no opportunity for interaction. When they had sat down and ordered their drinks, Lek began.

"You asked me to marry you. Do you still want to marry me? Good, I want to marry you too. Very much. In that case, there are some things that need to be arranged. It's the same in your country, eh? OK. First, we need to set a date. I want as soon as possible, don't you, darling?"

"Yes," he answered cautiously not knowing what was coming but sure that something was on its way.

"Good. You see, Goong may have to go away suddenly and as one of my oldest friends, I want her to be at our wedding. You can understand that, can't you, darling?"

"Yes, sure. Where might she be going?"

"Just away, I can't say where, because I don't know when or where..."

"To America to live with Bob?" he suggested.

"I told you I can't say. I don't know where or when. Goong doesn't even know herself. That is why we must hurry. When she is called, she will have to go immediately, with only a short warning. So, can we get married soon, my dear?"

"Yes, next week, if you want."

"Don't be stupid! How can we arrange everything by next week? Typical man! There is a lot to arrange. It cannot be done in a week. Do you know about Thai tradition for marriage?"

"No, I haven't a clue. Can't we just go to a registry office?"

"What and deny my friends and family a wedding and a party? What about face? What will people think?." She paused as she remembered Goong's words. "Well, no and yes. We must talk about this. Have you thought about how much you will give me to marry you?"

"What? You expect me to pay you to marry me?"

"It is normal in Thailand, but not pay to marry. Sin sod. I don't know the English. You must give me and my mother money. It is traditional. You don't have in the UK?"

"I'll pay you the same as you pay me. Nothing. Oh, wait a moment... You mean 'dowry'. In the UK the father of the wife used to pay the man to marry his daughter and he would also pay for the wedding party."

"Oh, no! In Thailand the future husband must give the girl gold and the girl's mother money. How much will you give for me? I am beautiful, not too old and will take care of you all my life. 250,000 Baht is cheap, neh?"

"£5,000 is a lot of money, Lek. That is six-month's work for a lot of people."

"Six months is not long! You have me for all your life, darling. OK, we can talk about how much again, but you must put money in the bank for the wedding. OK? Remember. That is your job and you must do it quickly. I will talk to the monk to ask for a lucky day to marry in three or four weeks. Maybe that is good for all of us, but there is much to do.

"We need to invite guests ... how many? One hundred and twenty again? I will ask the caterers how many can fit in our garden; order invitation cards; order a stage and entertainment, oh, many things. Do you want to come to see the monk about the date with me? No, you drink beer already and it smells; not nice for see monk. I will go alone. I go now, maybe he can see me today or maybe I must go back tomorrow.

"I must ask friend and my Mum to help too. You stay here and think, I go do something for us. See you later, much later. Maybe twelve o'clock. Bye-bye."

'She's gone again', thought Craig, 'I've hardly seen her for days, then she comes back, invites me for a beer, tells me to expect a bill for 250,000 Baht in the next few weeks and disappears again. You could not make it up.'

He ordered another beer and settled back to watch village life pass slowly before his eyes.

He wondered whether he ought to get out now or whether he was already in too deep. He was not a rich man and he still was not earning much from the Internet. The cost of building and furnishing the house had taken a large part of his savings, and the trip to Wales had also been expensive. On the other hand, everyday life in the village was very cheap even by Thai standards. Now he was expected to find another £5,000 in the next few weeks!

He had the money, but it was haemorrhaging out at an alarming rate with no real income to replace it. Once he was married, what would be next? Lek had already been dropping hints that 'a car would be nice – wouldn't it be nice to have a car?' To put the costs into perspective, a new car would cost about 750,000 Baht, a good second-hand car half of that. It made the wedding look cheap and his wife would keep forty percent of the money 'in the family'.

It was still more money going out though. Lek never seemed to ever think about where he would get money from. She seemed to think that he just had to ask the 'hole in the wall' and the bank would give it to him – no questions asked. She was like a child in a toy shop.

Lek had never asked for money for her family or her daughter, but perhaps that was to be the next financial bombshell. He wondered whether Lek was just milking him for all she could get. He didn't think so; he didn't want to think so, but then he didn't want to look back on his stay in Thailand in five year's time and realize what a mug he had been either.

His worst fear was to be deported for having no money, because then he would not be able to afford to get Lek a UK visa, which would mean that they would be separated. People would taunt him with the old saying: 'A fool and his money are soon parted'.

He decided that the least he could do was find out something about the dowry to see if Lek was telling the truth. It would be the first time he had checked up on Lek and he hated the thought of doing it, but he had to for his own peace of mind

Why hadn't he seen this coming? Craig ordered another beer – he had a lot to think about. He unpacked his laptop – he never went any-where without it these days – and fired it up. He typed 'thai dowry thailand' into Google and read an article on the subject.

<u>The Dowry in Thailand</u>

'The registry office wedding is the only legal ceremony as far as the government is concerned for taxes, inheritance, name change and the like. Despite this, the ceremony with the Buddhist monks is the tra-ditional way of getting married and many couples do not go further than that.

'The registry office wedding is cheap and simple for Thais, but can involve a long wait as they don't use appointments. If a foreigner is involved, you will need papers proving your ability to marry and trans-lations in Thai. Normally, the woman takes her husband's surname (and is eager to do so) and gets her ID card and passport changed to suit.

'Young Thais tend not to live together in the villages, but they probably do in the cities. Older or previously married ladies might live 'over the brush' as an old friend used to call it. However, it would be wrong to think that this is a result of prudishness or double standards.

'In Thailand, the man pays the dowry. Therefore a daughter with no 'history' - no children or ex's will be able to attract a richer husband. Some parents profit from this, but all the families that I know have given the dowry back to the couple to start their married life with.

'The dowry can be quite substantial. A young man I know re-cently paid $4,500 in cash and $4,500 in gold. When you consider that $300 p/m is an average decent wage for a young farmer, you can put it into perspective - he paid 30 months gross salary. That is a lot, but some pay more.

'It is also important to remember that the cash element is given back to and the gold remains with the couple, but it is an indication of the groom's ability to raise cash (or have it).

'If the girl has been to university, the dowry can easily be two or three times that, but then a girl like that would not be looking to marry a small farmer. A university educated girl from a rich family would command a great deal more – maybe ten times more.

'There are two elements to a dowry (sin sod in Thai) - cash and gold. The following is my wife's explanation of dowry, but not all my foreign friends agree. The cash is used by the mother-in-law to pay for the wedding party and she either keeps the balance or gives it back to the couple, but the gold is the bride's and is her divorce settlement in advance, since there is no compulsion for Thai men to support their children or pay maintenance'.

It made Craig happy to know that Lek had not been lying, but it was a double-edged emotion, because now he knew that he was morally-obliged to pay it, although he may be able to whittle the dowry down a little.

An Exciting Future

20 WEDDING PLANS

Lek had come in after Craig had already gone to sleep, so when they woke up, Lek said excitedly,

"Good morning, my dear. I have some really good news. You know that it is Loy Krathong next month? Well, the monk said that the following week is good for marrying. Loy Krathong is Tuesday, so we can marry on Saturday! Isn't that romantic? And we have about four weeks to get everything ready. Isn't that just perfect? Oh, we could not have wished for better luck. This is a very good sign."

"Yes, that's great, love. We need to talk about money too. I will give you the gold you want, but I am limiting the party here to sixty thousand Baht and we will use the other forty on a honeymoon in Pattaya, OK?"

"Yes, darling, that is fine. Come on, let's have breakfast and get started."

Craig let Lek go to the bathroom first. He lay there wondering whether he had won anything there or not. He had got what he wanted, but it didn't feel like a victory. He got up, put the coffee on and started up his computer, while listening to Lek singing in the shower.

He took her place when she came out and by the time he had showered, Lek was already cooking in the garden.

"Craig, I understand that you have spent a lot of money in this last year, but I want to live a normal life. If I am to give up my life in Pattaya, I must have a decent life which is better than most people here. Maybe you don't understand but I went away to work and stayed away for ten years. People must see that all that 'working away' was worthwhile or they are going to wonder why I bothered. They will think that I must have been stupid to do it.

"I could not bear that. I may be stupid, I cannot help that, but I can't do anything to make people think it. Do you see what I am saying? If we are going to get married it has to be done properly. The same as our house; we had to have one of the best in the village, which is why I did not like your idea to make it fit in. That is the last thing I want! I want to stand out. I want people to say: 'That Lek has done well for herself, hasn't she?'

"You don't like to stand out from the crowd, I know that and respect it, but I have to stand out. I have always stood out and it is not only too late for me to change now, but I cannot change because of my position in the village. I know it is not easy for you, but please trust me. It is the only way that we can do this.

"I will try to keep costs down, but the figures I gave you yesterday are not excessive. I must have something to prove how well-off you are and what you think of me – that is the gold. We must also give my mother face; that is the cash. Traditionally, she would spend half on a party and keep half. My mother has offered you all the money back, but you have to pay for the party. You cannot get fairer than that. Really… It is not as if the gold is going anywhere, is it? It is still ours, but I will wear it on special occasions to prove, well, to prove what I said before.

"Do you feel better about it now?"

"Yes, but in our country, the man is paid, although that tradition has died out."

"Well, I am sorry about that, but you chose to come and live in Thailand and this is the way we do things here. It's up to you, but please tell me soon what you want to do. I would die if I had to cancel everything once I have set the ball rolling."

"I'm sorry, Lek. You know me, I speak as I'm thinking. I should think first and then speak. You go ahead and I'll get the money. Let's eat and then you can start organising with your Mum and friends."

"OK, thanks, my dear. Loy Krathong is on the 16th of November and we can get married on the 20th. You get the money here by then and think about who you want to invite. I will do everything else. I want to go to Phichai today to order the invitations and look for things for me. Do you mind?."

"No, you do what you have to. I'll just get on as usual."

"Thank you, I'll bring you some food back later in the afternoon. How about roast chicken and a big salad?"

"Yes, that'll be great. See you later. Good luck." Craig went back inside to start work.

As Lek cleared away the breakfast things she was making a mental to-do list. Her memory was pretty good, but a task of the magnitude of organizing a wedding called for a notepad. When she was done, she walked to Nong's and bought an exercise book. Then she went to her mother's.

"Good morning, Mum, how are you today? I'm getting married! On the 20th of next month. That is four days after Loy Krathong. Do you have time to help me make a list of things I have to do?"

"Oh, how lovely! Congratulations! Sure, let's sit down. Did Craig agree the sin sod? Good. Did you tell him he can have all the cash back after the ceremony?"

Lek took out her notebook and pen.

"So, we need caterers and a stage with a disco and dancing girls. That's two things. And a hairstylist to do you and me – I know just the one, a friend of mine, if he's got the time – he's a professional make-up artist at Tiffany's in Pattaya. Then what?"

"Are you having monks? If you are you'll have to book them and seating, crockery, pots, tables and shelters from the Wat. Karaoke for the night before. Uh, food and drink..."

"Wedding favours, a cake, a wedding arch...."

"Security for the gates... stewards, fans, er... How many are coming?"

"I was going to ask the caterers for an idea of how many tables we can fit in the garden."

"Invitations... garden lighting … cloths, paper towels, serviettes, a few speakers to say something on your behalf, say, the mayor and a few of your friends...."

"OK, that'll do for now. I'll ask Craig about the monks and I'm going into Phichai this afternoon to look at clothes and gold and I'll order the cards at the same time. I'll ask that caterer by the bridge to pop round to measure up and leave a menu price list. Thanks , Mum, if you think of anything else, write it down. See you later, I'm meeting my friend, Su, she's coming with me."

Lek walked to Su's house to get a lift into Phichai. They first stopped off at the printers, where they looked at popular wedding invitations. Lek chose the one she liked the most and then customized it. She also had to give names and dates. She didn't know exactly how many to order but she guessed that a hundred and fifty would cover it.

Next came the caterer's. She wanted Craig's input here out of politeness, so she asked them to visit the house to assess the optimum number of guests and she took a price list of courses. She promised to give them a menu, if they came around the next day. Although Lek just loved spending money, the exciting part was last on the list: clothes and gold. They looked at the bracelets and necklaces in all three gold shops, but were not really enamoured of any of them so Lek placed a tentative order to be confirmed later for a five Baht bracelet and matching five Baht necklace from a catalogue – a total of just over five ounces of pure gold. She took the catalogue with her to check it with Craig.

Then they hit the clothes shops.

Lek didn't actually want a lot, but that wouldn't stop her looking. She was shopping for traditional Thai clothes: a sarong, a pretty blouse and gold-coloured shoes. There was plenty to choose from and Lek and Su saw them all before settling on their final selection. Not to feel left out, Su also bought a blouse for the wedding.

Lek invited Su to Ben's shop for a treat: a cup of coffee and a slice of cake. Lek was pleased to see that Ben was working herself that day, but the shop was empty.

"Hi Ben, this is my friend Su from the village. How are you today? We've been on a shopping spree... Go on ask me the occasion ..."

"Why what's she occasion?" she asked sitting down.

"I'm getting married next month! The weekend after Loy Kra-thong. You are invited and Murray and his wife. You are the first person we've invited. Isn't it great news? We've just been to the printers' and the caterers. We've looked at gold for the sin sod and we've bought some clothes. Will you come? Good. If you see Murray you can tell him, but you'll all get an invitation soon. Can I have an iced coffee, please? Su? Two and two slices of chocolate cake, please."

"Which caterer are you using?"

"Bridge Caterers."

"Ah, good choice. They are about the best around here. Who's making the cake?"

"I don't know yet."

"Good. Let me do it and I'll make you something really special, I promise. For the normal price and I'll deliver it free and help with the organization. What about the Wedding Arch? A friend of mine does a beautiful arch and I'll get a discount for you. Tell me to but out if you like. Some people like to do everything themselves. I love weddings! I just want to get involved."

"Sure you can help. Go ahead with the arch and the cake, but keep me informed on progress, please."

"What abut Loy Krathong? I'm thinking of booking a table at the council do. Murray and El are coming, do you want two seats. It's free, buy your own food and drink there and free entertainment."

"Yes, put us down for that too, we'll be in party mode by then."

"OK, we'd better get on. Don't forget to tell Murray and thanks for everything. See you soon."

"She's nice," said Su, as they were getting on the motorcycle, "She just took on a load of work for next to no money. That's a good friend to have."

When they entered the village, they called in at the Wat. Lek spoke to one of the monks:

"Last night, Ajan suggested that I get married after Loy Krathong, well I am going to take his advice and I want to book some equipment for Saturday 20th November. There will be about a hundred and fifty of us in my garden, so we will need chairs, shelters, crockery and utensils to suit and some pots and gas rings, but my mother will confirm what exactly tomorrow. Is that all right? Thank you."

Then they called in her mother's and told her how the day had unfolded.

"OK, I'll work out what you need and book it tomorrow. That Ben sounds helpful, I'm looking forward to meeting her."

"OK, Su, I think we've earned a drink. Let's go and join Craig in Nong's... Oh, shit! I've forgotten his chicken and I don't fancy cooking now. Su, will you do me one last big favour for today? I'll walk to Nong's and you go and buy a roast chicken and some sticky rice? I'll have a bottle of lao waiting for you when you get back. Thanks. Here's the money. You're a life-saver."

Lek walked around the corner to Nong's. Craig and Lek smiled at each other and she sat down.

"What a day! But we got a lot done. How have you been, my dear?"

"Lonely and hungry... most of the time, thanks, but at least you're here now. Do you want a drink?"

Oh, she thought, he's in a bad mood, he's going to love this: "Er, well, I told Su she could join us. She's been running me around all day, so, er, I'll share a ben, er, a half-bottle with her. Then we can go home. OK?"

"Do I have a choice? I only ever see you when you're asleep. Sometimes I feel like the washing machine — you load it up once a day and then leave it alone for the rest of the day till it's done your work for you..."

Su pulled up and saved a row. Lek squeezed his hand.

"You know Su, don't you? She's been helping me all day. She doesn't speak any English."

"That's no surprise, nobody does around here. Sawasdee kap, Su," he said standing up to waai, "Kapun kap chuay — thanks for helping.

Nang ni, sit here." He smiled at her – it wasn't her fault and went back to his notebook. As the two women talked as excitedly like school-friends after the summer recess, Craig took out his pen and began writing again.

He could often write two five-hundred-word articles a day sitting in Nong's. He found writing them quite easy, but was not so keen on typing them up at home. The final step was to upload them to his web sites, which were starting steadily to get more traffic, if not a lot more revenue.

Craig felt bad about criticizing Lek. He knew that there was no point in her sitting around the house all day while he was working and he also knew that the wedding would not organize itself. It was just that..., just that sometimes he felt like a greenfly or a washing-machine.

Lek was unwrapping a few parcels and laying them out.

"Here's your dinner, love: chicken, sticky rice and mangoes." She deftly peeled a mango and sliced it up with a knife that Nong brought for her, while Su dismembered the chicken.

He tried to keep from getting angry. He had told Lek a dozen times that he didn't like eating at Nong's where all the shoppers would stop to watch 'how a falang ate'. They used to stop to watch him write, but most of them had got over that novelty now, but they still seemed to be fascinated by his eating habits though, although he couldn't see any difference between his and theirs. Maybe that was the fascination; they had assumed that there would be a difference. Perhaps they wanted to see him use a knife and a fork.

He imagined that it must be how monkeys felt at feeding time in a zoo, if monkeys ever thought about it.

"All right, dear?"

"No," but he knew that he had to eat or it would go and Lek would not be cooking at this time of the evening just for him, if there was any food in the house to cook. As far as he knew there were only a few bananas left.

The thought made him smile, but he tried not to show it: quite apt really, bananas for a monkey at feeding time in a zoo.

So he ate and tried to follow the conversation and as the two ladies sensed that he was coming round, they tried to include him more by offering him morsels of food and smiling at him, which at least made him feel more like a human baby than a monkey.

Lek had been right in the warning she had given him years ago. There was nothing to do in the village but work. You had to make your own amusement and this usually meant eat, drink and sleep. It was what drove most falang back to living in Pattaya or Bangkok. They called it tedium. Craig didn't find village life tedious; he found that he was isolated. The isolation though was of his own making. There were hundreds of people who wanted to talk to him, to ask him questions, but he could not yet speak Thai well enough.

He doubted whether he ever would. He had to concentrate on making money or he would lose his visa and what good would it be to be able to speak Thai if he were not in Thailand? Thailand is the only country in the world that uses Thai – like Wales and Welsh, another difficult language. He had just told Su to 'nang ni', she had known what he had meant from the context, but 'nang' also means skin and 'ni' can mean this. So 'sit here' or 'this skin'. A Thai would never confuse them, but foreigners were hopeless with the tones that made the phrases sound totally different to a Thai.

In situations like this, where the company he was keeping were talking in a way that excluded him, Craig, usually retreated into his mind like a hermit crab into its shell. This was his solution to the isolation: to live in his head as he liked to think of it. He did a lot of living in his head in Thailand, but then he had always done it anyway: especially when his friends were talking about sport or babies. And, as a frequent traveller, he had often been in the situation where he couldn't follow the conversation in a different language.

The only difference here was that it was the permanent state of affairs. It was why he felt like a pit pony in Pattaya and couldn't stop talking. All the words were queued up in his head waiting to escape and when he met someone who could speak English properly they all poured out.

A stack overflow error caused cabin fever and the reset button was Pattaya.

"We are talking about Loy Krathong. All Thai people love Loy Krathong. Do you know about it? Craig?"

"Uh, I saw it once in Pattaya in my first year; we missed it last year, I think. I know a bit, but not much really. It's the Thai St. Valentine's Day, isn't it? Something like that?"

"Yes, Su wants me to tell you about it." He nodded and smiled at Su, who was beaming back broadly. "I'll tell you later."

Lek went back to her conversation and the food and Craig crawled back into his shell.

∞

The next morning as Craig was working, Lek came into the office with two cups of coffee.

"Craig, do you have time to talk, I want to tell you something."

He was not angry. Situations like the evening before were too common to make him angry for long and he was not the sort to bear a grudge – not for long anyway, but sudden interruptions like this were annoying. When he was working, writing or creating a web site he did it inside his head and no-one else could join him there. If he was just copying something out of his notebook, then he could talk or listen to the radio as long as it wasn't music. He usually listened to BBC Radio 4. He loved music, but could either listen to music or work, not both together.

This was a bad time for Lek to want to chat, but she was so rarely there that he had to acquiesce.

"Sure, what is it?"

"I want to tell you about Loy Krathong, so that you will appreciate it on Tuesday and you will keep it in your heart on our wedding day and always. It won' take long, but you must know." Lek sat down and put the mugs on the desk in front of them.

Lek settled herself, took a sip of coffee, looked at him and began in a theatrical manner:

"Loy Krathong takes place on the first full moon of the twelfth lunar month – November in English, which this year is next Tuesday. The time of the month ensures that the water is high because of the full moon and the time of the year ensures that the evening is cool. The tradition of Loy Krathong is very, very old. No-one knows how old. People want to say sorry and thank you to the goddess of water for using and polluting her. The word for 'river' in Thai is 'mae naam' which means 'Water Mother'.

"Anyway, the festival is old Thai - it probably started in Thailand's first capital city, Sukhothai, not far from here. Many people agree that the best place to celebrate Loy Krathong is still northern Thailand and that Chiang Mai and Sukhothai give the very best light shows in all of Thailand for this evening.

"They are good, very good, but I think that Phichai is very good too, just a little smaller and not so well-known, which is good because not many tourists come. In fact, there are local festivals all over northern Thailand. Phichai, or Fort Phichai, in the nearby Province of Uttaradit has a beautiful seven-day event to celebrate Loy Krathong.

"The krathong or 'boats' are traditionally made from a disk cut from the trunk of a banana tree, so they are about six to nine inches across and are decorated with banana leaves, flowers, candles and joss sticks.

"People often put some small money, er, coins in their krathong to increase their chances of having their wish granted before pushing them out onto the river or sea to float away. These krathong are bio-degradable, so do not hurt the 'mae naam' but some people, bad people want to sell cheap plastic krathong. This is not a good idea. It is strongly discouraged by environmentalists and traditionalists. The council in Bangkok often must remove over a million krathong from the rivers and canals. How many do you think go through to the open sea? It is shocking!

"People traditionally pushed their krathong out onto the water with a wish. It was hoped that the River Goddess, Kongkha or Ganga would be appeased and would grant the wish. Sometimes, Loy Krathong is called 'The Festival of Light' because of the hundreds of millions of candles that are lit on this evening and the flying lanterns of light launched into the sky.

"These days, Loy Krathong is still for good luck, but now more for romantic. Lovers push their two krathongs out together and hope that they stay together as the water takes them away. If they stay together, it is a sign that the couple will be happy together for the following year.

"In some parts of Thailand, especially here in the north, people launch small hot air balloons or lanterns into the night sky. These hot air balloons are about two feet in diameter and made of white paper. Some are like a pipe not round. The bottom is open and a candle or something like that is put below the opening.

"It is very hard to light the candle and heat the air in the balloon enough to get it to take off. It is very funny to watch! The light from the fire shines through the white balloon and they rise quickly into the wind. You can see them fly for miles. Some travel on high winds and some on fast wind until the fire goes out and the balloon comes down.

"Sometimes the balloon catches fire and falls to the ground from a great height in a most spectacular way. The government has tried to ban the balloons from the Loy Krathong Festival of Light. They say they are too dangerous, but not many people take any notice and tradition wins out in the end and so does love.

"What do you think – a romantic story, neh? I love Loy Krathong and I love you. I am sorry I leave you alone every day, my telak, but I cannot sit in here and do nothing all day too. The house, it is clean, neh? I am an outside girl. I am a farmer's daughter in my heart. I am not a city lady who can sit inside, drink tea and watch TV all day. I must get out. We are not the same in this way, you and me. You are happy in-side, where you not have flies and insects. I think flies and insects are a small price to pay for sunshine and beautiful flowers.

"If you want, I will try to be a better wife to you, but it may kill me and then you pay all sin sod for nothing, eh, telak?

"Oh, darling, one more thing, I need to get the money and the gold for the dowry today, tomorrow or the day after at the latest, so do you mind if I take the money and buy the gold on my own? I showed you the ones I like in the catalogue and you liked them too, didn't you? The only thing is, I will probably go with a friend so you cannot come with me... Is that all right? I promise not to go over budget. You trust me, darling, don't you?"

"See you later, I will cook something."

She laughed, kissed him and left.

"Yes. OK, you carry on. I'll be here. Or there, but nearby. Where else can I go?" he said quietly to himself and went back to work.

∞

The day of Loy Krathong itself was just like any other day, but as he sat in Nong's at seven o'clock waiting for Lek, Craig did notice a lot more vehicles on the road than usual. Presumably, they were heading for Phichai or private parties. For once, Lek was not late. She arrived on the back of a pick-up which was full of a family that were offering them a lift into Phichai.

"Hurry up! Hop on. I said that we would ride in the back so we could look at the stars, the fireworks and the fire lanterns."

He had heard a few fire crackers going off, but nothing much. There was a laser projecting into the sky like a call for Batman. He guessed that it was coming from Phichai. Lek was holding his arm tight and snuggling into him.

"No traditional Thai costume tonight then?" he joked. He had never seen Lek in traditional dress, although many girls in Pattaya did

246

wear it for this day.

"Did you want me to wear it? It is very expensive, you know? Four falang outfit for one Thai. I will wear one next year if you buy."

He had only been joking, Lek looked great as she was.

When they arrived in Phichai the streets were buzzing with people and cars. They were late by normal standards because all the parking for kilometres was already taken. They circled for fifteen minutes before they found a tiny space. The streets were absolutely full. A lot of schoolgirls were in traditional costume and make-up; it was eerie to see sixteen-year-old girls looking twice their age. Many girls giggled when they saw Craig and he wondered whether it was out of embarrassment.

The family went their way and Lek and Craig theirs. Craig had no idea where they were going, he just followed right behind in Lek's wake. Suddenly she stopped, grabbed his arm and moved off at a faster pace.

"Soom, Soom, Soom."

Lek had spotted her daughter, but Soom seemed to be pretending not to have heard her name. Lek was determined though and she grabbed her daughter by the shoulder.

"Didn't you hear me calling?"

"No, Mum, I was talking to my friends." She cringed when she saw Craig, but smiled sheepishly. Her friends were all giggling behind their hands.

"Doesn't she look nice, Craig? Quite the young lady in her traditional Thai costume, hair-do and make-up."

"I wouldn't have recognized her, but she does look great. Very pretty. Soom, you look lovely" and he wouldn't have recognised her either. She too looked twice her thirteen years and, still not being used to compliments, felt acutely embarrassed.

"I wish you hadn't. I feel stupid now."

"Did you win a prize, darling?"

"Second as a group - the six of us."

"Well done, you all look lovely, don't they, Craig?"

"They certainly do," brought another round of giggles with hands held before mouths and sent Soom to hide behind her mother from embarrassment.

"OK, see you later. You have a lift back, eh? Good. No later than eleven."

Soom agreed as she always did. She was an obedient daughter.

Lek led the way again past hundreds of stalls selling food and drink, traditional krathong, balloons and lanterns to a large public park area not far from the river. There were hundreds of tables and thousands of people. Ben's table was not far from a beer vendor and several food stalls. It was at the back, convenient for the toilets, but offered a decent view of the stage. It was a good choice and she must have been early to get it.

Murray was already sitting there with a woman that Craig presumed was his wife El. Everyone else was unknown to him so he waaied them and sat down next to Murray who was pushing a chair back for him. They shook hands and he waaied El before sitting down,

"Hi Craig, meet my wife, Pi El." El offered her hand so he shook it, smiled and sat down.

"Surely, her name is El, isn't it? Pi is only said to older people," Murray nodded. "But she is younger than me and you." He nodded again. "So why do you call her Pi El and introduce her as Pi El? It must make her feel ancient."

"Habit. I hear everyone calling her Pi El, so I picked it up. It's hard to shake off now. Here I bought this tower of beer for the table, grab a tumbler and have a drink."

Craig did as he was bid and surveyed the scene.

"So, you're getting hitched on Saturday, eh? Thanks for the invite. I'll be there. I think we both will in fact. Not sure yet, but I will be. We falang gotta stick together."

Craig smiled. The music had just started up, it was eight o'clock, and that killed all but the most intimate conversation because of the volume - even in a park. There were huge banks of speakers dotted around the edges of the field.

Lek wanted to put their krathong in the river shortly before midnight, so they had plenty of time to eat, drink and dance, although conversation was limited to talking and lip-reading. Still, there were plenty of people to look at and the music was good. The stage was too far away to get a good look at the dancing girls, but you could easily discern their general movements.

Some people went down to the dancing area immediately before the stage where you could get an extremely good eyeful – Lek, did. So did Murray, El and a few others, but Craig just sat there drank, ate and watched people. He had used to like to dance, but had lost the rhythm somehow, somewhere, some time ago.

When the speeches started at ten-thirty, Lek took Craig for a walk to see the exhibits. There was an annual Krathong competition and the winning entries were on display. Most were the size of wagon wheels and some were built up in tiers like wedding cakes. Each one must have taken many man hours to build, although none of the winners would go in the water, because they had to be on display to qualify for the not inconsiderable prize money. A double-edged sword for the winners.

Lek chose two pretty, little krathong of about eight inches in diameter. They had small waxy flowers, evergreen leaves, a few four-inch candles and a bundle of joss sticks stuck into them. They cost fifty Baht each. It was eleven thirty when they stood at a quiet spot on the river bank to launch their krathong.

"You must hold it like this in two hands before you, as if you were offering someone a gift. Then you make a wish, it can be romantic and you can close your eyes, then light the candles and incense. OK, ready, push them off gently together. Oh, look! See how they float away together?" and she took Craig's hand, "That is a good sign, a very good sign. The monk said that this would be a good week to marry and I think it will be too."

Craig instinctively bent to kiss her:

"No, not here. In the room – our room, the bedroom – not here someone will see."

They took one last look at their rafts and turned, still hand-in-hand to walk away. An older couple stood smiling before them awaiting their turn at the river bank. Craig smiled back, but Lek was blushing and could only look away, although she also had a smile on her face. When they were out of earshot, Lek said:

"Why didn't you tell me there was someone there," and punched him lightly on the shoulder.

"I didn't know either" and they both laughed out loud.

In an instant, they were half their real ages.

When they got back to the table, several people had already gone home and hundreds of others were heading away too, but their lift was waiting for them. They decided to buy another three-litre tower of beer, because they hadn't made a contribution yet, and wait for the traffic to die down. Their driver took a glass, although he looked as if he shouldn't drink any more already, although that could probably have been said about most men in Phichai that night, including the police.

"That was a lovely evening, Ben, thanks for inviting us. Nice to see you again Murray; lovely to meet you at last, El."

"This is just a warm-up for your wedding. It's going to be a hellova week!"

They all clinked glasses, drank up and reluctantly went home.

∞

Over the following two days, the Wednesday and the Thursday, Craig and Lek could not have led more separate and different lives, if they had been strangers. Lek was up at five or five thirty, Craig at seven or eight. Lek ate on the hoof, whereas Craig was brought food by Lek's mother when she came to feed the dogs. Lek got home at eight thirty to nine, showered and went straight to bed; Craig worked until midnight or later with two hours alone in Nong's for a rest and a few beers.

Craig knew that Lek was doing what she had to and he knew that he couldn't help, so he just stood aside and let her get on with it.

Lek knew that Craig didn't know chalk from cheese in these matters and forgave him for it. She had plenty of helpers anyway, although it would have been nice, she thought, if he had shown some more interest, but she knew it was not his way.

He was just as nervous as she was, probably more so, but he could just sit there and weather the storm whereas she had to be active so that time appeared to pass more quickly. She was really looking forward to the wedding and looking nice for her friends, but the preparations were doing her head in.

They were just different types of people with different ways of coping, but at least they were both sensible enough to know it, which was a godsend in itself. In fact, they rarely argued for long, not because they didn't care, but because they were both quick to fly off the handle. However, they were both just as quick to calm down again and neither held a grudge for long.

On the Thursday evening, Lek got both the calls that she had been waiting for. Goong phoned to say that she would be arriving the following afternoon and Beou rang to say that she had two minibuses full of friends from Daddy's Hobby and that they hoped to arrive before it got dark. Lek had been worrying about those calls for days.

On the one hand she had been desperate to know that her friends could make it to her wedding, but on the other hand she didn't want to put any pressure on them by phoning first – especially Goong, who could already be in hospital for all she knew. Beou too did not lead a life that was totally her own, what with her daughters, the bar and the absenteeism her wedding was sure to cause among the staff.

It was going to be a very busy few days, but Lek knew that she still had twenty-four hours to do anything that she had forgotten. Not that there could be anything, because there were just too many people joining in. In fact, Lek had probably done less actual work than anyone but Craig, although she had worried enough for three brides.

It had got so bad sometimes that she had felt paralysed with worry.

She had woken up in the middle of the night too as if from a nightmare, but couldn't remember what had caused her to wake.

So, at seven o'clock in the evening, Lek asked Craig if they could go inside early, lock the doors, switch the mobile phones off and be alone for the last night before bedlam erupted.

"I think that we both should get an early night, Craig. There is so much to do over the following four days and we will have house guests from tomorrow night. Goong will have the spare room, but there could be any number sleeping on the floor. I don't know what arrangements people have made and I don't even know who's coming except Beou, Goong, Ayr and two minibuses full of friends. How many is that? At least twenty-four, eh?

"If the girls are from the village, they can stay with their families, but we will probably have to put a few up. You won't mind, will you, dear? What am I thinking of? No, of course you won't! You'll love it won't you – a dozen young women in their pyjamas wandering around the house? Your own harem for the weekend. Well, I'll have my eye on you, that's all I can say and it still won't be too late for the carving knife.

"OK, now that we are inside, I want to do something. One last job – no not that! We can do that any time. Look in the bottom draw of your desk. Yes, a bottle of Bailey's and two small glasses. I'll pour, and I want you to look online for a nice hotel for us to stay in next week - our honeymoon. Let's stay on the waterfront overlooking the beach. What do you think?"

"I think that's a great idea. Cheers, my dear, and so was the Bailey's." They interlinked arms and drank from each other's glass. The sweet, warm, liqueur oozed down their throats pleasantly.

Lek topped their glasses up as a hotel comparison web site came on screen. She sat on Craig's lap and they scrolled through the better hotels in Pattaya. After forty minutes they had booked a hotel they both liked and drunk a third of the bottle of liqueur.

"OK, darling. Now it's time for a shower. Together? Like we used too? And then we'll take this bottle to bed. What do you think?"

It sounded just what the doctor ordered to Craig.
He was looking forward to the harem too.

253

21 THE STAG NIGHT

Lek and Craig woke up bright and early, as they always did, but there was a buzz of excitement in the air. At six o'clock in the morning, there was already music drifting in from somewhere, probably Lek's mother's house, and there had been for about an hour. They both knew what it was - it was the typical call to action for the women in the village who wanted to help prepare the food for the pre-wedding party – the hen night, although, since Craig had no family nearby with which to have a stag night, they would have a combined do.

They both also knew that Lek ought by rights to be with the women. She looked at him with a mock-sad face.

Craig nodded gravely.

"Go on then, I suppose you must, if you must."

Lek kissed him on the forehead and leaped out of bed. It was obvious that she could not wait to get involved. She was showered, dressed and gone within ten minutes.

Craig was pretty used to this sort of behaviour by now, although there was obviously ample cause to call this a special, even extraordinary, exception. He flicked the TV on to watch the news for a while before getting up. There was no rush for him, because men were virtually excluded from this preparatory fun.

When Craig did get up, he put his coffee on and awoke his computer. The confirmation slip for their hotel booking had come in over night, so he printed it off and pinned it to the fridge with a magnet so that Lek would see it.

One less thing for her to worry about, he thought. He hadn't been much help thus far, so it was the least he could do. Then he took his coffee into the office, read his email and listened to the laughter of the ladies in the garden in Mum's house.

He thought about making an effort to give Lek a reason to be proud of him, but being without transport in a village with only a few shops, all of which only sold basic food and drink, made it very difficult. He came up with three things though. He could bake a cake, iron his own trousers and shirt, and he could get a haircut.

It sounded pretty pathetic, but these days he never wore a shirt that needed ironing or long trousers and Soom usually did the ironing anyway as part of her training. She was also learning to cook and tend the garden. The haircut was a new phenomenon too, because a neighbour had just set up a barber's of sorts. He had been there a few times and decided to go after completing the other two tasks.

Then Craig had a brainwave and emailed the hotel to ask them to put two bottles of champagne in the fridge for their arrival on Sunday 'to start their honeymoon off with a bang'. He hoped that they would take the hint and do something else too: maybe put some flowers in the room or treat Lek a bit specially.

So while Lek was out, Craig rummaged through the cupboards for ingredients and then found a recipe online to use them. The most special recipe he could find with the ingredients that he had was a 'honey cake'. That would have to do. The honey was wild, very tasty and had been collected from the woods nearby by one of the local men. There were still two bees floating in it, but the neck of the whiskey bottle was too narrow to fish them out easily. They hung in the middle of the bottle like insects in amber.

While that was baking, he ironed his shirt and trousers and hung them up in plastic bin liners, by which time the cake was done. A sweet smell wafted around the house, which made Craig promise himself to bake more often. He tried to work, but there was no enthusiasm in him for it. He sat at his desk and just idly surfed the Internet, but it was not as enjoyable as it had been the day before. He put it down to nerves, although he didn't feel nervous. It wasn't as if he would have to make a speech – there was only Murray to listen to him.

He thought again and wondered whether it was because he was the only person he knew in Thailand who wasn't involved in a party at that moment. The girls on the buses would be whooping it up and the women at Mum's were all having a great time, but the groom was not. Craig was thinking that he would have to do something about that. He decided to have a shower, get a haircut and then go for a walk around the village.

He had to admit, even to himself, that when he stayed in the village for any length of time he had a tendency to let himself go. His standards dropped. Quite a bit in fact. Like dropping off a cliff. Lek liked him with a few days growth, so he only had to shave twice a week, but he often didn't even manage that. He tried to make it a rule to shave at least every Sunday, but he too often failed miserably at that too.

Sometimes it was the cause of an argument.

Not that it ought to have been. Shaving once or twice a week was nothing compared with what Lek put herself through to look good for him. Well, for both of them and he actually enjoyed going to this barber. Craig had a ritual, albeit a small one: before going to the barber's for a shave and a haircut, he would shower, don a collarless shirt and put a few mints in his pocket, real British sweets if he could get them, and then walk over the lane still damp.

The barber's name was Deo, which sounded like 'God' in Welsh, the way they say in the Valleys. Deo always seemed happy to see Craig, but then he didn't get many customers, so he was probably always happy to see anyone walk up his path.

Deo cut hair in a corner of his living room, which was a stand-alone building to the side of the sleeping quarters. It had two full walls to the sides, but the front and rear walls had a large gap in them, so that the family's motorbikes could be wheeled through to the safety of the backyard. There were no doors though. It was like a short hangar.

Often the family would be there too, eating or watching TV while Deo was cutting hair. The area assigned as a barber's had mirrors all over two walls and a dressing table in front of the chair. The table held all Deo's tools of the trade and also had a large mirror attached to it.

The effect was like being in a completely mirrored cul-de-sac. There were even mirrors on the ceiling like a French brothel in the films. The chair was a very comfortable, authentic barber's chair located in the middle of all these mirrors. It left just enough room for Deo to dance around its occupant. In fact, it would not have looked out of place in a museum, if it had been re-upholstered.

However, it had not been secured to the floor, so it wobbled precariously, especially when Deo threw it back to carry out a shave more easily. He laughed out loud at the consternation on his customer's face every time he did it. This was when Craig would get out a sweet and offer everyone else one too.

The haircut was very good though - very thorough, fairly quick and cost twenty-five Baht. He was the only barber that Craig had used, anywhere in the world, after whom everyone said that it is a good cut. No matter where else he'd been, someone wouldn't like it, but never with Deo.

A shave took a lot longer - maybe forty minutes. It started with the electric clippers. When done, he would ceremoniously insert a new Wilkinson Sword blade into his ancient safety razor and inspect it thoroughly and theatrically. Next he would spray distilled water onto a wisp of cotton wool and stroke that over a large bar of medicated soap. This he used to wet small areas of skin prior to scraping them with the razor.

Every bit of bare skin above the shoulders got that treatment: neck, nose, forehead, ears, as well as the more usual parts. He always made as if to shave the chest too, especially if it was hairy, like Craig's.

It was another of his regular jokes, which always make his wife and kids roar with laughter.

For the final treatment, Deo would take another wisp of cotton wool and put it in a tin of medicated talcum powder. This he closed and shook as if making a cocktail; then he retrieved the cotton wool and painted every square inch of bare skin white.

Finally, he would shave the talc off. This was his way of ensuring that he hadn't missed anything, because as everyone knew, and Deo readily admitted, his eyesight wasn't all that it used to be.

A shave at the village barber shop cost twenty Baht.

It was a real, old-time experience and was another thing that Craig vowed to do more often. He wondered whether Lek had invited him to the wedding. He hoped so, he liked old Deo.

When Craig left the shop, he gave any remaining sweets to Deo to share out or eat himself and headed up onto the main road that ran through the village. As he passed Nong's, Craig was tempted to have a beer, but he decided to keep that for the last leg before going home. He was on his stag party alone, but it didn't bother him much, because he was used to it now.

Halfway up the road, a taxi passed him going in the opposite direction. He saw Goong waving at him through the back window and he knew that Lek would soon discover he had gone walk-about. Not that that mattered, but he couldn't seem to be able to do anything without Lek finding out in minutes, whereas he had no idea where she was or what she was doing most of the time. If it wasn't for the fact that he trusted her, he would have gone mad by now.

Craig stopped at the second shop in the village, asked if he could sit down and drink a beer and took out his notebook and pen to write something. It had become second nature now to always have writing material and or the laptop with him at all times. He had never been frightened of writing and he had always written letters, but this was something different. A new approach to writing was getting a grip on him and he liked it. He wondered whether it was the feeling that reporters or authors had towards their work.

An hour later, Craig moved on down to Nong's shop, his stag pub-crawl over, but his stag night proper still to come. At least he wouldn't have far to go home from Nong's and it felt like a home-from-home anyway.

Lek was having a great time when Goong's taxi pulled up, but she noticed that her friend was a little slower than usual, that she was not her normal self. Lek had seen her with many a hangover, but none as bad as this, if it were drink-related, which she doubted. Narcotics, pain-killers probably. Lek took her bag and ushered her to a chair. Everybody stopped and stared which made Goong feel even more self-conscious.

"Goong's got a hangover again," said Lek to everyone and no-one. "Trust her to start the hen party early, eh? But, we've been having fun too, haven't we girls? Since six o'clock this morning! Can I get you anything Goong or will you wait ten minutes and then I'll take you to your room?."

"Oh, I'll wait. I'll have a drink when I've unpacked and had a shower. There's plenty of time. It's still early."

Lek didn't wait the full ten minutes before helping her friend over to their house.

"Ah, it's locked. Hang on a sec.."

"I just saw Craig. He was walking up towards the end of the village."

"Bored, nervous or jealous, I should think. He doesn't know anyone around here. Well, there is only one, Murray, as far as we know, and he lives a long way away, but he'll be company for Craig tomorrow. I can't remember whether he's coming tonight or not. My brain's like a sieve at the moment. How are you?"

"Really tired," she answered as they entered the house. "I think I'll lie down and have that shower later. You go back and enjoy yourself. What a lovely smell. Have you been baking?"

"No, it must have been Craig. He's got hidden talents, that man. The only problem is that he hides them too well. Anyway, OK, Ill go back, but can I get you anything first? I've put towels out for you and the fridge is full and... well, you know where everything is, just help yourself. See you soon if you're sure you're all right."

"Yes, I'm sure. Go on. Let me get some sleep, I'll be fine in an hour. Travelling is not as much fun as it used to be. It sort of takes it out of me now.... Makes me feel thirty years older."

Goong flopped on the bed and closed her eyes, a signal that she wanted to be left in peace. Lek said goodbye, closed the door and returned to the kitchen party.

Goong loved her friend very much, but at that precise moment all she wanted to do was rest. Even talking was too much effort. She quickly fell asleep, hoping that she would be well enough to last the weekend without giving her friends much cause for concern. She knew that they weren't stupid and that she would have to perk up so that they didn't ask too many embarrassing questions. If they did, she would parry them.

"Whoosh, Goong was glad to sit down. It must have been some journey or some party last night! You never know with her, she's a real party girl," said Lek when she got back, but nobody said anything. Someone was telling a funny story about her husband and a snake.

By six o'clock, most of the food had been cut, chopped or pummelled as required and just needed to be cooked when needed. There were bowls of different vegetables like soft banana tree core, pumpkin, Thai carrot, fresh leaves, beans, onions and garlic, herbs, noodles, chopped chicken and sliced pork and the bowls were huge. There were smaller bowls of 'naam pik', a red-hot, home-made chilli sauce, satay sauce and ginger sauce all made with a pestle and mortar the traditional way..

While the ladies were peeling and chopping, they drank very little. It was just too dangerous when wielding razor-sharp butchers knives, meat cleavers and axes, but that didn't stop them eating. Somebody was cooking something to be shared by their team all the time. Sometimes, a lady would leave the team cutting up chickens to join those peeling banana trees. There was a fluid, party atmosphere which would have had to involve lots more alcohol if men were allowed to take part.

As the ladies drifted off home to take care of their own families who would be returning from work and school, they all promised to come back later. Then the buses arrived and twenty-eight laughing hyenas stumbled out of them. It was all any of them could do, Lek included, to stop themselves from crying. Lek knew them all: some had been in Daddy's Hobby when she had been there and others were village girls that had gone down to Pattaya later for one reason or another, which usually meant money in the end.

None of them was wearing the short skirts, low tops and make-up associated with Pattaya bar girls, they were back home again and for a few days at least, they would revert to the girls that their families recognised from their school days. Except for the alcohol that is and the occasional cigarette. About a quarter of the girls were carrying an open bottle of lao and some were smoking.

Ayr and Beou got out last accompanied by a young man in his mid-twenties. Lek made her way over to them and hugged the women. She greeted the man in Thai, but he looked confused.

"Jaseem doesn't speak Thai. He's from India. You'll have to speak to him in English. Or Indian," giggled Beou a little drunk. "Jaseem this is my cousin Lek. She is getting married tomorrow and this is her mother's house. It is her party. Or our party, it's everyone's party! So, just join in and have a good time. Put your bag over there with the others, you can take it to my mother's house later. Lek, where is that future husband of yours?"

"He's right behind you. He must have seen the buses arriving."

There was a spontaneous rush of women towards Craig like water through an opening lock gate. He was being ravaged like a rock star by groupies and he was loving it. They squeezed him, kissed him, stroked him and patted him. Some called him Mr. Craig, some just Craig and others called him 'Papa'.

He wasn't keen on that at all since he had never been called 'Daddy' by anyone before, but he knew that it was a term of endearment. Maybe more like 'Pop' than 'Daddy'. He knew what to do: keep his hands to himself, not kiss back and not get the wrong idea. They were greeting him like a very special, older uncle, like children almost.

Lek broke it up after a few minutes, not out of jealousy, she really didn't mind because she trusted her friends, but she wanted to get on.

"Craig, this is Jaseem. He is from India and speaks English. Why don't you take him to Nong's and have a chat while we finish off here?"

"Hi Jaseem, how are you doing? Where are you from?"

Jaseem bowed slightly and waaied. It is very nice to meet you, Lek and you, Craig. Thank you for allowing our mutual friends to invite me to your wedding celebrations."

"Oh, it's our pleasure, isn't it, Craig? Any friend of my cousin Beou is a friend of ours. You came up from Pattaya with the girls, didn't you?"

"Yes, I just finished university in Kannur. My parents saved money for a present for me if I passed, which I did, so I chose a holiday in Thailand. I met your cousin in Pattaya. She was very kind to me. I did not know anyone there. I was telling Beou that I wanted to see more of Thailand and one day Beou said: 'Do you trust me? I have just the thing if you want to see more of Thailand'. Well, of course I trusted her and so here I am."

"Kannur, Kannur? Where is that exactly, Jaseem? India, but where precisely?"

"Yes, Kannur is a university city on the south-west coast - probably a little further south than Bangkok, if you see what I mean. It is very beautiful and has lovely beaches Like where I come from Muzhappil-angad Drive-in Beach.

"Anyway, we can talk again. I know you must be busy. I only wanted to say thank you. Sometimes I act like a tourist guide for Kannur, but I do love it so."

"Don't worry about it," said Craig, "I love Wales too. We'll compare notes later. Let's go for a drink and let the girls sort themselves out. See you later, Lek. Beou."

"There are many Muslims in Kerala who do not drink, but I am a Hindu, so I will take you up on your kind offer." Jaseem waited politely for Craig to take the lead and didn't speak again until they were seated five minutes later.

"What can I get you, Jaseem? A Chang? OK. So, tell me more about Kannur."

They clinked bottles and Jaseem continued as if giving a lecture: "Kannur is a seaside city in the northern part of Kerala State, which is in south-western India. It is one of the ten best cities in India to live according to economics research companies, based on housing, earnings and investments. But according to my heart, it is the very best place to live.

"Apart from its idyllic beaches and greenery, Kannur is an important industrial centre. Did you know that thirteen percent of the population are employed overseas? Well, no, I don't suppose you do. Anyway, experts forecast that emigration from North Kerala is bound to increase in the coming years and I want to be one of them, for a while in my youth, before I marry.

"My family comes from an area known as Muzhappilangad Drive-in Beach. It is located between Kannur and Thalassery. Muzhappilangad Drive-in Beach is the largest Drive-In Beach in Asia It is very beautiful in April. I hear that Thailand has Songkhran then, well we have The Beach Festival, which is celebrated in the month of April too. It is one of the most important tourist attraction in the district of Kannur. The youth try many driving stunts in cars like drifting and wheeling in bikes as this is a paradise for driving along the shore."

"Sounds lovely. Idyllic."

Jaseem had the look of a saint in ecstasy on his face as he let favourite images of home drift past his mind's eye. They chatted for another hour, exchanging pleasantries, discussing each other's land and their current mutual country of Thailand. Craig called up a second and final small Chang and two sachets of Koh Yoh anti-mosquito cream for them.

Small groups of women in Indian file strolled past them from time to time. Some of the bolder women smiled and gave a discreet wave.

Craig was trying to think of a suitable joke.

"Craig, all these people, are they going to your mother-in-law's house?"

"Yes, well, I'm not sure, I think so, but there will be a fixed number tomorrow of a hundred and twenty invited guests with tickets. Don't worry, there'll be room for you too."

"I do hope I haven't put anyone out. I didn't really think. I was invited by Beou and I just said 'yes'."

"Honestly, don't worry about it! What's one more mouth? I would have done the same. In fact, I have, several times. Go with the flow, I say, because you never know when you'll get the chance again. Come on, drink up, let's go and join the others. You can take it with you. Nong won't mind. It's the same price to drink here or take it away."

With that Craig told Nong that they would pay the next day and they went back to Lek and the others.

"How much is my bill, Craig? How much do I owe you?"

"I said we'd pay tomorrow, so don't worry. It is very easy-going here in the village."

They walked back to Mum's house but there was no longer much noise coming from there – voices rather than music. It was not what either of them had expected. When they turned the corner, they saw Lek, Beou and a dozen or so other women.

"Hello, what's going on here? I thought you were having a hen night? Where are Goong and Ayr?"

"Mmm, maybe I didn't understand what you meant exactly by 'hen party'. We have been having a party since six o'clock this morning and now it's eight o'clock in the evening. That's a long party or not? We have to get up again at five in the morning to get ready for the wedding. It is all right for you, you don't have to. Goong and Ayr are very tired. They have been working and travelling. Goong is asleep in our small bedroom and Ayr is with her family.

"We will sit here and talk, drink a little and eat a little, but only for an hour or so then bed for seven or eight hours. You don't want us all to look like old witches, do you? We need more energy for the morning."

"You're right, Lek, I didn't realise or didn't think I suppose. It's not a problem, but if you don't mind Jaseem and I will do one more lap of the village and come back at about nine-thirty. Are you up for that Jaseem or are you tired too?"

"I am starting to get tired too, but I can do a round of the village. I haven't seen it yet."

"OK, you two go off, but you will be lucky to find much to do. I know it's early, but don't forget that Jaseem is sleeping at Beou's and we have eight girls sleeping on our floor. I don't want you falling over them when you come in. You can't come in late. Not tonight. If you want to drink more, you can sit in the garden, in the sala, then you have not far to fall, neh? If you shout 'help' maybe a girl will come help you if I don't hear."

They set off, but in his heart, Craig knew that Lek was right, There would be nothing to do at this hour, but he didn't want to go to bed yet and he didn't want to sit with Lek either. It was as if she didn't want him there as well which may have been more than half true. By tradition, he should have had his own party; it was just that their relationship wasn't traditional. Neither Welsh, British, European, Thai nor Asian.

He thought about calling in on his future brothers-in-law, but they couldn't speak English and would probably be going to bed soon anyway, so he led Jaseem back up onto the road which would take them around the village, although his heart was no longer in it.

"So tell me, Jaseem, do you have any brothers or sisters?"

"One sister, Rajesh. She is two years younger than I. She wanted to come with me, but well..., you know. I wanted to be able to do what I wanted without sis looking over my shoulder."

Jaseem sensed Craig's detachment so he stopped talking for a while.

"Is everything all right, Craig? You seem..., I don't know, depressed. Is that the right word?"

"Maybe a little strong, but in that vein. I have never been married before and, well I thought that it would be more exciting than this when I did marry. No offence. If you weren't here, I'd be walking about alone."

"Perhaps, your expectations and not reality are the cause of your sadness, my friend. Did you want to be the centre of the attention of dozens of people? Would that have made you happier?"

Craig knew that it would not have.

They walked on in silence, Jaseem too polite to push the point and Craig knowing that he was right, but wondering what he had been expecting and why."

When they got back to Lek's mother's house, the party was ready to split up, so Beou took Jaseem back to her mother's house to sleep in a spare room and Lek and Craig went to their home to pick their way carefully through the mass of bodies that were sleeping on their floor. It would be the only night that Craig remembered Lek not showering before she went to bed, but she didn't want to disturb their house guests.

267

22 THE VILLAGE WEDDING

Although neither Craig nor Lek had slept well, the music seemed to start not long after they had gone to bed. It was five o'clock already, so Lek got out of bed quite cheerfully and tip-toed into hall-cum-living room, where some of the supine girls looked as if they were going to get up while a few others had covered their heads in a vain effort to block out the call to action. Nobody was obliged to help, it was supposed to be a happy holiday, so Lek went into the shower and left them to it.

The music was deafening even under the shower, but then the speakers were only thirty metres away and they were meant to be heard all over the village. No-one would complain about music like this if it were for a special occasion, because everybody did it and being farmers they were all up at five o'clock anyway.

She didn't spend long in the shower, because she knew that she would have another one in four hours time. Then she dressed and went to her mother's house, passing a group of girls taking their first cigarette of the day in the sala still wearing their nighties.

"Morning, sisters, in Mum's house for breakfast when you're ready. Help yourself to anything you want. See you soon."

It was no good. Craig tried to sleep on but there was too much going on in his head and outside it, so he got up, dressed and left the bedroom.

There were girls in pyjamas and girls in nighties everywhere and not just the ones who had slept there. Others had come to visit their friends. Some were laughing, some were hung-over and some were still half asleep. He felt like a janitor in a girls' dormitory.

It should have been heaven, but in truth, Craig didn't know where

to look or how to stop staring. They, however, seemed completely oblivious to his predicament. Craig put the coffee on quickly and retreated
into his office.

Presumably a lot of the helpers had arrived, because they turned
the music down to just loud. Again, he was having problems working.
He opened his email, but the computer didn't have much to tell him.
His British friends and family would probably email him in seven hours
time or even more due to the time difference, but it would all be over
by then.

He could hear the shower being used from time to time so he knew
that the girls were getting up. Nid brought him a cup of coffee:

"Here, Crai', I bring you coffee. You sleep well?"

He turned to look at her. She was wearing a very short teddy outfit.
It wasn't see-through, but it didn't hide much either.

"Great, Nid..."

"You li'? I buy special to come here. I sleep with nothing in Pattaya." She did a twirl.

"I meant, great, thanks for the coffee, but yes, now you come to
mention it, your erm, er... nightdress is very nice. It suits you."

"Thank you, Crai', I li' it too," she moved from behind to in front
of him. "Very sexy, no?"

"Yes, it's very nice."

"I mus' take it off now... Go ab naam, er... go shower. See you later.
You want more coffee later?"

"Yes, please, that would be lovely."

He turned to watch her walk out the door, he couldn't stop himself
and he saw her see him do so in the smoked glass of the sliding door.
She smiled and waved with a wiggle of the fingers on one hand also re-
flected in the glass.

By seven o'clock there were only two girls left in the house, but a
group of village elders arrived to transform the room, to make it suitable for a wedding and they quickly dressed and left more than a little

embarrassed to be caught not taking part in their hosts' wedding preparations.

The men set about preparing the living room for the wedding ceremony which meant that the walls and windows had to be covered with orange sheets so that the area where the ceremony was to be held was completely orange with no distracting widows to look out of. They dotted cushions about for those who needed them. They also set up a public address system so that the people in the garden could follow the service.

With the men came the alcohol and they drank small tots or lao khao out of a communal glass as they worked. When they had finished in the house, they moved into the garden trailing leads to plug into external speakers

Time was moving even faster now and Craig had no idea of the timeline. Nobody had told him what to do or when it had to be done by and he was starting to become more than a little concerned. He felt arms around his neck and he was relieved that Lek had come to put him at ease. He patted the hands that were patting his chest.

"Hello, darling, what's happening?"

"Nothing, darling, I've just come to say hello..."

It wasn't Lek, it was Ayr.

"Ha, that surprised you didn't it? I didn't see much of you yesterday and I want to see Goong, but I see you first. I can go say hello Goong, all right?"

"Yeah, sure, you carry on. I thought everyone had gone already, but if she's still here, she'll be in that room there. Nice to see you again. We don't see much of you now. We'll have to have a long chat later."

"Yes, I like that too. I think Lek come soon, she must change and do make up. You know?"

"OK, see you later." He didn't know. He didn't know anything, but he could have guessed that Lek would have to get ready, unless she was getting married in a T-shirt and jeans.

But, Ayr was right, because Lek was hot on her heels. She went into the small bedroom first but came out five minutes later.

"OK, I need your office, so you must go outside."

She looked very serious, liked a woman on a mission and not to be trifled with.

"Yes, OK, love. Err, what's happening?"

"We are getting married in two hours time! You forget?"

"No, I not forget, but I didn't know when..."

"You can't see people get up go outside? Can't see men put sheets up on the walls? Can' see thirty people in the garden and fifty more at Mum's."

He hadn't noticed the people in the garden and thought that he could not reasonably be expected to see people in her mother's house behind two brick walls, but he judged that this was not a good time to point that out. Lek was physically helping him out of his chair.

"Come on, go out. I want to have a shower get dressed and then man from Tiffany's come to do my make-up, but first he must put all his things out on a table. We do here and he come in five minutes. Please, Craig, go now. Go outside have a beer or two and in one hour, you have a shower, shave and get dressed. Monks come at ten o'clock."

He switched his computer off and closed the lid. Lek draped a towel over all his things, presumably to keep talc, hair spray and make-up off them, he thought, but Lek didn't explain. He left, a minute or two before Lek exploded. He couldn't help thinking that her English had deteriorated over night.

He put a normal, collarless shirt on, took a beer from the fridge and went outside to wait for an hour. Meanwhile, Lek showered and dressed in her wedding clothes with the help of Goong and Ayr. Lek was quite tense, but she gradually calmed down with the help of her closest friends.

"You chose traditional Thai, not a Western-style, white wedding dress. I like that. Either would have suited you, but I think that traditional Thai is better in the village. White would show the dust too much. It would look shabby after a few hours and there's nothing you can do about it. As we all know, dust is a fact of village life."

"Well, I chose it because I liked it, but also because you can only wear a Western wedding dress once, can't you? Once per marriage, anyway, but I can wear these clothes to any formal do and they will always remind me of today, my husband and my friends. That way I get to relive today a few times a year."

Goong kissed her: "What a lovely thing to say. The best of luck, my darling Big Sister" and there were six wet eyes.

There was a tap on the door:

"Hello, girls, are we decent? Is there room for a little one?" Dow held the door open,

"Ooh, Lek, you do look lovely! Nice enough to eat. If I was that way inclined, I'd marry you myself. Are you ready for me? 'Cause I'm ready for you, sister. Ready, willing and able. Are you done dressing?"

It was hard to get a word in edgeways with Dow. He was one of the top make-up artists at Tiffany's the top lady boy review nightclub in Pattaya. Lek had known him for decades. He actually came from Baan Suay, but had moved out of the village even before Lek working first in Phuket, before moving to Pattaya. The profession suited him perfectly: he got to meet the prettiest boys in the world and rarely got interrupted while talking, because his clients had to keep rigidly still while he was painting a face on.

His time cost three thousand Baht an hour to private clients, but he had been driven up in his car by a friend to donate his services as a wedding present to his friend Lek.

Lek sat on the swivel chair that Dow had brought with him and Dow draped a huge sheet over her head like a tent with a hole in the top. Later it could be unzipped and removed from the side. Then he put two towels around her neck: one from the front and one from the back.

Lek's hair was still wet from the shower so she was in the exact state that Dow had told her to be in, in order to be ready for him to work his magic. Goong and Ayr sat on the floor to watch the show with a bottle of beer and one glass between them. None of them knew anyone personally that earned more than Dow – his hourly rate was the same as that of a Pattaya bar girl's salary for a month and a bar girl earned fifty percent more than a shop girl. He was a mega star to them and he chose the Thai word for star as his nickname – Dow.

Nobody doubted that he deserved the name. He knew and worked for the rich and famous and if you didn't treat him right he wouldn't come back again. Lek mused that she was probably the only woman in the province, with the exception of Dow's mother, who had received such five star treatment at the hands of Dow.

Outside in the garden, people were starting to turn up. Most nodded at Craig, but were too shy to approach him and that suited him too. Or maybe it was his aura that kept them away. Or perhaps it was sympathy for a formerly free man that had succumbed to marriage. Craig was trying to stay light-hearted but he could feel himself becoming serious. He didn't know whether that was normal or not – not many of his friends had ever married and he didn't usually attend weddings outside his family anyway.

He was on his own again with no-one to ask. Murray would know, but he was nearly twenty years older than Craig – from a different generation maybe with different ideas. Maybe being Canadian made him different from Craig anyway. Jaseem would certainly have a different outlook being Hindu, Indian and Asian or were all men much alike wherever they came from? He didn't have much time to work it out right now, but it kept him occupied.

The dress code at formal events for men is log trousers, collar shirt and sandals and women may wear traditional Thai village or modern clothes and so was it here. It was the first time that he had seen most of the guests dressed formally and he knew that more than a few had had to borrow shirts. He knew because he recognised them. Lek had lent three of his shirts to friends who couldn't afford to buy one. He had told Lek to tell them afterwards that they could keep the shirts as a thank-you for attending their wedding. Wedding favours of sorts.

At nine o'clock precisely, Craig finished the last sip of his beer and went inside to get ready. He wanted to look in on Lek but was frightened to in case she would think it bad luck, but he caught a glimpse of her with Dow's hands hovering over her face, paint brush in one hand and a tissue in the other. Lek looked extremely serious, but Goong and Ayr seemed happy enough. He supposed that Lek was just trying to keep a straight face for Dow to work on.

Lek was doing precisely that, but in her mind she was running through all the tasks that needed to have been done before ten o'clock so that the event would run smoothly. She didn't want anything to go wrong in front of the monks. Afterwards was not so bad but definitely not while they were there. Once in a while, she would give a good impression of a ventriloquist and either Goong or Ayr would phone the relevant person, usually either Lek's mother or Beou, for assurances that all was as it should be.

The girls were starting to come back now. Some wanted a shower and some just wanted to get changed into suitable wedding attire. He could hear two girls in the shower together through the en-suite door between the bedroom and the bathroom. There were at least two in there laughing and joking, but then there wasn't much time left now and there was nowhere to change but Goong's tiny room or the large bathroom.

Craig had laid his things out and was drying himself off when the door to the bathroom opened and he stood naked before three naked women. They looked at him and he looked at them for a few moments, before Nid said: "You too big… you must lose some weight" and closed the door. He heard them giggling on the other side. He got dressed quickly and went outside with another beer from the fridge in his hand.

When the girls known as the 'Three N's', Nid, Noi and Nok came out into the garden, Nid made straight for him.

"I am sorry about that Papa, but is no problem, neh? I ask Lek if we can change in her bedroom and she say OK. We don' know you in there. Ooh, ooh or maybe you wait for us, eh? Maybe you are flasher and you want to show us your chang, no?"

"No, I..."

"Oh, you just want to see me and my friends with no clothes, neh? That is OK, I understand that. I like see you too. I want to say that you have a lovely, big, er, what is the name? Bedroom. You can do a good job, neh?"

"No, really, I was just..."

Nid smiled and walked back to her friends. He nodded at them and they all started giggling again.

Oh, well, no harm done, he thought and he knew there would not be a problem, even if he told Lek because it was just an accident, even though that minx Nid wanted to have her jokes about it.

At ten o'clock, Nid and her two water baby friends took Craig by the arms and walked him out of the gates. When he looked around for Lek, he saw that everyone from his garden was following him. As the passed Mum's house, Long, one of Lek's brother's put a sash around his neck and Gnat turned the music up. Craig was walking, held and urged on by the Three N's, but everyone else was dancing; people from Mum's house including Murray and Jaseem joined the procession. Many of the followers came to the front to touch him or and dance in front of him before dropping back again.

When they got to the front gates, they were barred by Lek's sister, girlfriends and mother. They did as if he were not welcome and asked questions of 'his support team'. There was a lot of laughter and Nid got quite rude touching herself and the women the other side of the gate. There was lots of laughter, the jokes seemed rude to Craig. He didn't understand any of it really, but he gathered that they were asking whether he was capable of supporting Lek and taking care of her every need. When Nid held her hands about a foot apart and pointed at him with her chin, she seemed to be saying that she could vouch for him.

When the gate was opened, Craig and the entourage were allowed in and led to the front door of the house, which was full and very hot, but there was a space for him next to Lek with a cushion and a stool. Lek looked an absolute picture. She was beautiful anyway, without trying, but with Dow's help and traditional Thai costume, she was stunning. She smiled at him hoping that he approved.

When he took his place next to her, he whispered: "You look beautiful, my darling, and I love you very much." She only gave the faintest of nods without looking at him directly.

The monks chanted and sometimes people repeated words. Then the dowry of gold and cash was displayed and everybody was invited to witness it and tie his left hand to Lek's right while they knelt together. Family and friends first.

Nobody had told him what to expect or what was going on, but he could feel the atmosphere and it was good.

Then food was brought in for the monks on nine huge trays, the same as for the house-blessing with many dishes on each. The guests watched the monks eat some of it and when they had finished, the 'left-overs' were taken away to be shared amongst the guests, also as before.

Craig was told to kiss Lek, which he did. Then he was told to kiss her again because people wanted a photo. Then again because some people hadn't been ready. Five or six times until it became obvious to Craig that this was another joke. People laughed as they saw realization dawn on his face. Lek laughed too, because she had seen and done it before.

The monks left at about eleven-thirty to return to the Wat for dinner. As soon as they had left, Craig's mother-in-law picked up the cash and ran out of the door. People exclaimed surprise with "Ooh!" and "Ahh!," but Craig sensed that it was another joke.

The master of ceremonies, a lay preacher-cum-helper, then took Lek and Craig by the arm and led them into their bedroom, where they were told to lie down. He watched for a moment and then left, closing the door behind himself. Now Craig was definitely unsure what was going on. Anyway, he thought it best to neither say nor do anything. He could see Lek's mouth moving silently. There was complete silence in the house. They were still tied together. Suddenly, the door opened and the man came back inside.

Lek had been counting down two minutes.

He led them back into the living room, where people cheered them. Then the guests got up and went outside, smiling as they passed them by. They were going out for some fresh air, some food and a drink.

When they were left alone, Lek cut the bonds between them, but the way they had been tied - around each wrist individually - they still had about fifty threads around their wrists. After a few minutes, Lek's mother came in again, gave Craig the money back and the three of them went out to join their guests for an afternoon party in the garden.

He was married and the hard part of the ceremony was over. He had already been asked whether he wanted to give a speech but he had said that it was pointless – he could tell Murray and Jaseem personally later, but in truth he was not much of a speech maker.

He found Murray and Jaseem waiting for him at the end of one of the large rows of tables under an awning at the bottom of the garden. They could not have gotten any closer to the huge loudspeakers. Murray was fairly deaf, but Jaseem would be too, if he didn't rescue him soon. Jaseem would be too polite to tell the much older Murray about the noise, especially if Murray had chosen the seats.

Craig relocated them to a position closer to the house and behind a small bush and sat down, glad that it was all over as far as he was concerned.

This was also a time when Lek could relax. She had to greet all the guests and thank them for coming, but as they were all friends and family of hers, that was not onerous. The more formal party would start at eight o'clock with invited guests only. Lek wanted to wear her wedding outfit for the evening, but she couldn't take it off without ruining her make-up and hair-do, so she had to make do with draping a towel over shoulders in order to keep her clothes free from dust and accidents.

It was lovely to be outside the house again. People laughed and joked as they ate and drank to the accompaniment of records and the roadies setting up the stage for the evening's entertainment.

By five o'clock, most people had gone home for a shower and a siesta so that they would be fit to come back for the evening do. The dancing girls and the DJ took advantage of the lull to set up their equipment and practice a few routines as before, but then it was the same troupe. The caterers set up their tables for the hundred and twenty invited guests, who would arrive between seven and eight.

∞

As the first guests started to arrive, Ayr stood at the gate with Craig to welcome them in, because Lek was having her hair retouched.

"Thanks for helping us out, Ayr, I wouldn't mind standing here alone, it is just that I don't know what people are saying to me. I know they are giving me money, but 'Kapun Kap' seems a bit lame, er, does not seem enough."

"I know, don' worry, that is why I stand here. I do what your wife must do, but she cannot because have hair fix. Just don' worry, Craig." She squeezed his arm.

There were security guards on the front and back gates to keep out those without tickets and an usherette to show people to their tables.

After an hour, the flow of arrivals had slowed considerably, so Craig left Ayr and went around to the back garden to join in. Murray, Jaseem and the family were seated at the head table. Everyone seemed to be having a good time. The eight girls on the stage danced their hearts out and so did most of the guests although it was a very hot evening. The eight female house guests and all the others up from Pattaya were dancing for all they were worth too.

Lek was thanking everyone for coming and picking up envelopes from those who had entered by the lane gate. When Lek and Craig were called to the stage, no-one could have been more shocked than

Craig.

First the mayor gave a speech, then his wife; then a few neighbours and Lek responded. Then there was some Thai and the microphone was handed to Craig. This was exactly what he hadn't wanted, but everyone was looking at him. He said something, but didn't remember what, then he saw Murray applaud, followed by Jaseem and soon after everyone was clapping.

He knew it was not real, but he did feel good and Lek felt proud too, although she was unsure of what her husband had said as well.

When they left the stage, Lek manoeuvred Craig around the tables to greet the people that she knew expected it – mostly local government officials, whom they both knew. Craig didn't have a problem with that, he liked most of them and didn't mind showing it.

When Lek deemed that Craig had done his bit, she escorted him to the table to sit by Murray and Jaseem.

"Hello, guys how are you doing?" he slurred after accepting too many shots of lao deng. "Everything peachy?" He had no idea why he had used that expression, he never had in his life before."

"Yes, certainly, Craig," said Jaseem. "It is a wonderful party – dancing girls, music and more young women than young men. You have many couples here but not many singles – very good for me."

The next day, Craig remembered hoping that Jaseem would behave himself, but there had been no worries on that score. Jaseem, Murray and all the guests danced, some more than others, but it was an active party. The caterers delivered the set meal to every table: dishes of chicken, pork, fish, vegetables and rice. Craig had wanted to put real bread on the tables too, but Lek had talked him out of it quite easily, when she pointed out that it was impossible to get in the area and that Thais would probably not eat it anyway.

Craig had reluctantly, but whole-heatedly capitulated, as he so often had to.

They did however share out the huge wedding cake that Ben had made. It was chocolate: Craig's favourite. Craig insisted on cutting his home-made cake too although there was not enough to go around more that those on the top table. Lek had tried to advise him to keep it for the next day, but he wouldn't listen.

Both English-speaking men at his wedding had been absolute rocks and Craig tried to show his appreciation, but he was finding it more and more difficult as the evening turned to night and the beers went down. Lek was not with them, she was on her own mission, but being more sociable than Craig.

"Are you guys all right?" he asked again, but staring at the girls on stage.

"Yeah, sure thing, Craig, great party. That's a good act too. Real beauties. Where do they get changed?"

"In my bedroom. You would not believe how many naked girls have been in our bedroom today. More in one day than in the last ten years of my life. What does that do to the imagination, eh?"

They both liked to see pretty, naked women, as do all men, but it was his wedding day, so somehow it sounded inappropriate. Today had meant to him that he would guarantee to do his best to take care of Lek and to make sure that, if it was within his power to do so, Lek would always have enough money to carry out her filial and maternal duties according to Thai tradition. It did not mean that he couldn't look, but it did mean that he shouldn't touch. And he was happy with that.

He hoped that Lek had a similar code, but he was pretty sure that she had had for quite a while already.

As the night progressed, Craig slowed down and other people caught him up in the drunk stakes, but the difference was that those people could go home to bed whenever they liked, whereas Lek and Craig would be the last to leave.

All of the people that Craig knew well stayed until the end, which was midnight.

When the band started to pack up, Lek tried to persuade them to play on, but they were not able to. It was a shame, but not a calamity.

Most people were going home anyway and the ones that were left were pretty tired. However, Lek and Craig had their second wind and felt that they could go on all night. Murray had to leave, because El was already asleep in the living room, which the elders had changed back into a normal room again. Some of the girls were asleep too. They had danced almost non-stop, before and after the meal.

Lek had no idea how supplies were looking, but she knew that she had thirty more bottles of beer and two of lao deng in the fridge in the house, which had been kept locked while the party was on for security.

As the band took the last planks back to their lorry, their dancing girls, back in civvies now, scooted around the garden with bin bags and picked up all the litter. It wasn't part of their job, but they said they did it as an extra, so that employers would remember them. Likewise, the caterers took away all their tables and the security staff stacked the plastic chairs to take them back to the Wat the next day.

At the end of the night, all that was left were the cooking things belonging to the Wat and most of them had already been washed, the chairs, which were stacked and the awnings. Craig fancied that it looked tidier after the party than before it had begun.

Murray and El took their leave and went home; Jaseem had already left; the girls were either in bed or going inside and the only ones left were Craig, Lek, Ayr and Beou. Just like old times in Pattaya. It felt like a staff drink after the bar had closed.

"Goong gone to bed already?"

Goong had done what most Thais do at parties when they want to leave – she had melted away without anyone noticing. It was something that had always amazed Craig. Thai people usually said 'hello' when they arrived, but rarely said 'goodbye' when they left.

"Yes, she's not well. She shouldn't be here really, but I understand that she didn't want to miss the wedding. At least she's in her own village if not in her own home. It is so sad that she doesn't get on with her family.

"She made an effort with her Dad a few weeks ago, but I don't think he knows what day it is. Neither of the brothers bothered though and they must have heard that she was around. She was here for, er, two days, I think or maybe three. Something like that. We went to the Wat and sat in Ron's, but nothing. She was quite a bit fitter then, even only a few weeks ago. A shame."

They all fell silent, so Lek went to get a cold beer for Craig and a lao deng and clean shot glass for themselves.

Nobody wanted to voice their feelings on Goong for fear of telling the others more than Goong wanted them to know, although, in fact, they all knew that she had cancer, except Craig, but Lek was the only one who had any idea how advanced it was.

They sat there for an hour, but everyone was pretty tired so they went to bed, hoping for some kind of a lie in the next morning before having to drive down to Pattaya, where they would take part in a civil marriage on Monday to have the matrimony recognised in Thai and British law.

23 THE SHIP HOTEL

It was not possible for Sunday to be a day of rest. Beou wanted to be back in Pattaya for her normal evening slot and most of the girls had said that they wanted the same, although if asked again now the answer might be different. Still, it was a journey of eight hours and there was nothing to stop them sleeping on the bus.

Lek got up at nine, which was a three-hour lie-in for her normal routine. Craig snored on and she left him there. She went for a shower, dressed and began to wake the girls.

"Come on, house-mates, get up! It's nine thirty and the buses are leaving at ten thirty. Hi-di-hi! Let's be 'aving you! Come on, get up and shower! Lively now!"

She had enjoyed having them as guests and she had enjoyed the weekend. She also hoped that she hadn't disturbed Goong. She lowered her voice:

"Come on, get a move on and be as quiet as you can, I don't want you waking up Craig. He deserves another forty winks."

They did as they were told by their matronly friend and started to pack their things away or move into the shower. Lek went outside to see what was going on. Nothing in her garden except Bpom and Bpouy looking for their breakfast which was three hours overdue, so she went to her mother's house.

"Good morning, Mum, how are you today? Did you enjoy last night?"

"Oh, yes! The ceremony was good too. Craig was funny! And the food was wonderful. I even liked the music and had a couple of dances for the first time since your dear old Dad passed away."

Lek squeezed her shoulder as she walked past. "Yes, I saw you dancing with Craig and Soom and with Murray, I think. Quite the raver! But I'm glad you had a good time. You put a lot of effort into it. It would have been nothing without you."

"Lots of people helped, dear. Su and your nice friend Ben. She did a lovely arch and cake. Ayr and Goong helped a lot too and Beou was stage-managing from the wings. Soom was washing up for hours and hours, bless her heart."

"Yes, there are a lot of people I have to thank. I couldn't get round to it all last night, so when the buses have left, I'll need to make a few phone calls. Have you seen Beou yet? The girls in our house are getting up and ready, but they may want something to eat before they go.

"Don't fret. I've got about two gallons of rice soup keeping warm. If they don't eat it, we'll have to for the next fortnight."

"OK, I'll go steer them over here and find Beou later."

She went back to the house, where two girls were dressing, one was in the shower and five were waiting in their towels.

"When you're done here, Little Sisters, take your things over to my mother's house and have some breakfast. The buses will meet you there later." She looked in on Craig. He was awake, but not getting up.

"I'll get up when I've heard the shower stop running. I'll see you in Mum's."

She nodded and closed the door tight.

Beou's mother's house was just two minutes up the road. She met her cousin outside. Jaseem was nearby and she was on the phone arranging a pick-up time for the buses.

"Is ten thirty all right? Can I rely on you? I'll have everyone there and ready to board, If you get there ten minutes earlier, I can promise you breakfast, but we leave at ten thirty on the dot, OK. We have to get back to work tonight. OK..., OK... It'll be on the table waiting for you. Thanks, see you soon.

"Hi Lek, great party.. What's it like to be married again?"

"I don't know yet, ask me again in a couple of days. Mum's laid on breakfast at her house and all my girls will meet you there. Is that all right?."

"Sure, my mother has told me about the breakfast already. That's where Jaseem and I are off now. Eh, Jaseem? Breakfast?'

He nodded sleepily.

"Come on then, we don't have a great deal of time." Beou lit a cigarette as they walked. "Back to work, eh? It's all right for some, isn't it?"

"Don't you believe it. I miss having a job and earning my own money. Don't get me wrong; I'm glad I'm here with Mum and Soom, but it would be nice to have a job too. I'm thinking of going back to school to get my high school leaving certificate. Did I tell you?."

"You may have done dear, but I don't remember at the moment. I think it's a great idea though. You go for it! Here we are! Good morning, ladies! How are we today?"

Lek wasn't sure whether that was real encouragement or not. It had sounded a bit glib. She decided to ignore it, because she knew that Beou would always support her and always be on her side. She was just stressed and hung-over. Nocturnal nicotine starvation too most likely.

Lek went over to get Craig.

Are you up yet? The buses are going, come on get a move on.

"They'll wait for us won't they? I'm nearly ready. Are the bags packed?"

"What are you talking about? Those who came on the bus are going on the bus right now. Do you want to say goodbye or not? We and Goong are going with Dow in his car. I told you all this last night. Dear me... I'll see you over there. And don't wake Goong up!"

And she left. Wow, he thought, sorry I opened my mouth. Welcome to married life, Craig, at least you escaped it for nearly forty years. That's better than most can say.

He finished dressing and strolled over to Mum's. The dog's played around him, trying to coax some food out of him in vain.

"What a beautiful sight to wake up to! Thirty beautiful ladies at breakfast!," he said.

The girls smiled or laughed; some said 'good morning' others said 'sawasdee, ka'. Craig loved it and was beaming from ear to ear.

"Hmm, you're still drunk and you can't count. Do you want any soup?"

"Yes, please, but with you, your Mum, your sister, Soom, Beou and her mother, there must be about thirty ladies here, surely."

"Mmm, eat your soup and stop talking rubbish. Bak wan - flatterer."

"Just, what is your problem, Lek? Hung-over?"

She blushed and saw some of the others looking at her unsympathetically. She decided to be conciliatory:

"Maybe. I don't mean anything, really I don't. The stress is off, you know... er, everything is fine." Lek could not bring herself to apologise. "I'll go and see if Goong wants to say goodbye too," but she had no intention of asking Goong anything, she just wanted to have a few minutes to herself.

After she had left, some people shrugged their shoulders and others looked down at the ground in embarrassment. They didn't know that side of Lek; they had never seen it before.

Lek came back as the buses pulled up, put a hand on Craig's shoulder and said that Goong had said that she would see them in Daddy's Hobby. The buses were late, so Beou ushered the girls and Jaseem on board quickly. When the drivers asked for their breakfast, Beou handed them a paper cup of rice soup each to eat at the wheel. Like it or leave it. They both accepted the food, but ungraciously. Beou was back in charge.

The buses departed to lots of shouting and waving, but when they rounded the corner, peace descended on the household once again. Everyone was glad that a good job had been done, a good time had been had by all and that they could get back to normal again.

Soom slumped back on the table.

"Oh, Mum, I still have wrinkles from scrubbing all those pots and pans yesterday. Look at me! I know what a fish feels like now."

"There's nothing there, don't be silly, but Craig and I want to thank you very much for all your help yesterday. You were a good girl. Wasn't she, Craig?"

"Yes, Very good. I didn't know where you were half the time. Washing up, were you?" Craig wanted to give her a thousand Baht, but he didn't know the protocol. "Can I give her some money to buy something, Lek, to say thanks?"

"You don't have to reward my child for helping her mother and her mother's husband, but on this occasion, yes, if you want to."

He took a thousand Baht note of his wallet and handed it to Soom, Thanks Soom from your mother and me. Lek thought that two hundred would have been enough but she refrained from saying anything. She couldn't allow Soom to keep so much money, a thousand Baht was a week's wages for many people, but only £20 to Craig – a few rounds for the both of them in a British pub.

Soom's face lit up at the sight of so much money. It was easily five times more than she had ever been given before.

"You can give me that, young lady, and we'll put it in the bank when we get back from Pattaya. Here's two hundred, don't spend it all at once."

There wasn't much chance of that; there was nothing that she had ever bought that had cost more than twenty Baht.

"Am I coming to Pattaya too then, Mum?"

"No, not this time darling. I didn't mean that, but we will all go as a family soon, won't we Craig?"

Soom looked at Craig from near her mother's lap.

"Craig, now you marry with my Mummy, do you want me call you 'paw', 'papa' or what? 'Daddy' in English?"

Craig switched his gaze to Lek for a second, looking for help. "I don't mind what you call me. Whatever you like, as long as it's a nice word. You have always called me Craig; you can still call me Craig, if you like or you can use any word that means 'Dad' or 'uncle'. Why not think about it and discuss it with your Mum? I'll be happy with your decision."

Soom seemed happy with that solution too.

"What time are we leaving, Lek?"

"I'm not sure. Dow said that he would give us at least an hour's no‐tice, but that it would not be before one. It only takes him five hours to get to Pattaya in his car, if the traffic is OK, so he said."

"All right, well, I'll go back to the house and check my email. See you later, ladies. Sawasdee, kap, pu-ying. Bye-bye."

He put some coffee on and sat at his desk. It was lucky for the towel over his stuff because there was talcum powder everywhere. There were also a few dozen mosquitoes on the walls. He sprayed his office and poured a mug of coffee. While he was checking his email, he heard movement and assumed that it was Goong surfacing at last, but he didn't look or say anything.

There were seventeen emails from friends and family all wishing them a great day, an exciting life together, sorry that they couldn't be there, a happy life together et cetera and one or two hoping that they liked their presents. What presents? He hadn't seen any. In fact, he had forgotten about wedding presents – there hadn't been any. Not one.

He replied to all the emails that didn't mention presents and then put the Internet radio on BBC Radio 4 and lay on the floor for a nap, It was just gone eleven o'clock and he was shattered, which was unusual for him. He didn't quite get to sleep, but could hear himself snoring and was vaguely aware of movement in the house around him.

Lek stayed at her mother's.

Mum said: "I forgot to give you these yesterday. No, I didn't forget, I thought it would be nicer to open them today when there was less to do. She returned with an armful of presents from the UK. I can't read who they are from, but I am sure they are from Craig's family for your wedding, so I put them aside for you."

"OK, thanks, Mum, that was he right thing to do. We wouldn't have appreciated them yesterday. This way, we can extend the fun. I'll take them to show Craig."

But she thought that Craig was asleep, so she went in to talk to Goong instead.

"How are you today, my dear? Are you OK?"

"A good night's sleep and a shower has helped a lot thanks. Have the others left yet?"

"Yes, just a few minutes ago. They told me to say 'goodbye and see you soon'. Are you coming back with us in Dow's car or do you want to stay in Baan Suay? You can stay here, if you like."

"No, I'll come with you. I'll be better off in Pattaya. I may even treat myself and stay in the same hotel as you, if you don't mind. I've always fancied The Ship, but never stayed there."

"Of course, you can stay in the same hotel. I'll leave you to get ready, we've about two hours, but I'm not sure as Dow hasn't rung and I don't like to disturb him."

Lek looked at the presents as she passed, longing to open them but wanting to do it with Craig. She could open the envelopes from the day before though and mark the amounts in her notebook as that was her money a fact that she had already established with Craig in the summer.

She dragged the silver-foil-wrapped crisp box out from under the bed, ripped it open and tipped its contents onto the duvet. She took her notebook from the cupboard and uncapped her pen. Then she thought that the job would be more fun with a companion, so she phoned Soom to come over.

"Right, Soom, you open the envelopes and I'll write the names and the amounts. Fun, eh? I love counting money, don't you?"

"Yes, Mum, I want to work in a bank when I leave school."

"Well, Little One, if that's what you want then you will have to do very well in school, then go to university and do very well there too. Then if you are lucky, you will get your heart's desire. I wish that I'd stayed in school too, but I... well, we can talk about that another day. Number one. Who is it? And how much?"

"Three hundred Baht..."

"Good start, neh?"

And so it rolled on. "Aunt Su... five hundred Baht. How generous of her. Next? Soom? Next one, please." She looked up, Soom was counting.

"Er, um Aunty Goong, twenty-five thousand Baht...."

"What? Let me see. Oh, that is too much. I will have to talk to her later. Let's carry on... Next!"

When they were done, they had over thirty thousand Baht from the afternoon and the evening guests combined plus Goong's outrageous gift of twenty-five thousand. She decided to give her mother twenty-five thousand to put in he bank for her, put five thousand in her purse for Pattaya and give Goong her money back.

She packed a bag for them to go to Pattaya and then awoke Craig.

"Come on, darling, you must get ready now. It is twelve-thirty and Dow may want to leave any time soon. Go for a shower, put what you want to take in the case and then take it over to Mum's house, please. Otherwise, we are ready. I want to talk to Goong a moment. She is coming with us and maybe will stay in the same hotel. Good, neh?"

Craig couldn't see what was good or bad about it. He liked Goong and if she wanted to stay in the same hotel fine, but he thought it better not to express his feelings honestly at the moment, given Lek's attitude earlier.

"Yes, great. Why not? Well, I'll go and pack my computer then and go to Mum's to wait for you. I won't come back here, so you lock up behind you, won't you?"

She went into the small room without answering him.

"Goong, what is all this? I can't accept twenty-five thousand Baht as a wedding gift. What were you thinking of? A thousand would have been ample. Five hundred even. What's going on?"

"Lek, sit down next to me. Big Sister, I have been vain and stupid all my life... No, no, let me finish. You had to leave the village to save the farm, but I did not. I used you as an excuse to escape a life that I didn't want, but could never have rejected without an excuse and that excuse was you. Call it a reason if you like, but a reason is only an excuse with substance.

"I didn't want to be groped in a field by some spotty farm boy and get married to a farmer who wanted a good-looking, hard-working wife who could also knock out a few sprogs. Could you see me doing that? Me? Not on your Nelly. You, yes and maybe even Ayr, but not me. I wanted what I got. 'The Good Life', Men with money drooling over me. And you know that I had that. I was vain and stupid. Stupid, because I am a miser.

"I made loads of money and was given lots of gold, which I sold for cash as soon as the punter was in the taxi, but I couldn't spend any of it. Once it went in my bank account, it was in there for life – funny expression now. I never touched anything that went in there – ever. My pleasure was to sit alone and read my bank book. I could look at it for hours and not get bored.

"I'm not saying that I put every Baht I earned into the bank because I didn't, but when I had surplus cash, in it went and never saw the light of day again. That money you have there could be twelve years old. Do banks pay out on the basis of first in first out or last in last out? I don't know.

"What I do know now though, is that I was stupid not to enjoy some of it with my friends and, yes, even my family. The bastards, eh? Now they will reap the rewards of my vanity and stupidity, but I want my friends to have some too.

"You have always looked after me, Lek, even when I had more money than you and I let you do it, because I'm a scrooge. But not any more, my friend, not any more. So, let's lock up, go over to your Mum's and wait for the chauffeur."

Lek was quite dumb-founded and could only hug her friend and say 'thanks'. They checked the windows, locked the door behind them and left arm in arm, at least until the gate.

"Hi, Mum, we'll wait here for Dow. Where's Craig?"

"He said he would wait for you in Nong's as you had to drive past that way anyway. At least, that's what he tried to tell me, I think."

"Don't worry about him, Lek, he's got the right idea. Why be miserable. Either we drink a ben here or go and join him. Why not? Let's join him at Nong's, give your mother a rest. You don't mind, Mum, do you?" asked Goong.

"No, not at all. Just one question. What presents did you get from Wales? I've been dying to know for a week now."

"Sorry, Mum, I forgot all about them. I clean forgot. But, I must do this. Please put this money in the bank for me when you go to town or hide it and I'll do it when I get back in a week or so. There's twenty-five thousand and another fifteen, making forty thousand Baht. There, OK?"

"Forty thousand Baht? Wow! I can't walk the streets with that much. My heart wouldn't stand it. I'll stash it here and you can sort it out again."

"OK. That's fine. We're off now then, Mum. Say goodbye to Soom for me. We'll wait in Nong's. Bye-bye and thanks for all your help."

"Bye, have a great time. Don't worry about the house or the dogs."

"Oh, shit, the dogs. Mum. I haven't fed them today... Could you take care of it for me?'

"Sure thing. Bye both."

No sooner had they arrived at Nong's when Dow phoned to say that he would be there in about thirty minutes and not to be late, because he had to work that evening. Lek assured him that they were already ready, sitting in Nong's waiting for him.

"That was Dow, he'll be about thirty minutes, so-oo, silly question, but someone has to ask it: Does anyone want something to drink? Goong? The usual? Craig? Another Chang? Nong! Ai Nong! A Chang, lao deng ben, two small glasses, ice, soda and mineral water, ka. Here we go again then, my frien... I suppose I have to call you hubby, now. My friend and my hubby, back to dear old Pattaya. I don't think we could stay away from there for long even if we tried. It seems to get a hold on you, doesn't it?"

"It sure does. Once bitten, forever smitten. I'll be there to the end, I couldn't live here again. I know why you do, Lek, but I can't understand Craig wanting to, coming from the West as he does. Craig sorry, we can speak in English for you. I say, I cannot un'erstand why you want to live in a village when you come from the West. Is not boring for you, no? It is boring for me and I come from here."

"No, Goong, it is not boring for me. I have never lived in a village before – that is true, but here is exciting for me because I am learning every day. I am learning a different culture, a different way of life, different people – even a different people, Asians – a different language, different animals, different dangers and different plants, every day. You know all these things, so they are boring to you, but they are brand new to me and nothing like where I come from.

"I find living abroad really exciting and especially here because Asia and Asians think and act so differently from people where I live. Sure, it can be frustrating to always be told that I'm making mistakes, but I don't really mind. I'm like a baby here. Like you were when you had everything to learn when you were six, ten or twelve. I think it's great."

"I think you are mad. I know what Goong is saying. We left all this behind us twelve years ago. No cinemas, no shops worth talking about, no bus service, no trains for miles, no clubs, not even a proper bar. We saw what it was like on TV in the cities and in other countries and we wanted the same! Not some crappy noodle shop and to get drunk every night and then have to go home early because we had to go break our backs again in the fields the next day.

"However, I will say this... now that I have a daughter and I missed the first ten years of her life, which I will never get back again, being part of Soom's life is exciting to me. Being married to a falang is exciting too, I have to admit that. We saw many falang in Pattaya, Goong and I, but I realise now that I never truly knew any of them. I learn from you too, Craig and yes, it is exciting. I understand what you are saying too.

"What a subject, what a peach! Let's have a top up, Goong." Lek refilled the glasses.

"I was always too selfish to have or even want children. Was it the same for you, Craig?"

"I suppose many people would think that and who am I to argue. They may be right, but it's not the way I see it. I just think that my way of life would not have suited children. Not only that, but I have never stayed with anyone long enough to think about children before they kicked me out or I left. I have always travelled a lot.

"To be totally honest, in my head, I am still a student hitch-hiking around the world. Half my age, seeing the world on the cheap. That's about it. You never wanted your village and I never wanted to be tied down in mine either, although I love going back. I think that this is the first time I've ever said all that."

"Cheers, everyone! See and experience Asia, Thailand and marriage, but not too cheaply, eh, hubby?" They clinked glasses again.

"No, OK, not too cheaply. I did forget to say marriage though. I have never been married and never had a wife and her daughter to rely on me before. That is kind of exciting in a scary way. I have had younger brothers, but I have never lived with a young girl growing up, so that's all new to me too. Every single thing here is new to me and if that doesn't make for an exciting life, I don't know what does. I'm even having to find new ways to make money and who knows where that will lead me or even us?"

"I like that... You're right... It is exciting, when you put it like that. Thanks, my dear."

"And that's what it's all about. Some people don't want an exciting future. They like it to be same-same every day. It's hard to make those people understand what we are talking about, so I guess it's better not to try. We just sit on the outside and look at them in amazement and they sit on the inside and think of us as crazy people.

"Craig, I want to tell you something... I will be going away soon on a long journey. I have come into some money and I will be going away."

He knew better than to ask questions, Lek was always telling him not to put people under stress, but he asked anyway, because Goong was his friend.

"Where are you going? Will you be gone long?"

"I don't know yet. I only know that I will be going, but I will see you again, have no fears about that, when we are ready to see each other again, I know that we will."

Craig felt that he was being fenced with by an expert so he gave up, offered his glass up to be clinked and said,

"Cheers to us all and our exciting futures! Have a great trip, Goong."

"Oh, I shall, I'm looking forward to it now. You know while we are on the subject, I should imagine that little Soom finds it exciting too to have a father for the first time that she can remember and a rich foreign one at that. I doubt if any other classmate can say the same.

"And you are the first falang to build a house here and actually live in it. I bet that a lot of villagers think that that is quite exciting too, although the novelty will wear off one day, I should think. Imagine that, Craig, your very presence has sparked a wave of excitement in the village that might last years! What do you think of that?"

"I suppose it's possible. If a foreigner, a rich foreigner, came to live in a village in Wales, I'm sure that it would cause a flurry of excitement. Tongues would wag with speculation and net curtains would be peered through to catch glimpses of his unusual foreign ways. I was the first to build a concrete bungalow Western style, but credit for that has to go to Lek and I was the first to have the Internet here. We have two satellite dishes – people used to stop and stare and ask Lek why I needed two dishes. It was funny.

"Another thing, we have smoked glass windows - people can't see in unless they refocus their eyes, so often, people would slip into the garden – before we had gates and a wall, and look into the house through the glass. They would press their faces right up close to the glass – usually in my office windows. I would give them a moment to get their focus and then wave at them! Oh, it was funny! Most of the old ladies would run, but a lot of old men just waved back as if they had every right to be nosing into our house.

"One day, a young woman sneaked in and used the window to adjust her make up and her bra, when she saw me two feet the other side of the glass she blushed bright red, screamed and ran out. Hilarious. This really is the best place I have ever lived, I can tell you. There is no contest.

"An exciting future? You don't even need excitement with all the funny things that you see around here."

With that a bright yellow - canary yellow - Mercedes sedan pulled up. Dow hopped out.

"Hello, darlings, are we ready? Having a little drinky-poos, are we?"

Lek handed him her glass.

"Yes, Craig was just making us laugh with stories about our house. Do you want to sit down a while or get going immediately. We're ready. We just have to pay Nong. Shall we take some supplies with us?"

"I think I'd rather get going if it's all the same to you, dear. Oh, Tommy, wait a moment, darlings, Oh, Tommy, dear, did you put those things in the cooler like I asked you? Oh, good. No, Lek no need to buy anything for us, we have vodka in the fridge, but no beer. I don't want to lose my figure. Oh, no, I couldn't be doing with that. What would the boys think? Still, if your Craig wants to put a few in there, there's plenty of room." Dow put a hand on Craig's shoulder: "You did look smart yesterday. What did you think of Lek? Did I do a 'star job' or what?"

Craig had no problems with Dow's familiarity.

"You did an excellent job, Dow. Thank you very much."

"Good, thank you. One tries one's best, you know. Anyway, you had better run off now and pay the bill for the ladies and get yourself a few beers for in the car. We can always stop for a few more on the way."

Craig got up and went inside. Nong was watching from behind a stack of crisp boxes. There were probably dozens watching the proceeding attracted by the Mercedes and Dow's flamboyant and fairly loud way of speaking.

Craig wondered whether he had learned to talk loudly to make himself heard over the hairdryers. When he got back, the women were getting in and Dow was rummaging in the boot.

"Pass them here, darling, and I'll put them in the fridge for you. That's it... keep one. Now hop in."

He sat next to Lek, directly behind Dow and the car took off immediately. Not too fast, but in a regal fashion allowing maximum viewing. When they had left the village, Tommy gunned the Mercedes up to 100kph effortlessly.

"OK, my friends, the cruise has begun and the bar is now open. Craig, you first, here's a bottle-opener for your big Chang. Yes, I'll have it back. It goes here, in it's place, neat and tidy so we can find it next time we need it. A place for everything and everything in its place. Now, that's Craig settled. Tommy, you're easy, aren't you? You know you are! A diet coke for Tommy, can't have him losing his six-pack! Oh, deary, me no. There you are Tommy. And now the girls... Will you join me with vodka? Vodka and coke or vodka and lemonade?"

"I don't mind. Vodka's fine, but I don't mind what with," said Lek.

"Nor me. Coke if it's diet. I'm not keen on too much sugar," rejoined Goong.

"Vodkas and diet coke with ice all round it is then. Here, Lek, here you are Goong and one for me. Bottoms up! Here's to a pleasant journey. Now a bit of soothing music, not too loud... sit back and relax. Watch the countryside whiz by. Just call when you want a top up, we've got plenty."

When they got to the motorway, Tommy increased the speed to 150kph, sometimes driving faster still, but he seemed a competent driver and the car was not being over-taxed in the slightest. Everybody fell into their own little world listening to the music and watching the scenery through the heavily tinted windows. An armchair or a sofa would not have been more comfortable.

They arrived at their hotel shortly after six. They had probably passed the buses on the road, but nobody had noticed them. Perhaps they were having a pit-stop, but they had also hoped to be arriving at about six o'clock. Dow offered to have Tommy take the bags in but they refused, so the yellow Mercedes pulled away with Dow hanging out of the window promising to catch up with them again soon

They walked up the steps and entered the Royal Cruise Hotel. The entrance hall was very chic. It was the best place that any of them had stayed in for quite a while. They allowed Goong to go first.

"Do you have a room available?"

"How many nights, madam?"

"I'm not sure yet... At least two."

"Certainly, madam, I'll just check. Does madam require a sea view?"

"Yes, I think so. I don't want to be on the seashore and not be able to see the sea."

"Yes, we have several available. Does madam have a preference for a high floor?"

"No, as long as I can see the sea from my balcony, that's fine."

"Certainly, madam, you can register, when you have unpacked, if you like, but please do it today. The boy will take you to your cabin now. We call them cabin's here, not rooms, you understand."

Everyone smiled.

"May I help you, sir?"

"We have a reservation, Craig Williams."

"Ah, yes sir, our honeymoon couple. We have been awaiting your arrival most eagerly. I will show you to your room myself." A woman waaied them and took the man's place behind the reception desk.

Goong left for her cabin and Craig and Lek for theirs. The manager stopped outside a door, opened it, went inside, took his shoes off and beckoned them in.

"Please come in, we have prepared this room especially for you. It is an upgrade on what you originally wanted. It is more spacious and the private terrace is larger. It affords a magnificent view over Pattaya beach. There are fresh flowers in the vases and fruit in the bowl, they will be refreshed every day of your stay.

"The champagne that you ordered has been chilling since yesterday in the refrigerator over there and there is ample ice in the freezer for the champagne bucket which is here along with four flute glasses. If you need more, just telephone down to reception. You have complimentary Wi-Fi – here is a ticket with the access code and the television has many international stations, including English, of course.

"We have full day spa, massage and beauty treatments and a fitness centre available and, as a special gift for the bride, please accept this complimentary voucher for one free hour in either the spa, the massage or the beauty salon. There will also be a complimentary first drink of the day at the bar courtesy of the management of the Royal Cruise Hotel.

"My name is Jacques, if you need anything, please ask for me personally or the desk manager at the time. Thank you for choosing to stay at the Royal Cruise Hotel. I hope that your honeymoon with us will be a memorable one. Will you please register later on today too. Bye for now." He put his shoes on, left and closed the door behind him.

They looked around for a few moments and then Craig picked Lek up and threw her on to the bed. He lay down next to her.

"Well, what do you think? Will it do?"

"Oh, darling, it's perfect... just perfect. Come on, let's take a look from the balcony!"

"Terrace', darling, not balcony. Wow! Look at that! I've never seen the beach look like that before. What do you want to do now, Lek?"

"What I want to do and what we ought to do are not the same and I'm afraid that duty must prevail. You go for a shower and I'll unpack, then we'll get Goong's room number and see if she's all right. OK?"

"Sure," he dropped his clothes on the floor where he stood and went into the bathroom, "This is quite something too," she heard him say as he turned the shower on and started to sing a Welsh song.

Lek began putting things away and hanging clothes up. When Craig came out of the shower, she was ready, with her towel wrapped around her to swap places.

"Can you finish off, while I shower now?"

He completed the unpacking and got dressed. Lek came out, got dressed and put a little make-up on.

"Right, let's find Goong." She phoned reception. "She's on he floor below us. 'Deck', I suppose," she muttered in Thai, not knowing the English word. "We can walk down, it's only one rung of stairs,"

"'Flight'," corrected Craig.

"No, it's a ship, not a plane," replied Lek.

Craig said nothing and followed her down to Goong's 'cabin'. When Lek knocked, Gong invited the visitor in, not knowing who it was.

"Hi … I was wondering whether to come looking for you. I didn't know whether you'd be at it or not. Nice roo.., er cabin, isn't it? Is yours to your liking? Hello. Craig, do you like your cabin? Great. Why not let's go down to the bar and work out what to do next?"

"Sounds good to me" and he turned to leave, giving the friends time to chat alone, if they wanted or follow on behind. He took a stool at the bar. He hadn't heard the door close, so they were obviously having a chat. In lieu of anyone to talk to himself, he ordered a Chang and gazed out over the deep-blue sea. The girls were only a few minutes behind him, but he had finished the small bottle of beer by the time they arrived. He was used to the pint-size bottles in the village so these small ones didn't seem to go anywhere. Three or four slugs and they were empty.

"What are you having, ladies?" They studied the bar then spoke to the barman in a flurry of Thai.

"Do you sell pitchers? Good. Pitchers of cocktails? Do you know how to make a Screwdriver? Good. When did you press the oranges? You do that as necessary? Good. Will you make it 3:1 orange juice to vodka. It is going to be a long night. We'll have a pitcher of Screwdriver, two glasses and a bucket of ice for us, and another beer for my husband. Put everything on my bill, please. We'll sit over there by the window."

Craig followed them over. The drinks arrived soon after.

"We phoned Beou, they have arrived. Some got dropped off on the way so they could shower, then they will come in so that the others can go home and do the same. We said we would meet them after this, in about an hour. We can walk, it's only around the corner. Cheers everyone. Here we are again in good old Pattaya by the sea!"

When they arrived at Daddy's Hobby an hour later, it looked the same as it had always done except half of the staff looked washed out, although that was the general feeling of all those who had been to the wedding at Baan Suay. Even Lek and Craig were worn out, but they had had to show their faces even if only for an hour out of solidarity. One suffers, everyone must suffer.

Craig really didn't have much to say. He knew that they were getting married for real, in the eyes of the law, the next day, but he didn't know where, when or how and didn't much care. He knew that they would tell him what he needed to know and probably minutes before he needed to know it, but that was OK, he was getting used to the style of management control called 'fire fighting'. He sipped his beer slowly and watched people go about their lives and holidays.

Meanwhile, Lek, Goong, Ayr and Beou were making plans for the following day.

Beou said: "Do you want a pig party tomorrow night?"

"It would be rude not to, wouldn't it? Yes, I think so. Show our appreciation and all that."

"OK, I usually charge nine and a half thousand these days, but I don't want to make any money out of you, my favourite cousin, so I can do it for seven and I'll pay half. I doubt whether my girls paid for a third of what they ate and drank up there anyway."

"Don't worry about them. They lost two days earnings and they made the party go merrier. You don't have to pay anything. I appreciate the price of seven thousand."

"Three and a half, take it or leave it. It's my bar and I can do what I like. OK? So, I'll set that ball rolling. Excuse me a moment." She walked a little way off, mobile already to her ear.

"Beou's done such a lot for us. She's been really great. You all have. I love you very much. Thanks, guys. I don't know about you though, but I'm fit to drop."

"Too much of the soft life," said Ayr. "You'll be a portly, old matron soon. Cooking dinner every day for your husband and feeding the chickens and watering the garden and … vacuuming behind the couch and…" They all laughed.

"I'm doing half of those things already. Anyway, what's wrong with vacuuming behind the couch? That's normal…"

"Precisely! Pre…cise…ly! When were you ever like that?"

"I'll have you know that I did clean behind the furniture when we all lived together… sometimes. Now I have more time on my hands and more visitors. Now it has to be done."

"My point precisely! You have to do it to fit in. So, that people don't call you a dirty cow, but not because you want to."

"I don't suppose anyone can say that cleaning behind furniture is their favourite job, Ayr, but it still has to be done and I do like the house looking nice for Craig… You're right, I am becoming a matron, but less of the 'old' and 'portly', thank you very much."

"Ah, that's phase two." And they all laughed again.

"Right, that's sorted. Nid, another beer for Craig, please, darling, keep your eyes open, there's a good girl. Now, where was I? Oh, yes, the party's on. How are you getting to the registry office? Do you want a taxi car, meter taxi, I mean? Or shall we private hire a Baht taxi and go char-a-banc style?"

"Char-a-banc. I vote for char-a-banc," blurted out Ayr.

"So, do I said Lek, but I'll go with the flow."

"Baht taxi it is then I can sort that out after I've asked the girls who wants to go. What time? There are no appointments, you just wait your turn. Monday morning probably won't be too busy. I shouldn't think that many young love birds jump out of bed early on a Monday morning to get married… and that's it. Oh, just one more thing. Maybe you should tell Dow that we'll be there at, what, say, ten thirty? And that there will be a party after that and a pig party with music starting at eight. He may have time to come along."

"Good idea, I'll ring him now."

"Well, my friends, that just about wraps it up for me, I'm done in. Kippered, so I'm going home. It will be a long day tomorrow, but first I have to have a word with the girls. Ayr, I'm putting this note pad here. Anyone that wants to go to the registry office tomorrow, will you ask them to put their names on this list? Ask Noi to take care of it and I will phone her in the morning… and that is definitely it. Goodnight."

"I think I'll go too," said Goong, "I'm feeling very tired as well. Travelling, even in a luxury car, just takes it right out of me these days. So, I'll be saying good night too, my dears. See you tomorrow, bright and early."

"Hang on, Goong, Craig and I will walk with you. Craig drink up or take it with you. We're going back to the hotel with Goong. You can have another one in the hotel bar if you like. Ayr, we'll settle up tomorrow, OK.

"Ayr nodded from her usual seat at the cashier's desk, the one that had been Lek's two years before.

24 THE PATTAYA WEDDING

On her way to their cabin the night before, Lek had booked an early-morning session in the beauty salon, so she got up at eight, showered and went down to that, leaving Craig sitting up in bed flicking through the TV channels. She would have an hour in there to spruce herself up, then have breakfast and walk over to Daddy's Hobby to chat with Noi and wait for the taxi.

This day and the forthcoming ceremony did not mean as much to Lek. The traditional Thai wedding had all the romance, this one would just be a question of filling in forms and paying fees, but this would be the one that counted. This would be the one that allowed her to change her name to Williams. This one literally made her a Williams by law. And she wanted that. She wanted to be legal, decent, honest and upright. Becoming Mrs. Williams was a step in that direction.

She phoned their room from the salon:

"Are you up yet, Craig? I'll be finished here in about twenty minutes, so why don't you go for a shower and I'll meet you in the restaurant for breakfast? We can go straight from there."

Then she phoned Goong's room.

"Good morning, how are you today? Are you coming with us this morning? We are going to have breakfast in about fifteen minutes and then go and see Noi. Do you want to join us? OK, good. Seen you soon."

After a hearty breakfast, they walked the short distance to Daddy's Hobby. Noi was making coffee.

"Coffee, everyone? Craig, a beer?"

"No, coffee for me too, thanks."

"I think she was joking, my dear," said Lek. "What are the plans for this morning, Noi?"

"Well, I missed the Baan Suay wedding, so I am going to this one. One of the girls will cover for me. The taxis are coming at ten fifteen, so people should be arriving soon. With that Beou arrived with her two daughters. They hadn't gone to Baan Suay either, but had stayed with their Aunty Noi. They loved their Aunty Lek and hurried over to her, Lek cuddled them, but they were still too shy of Craig to approach him.

"Say 'hello' to your Uncle Craig. He is your new uncle from Wales, the UK." They waaied, but kept their distance. Craig waved and said 'hello'. It was incorrect to waai children under about twelve years of age. He often struggled to remember the etiquette but got it right this time.

"Some people have gone straight there, so I'll phone the taxi up and get him to get a move on. Oh, there he is now. Speak of the devil. Come on let's get going. Joy, take care of the bar, won't you. If you have any problems, ask Or over there or phone me, but we'll only be an hour or two... I think."

When they arrived at the registry office, there were thirty-odd well-wishers packed into four Baht buses. Lek, Craig and Beou went into the government building to take their place in the queue. To their surprise, there was no-one before them, but the officer was not at her desk, so they had to wait for her to come back. The process of getting married took about fifteen minutes and Beou acted as a witness and took photos of them signing their names on the certificate.

When they went outside, there were two rows of friends lining their route to their taxi. They kissed on the steps to many cheers. Their friends were throwing rice and taking photos with cameras and mobile phones, but the big surprise was that Dow had brought two stars from the cast at Tiffany's. They were in full costume and Pattaya People's News was there to film the stars on their publicity stunt. Lek was thrilled to think that their wedding would be broadcast on television that night. The Tiffany girls were very generous and made certain that

Lek and Craig got into most of the scenes.

The four Baht buses had been decorated with ribbons, balloons and banners and so had Dow's Mercedes, so the five vehicles made quite a cavalcade as they drove back to Daddy's Hobby. Once back in the bar, the girls set to work decorating that too. They hung balloons all around the eaves of the roof and banners from the pillars supporting it. Craig rang the bell to buy all the girls a drink as they set about making sandwiches, soup and stew for the party later on. The pig, which was roasting on a spit over hot charcoal alongside the bar, was giving off a delicious smell.

All the preparations had been completed by three o'clock, so most of the girls drifted off to get changed. Beou went home too to meet her daughters from school and Goong wanted to go back to the hotel for a lie down. Lek and Craig decided to go back with her. Noi stayed behind to guard the bar and all the food until Ayr came back to relieve her. The girls would nave to be back as soon as possible, but Lek, Craig, Beou and Goong arranged to meet between seven and eight o'clock.

Craig passed the time by sitting on the terrace reading a book and drinking a beer but Lek wanted a few hours sleep before starting again. Goong went straight to her room too, where she slept like a baby absolutely worn out from even those few hours of activity and excitement. Lek was thinking about her too as she fell asleep. She decided that she would try to take her friend to see a doctor the following day, most likely in the afternoon as the party that night would probably last until midnight.

Craig went for a shower at six thirty and then woke Lek so that she would have plenty of time to get ready. When they were both set to go, Lek phoned Goong's cabin, but she didn't answer. They checked at reception on the way out, but Goong had not left the hotel. Either asleep or in the shower, thought Lek, so they went on without her.

A big cheer went up as they arrived at Daddy's Hobby. There must have been a hundred and fifty people there, but Beou had reserved two stools on the left side of the bar near the front. Drinks appeared as if by magic from well-wishers and they had a hard time working out who they had come from. Several dishes of food arrived to. They both particularly liked the roast pork. Lek had a penchant for crackling, although Craig was careful about his cholesterol intake.

There had probably never been so many people at the bar. Lek had been going there for twelve years and couldn't remember it ever having been so busy before. From time to time, Lek dived behind the bar to help out. She wasn't expected to, in fact she was expected not to, but she missed some of the people, liked the job and wanted to help out. She already had a good idea that Beou would make a small fortune from this party. Craig was quite happy about Lek leaving him, he just sat there and watched people singing on the karaoke and dancing in the space in front of the bar. As he finished one beer another arrived and as a plate of food disappeared another took its place. Some people came over to shake his hand, but in general it was too loud to talk.

At eight o'clock, Noi turned the music down and the TV up for the news. They didn't care about the plights of the world at that moment though, they were looking for Lek and Craig and themselves at the registry office. Sure enough, the last segment of the news broadcast showed the group of them posing with the dancers and Dow. The story was more about the girls from Tiffany's but Lek and Craig got a mention and a good showing too. That would be repeated on news highlights for a week as normally happened, so Beou offered to put it on a tape for them as a keepsake.

Beou brought the wedding cake out and Lek cut it up. Everyone had a tiny slice as they watched the rerun of the morning's events in the registry office car park.

Goong arrived at ten o'clock looking radiant. She sat down inside the bar as there was no room outside and right opposite Craig. Lek gave her the piece of wedding cake she had saved for her.

"You look marvellous, Goong. Not that you don't always look good, of course, but you look even better today. That's all I can say without getting into trouble."

She squeezed his hand. "I made a special effort, because this is such a special day, but thank you for saying so. A girl needs a boost sometimes. What can I get you? Lek, what do you want to drink?"

"What's the old flatterer saying to you now, Goong? Although this time he is telling you the truth, darling. You do look lovely. Anyway, look, we have so many drinks backed up that I don't think we'll be able to finish them all. Let us get you one. What is it to be?"

"OK, thanks, a Bacardi Breezer. Lemon if they have it, otherwise any flavour." Lek handed her a drink and some food on a paper plate. "I love these roast pork sandwiches. Mmm, great! Beou always did put on a good party. Are you enjoying yourself, Craig? Are you going to sing us a song later."

"I doubt it, Goong, when have you ever heard me sing on a microphone? No, I'll leave that to the experts. Anyway, they probably don't have any songs in English or Welsh. Don't ask them though, because I don't want to sing one anyway."

"Cheer up, it's a party. You are on your exciting voyage, your maiden voyage of marriage with your first wife ever and she is a very beautiful maiden too."

"Oh, I'm happy all right, I just don't want to sing."

"And you don't have to. Look here is a surprise for you. Teddy is a professional singer. He works all over Pattaya. He has finished work early to sing at your party."

Teddy seemed to be well-known because when he took the microphone many people applauded. When he heard Teddy start to sing Moon River, he applauded too. Lek was spell-bound and Goong wore a wide smile. Craig seemed to be the only person who had never heard of him, although he had an excellent singing voice and a really magnetic stage-presence. It was very obvious that all the girls thought that Teddy was a big heart-throb.

At about eleven o'clock, there was another surprise. Dow's Mercedes pulled up and the two lady-boys from the registry office car park got out. They went straight into the group of dancers and joined in. They had finished their spot and wanted to support their friend Dow's old friend Lek, They danced and flounced their long skirts as if they were in the Moulin Rouge. People stopped as they were walking past to watch and listen to the spectacular. Lek felt enormously proud and hoped that Craig did too.

"Craig what do you think? Teddy is one of the best singers in Pattaya and these katoi are stars at Tiffany's. They are dancing and singing at our wedding! Aren't you thrilled?"

"Sure, darling. They're really great. It is very kind of them. Do they know you from before?"

"Eh? No, I know Dow, but I don't know the dancers except from this morning. I meet Teddy one or two times, I think, but he does not remember me. He is a big star in Pattaya. He never remember me from just say 'hello' four or five years ago. I am not sure... maybe Beou or maybe Dow asked him to come here for us."

One of the visitors was making an impromptu video of the evening and promised to give Lek a copy for her wedding memorabilia. If she had known that it was going to be this good, she was thinking, she would have hired a cam-corder herself. She was looking forward to re-playing the video for her mother and Soom.

At about midnight, right at the end of the party, Will walked up totally out of the blue and sat down next to Craig, Lek, Beou and Goong.

"Hello, gang! What's the occasion?"

"Eh? Oh, for the party? Lek and I got married today."

"What? Why didn't you tell me?"

"You were in the UK. I didn't know you were going to be here, did I? You didn't say anything."

"No, well, I never do, to be honest, do I? I just turn up when I can. I don't like to say anything in case it puts the mockers on it. If it comes off, great, all well and good, but if it doesn't, then no harm done either. Wait a mo, Craig. How are you, my darling girl?" He leaned over and kissed Lek. Hiya, Lek. Mrs. Williams now then? Congratulations! Take care of the old duffer, won't you? He won't do it himself. Congratulations, Craig! Well done! You picked a cracker of a girl there. I always did like Lek. And Goong, of course. This is some hooley for sure. I didn't know about this, but my flight was delayed. I should have been here six hours ago. What can I get yous all to drink?

"Same again here, Beou, gin and tonic for me – make it a double - and one for yourself.

"I didn't see much of you in Barry when you were back and then, next thing, you were gone. What happened? I've been here a couple of times since then but you were up north. You won't get me going up there. No way, boy, not after your telling me that there are snakes up there. You know me and snakes. I ain't scared of no man, but put a little snake in front of me and I'll wet myself. It makes me shudder just to think of them."

"They are not all poisonous and you don't see one even every month. It's not that bad!"

"I don't care if they're poisonous or not and you can bet your life that I'd see one every day. Now let's change the subject. What was your wedding like, Lek? Sorry I missed it, but as I was just telling Craig, my plane was late and I hate snakes anyway."

Lek didn't quite follow what Will was talking about, but she was happy to tell Will about her two weddings. She liked this old friend of Craig's and Goong's who had introduced them to each other a couple of years ago."

Beou turned the music off and the lights down, so the technician started to clear away his karaoke and lighting equipment. Most people drifted off but Craig, Lek, Goong, Ayr, Beou, Will, Teddy and the lady boys stayed for a final drink. Teddy and the dancers made a good impression on the friends, but after the one drink, they too had to go to a party being held for the cast of the show at Tiffany's. They kissed Lek, shook hands with Craig and promised to keep in touch before disappearing in Dow's car.

"What lovely people," said Ayr. "Show-busy, but nice with it. Like normal people."

"Yes, they were, weren't they. It was kind of them to give up their time like that and make a fuss of us… and get us on the TV too. Will, watch Pattaya People's News this week and you'll see all of us at the registry office this morning. They filmed us with those two dancers from Tiffany's."

"Oh, yeah? I know Tiffany's. I went there a few years ago. Very glitzy and professional. Very good! I'll look out for that." Will rang the bell quietly.

"I was just about to do that," said Craig.

"So, was I," added Lek.

"Great minds think alike," replied Will, "but it's your wedding party and I missed it, so I'll pay. Not that anyone told me it was taking place, mind you. I'm going to sleep on that one to see if I should be offended."

"We didn't tell anyone really. I didn't even tell my family until it was too late for them to get here because we didn't want people to think that they had to come over. You know, it's expensive and people have other plans for their holidays. So, we thought it best not to give them the option."

"Your family did send presents though, Craig," said Lek.

"Did they? First I've heard of it. When? Where are they?"

"I'm sure I told you. You must have forgotten. Mum took them from the postman and put them aside until after the wedding. They're in our house still unopened. I forgot to bring them with us."

"I think you forgot to tell me too, but that's something to look forward too when we get home. How long are you here for, Will?"

"Six weeks, I think. Unless I get a phone call and then it could be more or less and you?"

"We booked into the Cruise for a week yesterday. We are now officially on our honeymoon, aren't we, Mrs. Williams?" and he kissed her on the nose.

She blushed despite the fact that they were with friends and in Pattaya.

Goong sighed. "I'm so happy for you I could cry. You have
everything that the three of us, and many others, always wanted."

"Yes," agreed Ayr, "I'm really happy for you too. Long live the
happy couple and may you ever be so."

Lek translated for Craig and Will. Will joined in the toast. Everybody was beginning to flag by one o'clock, so Beou offered one more
round to be drunk while she did the till and put everything ship-shape
for Noi who had already had a long day and now had to do the night
shift too, although the bar would be closed and she could sleep.

When the drinks were finished Beou put the glasses in the sink and
filled them with water for Noi to sort out later.

"OK, my friends, I'm going to bed and I think that Noi wants to
do the same. Tomorrow is another day and you all have homes or hotels to go to, so let's be having you. Lek, Goong and Ayr, I have made
us all up a bag of left-overs. Yours is over there in the fridge, Noi. Pork
sandwiches, more pork and some cakes. See you tomorrow."

"Good night, Beou, thanks for organising a great day for us. The
wedding, the party, the singer and dancers, the karaoke and the food. It
was marvellous, wasn't it Craig?"

"Yes, sure thing. Thanks very much, Beou, I suppose I can start
calling you cousin now too?"

"Yes, I suppose we can. Well, we are cousins now. In Thailand, I
don't know about in Wales, but here we are, so, good night, cousins,"
and she kissed them both on the cheek. "It has been my very great
pleasure to help in any way that I could."

Ayr took a motorbike taxi back to the flat that she, Goong and Lek
had once shared; Goong walked back with Will, Beou took her car and
Craig and Lek walked back to their cabin arm in arm because it was late
in Pattaya, there was no-one to see them and Lek didn't really care on
the day that she had become Mrs. Williams anyway.

An Exciting Future

25 THE HONEYMOON

They had been in Pattaya for two nights, but had not touched their champagne yet, so when they had finished showering together, Craig called reception and asked them to send a large pitcher of orange juice and breakfast on a trolley up to their cabin. They ate breakfast on their terrace accompanied by glasses of Buck's Fizz dressed in their bathing costumes. Lek said that she had never done that before. They sat there for an hour talking about their wedding the day before, when Lek seemed to remember something suddenly.

"Craig, you haven't asked me about the money and I forgot to tell you."

"What money? Oh, the party money? How much did you get?"

"No, not that money. The money you gave Mum for the party. The hundred thousand. Don't you remember?"

"Well, yes, of course I remember. What about it?"

"Don't you want to know how much is left?"

"Yes, of course I do. Sorry. It had slipped my mind and with the champagne so early. How much is left?"

Lek fetched her bag. "There is forty thousand Baht left. The party cost a little over sixty thousand, but I put the rest. Is that OK? Here look..." She counted it out in front of Craig and handed it to him with the air of a cashier, which of course she had once been for a brief spell.

"Ermm, thanks very much, but why are you doing this now and like this? I don't get it."

"I am not making a problem, I just want you to know, on the first day of our married life together that I will never steal from you. You paid, this is your change and that is fair."

"But I never thought that you were stealing from me or that you ever would. Why would I want to marry a thief?" He took her in his arms and kissed her. "I trust you my darling. You don't need to prove anything to me ever. I want you to remember that always. Thanks for the money though, I'll lock it in the hotel safe. Do you want to put anything in there for you? Purse, passports?

"By the way, how much was donated at the party?"

"Yes, OK. Put my purse and the passports in there too. Do you want more champagne? We have one more bottle and we have money to buy more."

"How much did you make on the party, Lek?"

"Quite a lot..."

"Yes, but how much?"

"Er, more than last time..."

"Lek?"

"A lot. I don't remember how much," she teased. "A girl is allowed to have some secrets. I'll treat us a little bit here on honeymoon and put the rest in the bank for a rainy day, but you know the rules with party money. I, not you, will have to give it back with interest one day, so it is not really my money. It is just play money. A loan. What do you call it, er, Monopoly money. It is best to forget it exists."

Lek was not being greedy. She didn't really mind telling Craig how much she had received, but then she would have had to say that Goong had donated twenty-five thousand and why and she didn't want to disclose her friend's secret until it was permitted to do so.

"OK, if you don't want to tell me, I don't mind. I trust you, like I said. I wouldn't have mentioned money, if you hadn't brought the subject up. You'll tell me if and when you're ready. I know that."

Lek hugged him: "You are the best husband in the world. Do you know that?"

"I'm not sure. It's early days yet. Not even that. It's just twenty-three hours since we got married officially. Now do you want the second bottle here in the room or go for a swim first or drink champagne at the pool side?"

"I would love to be seen drinking champagne a the poolside at ten o'clock in the morning. Let's do that, it is so decadent. But leave that bottle in the fridge. We can order one from the waiter. Loudly, so that people can hear us. Is that wickedly vain? It is, isn't it? Are you ashamed of me now?"

"Yes, it is pretty vain, but I'm not ashamed. It's not as if this happens every day and it is a first. You have never married a foreigner before and I've never married anyone, so what the Hell?"

She unembraced him and collected towels from the bathroom. They took a lift down to the pool wearing sunglasses and the dressing gowns provided by the hotel. Lek paraded all the way around the pool before leading Craig to two sun loungers near the entrance to the pool area. She had made sure that everyone saw them, even though she wasn't really looking forward to showing her body in the bikini that she had on under the robe. She adjusted the parasol so that she would be totally in the shade and invited Craig to draw nearer, which he realised was a wise thing to do in the blistering midday Thai sun.

You needed to be a dedicated sun-worshipper to be able to tolerate that sun for more than ten minutes at a time even using strong sunblock. Neither of them had any experience of sun bathing and Lek didn't even want to get a sun tan. She, like most Thai ladies, thought that tanned skin was common. All right on foreign film stars, but Thai stars tried to have the whitest skin possible.

Lek took the sun-block out of her pocket and rubbed it on Craig as he had taken his robe off, then she put some on her lower legs, arms, face and upper chest. She wasn't feeling brave enough yet to take off the dressing gown and she was too shy to allow even her own husband to put the lotion on her in public.

"Do you mind if I order the drinks, darling," she whispered quietly.

"No, you carry on."

"Oh, waiter! Waiter!" she cried, one hand waving up and down in the Thai style. When he was still five yards away and hurrying to her side, Lek said loudly in Thai so that all the Thai girls could hear, "A bottle of champagne in a bucket of ice and a pitcher of orange juice for two. How did I do, Craig?"

"Oh, I think everybody heard you, Lek."

"Good. I've always wanted to do something like that. I won't ever do it again, I promise." She surveyed the people at the pool like she thought a film star might. It wasn't Craig's way, but he was glad that Lek, his brand new wife, was having the time of her life. The waiter brought the champagne and poured it. They clinked glasses, Lek took a few small, lady-like sips, put the flute down and promptly fell asleep. The early-morning champagne had gone to her head and the heat had made her drowsy.

Craig had to smile. It had been so unlike Lek to show off like that, he thought, but little did he know really. Thai women are fiercely competitive with women outside their circle. He asked the waiter to bring him any English-language newspaper and a pen and settled back to drink the champagne and do the crossword. He dared not fall asleep, because he had to keep moving the parasol to keep Lek from burning. And burn she would despite her light-brown skin. She had not spent any time in the sun since she was about thirteen years of age. Craig guarded her like a lioness would her cubs, like he knew that she would do for him.

When Lek awoke two hours later, she wanted paracetamol, air conditioning, a cold shower and food in that order, so they packed up their things asked for two tablets at reception and went up to their cabin.

"Oh, never again... No more sun for me... I think that I am allergic to it. Did you see how it knocked me out down there. I only lasted a few minutes and then out like a light. That is why you have never seen me sunbathing before."

"You were drunk."

"No, I was not. You have seen me drink more than that many times. How dare you say that? Pass me the water and those tablets will you, darling? Thanks... Anyway, I was not drunk."

"OK, you were not drunk, but many people say that champagne goes straight to their heads. It's the bubbles. They get to some people. Maybe they got to you too..."

"Are you saying that I get drunk on bubbles? That's nonsense. Give me a 7-UP out of the fridge and I'll prove it to you."

"No, it's all right. I believe that you can drink lemonade without getting drunk."

"Good. It was the sun, I tell you. Pass me a banana will you, I'm a bit hungry. Then I'll shower, phone Goong and have another little sleep."

She phoned her friend still damp from the shower while Craig read the paper, but she couldn't get through. "No answer on Goong's cabin phone or mobile. She might be out with Will somewhere. You know, I'm pretty sure that she would marry Will if he asked her to. Do you think he would ever ask her?"

"What? Pardon? Are you speaking to me or down the phone?"

"I asked, do you think that Will would ever ask Goong to marry him?"

"I've no idea. He's never mentioned it to me. Has he said anything to you?"

"You're hopeless! Maybe the sun got at you today too. First you say that I got drunk on bubbles and now you don't know what I'm talking about. Why would Will say anything to me? I'm going to have a snooze. Wake me up before six will you, please. I want to try Goong again and phone Soom before dinner.

And she was out again. Craig really envied the way that Lek could just turn off and go to sleep like a cat, but it had been a hard, stressful seven days for Lek and this was the first day she had had to relax with nothing to worry about, although Craig knew nothing about Goong's predicament. He put the TV on low, found a Star Trek film to watch and curled up as much like a cat as he could beside his beautiful cat-woman.

∞

Lek woke up first, to find Craig snoring at her feet. It was six thirty – not a bad time, so she tried to phone Goong again on both phones, but to no avail. Craig was awakened by Lek's movements so she asked him to phone Will, but there was no answer there either. She was worried, but she drew some comfort from the fact that Will couldn't be contacted either and that she still had her cabin in the hotel. She made her daily phone call to her daughter and was relieved when Soom answered it quickly.

"Are you all right, my dear? How was school today. Oh, that's good. Have you eaten yet? Make sure you help gran with the dishes, won't you and get an early night for school in the morning. We'll be back on Sunday morning. Miss you, my darling. Bye for now we're going for something to eat in the hotel. See you soon." Speaking to Soom always cheered her up.

"Come on then! Let's go down, claim our free drink and see what's on the menu for tonight." Craig put his arm around her which she removed once outside the cabin. Old habits died hard.

After a fantastic dinner, they moved to the bar to watch a cabaret. The main act was a Thai singer / comedian. Craig could vouch for his singing voice, but could not understand more than the odd word of his humour. It must have been good though because he had Lek and all the other Thais in stitches, their falang boyfriends trying to look happy, as did Craig.

The cabaret ended at midnight, so they got one of their first 'early' nights in Pattaya ever. It surprised them both, but they actually liked this more normal style of holiday, and they promised to do it more often and even to stay away from Daddy's Hobby while they were on their honeymoon. It was more romantic to do things together anyway. They both thought that. It was nice to sit and appreciate something together, just the two of them and not the three, four, five, six or more.

However, the next day, after what had become their routine of shower, breakfast, swim, room and shower again they decided to take all their surplus money to the bank. They checked on Goong and Will again, but in vain. However, the girl on reception said that the room was still being paid for although she declined to say whether it was being occupied.

It was just too baffling. Beou didn't know anything either so at four o'clock they broke their resolution and went to Daddy's Hobby. Neither Ayr nor Noi knew anything either.

"I just don't understand it," said Lek, "Where on Earth can they be and why don't they phone us? Or at least answer their phones?"

Mystified, Craig and Lek strolled back to their hotel to pick up their new routine: shower, drink in the bar, dinner, show in the bar and bed. They tried to phone again, but it was becoming tedious.

The fifth day of their honeymoon proceeded as had become customary. They didn't find it boring at all. They had not spent so much time together without friends being around since they had fallen in love years before. This was a reminder of how close they could be when there were no other people that they knew around and in their own different ways they were relearning something that they had both forgotten. The bad times of building the house seemed as if they had happened to other people or to people that they had become but no longer were.

Their love had been reborn and with it, so had they. Somehow over the last two years they had forgotten what they were supposed to be doing – enjoying one another's company. They had become too bogged down in the nitty-gritty of life and had forgotten to enjoy themselves.

When they awoke from their now customary post lunch nap, they sat on the verandah to watch the sun go down.

"Let's have a cold one, Lek. Do you want a beer?"

"Yes, sure, why not. There's still an hour and more before dinner is served, if we want to catch the beginning of the show, and the sunset from here across the bay is fabulous."

Craig got up to get two bottles of Heineken, Lek's favourite beer of late and put on a Neil Young CD.

"Here, Lek. Cheers. There was also this note by the door."

Lek read it. "How intriguing," she said getting up. "It says that there is a parcel waiting for us at reception. I'll have it sent up."

A boy delivered a large Jiffy bag with another note attached to it. In Thai it read: 'This bag was found in Miss Nattaporn's cabin at noon today. I apologise that we forgot to inform you earlier. We have no further information.'

"This was found in Goong's cabin when they went to clean it at midday because she had checked out. It is addressed to us in this cabin." She opened the envelope and tipped the contents on the table. There were two mobile phones with their backs and batteries removed and a letter. Lek read the letter slowly to herself before translating it for Craig:

My Dearest Lek and Ayr,

You are the only true people that I have met in the world and the only two that I really care about, which makes me doubly sorry that I had to deceive you in order to achieve my goal.

I have asked each of you to send my father or to give my father 200 Baht per week until his demise. I used this as a means of getting your bank account numbers. The truth is that I want you both to have all my savings.

I would count it as a personal favour if you would both continue to pay this money to my father for the rest of his life, which I don't expect to be long. In fact, he probably won't even notice it going into his account.

Keep the balance to do with as you please after his death. He would not know what to do with the money anyway. Not that it is a huge amount, but neither is it inconsiderable.

After the cheque for my hospital and funeral bills are deducted, you should be left with just over a half a million Baht each.

I hope that you have as much fun spending it as I had collecting it. I like to think that collecting that money, as a boy collects stamps, is my only vice, but you and others will be able to judge that better than I.

Please don't feel sorry for me because I am going on before you. I don't. I see myself as a trail-blazer and if I can, even in any small way, make your passages easier, be assured that I will, my friends.

Never forget that everything that you are going through is Maya. It is illusion. It cannot hurt you unless you allow it to.

I will never forget your help and friendship.

We are Mountees, the Three Musketeers and I love you.

Your friend always,

Lots of love,

Goong

PS: The phones are mine and Will's. I knew that he was going to Bangkok for a few days so I stole it to prevent you all comparing notes. Please apologize to him for me and tell him I always thought that he was a lovely man.

I have spent my last couple of days in a clinic, but kept the room in the Ship to maintain the illusion that I was still about – I hoped you would guess that I was with Will and I hope that he thought that I was with you.

I have paid a nurse to signal the Pattaya People's News to run a pre-paid personal ad when I died and I asked Ayr to look out for it and phone you when she saw it, although she may not know what it means. It will read: "Nattaporn had to go home early."

Please show her this letter when you can, but don't allow news of my departure to reach the village. I have sent my father a letter saying that I have moved on and will see him soon, which I truly hope to do.

I know that you will get where you are going because we all do, I just hope that you have as much fun getting there as I did.

Tell Craig that I think that he is a lovely man and that I am pleased to have met him too.

God bless you both,
Your loving friend for all of time,
Goong.

There was silence for minutes until Craig broke it with:

"What a shock! Are you all right, my darling? You and Goong... and Ayr, were long term bosom buddies, weren't you?... I don't know what to say... She looked great on Monday. What did she die of? Did she say? Let me give you a hug, darling."

"It is all right, Craig. Really it is. I would rather explain something than hug at the moment, if that is all right. Open that last bottle of champagne and sit down. She waited until he had poured two glasses before continuing.

"You see, we three went to Pattaya together. I had to go, but Goong and Ayr came with me to support me They were both stronger than I was, but Goong was the toughest because she really believed in the Buddhist concepts.

"I am not saying this right, excuse me. We all believed, but I wanted safeguards in case the teachings were wrong. My faith was … is weak. Goong's was or I should say is strong. Nothing and no-one could ever hurt her because she didn't believe that they could. She could live like what we had all been taught, but did not really believe... not deep own, where it matters.

"Goong was the most powerful person that I have ever met. When she came up to see us before the wedding, she told me that she didn't have long to live, but that she didn't want anyone to know... and she still doesn't. Ayr knows and I think Beou will work it out soon, but no-one in our village must know. They must just think that she has gone away, perhaps with some bloke ... abroad, but that she will come back some day. Maybe even often... Just let people work that out for themselves.

"Is that OK with you, my dear?"

"Yes, Lek I have always believed in life after death too. I talk to friends and family that have passed on in my dreams every week. I don't have a problem with it."

"I knew that you wouldn't, my love, so let's raise our glasses and wish Goong a happy voyage and an exciting future. No tears. She wouldn't want that and neither do we, do we?

"Look at that beautiful sunset. Good luck, Goong, see you again. May you always look as beautiful as the last time I saw you." Craig and Lek held hands, clinked glasses and downed them in one to their friend.

They watched a small fishing boat head out into the bay with the yellow-red backdrop of the setting sun to Neil Young singing.

Both had the same thoughts but in different languages.

The End
(for now)

An Exciting Future

Look out for the third book in the trilogy:
"Maya - Illusion"

Please leave a short review where you bought this book. This kind of
feedback is extremely important to authors and other readers, so please
make your voice heard, and join me as my fiend on Facebook and
Twitter.
Thanks,
Owen.

Glossary

These are a few commonly used terms in the book:

Auw: to want

Baan Suay: properly called Moobaan Suay, 'Beautiful Village', Lek's home village in northern Thailand

Baht: Thai currency: 1 Baht = 2p or 3c, but also 15.2 grammes of gold

Baht Bus: most common form of transport – a covered pick-up with bench seats, now 5 Baht for Thais and 10 Baht for foreigners

Bak Wan: literally: 'sweet mouth' – a flatterer

Beer Chang: Thailand's most popular beer – 6.4 % ABV

Bpombpouy: chubby or 'fatty', or the name of Craig's dogs, Bpom and Bpouy

Daddy's Hobby: bar in Pattaya where Lek works

Dam: the colour black

Deng: the colour red

Falang: properly 'farang', white foreigners, Caucasians. Confusingly 'man falang' means crisps (potato chips). It comes from the name given to the first white foreigners in Thailand, the French or 'Falangset' ('Farangset').

Kapun Ka: or just 'Ka', 'thank you', spoken by a woman.

Katoi or Lady Boy: a boy who would rather be a girl. Some have the operation, some don't.

Kapun Kap: or just 'Kap', 'thank you', spoken by a man.

KY: pronounced Koh Yoh – the best mosquito repellent in the world

Khao: can mean rice, or food in general or the colour white or just 'clear'.

Lao: can mean Laos, but usually means alcohol 30-40% ABV – clear (white) or red

Lickay: a play with a set storyline. The dialogue is usually interspersed with topical comments like a pantomime.

Ma: a dog, a horse or the verb 'to come'

Lek: means small or 'Little One"; but is short for Leynou Suksawat, Lek's full name

Mai: makes a negative like 'not' – 'mai auw' – 'I don't want' (or he, she, he , we, they).

Maak: or 'maak, maak', much or many

Mee: to have

Naam: water

Nattaporn: Goong's nom-de-plume

Neh?: Thai equivalent of 'Eh?'

Nid Noi: little bit, some

Phitsanulok: city 'not far' from Lek's village

Phom: I, me, mine or my

Pig and Whistle: Pub-restaurant in Pattaya Soi 7 where Craig stayed first time.

Poot-poot: faeces

Pu-ying: literally 'female people' – lady, ladies; woman, women; pu-chai: 'male people' – (gentle)man or men

Sala: a small outside shelter without walls, somewhere to sit and eat

Satang: money – 'mai mee satang' = 'I don't have any money'.

Sawasdee: hello or goodbye

Sin Sod: the dowry

Soi: a lane or narrow street. Soi 7 is the busiest soi in Pattaya, except Walking Street.

Soi Buakhao: White Lily Lane, a street where many ex-pats hang out In Pattaya

Soom: Lek's daughter

Suay: beautiful or pretty.

Telak: Darling

Uttaradit: city 'not far' from Lek's village

Wat: Buddhist Temple

Bonus first chapter of volume three:

MAYA – ILLUSION

Book Three: Chapter One

1 A BOLT FROM THE BLUE

Lek was waiting in Craig's study. She had been building up the courage for this moment for days and at the precise moment that she had chosen to do it, he had gone to the toilet. She knew that if he didn't get back soon, she would be in tears before she could tell him her news.

She heard the flush go, so she steeled herself, but then the shower started. He would have to pick just this moment to have a shower too, she thought, but to be fair, he didn't know that she wanted to speak to him. They spoke so seldom to each other these days.

Lek started to dust his desk with her handkerchief and tidy his bits and pieces for something to distract her, but she could feel the tears welling up in her eyes already. What the Hell was he doing in there?

She went into the kitchen and poured Craig his second daily cup of coffee, took it back into the office, cleared a space for it among the clutter on his desk and carefully and put it down.

Clack! The bolt was thrown on the bathroom door with the sound of a rifle being cocked.

As he came into the office moments later, he was surprised to see Lek standing there – she would normally have left the house hours ago to embark on her quotidian routine tour of friends for coffee and then lunch.

"Hello, telak, how are you this morning?" He kissed her on the temple and sat down. "Thanks for the coffee. Just what I need."

That was it, she was crying. Tears flowed down her face although unaccompanied by any sounds of sobbing at all.

"Oh, Craig, my darling! I am so unhappy... I think that I must go back to Pattaya and start work in Daddy's Hobby again, if Beou will have me. I am so sorry, my dear."

"I don't understand... 'if Beou will have you'. We have talked about your going to the city to get a job. The costs of our living in a city would outweigh what you could earn..."

"No, dear. I don't mean that we go to Pattaya... I mean that I go alone. I can live in a cheap room; share with other girls, like I did before. You... cannot come with me. You must stay here..."

"What? You are telling me that you want to go back to Pattaya to work in a bar and that I should just sit here and wait at home?"

"Yes, but not wait... I will not come back... You can stay here... get a divorce.... go wherever you like. You can find a new lady, a good lady to take care of you and I will... I don't know what I will do, but it will be without you. I am so sorry."

Once she had spoken, Lek regained her composure and the tears ceased to flow, but as the magnitude of what Lek has just said sank in, Craig began to cry.

It had been so unexpected. He had seen no signs. Not a dicky bird. He looked up at Lek, who was calmly staring back into his watery eyes.

"But why, Lek? What has brought this on now? I just don't understand."

"I don't know where to start, Craig, but I have been unhappy for some time. I expected more than this. I thought... I spent ten years waiting for my hero to rescue me and all the time I worked and put up with crap, but worked on and dreamed of a better life. Then I met you and thought that my dreams had come true... I am not saying this well. It is not your fault, but I expected more and I want more than.... this.

"We have been together for about eight years and married for five or six years, but I am poorer now than when I was working. I know that it is not your fault, Craig, you work hard, but... well, you know, we have nothing and I don't want to live like that.

"Soom has been at university for a year now and it costs... I want my daughter to go to university and I cannot see how we can afford it on the money you earn. I tried to better myself too; I went back to school, but there is no work for people like me here in Baan Suay. If we had a car, maybe I could get a job somewhere near, but... not have.

"I do not have a choice, Craig. My family means everything to me and my daughter more than all that put together. I am so sorry."

Craig thought before replying, his tears had also dried up, "So, I do not count as family after eight years? How long does it take to become a member of your family if you're not born Thai? You know that I gave up my friends and my family to come here – or at least I put them after you... and now you are saying 'bye bye'? I can see that you want Soom to have a better life, so do I, but you also know that I sit here working for fifteen hours a day, while you go out and socialise or whatever."

"I am not blaming you, my dear. You did a very brave thing to come to try to help me and my family, but it has not worked out and now we must move on. I am very sorry."

"Way! I did not come here to rescue you and help your family, I came here because I loved you and thought you loved me. Helping your family was secondary to me. I always told you that I would do whatever I could to help your family and I have, not that they have ever asked for anything."

"Yes, I know, but I did not understand the differences between falang and Thai then, same as you did not understand. It was just a big accident..."

"What? Us falling in love was a 'big accident'? My coming over here, building a house that I will never own and working fifteen hours a day for eight years is just a 'big accident'?

"Lek, Lek, Lek, you hurt me now very much..."

"OK, lovely accident, but now my daughter must have money and I don't have. You have?... No? So I must go get. Or can you go get? If you cannot, I must. My mother cannot give; my family cannot give. You think that Soom must work on weekends and at night? She cannot make enough money in a hamburger bar to pay for university, so what you want her to do? Work in a bar same me before?

"I kill someone first. I steal from someone first... but I go to work first and kill and steal later... If you have a good idea, Craig, please tell me, because I don't want to go away again."

Now they were both crying and Craig stood up to hug his wife, his mind racing with possibilities to save their marriage.

After a few moments, Lek pulled away, "I am sorry, Craig, but it is no good getting close and crying. Something has to be done and if I am going to go away, this is not helping either of us. You understand why I must do this and I understand that you cannot help me.

"I will leave in two days. Do you want me to move out now?"

"No, no, not yet, Lek... I think that you ought to at least tell me the costs and the shortfall. I have never asked you because you always seemed to have everything in hand and now you hit me with this! Or do you actually want to go?"

"I do not lie to you, my husband, but it is true that I do not, or have not always told you the truth one hundred percent. I tried to many times, maybe every time in the beginning, but the language was between us and ... well, it was easier not to.

"When I worked in Daddy's Hobby, I did lots of things that I did not want to do because I had to do them. I do not want to say any more about that unless you ask me and that is your right, I think.

"Anyway, I saved some money for Soom's education. Goong also left me 500,000 Baht when she died four or five years ago. I gave some of it to her family, but kept most of it.

"I don't have much of it left now. I was bored here for years with nothing to do and gambled a lot of it away on cards. I paid Soom's university fees last year and I have supplemented the money that you gave me for food for several years.

"Now, I cannot pay Soom's university fees when they come up next year and cannot buy her the clothes, books and laptop that she needs right now to be comfortable with her studies. I don't want her to look poor in university! She is the first person in my family to go to university and I want to give her every chance.

"That may mean losing you... but I will do it, if I have to, my darling, because I don't know what else I can do."

A few tears escaped her eyes, but she quickly wiped them away with her hand.

Craig was looking down at the beautifully-tiled floor, feeling like a total failure.

"So, you have paid the fees for now, right?" he said not meeting her eyes. "When do you need more money for Soom?"

"About six months. I pay university fees two times a year, but I give Soom money for her room and living every month."

"So you have six months?"

"No, I must start working now to give Soom money every month and then more fees in six months. If I wait, it is too late."

"OK, Lek... I wish that you had brought this up before, but, please give me a few hours to think about the problem, before you do anything quickly. Let's say that you have... two weeks, eh? Can you wait two weeks?"

Lek nodded and put her hand on his shoulder, "Sure, I can wait two weeks."

Craig was still shell-shocked. He put his hand to hers and patted it a few times, slowly. "I wish you had told me your problem before, Lek, I really do. Now, it's hurry, hurry, hurry, but thanks for... Er, well, we have two weeks, eh? … What are your plans for today?"

"It has taken me days to say this... I don't have any plans now. Do you?"

"No, but I know that right now, work is not the answer... Why don't you go off to your mother's and I'll have a think?"

Lek was glad of the excuse to get out and be alone and, having recovered somewhat from the initial shock, so was Craig.

After Lek had left, he finished his cold coffee in one, packed up his laptop and went to the shop where he did a lot of his thinking. The office was for slog work, but Nong's shop was for deep cogitation, usually over a few ice-cold beers. Watching the people in the village coming and going, carrying out their daily lives had always had a calming, yet inspirational effect upon him.

He sat down at the one table outside the shop and waited for Nong to notice him. He had been drinking at Nong's shop for eight years, but they still could not talk to each other in any meaningful way. Nong appeared not to have an aptitude for English and Craig had spent most of his time trying to earn money rather than learn Thai.

As he was staring out before himself, he heard Nong say, "Hello Mr. Craig, how are you today?" in Thai.

"Sabaai dee, kap - I'm fine thanks. Khun duay, mai? You too?"

"Yes, thank you. The beer is very cold today."

Nong always said that, but then the beer was always cold too.

Craig slouched in the bench seat and stretched his feet out in front of himself. He thought with a smile, that if he smoked, this would be a two-pipe problem, as Sherlock Holmes would have said.

"Why hadn't she mentioned it before? Why the sudden crisis? The real bottom line was, if she believed in karma, as she insisted she did, why did she think that she could change her daughter's karma?" It did not make sense now, although Lek's news had hit him like a bullet.

The problem was that Lek seemed to be sure that her only way forward was to go back to work in a bar. So, whether she was right or wrong in her religious philosophy, she would probably leave him in fourteen days.

Craig knew that Lek had an iron will. If that was what she had said she would do, that was what she would do, unless there was a very good reason not to. And the only reason that was good enough was money, so he needed a supply of money.

Or he needed to shed the chains that held him and Lek together – he needed to stop loving her.

Money or love?

That was the dilemma.

Lek had already decided that she would choose money, although not for entirely selfish reasons. Selfishness was in there though, he was sure. He knew that she would not be able to bear the shame of having to withdraw Soom from university for lack of funds.

Although that was the mechanics of the situation, it did not help his predicament. He loved Lek, but he was being offered an honourable way out. No-one would blame him for cutting and running now. Lek had told him that he was on his own.

Craig wondered for a little while whether Lek was offering him this easy exit because she had found someone new, but he dismissed the idea as much for lack of evidence as the fact that it would have hurt him too much to countenance it. He believed that Lek was genuinely concerned about her daughter's future and that helped him with the next choice, which was whether he should stay or go.

That would take another beer. It was not that he didn't want to stay. It was more a question of whether this problem would erupt again over an unrelated issue like Soom's first home, Soom's first car, Soom's babies, when she had them, which she inevitably would. Soom had been brought up by her grandmother as had Lek and he knew that Lek was looking forward to the role in her turn.

Craig, however, was not, yet the likelihood of it coming to pass was only three or four years away.

Nong saw the empty bottle and swiftly brought another one.

The ultimate decision was between selling everything that he had left in the UK, looking after Soom's children and staying with Lek in the village that he had come to call home or to call it a day and move on.

It was a tough one.

∞

Lek had gone to her Mum's house, which was just over the lane from their place, less than half-way to Nong's shop. She hadn't discussed her predicament with anyone yet, because so much depended on Craig, but she was ready to bite the bullet and go back to work if things worked out that way.

She was prepared to accept her own bad fate, but she was not prepared to allow fate to affect Soom's future, if she could do anything about it.

If Craig fell by the wayside, then so be it. The ball was in his court now. She had given him an out and a two-week period to come up with a solution. There was nothing more to do than steel herself again and wait for what her karma would throw at her. She did care about Craig, but she cared more about Soom and she cared nothing for herself.

After the dreams she had had for and the nightmares she had had about Soom's future over the last eighteen years, Lek was not about to leave anything to something as intangible as fate. Her daughter might not be clever enough to pass the examinations, that was something else, but she would sit them, shortage of money notwithstanding.

She sat with her mother, but her mother could see that she was troubled, so she cut and peeled some fruit for them both and pretended to be busy until her daughter made the first move.

"What would you think if I moved to Bangkok, Mum, to be closer to Soom if she needs me? I think that I can be more use there than here now. What do you reckon?"

"I reckon that that is your decision, Lek, but what does Craig think about it? He is your husband and therefore the one you should be asking this question, not me."

"Yes, I know, but... I'm just not sure..."

"I never followed you around when you were growing up. Did I do wrong? Why do you think that you have to be at your daughter's side and not your husband's?

"Soom has her own mistakes to make like we all did and still do – it is part of growing up. Will you be there when she meets her first lover too?"

"I would like to be, yes! And if he's not good enough I'd..."

Lek could see her mother's smiling eyes although no mirth showed around her mouth.

"You can only do what you can do. You could not be here for the first part of Soom's life, but that is not so bad. I did my best and you were here for the last eight years. Soom is a good, level-headed, intelligent girl, now is the time to give her some headroom – let her practice what she has learned – don't keep her hemmed in.

"She may start to think that you think that she's stupid and you don't want that do you? Not when she is in a big Bangkok university with all the rich kids. They will give her enough complexes already.

"What is your true concern?"

"Money, Mum, if I am honest. I want the university fees for the full, four-year term of the course in my bank account right now, so that I know that money will not stop her staying at university. I want to see it, in a bank book."

"Yes, I see. We would all like enough money in the bank to be safe, but that is not how it is for working class people like us, unfortunately. What does Craig have to say about it all?"

She didn't want to say that she hadn't consulted him or that she was thinking seriously of going back to work, so she said, "He doesn't want to live in Bangkok. Nor do I really, since I don't know anyone there except Chalita and her husband and I couldn't just hang around with them all the time. Sis has her own life to lead. Maybe I could live in Pattaya, it's only an hour or so away.

"Craig doesn't think we can afford to live in a city and he's probably right. I would have to find a job to pay the rent and most of the university fees..."

"I see," said her mother slowly. "Like that is it? How old are you now? Thirty-nine, forty? Not old certainly, but getting old to be doing some types of job, don't you think? Your job opportunities would be limited by your qualifications, lack of experience and age, I imagine. What sort of work did you have in mind?"

"I don't know Mum. I only know bar work and basic bookkeeping. Perhaps I could get a job as a cashier in a bar, or a receptionist in a hotel or working the till in a shop."

"Don't you need qualifications to be a bookkeeper these days? I think you do, unless your family gives you a job. Have you spoken to Beou about it?"

"No, not yet. I just told Craig and he's gone to Nong's to think about it and get drunk, I suppose. He took it rather badly although I did kind of hit him with it out of the blue."

"It is a shock to me, I can't imagine what he is going through. He gave up everything to come here to be with you. All his friends, his family, his connections... and now you are dumping him. Not a very nice prospect, is it? Now that he's spent most of his money too. It makes you look heartless, my dear, although I know you are only thinking about the security of Soom's future.

"However, you are married now and you and Craig must work as a team. This may sound like your concern alone, but it is not. We might not be able to help you financially, but we would miss you if you left again. It has been so..., so homely, like the good old days, having you around again for the last eight or nine years.

"Then there is Soom. Have you asked her about your idea of moving down with her? Perhaps she was looking forward to a lot more freedom. That is one of the perks of going away to study, isn't it? To learn about life in the 'real world', learning to stand on your own two feet? And she'll have you hanging around criticising her every mistake.

"If you want the advice of an old woman, I would say not to abandon the people who love you the most. Look for ways that we, or you and Craig can sort this problem out together. Talk to him properly, don't just tell him 'this is how it is going to be...'. He has his pride too and if you push him into a corner, he may leave you and I think that you would regret that sooner or later. Probably sooner too.

"Soom would miss Craig too. Well, we all would. We have all become fond of him and his funny little ways. He's a breath of fresh air sometimes."

"Do you think that I should go to him now, Mum?"

"That is up to you, Lek, but maybe it is better if he thinks things through on his own for a little while longer. Give him an hour longer and that will give you time to think what to say to him and cook him something nice. What is his favourite? Oh, yes, Paneng. Put some of your love into a Paneng for him and if he's not back by the time it's ready, take him a bowl to the shop."

"Thanks, Mum, you always know what to say just at the right moment... whereas I, well I just rush in and... Do I get that from Dad? I'll give it a shot. Do you fancy some curry too? I'll make enough for all of us."

∞

Craig was well into his fourth pint when Lek appeared at his side. He actually smelled her coming before he saw her, or at least he had caught a whiff of his favourite Thai meal being cooked somewhere near by.

"Hello, telak. I have brought you something to eat. You not eat all day and drinking with no food is no good." As soon as she had mentioned drinking and an implied criticism, she regretted it.

"Who cares? Go to Bangkok, then you won't have to watch, will you?"

"I did not mean anything, my dear, honestly. May I sit down and join you? I think I need a few beers too."

"I don't **need** a few beers, I **want** a few beers... Sure sit down, what do you want? A Leo? Nong! Can I have a Leo, a glass, some ice and another Chang, please?"

Lek was unwrapping her parcel of food and two dishes that already had servings of white, fluffy rice in them. She passed the bowl of curry, a bowl of rice and a spoon to Craig, so that he could serve himself first in the traditional way.

"Thank you. It smells very nice. Thanks, Nong. Cheers, my dear, bottoms up! When are you off? Oh, yes, in two weeks..."

"I want to talk to you about that, Craig. I am so sorry that I sprang it on you so suddenly like that. It must have been a terrible shock. I should have been more... more subtle. Is that the right word?"

"Well, it's one of them and you certainly were not it."

"Yes, I know and I am sorry." She put some more curry into Craig's bowl before taking a little for herself. "You understand the problem though despite my inept way of putting it, so I have come to you now for advice. You have more experience in money matters than I. I am only a blunt farm girl at heart, what do you think that we could do together as a family to solve this crisis?"

Craig knew that he was being buttered up, but he also knew that it was Lek's way of apologising. It was very rare for her, or any Thai for that matter, to actually say the word 'sorry' and she had said it at least six times today already – she preferred to show it in deeds.

"I know how important Soom's education is to you. I know how much you blame your own previous circumstances on your own lack of a formal education and I know that you don't want the same for Soom. An education with papers – qualifications – is like a guarantee. I know you think all that and I agree with you.

"So, I propose using my visa guarantee money to help you and Soom. That takes the pressure off for now. It means that I will not get a twelve-month visa extension next month, but maybe it's time we had a holiday anyway. We could go to Laos – Vientiane – for a holiday and pick up a three-month visa while we're there. I have a few ideas for replacing the visa money, but there is no rush for that. How much do you need right now for Soom?"

"I give her twelve thousand Baht every month for expenses. Later I will need sixty thousand, but not right now. In six weeks. I have most of that money, but then I have no reserves for if there is a problem. That is what worries me."

"Yes, OK, Lek. Tell Soom that you will transfer the money into her bank account on Monday and in the meantime, we can start planning our holiday to Laos. Cheers! I mean it, cheer up. We both need to."

Lek felt a lot happier now that the foreseeable problem had been sorted out. She had a year to find next year's payment and she still had fifty thousand in the bank.

Craig could see that the storm had passed, but the sky was definitely still very overcast.

An Exciting Future

342

Behind The Smile

The story of Lek, a bar girl in Pattaya

The *Behind The Smile* Series is the story of Lek, a bar girl in Pattaya, Thailand. Lek was born the eldest child of four in a typical rice farming family in the northern rice belt of Thailand. A catastrophe occurred out of the blue one day – her father died young with huge debts that the family knew nothing about. Lek was just twenty years of age, and the only one who could prevent the foreclosure of the family farm, and allow her younger sister and two brothers to continue their education. However, the only way she knew how was to go to work in her cousin's bar in Pattaya.

Can a Pattaya bar girl ever go back to being a regular girlfriend or wife?

'Behind The Smile' is a look into one part of Thailand, a country known around the world as 'The Land of Smiles'.

1] Daddy's Hobby: Lek went to the bar *'Daddy's Hobby'*, in Pattaya, as a waitress-cum-cashier, until she realised that she was pregnant by her estranged husband, and everything changed. After having the baby, a girl, whom she left with her mother on the farm, she needed real money to provide a better life for her child and drifted into the tourist sex industry.

The adventures, dreams and sometimes nightmares, this is Lek's point of view of what it's really like to be a Thai bar girl... the exhilarating hopes that cover up the frustrations, let-downs, lies and deceit of daily life, give way to the dream of a normal life when she meets a new man, yet again.

When this new man returns for a real life relationship, Lek finds it's not so easy going through the good and bad of couplehood.

Will they stay together, and for how long? Will she ever be able to trust a man enough again either? Or will she go back to the bar girl life?

2] An Exciting Future: *An Exciting Future* starts where volume one ends. Lek and Craig, her new 'permanent' boyfriend are flying back to Bangkok from Craig's home in Wales. The holiday atmosphere continues in Pattaya for months, but then reality dawns, and they have important decisions to make such as: where are they going to live, and how are they going to make a living. They start squabbling, and both wonder whether they have done the right thing in joining forces. They persevere, and, after many trials, tribulations and happy times, begin to settle down into, what, for them at least, could be called a normal life. One of the trio dies tragically, but gives the other two new hope. However, will the old villagers forgive Lek for going to Pattaya? And will Lek and Craig be able to adapt to rural village life after all that Lek has seen and done, and Craig being used to living in large towns? What chance do they have of really fitting in?

3] Maya – Illusion: *Maya – Illusion* refers to the Buddhist concept that life on Earth is not real. More than 95% of Thais are Buddhist, and so have a totally different outlook to most Christian Westerners. Lek and her best friend Ayr go into business together, when she retires from Pattaya, and brings a surprise Australian fiancé with her. A natural disaster occurs in the village but the two friends come up with an innovative form of help. Ayr proves to be quite a business woman, and teaches Lek, a willing student, how to make money and fit into the community, while Craig plods along with his books and websites.

4] The Lady in the Tree: *The Lady in the Tree* continues straight on from book three, Maya - Illusion. Lek is still in business with her old friend Ayr and they mean business as well, especially when rivals from nearby try to intimidate them. The two friends come up with a daring solution, which they can't even discuss with their friends, family or husbands. Soom is still at university in Bangkok and doing well in spite of having problems of her own, let alone looming final exams, which political upheaval in the capital threatens to disrupt. Craig continues to write, but he realises all of a sudden that he has bigger problems than finishing and selling his books. An old friend and an old lady give the three women some remarkably similar and accurate advice, but where will it get them?

5] Stepping Stones: *Stepping Stones* picks up the story of Lek, her family and friends in the village of Baan Suay four years on from where The Lady in The Tree finished. Lek and Ayr are still looking to expand, but especially Lek's career in the political arena, where she finds evidence of disturbing activity. Craig is still trying to write a best seller and Soom has graduated from university. In Stepping Stones, we are introduced to the Champunot family from Bangkok, the members of which have a profound effect on Lek, Craig and Soom - one which none of them will ever be able to forget. Stepping Stones reveals more in-depth details of life in a Thai family that has been affected by the inclusion of a falang like how they deal with the strange mixture of traditional and modern Thai life that that situation often creates.

6] The Dream: *The Dream* takes up the story of Lek, her family and friends from two years further down the line. In the past, it has always been Lek who issued the ultimata, but this story opens with her having received one and it throws her. She is offered the fulfilment of her oldest dream, but can she take it? The fulfilment of any dream requires sacrifices, but is Lek prepared to make them now that her goal is within her grasp? It is a tough one, which means a hard time for her, although her family and friends are behind her as always. Which way will she go? The instinct to follow her dream and the inertia of a comfortable life in the village, as she gets older vie for supremacy in her mind. As is usual in this series, nothing is hidden from the reader, we are privy to all of Lek's agonizing thoughts.

7] The Beginning: At twenty-one years of age, Lek, an ordinary, contemporary, farm girl from the northern Thai Rice belt, had to go to Pattaya to work in the leisure industry to help her widowed mother pay off the mortgage to save the farm from foreclosure and keep her siblings in school. This book, The Beginning, shows what her life was like before she had to leave her small, hard-working, but happy village and the only people she had ever known. It depicts the events that made her happy and those that saddened her in her early life from living with her grandmother to surviving with her husband, Tom. At the very last moment, some friends step up to make Lek's transition to life in Thailand's number one sex city just that little bit easier.

An Exciting Future

Books by Owen Jones

Alien House
A Story of Love, Hope and Alien Intervention

-

Andropov's Cuckoo
A Story of Love Intrigue and The KGB

-

Annwn – Heaven - *series*
A Night in Annwn
The Strange Story of Old Willy Jones's NDE
Life in Annwn
The Story of Willy Jones's Life in Heaven
Leaving Annwn
Returning to Earth on a Mission!

-

Asian Shorts
An Anthology of Short Stories Involving Asians or Asia

-

Behind The Smile - *series*
The Story of Lek, a Bar Girl in Pattaya
Volume I: **Daddy's Hobby**
Volume II: **An Exciting Future**
Volume III: **Maya – Illusion**
Volume IV: **The Lady in the Tree**
Volume V: **Stepping Stones**
Volume VI: **The Dream**

An Exciting Future

Volume VII: **The Beginning**

-

Daisy's Chain
A Story of Love, Intrigue and the Underworld on the Costa del Sol

-

Dead Centre - *series*
Dead Centre
Not All Suicide Bombers Are Religious!
Dead Centre II
Even The Wrong Can Be Right Sometimes!

-

The Bull at the Gate
The Day the Sky Fell !

-

The Disallowed
The Story of a Contemporary Vampire Family

-

Fate Twister
The Strange Story of Wayne Gamm

-

The Bull at the Gate
The Day the Sky Fell!

-

The Ghouls of Calle Goya
When Malice Results From Good Intentions!

-

The Psychic Megan Series
A Spirit Guide, A Ghost Tiger, and One Scary Mother!
The Misconception
Megan's Thirteenth
Megan's School Trip
Megan's School Exams

An Exciting Future

Megan's Followers
Megan and the Lost Cat
Megan and the Mayoress
Megan Faces Derision
Megan's Grandparents' Visit
Megan's Father Falls Ill
Megan Goes on Holiday
Megan and the Burglar
Megan and the Cyclist
Megan and the Old Lady
Megan's Garden
Megan Goes to the Zoo
Megan Goes Hiking
Megan and the W. I. Cooking Competition
Megan Goes Riding
Megan and the Radio One Beach Party
Megan Goes Yachting
Megan at Carnival
Megan's Christmas
Megan Catches Covid-19

-

The Bull at the Gate
The Day the Sky Fell In !

-

Tiger Lily of Bangkok – *Series*
Volume I: **Tiger Lily of Bangkok**
When the Seeds of Revenge Blossom!
Volume II: **Tiger Lily of Bangkok in London**
The Tiger Re-awakens!

-

Non-Fiction

Owen Jones

How to Give Your Dog a Real Dog's Life
(and make him love you for it)

-

The Eternal Plan
– Revealed
(written by Colin Jones, compiled by Owen Jones)

-

Authorship
Publishing Your Book On You Own